Refuge

Karen Lynch

ISBN: 0692317333
ISBN-13: 978-0692317334

Cover Designer: Nikos Lima

To my mother, Margaret, and the memory of my father, Sandy, for giving me a home filled with love and for empowering me to chase my dreams.

ACKNOWLEDGEMENTS

First and foremost, I like to thank my family and friends for their encouragement and unfailing support. Thank you to my amazing cover artist, Nikos, for his patience and ability to know what I want before I do. Thank you to my friends in my writing group, Prolific Pens, for your support and for helping to keep my creative batteries charged. Thank you to my editor, Kelly, and my wonderful beta readers: Anne Marie, Teresa, Rachel and Melissa. A special thanks to two amazing authors: Melissa Haag and Ednah Walters for their advice and guidance and most importantly, their friendship. And last but not least, thanks to my brother, Alex, for being a surly old dragon and providing a little extra inspiration for this story.

CHAPTER 1

I FELT IT coming even before he slammed into me and sent me flying back a dozen feet to land in a heap against the wall. "Ow." Little pinpoints of light floated before my eyes, and I tasted blood in my mouth where I'd bitten the inside of my cheek. That pain was nothing compared to the bone-deep aches all over my body. God, how much punishment could a body take?

A shadow fell across my face. "Is anything broken?" asked a gruff Scottish voice that rang more of impatience than concern.

I rolled onto my back and stretched my sore limbs to test them for injuries, grunting when my shoulder made a small pop. Satisfied that my body was still in one piece, even if it was as bruised as a ripe peach, I peered up at the dark-haired man standing over me with his feet planted apart and his hands on his hips. "I'll survive," I muttered, not sure if I was happy about it.

He extended a hand, and I took it reluctantly, letting him pull me to my feet. When he let go of me, I leaned against the wall as the training room did a little spin before my eyes. I didn't need to see straight to know that my painful flight had been witnessed by Terrence and Josh – the two other trainees in the room who were watching us while pretending to focus on their own workouts. I couldn't blame them. My daily training sessions were something of a spectacle, like a pileup on the highway that you can't help but slow down to watch.

Callum crossed his arms over his wide chest and fixed me with a reproachful stare. Solid muscle and taller than me by almost a foot, he was my penance for every one of my past screw-ups. At least that was what I told myself every day when I lowered my freshly bruised body into the healing bath. How I ever thought it would be fun to train with the smiling warrior with the sexy ponytail and chocolate-brown eyes was beyond me. It

3

took less than five minutes of our first session for me to discover the scourge hiding behind that pretty smile.

"You are still not working with your Mori, and you will never be able to fight or defend yourself unless you open to it. Remember, without that demon inside you, you're only human and just as helpless as one."

Not quite human. Not that Callum or anyone else in this place would know that. Only a handful of people knew my secret, and they were all far away from here.

I rolled my shoulders to work out a kink. "I know what you told me. I'm just not sure how to do it. Maybe my demon is defective."

His scowl deepened. "Your demon is not defective, and this is nothing to joke about. How do you expect to become a warrior if you cannot fight?"

"Maybe I don't want to be a warrior."

Callum barked a laugh. "You attract a lot of trouble for someone who doesn't want to be a warrior." I blinked in surprise, and he shook his head. "Oh, I've heard of your little adventures, and how you kept a whole unit – not to mention two of our best warriors – running around Maine for the better part of a month."

His remarks conjured an image of a dark-haired warrior with smoldering gray eyes. I brushed it away angrily. "They were there because of the vampires, not me, and they could have left whenever they wanted. In fact, I told them to leave more than once."

"So I've heard." Was that actual amusement I saw in his eyes? "There are not many people who would challenge Nikolas Danshov. I expected more from someone who did."

He was baiting me, and I refused to bite. "Sorry to disappoint you. Maybe you should find another trainee who will meet your expectations."

I got three steps away before he growled, "Where do you think you're going? We are not done with this lesson, and you leave when I say you leave. Now assume your position."

So much for pleasantries. I adjusted my padded vest and went to the area he had marked off for us. There was a painful twinge in my lower back and my butt was already protesting the punishment that was sure to follow, but I pushed the pain aside and turned to face my trainer. I might suck as a fighter, but I still had my pride and I'd see this through if it killed me.

Callum, however, was not where I expected him to be. I looked around and found him by the door talking to two men and a woman I had not seen before. The woman was tall and beautiful in a knee-length red dress, with flawless skin and long, straight black hair. I could not help but notice that the boys had stopped pretending to train and were ogling her. She seemed not to notice them as her emerald eyes found me and her nose wrinkled delicately. I almost laughed because I could only imagine how I looked and smelled after two hours with Callum.

My attention shifted to the men with her. They were both tall like all Mohiri males but very different in appearance. One had a plain face with curly brown hair and tanned skin. The second man had long blond hair pulled back in a ponytail that suited his finely sculptured face. His blue eyes swept the room as he listened to whatever Callum said to him, and they lit on me briefly before returning to my trainer. The man's commanding air and the way the other trainees had perked up told me he was someone important. This place was a hive of activity with warriors coming and going almost daily, so it was impossible to know everyone. But I was obviously the only person in the room who did not recognize the blond stranger.

Callum smiled at the man and turned back to me with his training face on again. I expected the newcomers to leave, but they leaned against the wall like they were planning to stay and watch. Great. All I needed today was more people watching me get my butt handed to me.

I watched Callum warily as he moved to a spot ten feet from me and faced me with the calculating gleam in his eyes that I had come to dread. "Open yourself to your Mori, Sara. Feel its power, and let it guide you. Its survival instincts are strong, and it wants nothing more than to protect you. Without you, it cannot exist."

Do you hear that? I said to the beast crouched sullenly in the back of my mind. *You need me a lot more than I need you, so you'd better behave.* I forced my mind to block out everyone else in the room and focus only on Callum's face. His eyes always gave him away a split second before he made his move, not that knowing when he was about to strike had ever helped me. I lowered the wall holding back the demon, feeling it flutter with excitement as its cage opened. At the same time, I reached for the glowing power at my center and pulled back a thread to wield if the need arose. The demon was strong, but it was no match for my Fae power and we both knew it.

My Mori and I saw Callum's eyes flicker at the same time, but the demon reacted first. It rushed forward in an attempt to fill my mind and make my body obey its commands. For a second, I allowed it – before the old memory surfaced. I could still feel the scorching heat of the demon beneath my skin, and the helplessness of floating in the vastness of the demon's mind.

My walls shot back up a split second before Callum plowed into me and sent me soaring backward again. This time, instead of colliding with the wall, I found myself snatched from the air and pulled against a hard chest.

"I think our little bird has had enough flying for today, Callum." Laughter rumbled through the chest of the man holding me before he set me on my feet. Embarrassed, I looked up into the sapphire eyes of the blond stranger, but there was no mockery in his expression. If anything, his smile was kind, indulgent.

"I think you are right," Callum agreed, looking at me. "No less than thirty minutes in the baths, Sara, and take some gunna paste." I made a face, and his expression grew stern. It was no secret that I would rather suffer a few aches than eat the awful putty-like medicine. "If I see you limping at dinner again, I will hold you down and feed it to you myself."

I nodded reluctantly because I knew he would follow through with his threat. Mumbling a good-bye to the newcomers, I hurried to the equipment room to shed my padded armor. Then I escaped the training area before Callum decided to feed me the nasty gunna paste himself, like he'd done on my second day of training.

The dark paneled hall in the training wing was quiet except for the muffled sounds of combat coming from behind the closed doors. Mohiri warriors spent a lot of time training when they weren't out saving the world. The stronghold housed between thirty and forty warriors on a given day – not including the teams that came and went – so the training rooms were always busy this time of day.

I pushed open the heavy door to the women's baths, relieved when I saw the empty chamber. Mohiri women were not timid or self-conscious, and they thought nothing of stripping down in front of each other, something I was still getting used to. If I was lucky I could get in and out of the bath before the room got too busy.

The first thing I did was go to a cabinet in the wall and retrieve a can of gunna paste. Scooping out some of the green paste with my finger, I grimaced and put it in my mouth. Within seconds, a dry, bitter taste coated my tongue and every corner of my mouth, and I had to force myself to swallow the paste instead of spitting it out. Even after the paste had gone down, the foul taste lingered, and I knew it would take at least another five minutes for it to go away. I silently cursed Callum as I did every day after training. It didn't change things, but it made me feel a little better.

Stripping off my sweaty clothes, I immersed my body in the nearest of the six rectangular tubs sunken into the tiled floor. The hot cloudy liquid bubbled gently, and I moaned in sheer bliss as it began to soothe my aches and pains. I didn't know what was in the water; just that it came from a deep underground spring that fed into massive tanks somewhere under the building. There, it was treated with special salts and purifiers and piped into the healing baths in a constant flow. That was as much as I cared to know about it, other than the fact that it did wonders for the body if you stayed in it long enough.

I closed my eyes and tried to relax and not think about my abysmal training session, or the dozen other negative thoughts that often plagued me in the week and a half I'd been here. *It's not as if you expected it to be like home.* I just had to give it some time, to get used to the people and my surroundings. I had never been comfortable getting to know people, and making new friends didn't come as easily to me as it did to Roland and Peter. A wry smile touched my lips. One more thing I had to work on.

When my thirty minutes were up, I climbed out of the tub to stand beneath the shower. Cleaned, dried, and dressed in a fresh pair of drawstring pants and T-shirt, I left the bath chamber and headed to my suite on the third floor of the north wing. Westhorne was a Mohiri military stronghold, but there were no barracks here. My suite was almost as big as my loft back home, with a much larger bathroom and a small combined living room and kitchenette. The furnishings were richer than I was used to, but I did love the antique four-poster bed. And the fireplace would come in handy if the winters in Idaho were anything like I'd been told.

I opened the window and took a deep breath of fresh air. The view outside my window was so different from the one I'd grown up with. I missed the ocean, but there was something about snowcapped mountains that made my breath catch every time I saw them.

If only I had the freedom to explore them, I might have felt better about my change in scenery. So far, I had been pretty much restricted to the grounds. Not that I hadn't tried to go beyond the border of the property, only to be caught and returned twice. They told me it was standard procedure for new orphans and it was for my own good, but I suspected my past escapades might have had a little more to do with it. I longed to walk in the woods and hike on the mountain trails without someone treating me like a five-year-old who had wandered away. It wasn't like I was going to run off. We were in the middle of nowhere and the closest town was five miles away. Even if I did head for town, Butler Falls had a population of a whopping four thousand and more farm supply stores than restaurants. Not exactly a magnet for vampires, especially with a Mohiri compound next door.

I turned away from the window with a sigh and hunted for a pair of jeans and a shirt in my ridiculously huge closet. Who needs a closet the size of a small bedroom anyway? My clothes took up half a rack and two shelves. A few days ago, the rest of my boxes from home had arrived, and most of them still sat unopened on the floor of the closet. That still left almost three-quarters of the closet bare. Claire, the woman who had shown me around the day I arrived, told me they had set up a line of credit for me to buy anything I needed, but so far I hadn't bothered. It wasn't as if I had anywhere to go, and my old clothes served me well enough. Besides, I felt weird about spending Mohiri money when I barely knew them.

I grabbed a warm coat and a paperback from my nightstand. The book was one of Nate's and I'd read it before, but reading it again made me feel a little less homesick. I tucked the book in my pocket as I left my room.

As I descended the stairs, the murmur of voices grew louder. It was lunchtime, but the last place I wanted to be was in the crowded dining hall.

Instead, I left by the door in the training wing that opened to a courtyard at the rear of the building. To my right was the wide, deep river that bordered one side of the property. I started that way, but the call of the woods was stronger. Besides, I always had the feeling someone was watching me when I went near the river. No doubt they were making sure I did not fall in and drown myself.

I passed a group of warriors carrying bows and swords, and they nodded politely but didn't speak to me. As beautiful as Westhorne was, I was constantly reminded that it was a military holding. The Mohiri had dozens of compounds across the US alone, and at least ten of them were like this one. The rest were community compounds that were even more fortified than Westhorne, but were less involved in military operations. I did not have to ask why I hadn't been sent to one of the Mohiri communities. No one wanted to take a chance of the Master attacking a compound full of kids if he ever figured out I was alive. So I came here instead.

Home sweet home.

The scent of pine surrounded me when I entered the woods. Overhead, I could see only patches of blue sky through the canopy of branches, but the sun still managed to seep through, its rays casting a dappled pattern of light across the ground. It was so quiet here, and the only sounds came from the birds in the branches above my head. I took a deep breath, imagining I was in the woods back home in New Hastings, and I could almost pretend Remy or one of his little cousins was about to sneak up on me like they used to.

I shook off my melancholy because the woods were too beautiful to allow sadness to mar them. Sticking my hands in my pockets, I wandered aimlessly, content just to be outdoors and alone for a while. *It will get easier,* I told myself like I did every day. They had a lot more rules here than I was used to, but the people were not unkind, even if they were different. Just because I didn't feel at home here, it wasn't fair of me to judge the whole Mohiri race after less than two weeks.

You mean it's not fair to judge them because of him.

Thinking about *him* would only make me angry, so I made an effort to focus on anything but him. I stepped into a small sunny glade where the air felt ten degrees warmer than in the shade of the big trees. It was a chilly day, almost too cold to sit outside, but it was infinitely better than being inside. I closed my eyes and raised my face to the sun, listening to the quiet sounds of the forest and breathing in its rich, earthy smell. *Yes, this will do nicely,* I thought as I stretched out in the grass with my book.

I barely got through two chapters before a small brown rabbit hobbled into view and stopped at the edge of the trees. Even when I'm not using my power, it seems to broadcast to animals and other creatures, letting them know I am not a threat. But gentler creatures like rabbits are still a bit wary.

I laid my book by my side and reached for my power, sending a stream of it toward the rabbit. His nose twitched, and he sniffed the air for a minute before he started moving forward. I let him come to me, not moving even when he touched his nose to my hand. I let power flow from my hand into him until he lay against my side trustingly.

I sat up slowly, so I did not startle him, and laid my hand on his back to feel for the source of his injury. It didn't take long to find the swelling and inflammation in one of his hind legs. I moved my hand until it closed around the injured leg and felt around for the extent of the damage. "Don't worry, little guy. I'll have you fixed up in no time."

A familiar heat welled in my chest and flowed down my arm to my hand where it sought out the injury, enclosing it in a healing fire that easily knit the hairline crack in the bone and burned away the swelling. I felt the leg return to its normal size, and I withdrew my power and lifted my hand from the rabbit. "There you go, as good as new." *I'd like to see Callum do that.* I might not be warrior material, but I had other gifts. Perhaps I'd be better off if I stuck to healing and left the killing to the real warriors.

The rabbit shifted his weight and took a few hesitant hops before he decided his leg was working right again. "See you around," I called to him as he went happily on his way. I lay back in the grass again to recover from the healing, and I was surprised to realize I wasn't feeling drained at all. Strange, even a small healing usually required a little recovery time. If anything, I felt energized, restless.

I got to my feet and started walking again. There was a small lake less than a mile from the estate. I'd seen it on a map in the library, but the first time I tried to go to the lake I was detained. Maybe this time I'd get lucky.

"What the – ? Not again." I came to a halt when my scalp began to tingle and my hair crackled like it was charged with static. My palms and the bottoms of my feet started to grow warm and itchy, and currents raced along the skin of my arms beneath the sleeves of my coat. A rustling sound made me look down to see the dead leaves around my feet quiver, even though there was no wind.

As quickly as it had started, it was gone. *What is going on?* It was the second time I'd experienced something like this in last four days. I suspected it was an undine thing because Aine had told me my powers were still developing, but there was no one I could ask about it. I wished I knew how to contact her. She promised to visit me soon, but I had a feeling that the Fae had a different concept of time than everyone else. For her, soon might mean a few weeks or a few years. I had no idea.

"Ugh!" I yelped as a spot in the center of my chest began to itch and a cold knot formed beneath my breastbone. This was new. The coldness was not painful but it did feel uncomfortable, and it alarmed me that it was exactly where I'd been stabbed a month ago. Aine said the faeries had healed me completely, but what if she was wrong? Even the faeries had admitted they were not sure how my body would react to the vampire blood that had been on the knife.

Rubbing my chest, I resumed walking and hoped the cold knot would go away. I turned and started back toward the stronghold, and to my immense relief, the knot began to ease. Whatever it was, it seemed to be going away on its own.

"Someone's been a bad girl again."

I jumped a foot in the air and spun around to face the man who had so easily snuck up on me. The red-haired warrior standing less than five feet away shook his head and gave me his "you know you're not supposed to be out here" look.

"I really wish you wouldn't do that," I grumbled.

"Do what?" asked another voice, and I let out a small squeal as I whirled around again to find a grinning mirror image of the red head. "Damn it, guys! Stop it!"

Laughter filled the woods as the twin warriors moved to stand side-by-side in front of me. Seamus and Niall were so identical that I doubted even their mother could tell them apart. They were the same size with bright green eyes, spiky red hair, and boyishly handsome faces. Right now they sported identical smirks.

"Now where would you be off to on this fine day?" asked the one I thought was Niall.

"Just taking a walk and I was already heading back. You can go back to patrolling or whatever it is you do out here."

"Well, unless you are planning to spend the night in the mountains, you're headed in the wrong direction," said the other who might or might not be Seamus.

Mountains? I must have been thrown off by all the weirdness I'd been experiencing a little while ago. It wasn't like me to get turned around in the woods.

"Come on, back you go." The twins moved to flank me, and I held up a hand to stop them.

"I can make it back on my own. Just point me in the right direction."

"Sorry, lass, we have our orders."

"Oh come on, you guys, not again." My plea fell on deaf ears, and I found myself being escorted along a trail I hadn't even known was there. The twins were watchful as if danger was hiding behind every tree, walking with me between them like a wayward child . . . or a prisoner.

"I was only getting some fresh air. You can stop treating me like I'm some fugitive."

The twin on my right spoke – I'd given up trying to tell them apart. "Isn't that what she said the first time, brother?"

"Aye, and we were near fool enough to be taken in by that sweet smile."

"That was over a week ago. How long are you going to hold that against me?"

"And what about three days ago?" asked the twin on my left.

"I told you I just wanted to hang out by the lake for a while. Where is the harm in that?"

The right twin snickered. "Like the last time you went to hang out by a lake, huh?"

"How do you know about that?"

He gave me a lopsided grin. "We've heard lots of stories about you."

"Which is why you won't be pulling the same trick with us," added his brother. "Though I am starting to feel a wee bit sympathetic to those guys."

The trees thinned and I saw the stone walls of the sprawling building I now called home. We passed the edge of the woods and stepped onto the wide green lawn. "I think I can make it from here," I told them.

Neither of them took the hint, and they stayed on either side of me as we walked toward the building. I folded my arms and went with them. No one had told me when I came here that being under Mohiri protection meant being treated like someone in a juvenile detention center. The twins were always good-natured about it, but they were still my guards no matter how you looked at it.

We neared the courtyard outside the training wing where two men stood talking, and as we approached they turned to watch us with knowing looks. Two more men walked around a corner, and I recognized them as Callum and the blond man who had shown up in training earlier. Callum gave me an amused nod, but the blond man's expression was unreadable.

I pulled away from the twins without a word and marched toward the door, trying to hide my anger and embarrassment. I'd promised to give this place a try, but I couldn't take much more of this. If this was going to be my life from now on, I wanted out.

I was almost at the stone archway of the courtyard when I heard shouts and saw the two men in the courtyard staring behind me with horrified expressions. *What now?* My heart raced as I whirled, expecting to find an army of vampires descending upon us.

At first, all I saw was Seamus and Niall drawing their swords along with Callum and his companion. "Run, lass!" yelled one of the twins. He jerked his head to the left to look at something. I followed his gaze and gasped at the sight of two monstrous creatures bearing down on us.

Bearing down on me.

Chapter 2

THE WARRIORS FORMED a defensive line in front of me a second before I realized what I was seeing. The creatures were coal black and so big they made a Great Dane look like a lap dog. Their huge jaws opened wide to reveal massive fangs.

The last time I had seen these two beasts had been over a month ago in the wine cellar of a mansion in Portland, and they looked just as ferocious in the sunlight as they had in the dimly lit cellar. Back then, I'd used my power to soothe them, but from the looks of them they were not so friendly anymore. All I could do was stand and watch huge claws gouge the ground and saliva flying from snarling jaws as the hellhounds thundered toward us.

The four men in front of me raised their weapons, and my mouth went dry with fear. My knowledge of hellhounds was very limited, and I had no idea if the Mohiri were even a match for the powerful beasts. I didn't think my power was going help much this time.

Or was it? What was it Nikolas had said about the hellhounds? *They are yours now. Once a fell beast imprints on a new master they are incredibly loyal. They will only answer to you.* Was that true? Had they really imprinted on me?

I backed away from the men who were too focused on the approaching beasts to watch me. When I had put a dozen or so feet between us, I turned and ran to the left, gathering my power as I went. If Nikolas was right, the hellhounds would not harm me because I was their master now. If he was wrong . . . I swallowed hard. I didn't want to think about that.

I stopped running and whirled around just as the hounds changed direction and headed straight for me. The warriors looked my way, and I saw horror on their faces as they realized what I'd done. They spun to intercept the hounds. I'd seen how fast Mohiri warriors moved, and I knew they would engage the hounds first. I had to do something before it was too late.

"STOP!" I bellowed at the top of my lungs, and the power building inside me made my voice resonate across the lawn in a way it had never done before. Men and beasts skidded to a stop and stood just feet from each other, watching me with startled expressions. My hand went to my throat. Had that sound really come from me?

I lowered my voice. "Don't move." When one of the twins opened his mouth to speak I cut him off. "I know these boys, and I think I can handle this." I had no idea if that was true, but it sounded pretty good, and I was encouraged by the fact that the hounds had actually stopped.

Before anyone could object, I pointed at my feet and said in my most commanding voice, "Come." The hounds tilted their heads to one side and looked at me like they weren't sure what to do. I spoke louder. "Come."

I didn't really expect it to work. I could barely get our beagle, Daisy, to come on command, even though I had saved her life and allowed her to sleep on my bed whenever she wanted to. I wasn't prepared when the two hellhounds sauntered over and halted right in front of me. *Holy crap!* I sucked in a sharp breath when I found myself face-to-face with two pairs of red eyes and two of the scariest looking mouths I had ever seen. Their hot breath fanned my face as they panted, and I resisted the urge to wave my hand in front of my nose at the awful smell that was like a combination of raw meat and bad foot odor. *God, I really hope these guys didn't just eat someone.*

"Sit," I commanded, and they sat back on their haunches. Their faces were still at eye level with me, but they didn't look nearly as threatening with their tongues hanging out. "Good boys," I praised while trying not to cough from their noxious breath. If you overlooked their size and their red eyes and their bone-crushing jaws, they were just big dogs really.

"Now, how did you two end up here?"

Their tails began to thump against the ground, and I smiled in relief. I reached out and rubbed the top of one hound's head, giving him a good scratch behind the ears. He shifted until he was pressed up against my side, and his weight almost tipped me over. A whimper made me look at the neglected hound on my other side, and I patted my hip. I found myself crushed between two heavy hellhounds clamoring for my attention. It occurred to me that I might be the only person to ever show them kindness. Hellhounds were bred for one purpose and that was to maim and kill. They were weapons, and weapons did not need affection.

I scratched their heads and grimaced when my face was bathed by two very long, wet tongues. "Ugh! This is not very hellish behavior." I tried to shove their mouths away, but they pushed back harder until I almost toppled backward. "Stop, stop," I wheezed, and when that didn't work, I choked out, "Down." The two of them immediately lay down and ceased their play. They were well trained at least.

I wiped my wet cheeks with my coat sleeve, grimacing at the wet tendrils of hair that hung around my face. My hand stilled in the act of pushing my hair out of my eyes when I realized how quiet it was. I looked up to find the four men watching me with expressions of shock and disbelief. I let out a sigh that only the hounds could hear. Just what I needed – another reason for people to stare at me.

The men recovered from their surprise, and the twins took a step toward me. The hellhounds leapt to their feet in front of me and bared their teeth, letting out low threatening growls. Niall and Seamus stopped in their tracks.

"Stop that," I ordered, putting my hands on the back of the hounds' necks. The growling ceased, but I felt the tension in their bodies as they maintained their protective stance, ready to pounce at the slightest provocation. *What do I do now?*

"If I wasn't seeing it with me own two eyes, I wouldn't believe it," said one of the twins without taking his eyes off the hellhounds.

His brother shook his head. "I'm seeing it and I still don't believe it."

I felt a low rumble in the hellhounds' chests when the men spoke, and I wondered how in hell I was going to stop the beasts from hurting someone. The hounds seemed docile enough with me, but apparently that did not extend to anyone else, especially armed men.

"Um, can you guys lower your weapons?"

None of the men moved to do as I asked, and they all stared at me like I had lost my mind. I understood their hesitation, considering what they were looking at, but I could not see any other way to end this peacefully.

"They are protecting me, and you all look pretty dangerous right now," I explained, still petting the hounds' heads. "They don't know you are friendly, so could you please just put the swords away?"

The blond warrior was the first one to comply, sliding his sword into the sheath on his back. The others followed, and as soon as the last weapon was out of sight, I felt the hellhounds' hackles go down.

"Much better. Now, I don't suppose any of you know how my hellhounds ended up here."

One of the twins gaped at me. "*Your* hellhounds?"

I patted one of the huge heads. "Do they *look* like they belong to someone else?"

Callum chuckled, and the blond warrior gave me an appraising look. Seamus and Niall stared at the other two men as if expecting one of them to say something. When neither spoke, one of the twins said, "They got here yesterday. That's all I know. I don't normally handle any of the beasts."

"You have other animals here?"

He made a noise. "I wouldn't call them animals, but yes, I think there's usually a few in the menagerie."

The image of young trolls trapped in a cage flashed through my mind, and outrage filled me. "You have a menagerie here? You put creatures on display?"

"That's just what we call it. It's where we keep some of the creatures we capture that are causing problems for the humans, until we can figure out what to do with them."

"I want to see it." He looked like he was going to object, so I said, "If my hounds are living there, I want to see it. Besides, how else do you plan to get them there?"

His eyes flicked warily to the hellhounds, and he sighed. "Follow me."

I trailed him, keeping a safe distance as he led me to a cluster of stone buildings at the back of the property. The hellhounds walked beside me, but I saw how they constantly surveyed our surroundings, looking for anything they perceived to be a threat.

Claire hadn't taken me near these buildings during my tour, and I'd figured they held weapons or more training rooms. The largest one was a long rectangle two stories high with windows on the second story only, and a domed roof that looked like thick glass but was most likely a much stronger material. There was one entrance, and my guide pulled open the heavy reinforced steel door, allowing me and the hounds to go ahead of him.

Whatever I was expecting, it was not the bright, airy, two-story room separated into eight caged enclosures of varying sizes. Between the cages were solid walls, presumably to keep the inhabitants from bothering each other, and metal bars lined the front of each cage. I could not see inside the cages when we first entered the building, but shuffling noises at the far end of the room told me that at least one of them was occupied.

"Can I look around . . . which one are you again?"

He grinned. "Seamus. Go ahead, but you'd best be putting up your beasts first because they make the other critter nervous. And me, too."

"Where do they go?" I hated the thought of caging any animal, but common sense told me the hellhounds could not be allowed to run free. At least not yet.

"There." Seamus pointed to the first enclosure that was at least twenty feet wide and fifteen feet deep. There was a slot at the front near the floor where food and water could be pushed inside, and at the back I saw an opening that led to a dark cave-like structure.

I waved at the open door to the cage. "All right, in you go, boys." The hounds hesitated for a moment, and I thought they were going to refuse to enter the cage. I couldn't blame them. I wouldn't want to be caged either. But they went in without any further urging, and I closed the gate behind them. "I'll come visit you every day. Maybe they'll let me take you for walks if you behave yourselves."

Seamus made a face that suggested no one would ever trust the hellhounds enough to let them walk around freely no matter how well they behaved. We'd have to see about that. These hounds were my responsibility, and I would not keep them locked away like zoo animals.

Seamus examined the locking mechanism on the gate after I closed it. "Hmmm, this doesn't appear to be broken. How did these two get out?"

"Maybe someone forgot to lock it."

He shook his head thoughtfully. "The locks engage automatically on the cages, and they can only be unlocked from the main control panel or with a coded key. I'll have to get security to pull up the surveillance for today."

I looked around until I spotted a number of security cameras fixed at regular intervals high up on the walls. There was one camera for each enclosure and two near the entrance. It made sense that if you were housing dangerous creatures, you kept them under close surveillance.

I left Seamus muttering over the lock and walked toward the other cages, intensely curious about what kinds of creatures they kept there. The first three cages I passed were empty, but my pace picked up when I saw what looked like wisps of smoke drifting out of the fourth one.

"Watch it, lass. Don't get too close to that one," Seamus called just before the interior of the cage came into view. Heeding his warning, I moved to the other side of the floor before I turned to see the occupant of the cage. My jaw dropped and my eyes nearly bugged out of my head.

"What the . . . ? You have a freaking dragon in here!"

I gawked at the greenish-brown creature breathing small puffs of smoke as it watched me with large green eyes eerily similar to those of a crocodile. Leathery wings were folded against its scaled body, and it crouched in the back of the cage like a cat about to pounce. It was small for a dragon, roughly the size of a very large bull, so I figured it must be young. Dragons are not native to North America so I wondered what in God's green earth had brought this one here.

"Not a dragon, a wyvern actually." An olive-skinned man with short black hair walked up to stand beside me. "And a mean one at that. This one burned five people and killed two in Utah before we managed to catch him."

I tried to remember what I had read about wyverns. They are smaller and faster than their dragon cousins but not as powerful. They breathe smaller flames, and they have two legs instead of four. Whereas dragons are intelligent, wyverns are closer to animals, kind of like a crocodile with wings and just as deadly.

I shivered. "What will they do with him?"

"We have a place down in Argentina where they actually train them to hunt vampires. We're holding Alex until they can send someone to get him.

Don't get too close to him. His flame has a good three-foot reach, and he won't think twice before trying to fry you."

I couldn't stop the laugh that burst from me. "Alex? You named a wyvern *Alex?*"

The man chuckled. "One of the men who caught him gave him that name. He said the beast was as surly as his older brother."

Shaking my head, I smiled and held out my hand. "Hi, I'm Sara."

"Sahir." His dark eyes were warm when he smiled. "I have heard much about you."

I made a face. "Yeah, you and everyone else, apparently. I think warriors gossip more than the girls at my old high school."

Sahir's laugh was deep and rich, and I liked him immediately. He moved toward the hellhounds' cage, and I followed. The hellhounds growled menacingly, but he ignored them. "I have cared for many creatures, but this is the first pair of fell beasts I've ever had in my care. They are extremely rare. When I heard how they were captured, I must admit I thought the story was fabricated – until I saw you walking with them."

"Damndest thing I ever saw," said Seamus, who had finally stopped studying the lock on the hellhounds' cage. "I thought for sure someone was going to die when I saw them coming at us. Sahir, you have any idea how those beasts could've gotten loose?"

Sahir shook his head. "No one's been here since they brought them in last night, and the keys are in my office. Perhaps we should check the security footage."

Seamus and I followed Sahir to his brightly lit office at the back of the building where Sahir logged into a computer. A few clicks later, he brought up the feeds from the security camera in the building. "All camera feeds are stored in the central security database, but you can view them from any computer if you have clearance," he explained to me as he clicked on the camera for the hellhounds' cage. He opened the digital footage and went back an hour. Then he slowly fast-forwarded until we saw the door to the cage click open and the hellhounds leave the cage. Sahir switched to one of the outdoor cameras, and we watched the hellhounds push open the main door and run from the building.

"Could it have been unlocked by mistake?" I asked, and their expressions told me that it was unlikely.

Seamus rubbed his chin. "Not many know the beasts are here, and I can't see why anyone would set them free."

"As a precaution, I'll ask security to put a second lock on the cages," Sahir said as he reviewed the footage again. "I'm just thankful Alex didn't get loose as well."

I shivered at the thought of the wyvern flying around the grounds shooting flames at anything that moved. "Yeah, same here."

Seamus left after we finished going over the surveillance videos, saying he had to get back to work. I stayed with the hellhounds for another hour and spent a little while getting to know Sahir who was new to Westhorne, too. He'd come here from the compound in Kenya two months ago, and before that he'd lived all over Africa and the Middle East. He was originally from Afghanistan, but his interest in supernatural creatures took him far from home. He considered himself more of a scholar than a warrior, and he obviously cared a great deal for the welfare of the beasts in his care. He told me few people came to the menagerie, but I was welcome to visit the hellhounds whenever I wanted.

I was in much better spirits when I returned to the main building later that afternoon. It felt strange to have so much free time here, but Westhorne did not offer regular classes for the trainees. Mohiri children went to school until they turned sixteen, and then they began their warrior training either at their home compound, or at a place like Westhorne where the seasoned warriors took over their education. There were six trainees here besides me, and I'd noticed their days were a lot fuller than mine. In the mornings, I trained with Callum, but so far my afternoons were free. According to Callum, it was to allow me a period of adjustment before full training began. Eight hours with that Scottish brute? I couldn't wait.

Back in my room, I fired up the killer new laptop that had been waiting in my room for me on my first day here. It made my old one look ancient, and I was immensely grateful the Mohiri loved technology. Their network connection blew my old cable modem out of the water. I went to my happy place every time I logged in.

The first thing I did was log into the new email account my hacker friend, David, set up for me. David was hiding from the Master, too, and he was pretty paranoid about communication, which considering our shared history wasn't a bad thing. He had also shown me how to check for any kind of surveillance software on my new laptop, in case the Mohiri were keeping track of my online activity. I hated to be mistrustful even before I got to know them, but I had to be sure. Thankfully, the computer was clean.

There was one new message from David, and I opened it, eager to see if he had any news. I knew the Mohiri had to be looking for Madeline and the Master, but in the week and a half I had been here, I hadn't heard a word about their progress. So, David and I were doing our own search for Madeline. Well, David was doing most of the work, but he had as much vested in finding her as I did.

The last lead I told you about turned out to be bogus. I have a few more I'm checking out and I have some of my friends helping. It might take me a few weeks, but if M is in the country, I'll find her. I'll keep you posted. Stay safe.

I read the email again. David was really good at what he did, and I bet his friends were, too. If anyone could find Madeline, it was him. When he did, she was going to tell us everything she knew about the vampire that had torn our lives apart. I still hadn't figured out how I would make her talk, but I'd think of something. Maybe I'd threaten to feed her to the hellhounds.

I tried for the hundredth time to think of a reason why she didn't just pick up a phone and call the Mohiri to tell them who the Master was. Why spend your life on the run when you could eliminate the thing you are running from? She was a warrior, a vampire hunter. She should be ridding the world of vampires instead of protecting the identity of one as dangerous as a Master. I did not waste my time wondering why she didn't give up his name to protect me. Madeline had shown her lack of maternal feelings a long time ago.

I closed my email and checked out a few of the message boards to see what was going on out in the world. According to my old pal, Wulfman, it was very quiet in Maine these days, and I suspected that was because every werewolf in the state was still on alert after all the vampire activity there a month ago. I worried about Nate there alone after what had happened to both of us, but Roland kept assuring me that Maxwell was monitoring the area and the pack was keeping an eye on Nate, too.

The rest of the country wasn't lucky enough to have werewolves guarding it, and I read about at least two dozen disappearances in California, Texas, and Nevada that looked vampire-related. I shuddered every time I thought about a human in the hands of one of those monsters. I still had nightmares about Eli even though I'd killed him. I had no illusions about my ability to fight off a vampire, and I knew things could have turned out horribly for me if circumstances had been different. If Nikolas and the werewolves had not arrived when they did. If Eli hadn't been too distracted to see me reach for my knife.

My phone rang and I reached for it, knowing it had to be one of two people since only Roland and Nate called me at this number. I was already smiling when I answered it.

"You owe me big time, demon girl," Roland quipped, snickering at the nickname he'd made up for me last week.

I leaned back in my chair and scowled at the wall. "If you don't stop calling me that, I'm not talking to you anymore."

He laughed at my weak threat. We both knew that would never happen. "I think you'll forgive me when I tell you about my little trip to a certain cave today."

My stomach quivered in excitement. "And?"

"And that place is a bitch to get to. You couldn't find a less dangerous hideaway?"

"Remy found it, not me, and you have to admit it's the perfect spot.

Now tell me."

"Do you know how bloody cold it is up on that cliff?" he moaned. "I think my toes are still frozen."

"Roland!"

He sighed. "Message delivered and answered."

I jerked upright, my heart racing. "Answered? He left something for me?"

"More like he drew something on the wall of the cave. I took a picture of it with my phone. I don't know how you can read this stuff. It looks like hieroglyphics." I heard him playing with his cell phone. "I just sent it to you."

I scrambled to check my email, and I had to wait another thirty seconds for his message to show up. When I opened the attachment, I stared at the picture for a minute before tears pricked my eyes. Leaving home had been hard enough, but leaving without saying good-bye to Remy had killed a little piece of me. After a lot of pleading on my part, Roland had agreed to leave a small note in the cave for me. Remy could not read human writing, and I knew how to write a few dozen troll words, so my short message translated to, *I miss you. Sara.* On the cave wall, written in Troll was, *I miss you too, my friend.*

"Well? What does it say?"

I translated the writing for Roland, and he huffed loudly. "That's it? You made me freeze my ass off climbing down a cliff twice to find out if he was still your friend? Hell, I could have told you that and saved myself the trip."

"You don't know trolls, Roland. They have very different ways, and the elders are really strict. If they told Remy to stay away from me forever, he would obey them."

He sighed again. "Sara, I might not know troll ways, but I saw you with Remy. Meeting him is not something I'll ever forget. No matter what happened back then or what orders he got from his elders, that troll will never stop being your friend."

Roland was usually playful and goofy, and sometimes I forgot how insightful he could be. "I think I just needed to hear it from him. Thanks for doing this for me. You're the best."

"I know. I get that a lot."

I rolled my eyes and laughed. "Good to know some things will never change."

He laughed with me. "What can I say? Women love me."

"You're hopeless, you know that? One of these days, you're going to meet someone who doesn't fall all over you, and I hope I get to meet her."

"I have met her, and she broke my heart back in elementary school."

"Oh, don't start that again." I closed my eyes, still embarrassed by his and Peter's recent confessions that they both had crushes on me when we were kids.

"I bet your face is red right now," he teased.

"Stop it or I won't tell you about what happened today."

"More exciting than my day?"

I told him all about the hellhounds, the menagerie, and the wyvern. He whistled and told me I had to send him some pictures. "I'm not sure if I'm allowed to do that, but I'll ask. Maybe you can come visit me and see them yourself."

"Yeah, a werewolf visiting a Mohiri stronghold, that should go over well."

"You never know. Stranger things have happened." I picked at the label on a bottle of Coke on my desk. "So, any special plans for the big birthday next week?" I felt a pang of sadness at the thought of not being there for his eighteenth birthday. It is a huge milestone for a werewolf because they are considered an adult at eighteen, and they are included in hunts and start doing patrols with the other adult wolves. It was bittersweet for both of us. We were excited for his coming of age, but sad that we wouldn't be able to celebrate his birthday together. My own birthday was a little over a month away, and it was hard to imagine him and Peter not being here for it.

"No big plans. I think I have to work the next day anyway."

"You have a *job?* Who are you, and what have you done with Roland?"

He groaned. "And what's worse is I'll be working for Uncle Max at the lumber yard. Every weekend."

"Didn't you always say you'd rather work at a fast food joint than for Maxwell?"

"I have no choice. I gotta make some cash if I'm ever going to get some new wheels, and the lumber yard pays good money."

Guilt settled over me. Roland's pickup had been ripped up by a pack of crocotta trying to get to me. He loved that old truck.

"I know why you're quiet all of a sudden, and you better stop it," he ordered. "That was not your fault. Besides, one of the guys in the pack might sell me an old Mustang he has in his shed. It needs some work, but my cousin, Paul, said he'd help me fix it up. You remember him; he's the mechanic. I just need to get enough for a down payment and it's mine."

I smiled at the excitement in his voice. "I wish I was there to see it. You never did finish teaching me how to drive."

"Forget it! I saw what happened to the last car you drove."

"Hey, that was so not my fault, and I got away from the bad guys, didn't I?"

"They must have lots of cars there you can practice on, and they can afford to replace them." He made a sound like a snort. "I bet Nikolas could teach you, if you don't kill each other first."

My hand jerked, almost knocking over the bottle of Coke. I pushed it out of my reach and glared at it. "I haven't seen him since he dumped me here and took off."

Roland was quiet for a moment. "I'm sure he has lots of work to catch up on and he'll be back soon."

"He can stay away for good for all I care."

"Come on, you don't mean that. Nikolas is not such a bad guy, and coming from me, that's something."

"I don't want to talk about him." My face heated up, and my palms prickled as resentment flared in me at hearing my best friend defend *him*. I knew I was overreacting, but I couldn't stop the angry hurt that came every time I thought about Nikolas leaving the same day we got here. After everything we went through, he couldn't even be bothered to say good-bye.

A soft *hissing* pulled me from my silent rant. I looked at the Coke bottle a few inches from my hand, and gasped at the brown soda bubbling up as if it had been shaken. My hand closest to the bottle was crawling with blue static, and sparks leapt from my fingers to the bottle that looked ready to explode.

I jerked my hand back and tucked it under my other arm, and almost immediately, the soda began to settle down. What was happening to me? Whatever it was, it was getting worse.

"Hello? You still there?"

"Yeah, sorry." I tried to keep the tremble from my voice. "I got distracted for a minute. I need to tell you something."

"Okaaay," he said warily. "You haven't been selling troll parts on the black market have you?"

"Roland!"

"Sorry."

I sucked in a long, slow breath. "You know how my friend Aine said my Fae powers might start to grow? I think it's happening – or something is going on anyway."

"What do you mean?"

"I don't know. It's like my power is on the fritz or something." I described the little flare-ups I'd been having, including the strange cold spot in my chest. "I almost made a bottle of Coke explode a few minutes ago, just by touching it."

"Hmm." He was quiet for a minute. "Maybe it's tied to your emotions."

"What do you mean?"

"You haven't been very happy since you went there, and you got mad when I mentioned Nikolas. Faeries are supposed to be, like, happy all the time, right? Maybe being negative screws with your Faerie magic."

I snorted. "Great explanation."

"No seriously. Or it could be hormones. It's not that time – ?"

"Stop! Do not go there if you know what's good for you!" My face really was flaming now.

Smothered laughter reached my ears, and I called him a few not-so-nice things, which only made him laugh openly. The thing about Roland is that it's really hard to resist his laughter.

"Feel better?" he asked when we'd both finally stopped cracking up.

"Yes." I wiped my eyes. "You're an ass."

"But you love me anyway." His voice grew more serious. "I'm sure this thing with your power is nothing. You've been through a lot lately, and it's probably messing with you."

"Maybe you're right." What he said made sense. This had only started up since I came here. I wasn't miserable, but I wasn't happy either.

"Of course I'm right. I'm not just a pretty face, you know."

"No, you have that huge ego, too." I felt lighter than I had in days.

"Well, my job here is done." He heaved a weighty sigh. "Now I have to study. We have a chem test tomorrow, and *I* still have to graduate from high school."

Chemistry was Roland's worst subject. It used to be mine, too, and we used to help each other cram for tests. Chemistry was one thing I did not miss. "Good luck on the test, and thanks again for going to the cave for me."

"Anytime. No, scratch that. Please don't ask me to do that again," he pleaded. "Talk to you tomorrow."

I hung up and rubbed my damp hands against my thighs. The static was gone and the Coke was back to normal, but that didn't lessen my anxiety. My power was acting weird, and I had no idea what to do about it. I wished Aine was here, or Remy. He was so knowledgeable and would have helped me figure this out. I let out a ragged breath. I missed him so much.

"Enough of that." I pushed away from the desk and glanced at the clock. It was a little early for dinner, but I had to get out of this room and stop wallowing in self-pity. I grabbed my laptop, tucked it under my arm, and headed down to one of the common rooms. There were three such rooms where people could hang out and watch TV or talk. They had wet bars if you wanted a drink, and no one seemed to care how old you were. Roland and Peter had been so envious when I told them that part.

TV sounds drew me to one of the rooms, and when I peeked in I found a single occupant, a blond boy named Michael, who I'd met on my second day here. Michael was fifteen, and he was quiet and reserved compared to the other kids here. He was a bit of a computer geek, too, and he spent most of his free time on his laptop, gaming and talking to his friends online. On my third day here, I was struck down by a vicious migraine, and it was Michael who had come to my room to see how I was doing and to ask if I needed anything. The healers said my headache was probably brought on by stress, but it was so bad that even the gunna paste had no effect on it. I lay in bed suffering for the better part of a day before I remembered the tiny vial of troll bile I'd brought with me. I'd planned to destroy it, but thankfully I never got around to it. A single drop of bile in a glass of water was all it took to rid me of the horrible pain.

Michael was sitting in an armchair, engrossed in his laptop as usual, when I took a seat on the couch. "Hey, Michael."

"Oh . . . hi, Sara," he stammered, smiling shyly. Poor guy, I didn't know how he would ever make it as a warrior if he didn't get over his nervousness. I almost rolled my eyes. Like I had room to judge others. I was probably the worst trainee in Mohiri history.

"What are you up to?"

"Not much, just talking to a friend." He leaned on the arm of his chair and his face lit up. "Did you hear that they wiped out a huge nest in Las Vegas yesterday?"

"How big was it?" The last time I saw a vampire, he had twelve of his friends with him. I couldn't imagine facing more than that.

"I heard it was thirty suckers, and it only took two units to take them all down. Of course, that's because Nikolas Danshov ran the mission. He probably took out half of them himself."

My mouth went dry. "Nikolas was there?"

His eyes practically glowed from excitement. "Yeah. What I wouldn't give to see him in action. They say he can take out half a dozen suckers at one time without breaking a sweat."

"Yep," I replied absently, remembering Nikolas facing down a dozen vampires and easily disposing of three of them.

"What's he like? You know him right? Everyone says you even fought suckers together."

I held back a sigh. It had taken less than a day here to learn Nikolas was something of a superhero among the younger Mohiri. "Nikolas is an amazing warrior."

Michael rolled his eyes. "I know that. I mean, what's it like hanging out with him?"

I let out a short laugh. "Nikolas doesn't hang out. He glares at you and tries to boss you around. Then he leaves. We spent more time fighting with each other than the vampires."

Michael's cornflower-blue eyes widened. "No one argues with Nikolas."

"He might be a great warrior, but he's still just a person, Michael, and half the time he's an arrogant pain in the butt."

"Who's an arrogant pain in the butt?" asked a new voice, and I looked at the two boys entering the room. Josh ran a hand through his unruly blond hair and elbowed Terrence before sitting beside me on the couch. "She must be talking about you, buddy."

Terrence scoffed as he plunked down in one of the other chairs. With his mocha skin, artfully spiked black hair, and stunning hazel eyes, he was easily one of the best looking guys I had ever seen. He looked at Michael. "Whatcha up to, Mike?"

"Nothing," Michael mumbled. He gathered up his laptop and stood timidly. "Um, I have some stuff to do. Talk to you later."

I watched him hurry from the room, feeling bad that we had scared him away. "He doesn't seem to fit in here much. He's an orphan too, right?"

Terrence nodded, wearing a sympathetic smile. "Yes, poor kid." I gave him a hard look, and he quickly added, "Oh I don't mean it that way. I have nothing against orphans. He's just never gotten over losing his family."

I was afraid to ask, but I did anyway. "What happened to them?"

"What else? Suckers got them. He and his brother were living with their mother in Atlanta when our people found them. But the same night they went to get them, the suckers went after them. Only Michael got out. His mother didn't make it, and the warriors couldn't find Matthew. The suckers took him."

"How old was his brother?"

"Matthew was his twin, and they were seven when it happened." Terrence sank back heavily in his chair. "They never found Matthew, and Michael still believes his brother got away. No one can convince him otherwise. He spends most of his time searching the Internet, looking at missing persons websites, public records – stuff like that."

"That's awful." I'd lost my dad to a vampire, but at least I knew he was dead and I didn't have to go through life wondering what had happened to him. I'd spent ten years just trying to understand why he was killed, and I could not imagine how hard it would be if he had gone missing like Michael's brother.

The three of us sat in silence for a minute before Terrence asked, "So, Sara, what did Tristan say to you today?"

"Tristan?" The only Tristan I knew of was Lord Tristan, who sat on the Council of Seven and ran Westhorne. He'd been away on Council business since I got here, and I had yet to meet him.

Terrence shook his head like I had asked who Michael Jackson was. "You know, Tristan, the head honcho? He showed up in training today."

"Oh . . . which one was he?" I resisted the urge to bury my head in my hands. Callum had wiped the floor with my butt in front of Lord Tristan? After that exhibit, the man must be wondering why Nikolas had wasted so much time trying to bring me in.

Both boys snickered. "He would be *that* one," Josh informed me. I looked through the doorway, which gave us a clear view of the main hall, and saw the blond man from this morning talking to a red-haired woman I recognized as Claire, who had shown me around on my first day here. I felt heat rise in my neck. "Oh, him. He didn't say anything to me. He was talking to Callum."

The boys looked disappointed that there was nothing more to it, but Josh quickly switched gears. "We heard some things about you, and we were wondering if they were true."

"And what would that be?" I asked warily.

"Is it true that you actually hung with a pack of werewolves?"

At the downward turn of his mouth, irritation shot through me. I knew the history between werewolves and the Mohiri, and I was well aware of how the two races felt about each other. But Roland and Peter were like family to me, and I would not listen to anyone put them down. "Yes, I hung with them all the time. I even slept at their houses and ate with them. In fact, my best friend is a werewolf."

Josh put up his hands. "Touchy. Okay, we get it; the wolves are off limits."

Terrence leaned in. "We heard a lot of other stuff, too."

"Such as?"

"Did you *really* kill some suckers?"

"And fight off a pack of crocotta?" Josh asked.

"And rescue a baby troll?"

I looked at their eager faces and shrugged. "Yes."

"Yes to what?" Josh asked impatiently.

"Yes to all of it. Only there were three young trolls and I didn't rescue them alone. I did fight one crocotta, but it probably would have killed me if one of my friends hadn't killed it first. And I did kill a vampire." I had killed two vampires if I included the one Remy held for me, but Eli was the only one that mattered to me.

"No way!" exclaimed a new male voice, and I looked up to see that Olivia and Mark, two other trainees, had joined us. I hadn't spoken to Mark much, but Olivia and I had talked a few times and she seemed nice. Olivia was pretty in a girl-next-door kind of way with long dark hair, a smattering of freckles, and a sweet smile. Mark reminded me of a grunge rocker with shaggy blond hair that fell into his eyes. He didn't smile as much as Olivia. I had noticed they hung out together a lot, and I wondered if they were a couple or friends like me and Roland.

Mark took Michael's vacated chair and stared at me in disbelief, making me want to scowl at him. Olivia was a little more hesitant. "Do you mind if we join you?" she asked.

I shrugged. "The more the merrier, I guess."

"So, let me get this straight," Mark began. "You expect us to believe that you did all that with no training whatsoever? I hate to point out the obvious, but from what I've seen, you can't fight . . . at all."

I flushed at the reminder of my training. "You can believe what you want."

"Don't mind him. Tell us about the suckers," Terrence urged.

Josh leaned closer. "Forget the suckers. I want to hear about the trolls."

I told them about how the young trolls were kidnapped and we had to find them before they were taken overseas. "They were holding them at this huge house in Portland. Nikolas and Chris went in first to take out the security, and we went in after. We had no idea those guys were crazy enough to work with vampires, and we had to kill a few of them to get to the house. Nikolas, Chris, and my friends took out most of them. I did one, but I had help."

"So, you found the baby trolls?" Olivia asked breathlessly.

"Yes, they were in the wine cellar."

Her eyes were like saucers. "What happened next?"

"A bunch of Mohiri warriors showed up and took over and we left." It was only half the story, but there was so much I couldn't tell them without revealing things I couldn't share.

Terrence whistled. "How did you guys know about the trolls in the first place?"

People did not understand my relationship with Remy and I was not in the mood to answer the questions that would arise if I mentioned him. "The werewolves know everything that goes on in their territory."

"That is too frigging cool," Josh said, his blue eyes wide.

Mark frowned. "Wait. What did you use to kill the sucker if you didn't have any weapons?"

"I did have a weapon. I had a knife Nikolas gave me when we met."

"You have one of Nikolas's knives?" Olivia asked, and I almost shook my head at the worship on her face.

"Not anymore." It was either at the bottom of the ocean or somewhere in Faerie, and I wasn't going to explain either of those possibilities.

"Convenient."

A girl with a cute blond pixie cut walked up to our group. Jordan was eighteen and, from what I'd seen and heard, the best trainee here. According to Michael, she was the oldest orphan ever reclaimed at ten years old – before I came along.

"What do you mean?" Olivia asked.

"It's a great story, but I've seen your girl here in training." Jordan scoffed. "If she killed a sucker, it's probably because it tripped and fell on the knife."

Terrence smiled at me. "Don't mind Jordan. She's actually a nice person when she's not being herself."

Jordan scowled, and I couldn't help but think she would be prettier if she stopped glaring at everyone. She walked away, calling over her shoulder, "Whatever. Make sure you get plenty of sleep tonight, Terrence. You wouldn't want to lose your grip on your sword again tomorrow."

Terrence muttered under his breath, and Josh said, "Don't let her get to you. She got lucky today."

I didn't say anything. I'd seen Jordan handling the long thin sword favored by the Mohiri, and I didn't think luck had anything to do with her skills. That girl was scary good. Not as good as Nikolas, of course, but she might be someday.

My stomach rumbled, reminding me I hadn't eaten lunch. I grabbed my laptop and stood.

"Hey, don't go," Terrence protested. "I want to hear about the crocotta."

"The crocotta will have to wait. It's dinnertime, and I'm starving."

He and Josh stood at the same time. Terrence gave me a wide smile, showing off his dimples. "Perfect. You can tell us all about them over dinner."

Chapter 3

I TOSSED MY sketchpad and pencil down on the bed after staring at the blank page for the last ten minutes. I was trying to draw the hellhounds, but even though I could see them exactly as I wanted to sketch them, my fingers didn't seem to know where to start.

Rolling off the bed, I went to open the window and listened to the heavy silence of the valley. It was too quiet here at night. I'd give anything to hear the familiar sounds of the waterfront or open my door and hear Nate clicking on his keyboard. I missed Daisy's three-legged gait and Oscar's motorboat purr. Hell, I even missed the imps scratching and chattering behind the walls. I missed everything.

It was too early for bed, and watching TV alone in my room didn't appeal to me for once. I opened my door, wondering if any of the other trainees were hanging out downstairs. Seeking out company was a new experience for me, but I'd never really felt lonely before I came here. I'd enjoyed having dinner with the others tonight, instead of eating alone like I normally did. For the first time since I arrived, it felt like I'd connected with other people. I hadn't realized how much I missed that until today.

The common rooms were empty except for a warrior I didn't know watching an old black-and-white movie in one of them. I stood in the main hall and debated where to go. The north wing and west wing housed mostly living quarters like my own, so there was nothing to see there. The first floor of the west wing was training rooms and I'd seen more than enough of them already. The south wing held the offices, meeting rooms, security, and the living quarters for Lord Tristan, some of the senior warriors, and important visitors. That left the east wing. During my tour, Claire had pointed out the medical ward on the first floor. She'd also told me there was a sick warrior recuperating in the wing. I stayed away from the first floor so I didn't disturb him, and I was very quiet when I took the stairs to the second floor.

Strolling down the long second-floor hallway, I ran a hand lightly along the dark paneling, struck for the hundredth time by the grandeur of my new home. The walls on this floor were hung with beautiful oil paintings and ornate wall sconces that had been converted from gas to electric. I had not asked anyone how old the building was, but I suspected it was well over a hundred years old. The Mohiri lived for centuries, so it was no surprise for them to hold onto their homes for a long time. What was it like to live that long and to witness the coming of electricity, automobiles, and the age of technology? What wonders and changes in the world would I live to see over my own lifetime?

At the end of the hallway, light spilled from a room with the door slightly ajar. I pushed it open and I could barely contain my excitement at the sight of the shelves of books lining the walls from floor to ceiling. There was a large library off the main hall, but it didn't hold a candle to this room. This one looked like something out of an English manor with dark walls, floor-to-ceiling windows, and a large fireplace at one end of the room. Two high-backed chairs faced the fire that crackled in the hearth, and a lamp on the small table between the chairs cast a soft glow over the room. It looked like someone had just stepped out of the room, and I hesitated, worried they would mind my intrusion. I turned to leave, but one more look at all those books changed my mind.

The only problem with so many books was choosing one. I liked a lot of the classics, but I had tons of them in the boxes of books that had come with me from home. I inhaled the smell of old paper, and a smile spread across my face. I had a feeling I was going to be spending a lot of time here, and I couldn't help but think that my dad would have loved this room, too.

I scanned the titles to see what treasures the little library held. Automatically, my eyes searched for the Bs because something told me there had to be some Brontë on these shelves. I found what I was looking for high above my head, and I had to roll the squeaky wooden ladder over so I could reach the books. Reverently, I pulled out the copy of *Jane Eyre* and fingered the cloth-covered spine. My copy was a dog-eared paperback that was falling apart from too many readings. I opened the cover to the first page and felt my eyes bug out. A first edition *Jane Eyre* in perfect condition!

I shouldn't be touching these. Regretfully, I reached up to slide the book back into its place on the shelf. My old copy would do just fine. I'd be too nervous about damaging the rare book to enjoy it.

The thought had barely passed through my mind when my hold on the ladder slipped. I let out a loud gasp as I lost my grip on the precious tome and it fell to the floor with a thud. I grabbed the ladder again, just in time to keep from falling. Climbing down, I picked up the book, relieved to see no damage to the cover.

"If you are quite finished making a racket, I'd like to get back to my book now," said a voice in clipped English from behind one of the chairs.

Startled, I almost dropped the book again. "I'm sorry. I didn't know anyone else was here."

"Well, now you do. There is a perfectly nice library downstairs where you can bother someone else."

I bristled at his rudeness. I might have disturbed him, but that was no reason to be nasty. I'd dealt with too many bullies in my lifetime to let a faceless person push me around. "Thank you for pointing that out, but I am perfectly content here." I moved toward the chairs near the fireplace, fully intending to make myself at home.

With an irritated sigh, a man stood up and came around the chairs. He was tall, and his dark auburn hair hung in unkempt waves to his shoulders. His complexion was pale as if he did not see much sun, but that did not take away from his handsome aristocratic features. Hooded brown eyes glared at me, and his mouth was turned down as he crossed his arms and blocked my passage. I couldn't help but notice that his pants and jacket looked like they were from another era, and they were wrinkled and lightly soiled.

I stared at him for several seconds, not because I was afraid of him, but because he looked so much like Stuart Townsend in *Queen of the Damned*. The resemblance was uncanny. I think I smiled, which only made the man scowl even harder. After a month of fighting with Nikolas and coming face-to-face with real vampires, this guy was about as scary as Michael. There was something slightly off about his stare and his disheveled appearance, but I couldn't put my finger on it.

"You must be new or you would know no one comes up here. They prefer to use the other library. I am sure you would be happier there."

I met his dark gaze without wavering. "I appreciate your concern, but I like it here." I moved to go past him, half expecting him to try to block me again, but he only watched silently as I took the other chair and opened my book. I felt his eyes burning into me for a long moment before he made a grumbling sound and went back to his own chair.

Once he sat, the only sounds were the whisper of pages turning and the soft cracks and pops from the fire. It was hard to believe I was reading a first edition of one of my favorite books, which had just been sitting on a shelf for anyone to read. Maybe a book like this didn't hold as much interest for people who had been around when the book was first released. I ran my hand along the open page and hoped I never got too old or too jaded to appreciate things like this.

It took me a few minutes to realize I was the only one turning pages.

Something told me my companion was staring at me again, but I was determined not to give him the satisfaction of reacting to his behavior. If this was his attempt at scaring me off, he'd have to try a lot harder. To prove it, I pulled my feet up under me and prepared to lose myself in Jane's world.

He seemed to settle down after that, and it was another twenty minutes before I heard him shift in his chair and make small huffing sounds. I was tempted to tell him there could be no way I was disturbing him now, but I refused to acknowledge him. Maybe he would give up or just go away once he realized I was here until I was ready to leave. However, after another ten minutes of listening to him fidget and grumble under his breath, I was ready to throw a book at him. *And he said I was making a racket.*

"She was a beautiful woman, but always so serious."

His voice startled me into looking over at him. "Excuse me?"

He waved a hand at the book I held. "Charlotte. Most people said that Emily was the fairer one, but she really had nothing to her older sister. Such a gifted but tragic family."

It took me a moment to understand what he was saying. "You knew the Brontë sisters?" I didn't try to keep the disbelief out of my voice.

He looked affronted, and his voice rose a notch. "Are you insinuating that I am lying?"

I shrugged. "I'm not insinuating anything."

"Still, I don't think I like your tone."

I turned my attention back to my book. "Then don't talk to me."

He made another series of huffing sounds and got up to go to the other side of the room. After a few minutes of quiet I figured he had gone. I felt a little bad because I hadn't meant to drive him away, but I had as much right as him to use this room. And it wasn't like I had been disturbing him, except for dropping the book. He looked like a twenty-year-old, but he behaved like a crotchety old man who was put out because he couldn't have his way.

It surprised me when he appeared beside his chair again with a different book in his hands. His body shook a little as he sat, and I noticed a fine sheen of moisture on his face.

"Are you ill?"

Apparently, that was the absolute wrong thing to ask him. His nostrils flared and his eyes darkened even more. "What is that supposed to mean?" he snarled, and I felt the hairs rise up on my arms. Okay, maybe he was a little scarier than Michael.

"It doesn't mean anything. I just thought you might not be feeling well." Something told me he would not react well to a sympathetic voice, so I kept my tone as normal as possible.

"I am perfectly fine."

"Good."

"Why do you care anyway?" He still sounded angry, but the snarl was gone at least.

"I don't know. I guess it's one of my many faults."

He was quiet again for a few minutes before he griped, "Do you do this often, invade others' privacy and tell them they look awful?"

I looked up from my book again and met his challenging stare. "As far as I know, this library is open to anyone, and I did apologize for disturbing you. I did not say that you looked awful, so please stop scowling at me. If I didn't know better, I'd say you were fishing for compliments."

"I do not *fish* for complements." He narrowed his eyes at me. "You are an annoying little imp. It is no wonder you came here instead of being with the other children. They probably can't abide your company."

I stood, fed up with his churlishness and insults. "Listen here, Lestat, you are no charmer yourself."

"*Lestat?*" His eyes widened and he jumped up, sputtering. "Did you just compare me to a vampire – a *fictional* vampire?"

I didn't know what had made me call him that, but there was no taking it back. "You called me an annoying imp."

"Because you are annoying."

"You're not too much fun to be around either."

His mouth opened and closed like a fish out of water. "You are an irritating person, and I am not used to people talking to me this way." He pulled himself up to his full height, sounding every bit like a haughty lord. For all I knew he was one, but that didn't give him the right to treat people like crap.

"If you don't like how I talk, then don't talk to me. You read your book, and I'll read mine."

"I can't read now. You've ruined it for me."

Good Lord, this guy would try a saint. "Then leave if you don't want to read."

He looked like he was about to stomp his foot like a little boy. "I was here first."

I let out a heavy sigh. The man was infuriating and rude, and I really didn't need the aggravation. "Fine. I'll leave. Good night."

"You showed up here and ruined my evening, and now you are leaving?" Was that disappointment in his voice? I could not understand this guy for the life of me.

"Yes." I stopped at the door and wrinkled my nose at him. "Something in here smells really *old* and musty. Maybe the room just needs a good cleaning." Turning away, I left before he could see the satisfied smile on my face.

* * *

I barely noticed my surroundings as I walked back to the main building from the menagerie. I still couldn't believe the hellhounds were here, and I had no idea what I was going to do with them. They were huge brutes, and they growled menacingly whenever anyone but me went near their cage. I couldn't leave them locked up in there forever, but Sahir was afraid – and probably rightfully so – that they would harm someone if they were let out. Their welfare and happiness were my responsibility now and it weighed on me. I was determined to spend as much time as it took to train them and make them safe for other people to be around.

The hellhounds were not the only things on my mind. My power was going haywire all of a sudden, and I had no idea why or what to do about it. Just this morning, I was soaking in the healing baths after training when my scalp began to tingle and static crackled in my hair. I could have sworn I saw tiny sparkles of light in the cloudy water. Fear drove me from the bath before my time was up, and I'd cast a furtive glance at Olivia who lay with her eyes closed in her own tub. But the other girl had shown no signs of noticing anything out of the ordinary. How long could I hide this before someone saw it and started asking questions I couldn't answer?

"Sara."

I turned to find Claire hurrying toward me. Judging by her amused expression she had called to me several times. "Hi, Claire. What's up?"

She returned my smile. "I thought you would have forgotten my name with all the new faces around you. How are you settling in?"

"Great."

Claire laughed at my unconvincing tone. "Give it another week or so. All orphans have an adjustment period. It took me almost a month to even speak to anyone."

"You were an orphan?" It was hard to think of cheerful, outgoing Claire as a shy orphan. "How long have you been here?"

She put a hand to her chin. "I think it's been eighty years. You lose track after a while. I was four when Tristan found me."

"Lord Tristan?"

"Yes. It was during the Great Depression," she said as we walked together. "He found me at an orphanage in Boston. I have vague memories of my mother, but I don't remember what happened to her. The people at the orphanage told Tristan they were overflowing with abandoned children whose parents could not feed them anymore. Tristan *adopted* me and set up a monthly stipend to help the orphanage. I think he did that for a lot of orphanages at the time."

The last two weeks, I'd resented the absent leader who had enforced so many restrictions on me. Hearing Claire's story about how generous Tristan was improved my opinion of him.

"Speaking of Tristan, he'd like to see you in his office. I'll show you where it is."

Lord Tristan wanted to see me? Maybe after my awful training session yesterday he had decided I wasn't cut out to be a warrior after all. Or maybe the incident with the hellhounds had made him question the wisdom of having me here.

Claire led me to the first floor of the south wing and stopped in front of a closed door. "He's waiting for you. Go on in," she said and left me alone in the hallway.

I couldn't just walk in, so I knocked on the door and waited for it to open. Lord Tristan's blue eyes were surprisingly warm and his smile welcoming when he saw me standing there. He opened the door wider and waved me inside. "Sara, come in."

His office was impressive. One side was taken up by the usual office furniture: desk, chairs, filing cabinets, and a computer. On the other side of the room was a sitting area with a couch, a chair, and several small tables. Large windows overlooked the front lawn.

He shut the door and surprised me again by leading me to the sitting area instead of going to sit behind his desk. I took a seat on the couch, and he sat in the chair.

"I'm sorry it has taken me this long to meet you. I wanted to be here when you arrived, but Council business kept me abroad these last few weeks."

"I understand," I told him, but I really didn't get why an important man like him with so many responsibilities would bother to explain his whereabouts to me.

"Tell me, how are you doing since you moved here?"

I made a face. "You really need to ask that after watching my training yesterday? I'm not exactly good warrior material."

His laugh was rich and warm instead of mocking. "I think it will take more than a few weeks to determine what kind of warrior you will be. From what I have heard, you have other very special qualities to commend you." I gave him a questioning look, and he said, "Nikolas told me about your unique heritage. Do not worry; your secret is safe with me."

"Thank you."

"Training aside, how do you like it here? Are your quarters to your liking? Have you made friends?"

His questions caught me off guard. Why would he care if I liked my room or made friends? Besides I had no doubt that he already knew everything there was to know about my first two weeks here.

"You want the truth?"

"Of course."

"This place is amazing, but I don't fit in here. I hope that doesn't sound ungrateful because I really do appreciate everything you've done for me, and I know why I have to be here. I just . . . I miss home." My throat tightened, and I looked away from him. My eyes found an oil portrait of a beautiful blond girl on the wall behind his chair. Her hair was the same shade as his, and I knew they had to be related.

Lord Tristan's blue eyes filled with understanding. "The transition to this life can be difficult for orphans, and I think we assumed it would be easier for you, given your age. We did not take into account the strong ties you have to your old life. All I can say is that it will get easier and you will find your place with us. I hope you will trust me in that."

I wanted to believe him, but I'd been burned once already. "The last person I trusted dumped me on your doorstep and took off."

He raised an eyebrow. "I was under the impression that you and Nikolas couldn't spend ten minutes together without needing a referee. Perhaps you both needed some space."

"You mean he was glad to get me off his hands."

He laughed. "I doubt that. Nikolas plays by his own set of rules. Don't read too much into him not being here right now. When he is hunting, he often spends weeks away at a time."

"Busy guy. From one job right into another." I smiled even though I did not feel like it. "If you don't mind, I'd rather not talk about him."

Lord Tristan nodded. "I understand. I did have another reason for asking you here today. Nikolas told me you might be open to meeting your Mohiri family once you feel comfortable among us. I wanted you to know they are very eager to get to know you – when you are ready, of course."

"They're here? I have family here . . . now?" His news floored me. I had been living under the same roof with family for almost two weeks without knowing it? Had I passed them in the halls? Sat near them at meals? They could be one of the other trainees or even my trainer. I crossed off that last thought. After everything I'd been through, there was no way God would be cruel enough to make Callum my family.

His face gave nothing away as he nodded. "You have a cousin who lives here, but he is away at the moment. And your mother's sire is here. You would call him your grandfather."

"My grandfather is here?" When Nikolas told me that Madeline's father was still alive and wanted to meet me, I was curious but nowhere near ready to meet him. The knowledge that my grandfather was at this stronghold right now filled me with trepidation and excitement at the same time.

"Would you like to meet him?" Lord Tristan asked.

My stomach twisted nervously. Was I ready to meet Madeline's father? The man wasn't Madeline and I could not hold her behavior against him, but was I ready to have him in my life? "No . . . I mean, I don't know. I'm sorry, you took me by surprise and it's a lot to take in."

He settled back in his chair. "It's understandable. This is a big adjustment for you and you need more time. He only wants you to know that he is here for you when you are ready to meet him."

I lowered my gaze as guilt hit me. Great. Now I felt like a total jerk. My grandfather sounded like a nice guy, and I didn't want to hurt his feelings. It wouldn't hurt to just meet him, right? It wasn't like we had to start having family dinners and all that. And how could I walk around here after this, knowing he was here and not be able to identify him?

"I'm ready," I said at last.

"Are you sure?"

I raised my eyes to his again and nodded. "I'm a little nervous, but yes."

Smiling, he stood and went to his desk. Instead of reaching for his phone as I had expected him to, he opened a drawer and pulled out a thin book. It wasn't until he returned to the sitting area that I saw it was not a book, but a photo album. He passed the chair and sat beside me on the couch. I looked up into his eyes, and the tenderness I saw in them punched me square in the chest.

"You have been through so much, and I can see how unhappy you are right now. I can't tell you how sorry I am for all the pain you've suffered. More than anything, I wish I could have been there for you all these years. Nikolas told me about your uncle and how much you care for each other, and I'm happy that you have someone like him in your life. I don't want to replace him. All I ask is the chance to get to know you and that you will come to think of me as family, too."

I struggled for words. What do you say when you find yourself face-to-face with a grandfather you never knew? Especially one who looks like he should be in college. "You're Madeline's father," was all I could manage.

His eyes grew sad. Nikolas hadn't told me much about Madeline or under what circumstances she had left the Mohiri, and I wondered what her relationship had been like with her father.

"I know Madeline hurt you deeply. My daughter has a lot to answer for when we find her." He reached for my hand, and I let him take it despite my conflicting emotions. "When I learned of your existence, it took everything in me not to go to Maine myself. But Nikolas advised against it. He told me about your anger toward Madeline and your refusal to have anything to do with us. With everything else that was going on at the time, he was concerned about overwhelming you."

I let out a tremulous laugh. "He was right. I kind of freaked out when he told me what I was. I'm still getting used to it all."

He squeezed my hand lightly. "All I ask is for the chance for us to get to know each other."

The hope shining in his eyes touched me, and I suddenly felt very shy. I nodded because I couldn't trust myself to speak.

He let go of my hand, but he didn't move away. "Why don't we start slowly by getting to know each other a little better? Nikolas told me what he could of your life, but I would rather hear about it from you. I'm sure you must have questions for me as well."

"Okay. Um, what should I call you?"

"We don't use most of the familial terms humans do, so you can call me Tristan."

"Not Lord?"

His smile grew. "That is my formal title, but everyone here calls me by my first name."

I returned his smile, feeling a little more at ease. "I have to tell you it feels very weird to have a grandfather who looks a few years older than me."

Tristan chuckled. "I can imagine." He settled back against the couch. "Why don't you tell me about yourself, if you want to, that is?"

I started with my early childhood. Tristan's smile faded when I spoke of Madeline leaving us when I was two, but it returned when I described my dad and recounted the many ways he had made my life so full and happy. I told him about my dad's love of books and his penchant for creating games to encourage my interest in reading and music and poetry.

When I talked about losing my dad, Tristan waited quietly while I struggled to get through it. I told him about my life in New Hastings with Nate and my friends – human and nonhuman. I made sure he understood that my life there had not been an unhappy one and that it had taken a Master to drive me from my home.

Tristan began to talk about himself then, and I was shocked to learn he was born in sixteen eighty-four. He told me about growing up in England with his parents and older sister, Beatrice, training to be a warrior and then travelling around Europe and living at various strongholds. I discovered that he had been to almost every corner of the earth, he was the youngest member to ever join the Council at the ripe old age of thirty, and he spoke fourteen different languages, including a few words of Troll. He met my grandmother, Josephine, in Paris in eighteen sixty-one, and she moved back to America with him.

When I asked him where Josephine was, he grew quiet before he told me she was killed during a raid on a vampire nest in southern California in nineteen thirteen. Their scouts had misjudged the size of the nest, and when Josephine's team of six went in, they were overwhelmed and only one of them made it out.

"It was a very dark time for me, and I might have done something reckless and gotten myself killed if it were not for Madeline. She was only ten, and I could not leave her without a parent. Nikolas took a team and wiped out the nest. He avenged Josephine for me because I could not leave my daughter, and he brought her body home to us."

"People here talk about Nikolas like he is some kind of superhero, but they seem almost scared of him, too."

"But you are not?"

I couldn't deny how good a warrior Nikolas was, having seen him in action more than once. "He is pretty good, but don't tell him I said that because he's arrogant enough already. He's way too bossy, but there's nothing scary about him."

"Our young people grow up hearing stories about Nikolas's missions and his fighting skills, so it's natural they look up to him. He is a fierce warrior, and there are few who could stand up to him when he sets his mind on something."

"No kidding. Been there, got the T-shirt."

Tristan laughed heartily. "In the short time I've known you I can already see why you were such a challenge for him. You seem to have a very strong sense of self and a quick mind. And you are not easily intimidated."

"I guess I had to grow up fast." I didn't tell him I struggled every day to figure out who I was and it wasn't getting any easier. "Can I ask you something?"

"Yes."

"I know you guys are looking for the Master, but every time I ask someone about it they tell me not to worry. Will you tell me what you've found so far?"

He gave me an indulgent smile. "You don't need to worry about him anymore."

"See, you're doing it, too." I threw up my hands in frustration. "I'm not a five-year-old, and I didn't move here to be coddled and kept in the dark about things that affect me."

Tristan was taken aback by my outburst, and silence stretched between us. "You're right. I'm sorry," he said at last. "We are naturally protective of our young people, and we don't include them in such things until they become warriors. It is a dangerous world, especially for our kind."

I watched his gaze move to the portrait of the beautiful blond girl with the dainty, heart-shaped face and angelic smile. Pain flicked across his face, long enough for me to realize who she was. Nikolas had once mentioned Madeline's aunt who was killed by vampires a long time ago, and there was no mistaking the resemblance between Tristan and the girl in the painting.

"Just because I want to know what is going on it doesn't mean I will go out looking for trouble. Trust me; I plan to stay as far away from that vampire as I can."

He came out of his reverie. "We cleaned out three nests in Nevada and two in California that we suspect belonged to him, but so far we have found no clues to his identity or his whereabouts."

"I guess he wouldn't be a Master if he was easy to find, would he?"

"I have hunted six Masters during my life, and this one is the most evasive by far. We did not even know of his existence until you told Nikolas about him."

"Six Masters? Did you get them all?"

"Yes, and we will get this one, too," he replied with conviction. "I just don't know how long it will take. Today's technology makes it easier to follow leads, but it also makes it easier for someone to disappear if they are good enough."

The phone on his desk rang, interrupting us. When I glanced at my watch I was surprised to see that nearly two hours had passed. Tristan stood, wearing an expression of regret. "That would be my reminder that I have a Council call in five minutes. I hate to cut our time short."

"I understand. We can talk again some other time."

"I'd like that very much."

We were walking to the door when my eyes lit on his large bookcase, reminding me of the strange man in the library. "Two nights ago, I went into a small library on the second floor of the east wing and I met a man who was upset about me being there. He didn't look like a warrior. I mean, there was something different about him. I think he was sick."

"Did he frighten you?" He didn't ask what the man looked like, so he obviously knew who I was talking about.

"No, he was pretty agitated though. There was one point where I thought he was going to freak out, but he was mostly rude."

He looked amused. "His name is Desmund, and he lives in that wing. He has been suffering from illness for a long time, so you'll have to excuse his bad behavior."

"Oh, I should have known. I heard there was a sick warrior living in the wing, but I assumed he was on the first floor." I felt terrible. I'd upset a sick man who probably needed peace and quiet so he could recover. No wonder he'd been so irritable.

Tristan's chuckle took me off guard. "Desmund has been closed off up there for too long, and it will do him some good to be around other people." He opened the door for me. "Desmund's had a very long and interesting life, and he was a different person before he became ill. I think you will like him when you get to know him."

"Maybe I will."

"Feel free to use that library whenever you wish. He can be difficult at times, but don't let him drive you away. I think you will be good for him."

I made a face. "Great, just what I needed, another difficult warrior."

Chapter 4

"DO YOU KNOW what this is about?" I asked Olivia, walking beside her around the back of the main building. When we'd arrived at the training wing a few minutes ago, we found a notice telling all trainees to head to the arena. I'd never seen anything here resembling an arena, and I was starting to wonder if this was some kind of joke on the new girl.

Olivia pointed to the left of the menagerie at a square stone building about as big as a small church, with a domed roof like the one on the menagerie. Tall thin windows covered by iron bars shaped like leafy vines lined the side facing us, and I could see an arched doorway framed with the same decoration. Standing in front of the building were the other trainees, Sahir, and the woman who had come into the training room with Tristan several days ago. Everyone but me seemed to know her, and it was obvious from the infatuated stares from the boys that she was very popular among them.

"Who is that?" I asked Olivia, who made a face.

"That's Celine. She lives in Italy, but she comes here three or four times a year. God, I hope she's not training us."

We reached the group before I could ask her what she meant. Celine stopped talking to the assembled trainees when we arrived, and I was taken aback when her frosty green gaze settled on me. "Now that everyone has decided to show up, we'll get started, shall we?" Her attention shifted back to the others. "Today we are going to add a little practical training, so I hope you studied hard in school."

An excited murmur rippled through the other trainees, and Sahir stepped forward, his dark eyes sparkling. "Before your imaginations run away with you, you are not going to be facing a vampire or anything that dangerous."

Celine walked to a cloth-covered cage I had not noticed. "We are going to start you on something less life-threatening." She pulled the cloth back to reveal a brown rat-like creature the size of a pug with large curved incisors and clawed feet huddled inside the cage. Unlike a rat, it had a short stump of a tail and yellow eyes.

"This is a bazerat, for those of you who are not familiar with them," Sahir said. "They are found mostly in the Amazon where they live off snakes and birds. They have been known to attack humans if provoked. They are sometimes bred in captivity, and they can be quite dangerous in the wrong hands. One bazerat is not much to look at, a couple of them are a nuisance, but a pack of them is like a school of piranha when they pick up the scent of blood. I have seen a pack of thirty or so bazerats kill and consume a twenty-five foot anaconda in less than an hour."

Celine smiled as her eyes moved over our group. "Fortunately for you, you will not have to face a whole pack today. You each have to face only a pair of bazerats, a task I'm sure *most* of you will have no trouble completing." I couldn't help but notice that she was looking at me when she said the last part and her smile had become more of a sneer.

"Oooh, someone doesn't like you," whispered Jordan close to my ear. I started to ask her what she meant, but Celine spoke again.

"Here is how we'll do this. One by one you will enter the arena where we will release two bazerats. Your task is to neutralize them. Before you go in, select your weapon of choice from the pile by the door, but remember bazerats are fast, so choose wisely."

The group of trainees surged forward to find weapons, and I was left standing alone in front of Celine. "You want us to kill them?" I looked from Celine to Sahir, and they both nodded. "Why?"

"*Why?*" Celine repeated as if she couldn't understand the question. "Because they are vermin and they would not hesitate to kill you."

"But they only kill when they are hunting for food or when they feel threatened, right? They are no danger to anyone now." I pointed at the bazerat in the cage. "That creature is terrified of us."

Celine arched a perfect eyebrow. "Would you rather we had you face the entire pack to make it feel more dangerous to you? This is how we train. Think of it as a sport."

My nostrils flared, and I shook my head. "I don't kill for sport."

The other trainees had joined us again, holding their weapons, and they quieted when they heard my declaration.

Celine's lip curled. "How do you expect to be a warrior if you can't kill? Do you think vampires will cut you a break because you won't kill them?"

"I have no problem killing in self-defense. I've already killed two vampires." I ignored the whispers around me. "But these creatures are not vampires. They're not even malicious."

"You'll change your tune when you face a couple of them with no bars between you. In fact . . . " She put a manicured finger to her chin. "Why don't you go first?"

"Fine by me." I saw a flicker of surprise in her eyes. Did she expect me to refuse, to run away? I started for the door of the building, but stopped when someone grabbed my arm.

Terrence pushed a knife into my hand. "Don't be stupid," he said when I tried to refuse it. "You don't have to use it if you don't need to, but don't go in there without some protection."

Nodding, I gave him a small smile and took the knife, immediately noticing that it felt different in my hand than the one Nikolas had given me. This one was larger and heavier, and the blade had a jagged edge instead of a smooth one. I held it flat against my thigh as I pulled the door open and stepped inside.

The door shut behind me with a loud click, and I found myself in a short hallway that opened into a large room. It was much darker inside the building and the only light came from the windows, but it was enough for me to make out the bleacher-style seats on three sides of the room and the polished wooden floor beneath my feet. The floor in the middle of the room was roughly thirty feet long and wide, and in the very center sat two empty crates.

"Great," I muttered, scanning the room for the bazerats. It was difficult to see anything in the deep shadows beneath the seats, so I stood still listening for movement. All I could hear was my own breathing. There was a shuffling sound as something moved beneath the seats to my left. I looked that way, but it was impossible to distinguish between shadows and the dark shapes of the bazerats.

From the other side of the room came the scratch of claws on wood, and I caught a glimpse of two glowing yellow eyes beneath a seat. *How the hell did he get over there so fast?*

I jumped when I heard a sound on my right again, and I whipped my head around in time to see a second pair of eyes peering out of the shadows. The hair stood up on the back of my neck as my heart sped up.

I clenched the knife in my fist, glad now that I had taken it from Terrence, and walked slowly toward the center of the room where the crates sat. There was nothing to be afraid of. If they attacked, there were only two of them and I had a very sharp blade. I would just rather not kill something if I could avoid it.

Hell, maybe I wouldn't even need to use the knife. I'd used my power to calm a crazed werewolf and two hellhounds, so surely it would work on these little creatures. I hoped so, because if I had to rely on my fighting skills, I might as well serve myself up to them on a platter.

That's not true, a little voice inside me argued. *You fought off a crocotta and killed Eli. You are not weak or helpless.*

I stood up straighter. For some reason, Celine didn't like me, and she was out there waiting for me to fail. But I wasn't weak, and I certainly wasn't a coward. She wanted these things neutralized, and that is exactly what she was going to get.

"All right, guys, I really don't want to hurt you and I know you'd probably rather be in home in the jungle, but none of us can change that right now. So what do you say we make a truce so we can all get out of here?"

The bazerat to my left gave a low *hiss* that did not sound friendly.

"Okay, so no truce. Suit yourself." I walked slowly toward the hissing as I released my power into the air around me. When I was three feet from the seats, I stopped. My plan, if it worked, was to draw the creature to me. It was certainly preferable to going under those seats after it.

A loud thumping made me jump, and my heart leapt in my throat before I realized it was someone banging on the door.

"Are you taking a nap in there or what?" Celine called, and I could hear the laugher in her voice. "If you need some help, just let us know."

"No thanks. I'm doing great," I called back, wishing it was true. I peered under the seats and thought I saw a patch of darkness that might be the bazerat, but I couldn't be sure. *I bet the others will have no problem seeing in here.* Callum kept telling me that my vision and hearing would be enhanced if I learned to use my Mori's power.

"Hey there, little guy. Why don't you stop all that noise and come out here so we can become friends?" I sent a wave of power toward the spot where I believed the creature was. "I know you're scared of people after they put you in a cage and I don't blame you for being upset, but I won't hurt you." *If you don't hurt me.*

Something shuffled under the seats, and I was about to smile when I realized that instead of approaching me, the bazerat was moving away from me. I frowned. When had a creature ever run from my power? I didn't know anything about bazerats except for what Celine had told us, but they looked like large rodents and I knew for sure that my power worked on rats.

I moved forward until my hand was touching the seats. Then I bent and strained to see through the darkness. It looked like I was going to have to go in after it. Wonderful. No so long ago, I had stood up to my chest in freezing sea water facing a pack of possessed wharf rats. I'd rather go back and do that all over again than go under these seats. If I could get close enough to touch the bazerat, I should be able to calm him – if he didn't try to eat me first. I just hoped the other one kept his distance until I worked my magic on his brother.

The world sounded hollow under the seats, and every move I made seemed to resonate in my ears, though I was going as quietly as possible. It wasn't as dark as I thought now that I was down here and my eyes were getting used to the gloom. Light from the windows made its way between the seats to create lighter patches, and I tried to stick to them as much as possible. Unfortunately, the bazerat kept away from them, which meant I was going to have to leave them as well.

All right, where the heck are you? I stopped and listened, but the room was silent. Taking two more steps, I stopped again and stared ahead of me at the dark shape huddled a few feet away. It wasn't running away so at least that was something. Now if it would only stay still . . .

A thump followed by the sounds of scurrying on the other side of the room made me whirl around, fearful of an attack from that direction. My head knocked against the bottom of a seat, and I stumbled before I tripped over my own feet and fell forward. I landed on my stomach, knocking the air from my lungs and sending the knife skidding across the floor. Letting out a moan, I looked up into the furry face of the bazerat standing less than a foot away. Before I could move, its mouth opened impossibly wide, like it was on hinges, and I got a close-up look at the rows of sharp teeth inside.

"Oh shit!" I squealed as it leapt at my face.

My arms came up to protect my head, and one of the long incisors scraped my palm, leaving a shallow cut that burned like the devil. There was no time to worry what kind of venom the bazerat might have because I was too preoccupied with wrapping my hands around its neck to hold it away from my face.

As soon as I touched it, the bazerat began to twist and screech, trying to get away from me. The only time a creature had reacted to my power like this was when I had encountered a rat possessed by a Hale witch. But I could sense no foreign presence in this creature. The bazerat was truly afraid of me, and I didn't know what to do.

I felt it then, the strange prickly static sliding over my skin. The bazerat went nuts, clawing at my arms, which were protected for the most part by my sleeves, and struggling so violently to break free of my grasp that I knew I wouldn't be able to hold it much longer. I began to pull my power back inside me, hoping that would calm the bazerat. I thought it was working until a small surge of electricity shot from my hands and right into the creature. The bazerat went stiff for a few seconds then collapsed limply in my hands.

"What the hell?" I sat up, holding the unconscious creature. I knew it was still alive because I could feel a pulse, slow and steady beneath my fingers. How long it would remain knocked out was another matter. I freed one hand to fumble around for the knife, and once I found it, I staggered to my feet. There was no telling where the other bazerat was, and I'd rather get this one locked safely in his crate before his brother decided to come looking for him.

I released a sigh of relief when I slid the lock into place on the crate holding the unconscious bazerat. "One down, one to go." I felt a lot more confident now that I only had one left to contend with.

The second bazerat proved to be a lot more slippery than the first one, and he led me on a crazy chase before I finally managed to corner him. He wasn't nearly as brave without his brother, but he still hissed and bared his teeth menacingly at me whenever I got close. He freaked when I dived, got my hands around him, and gave him a taste of my power. Once again the weird static electricity surged through me, and I had to fight to keep it from zapping the life right out of the creature. I wanted to capture him, not kill him. Still, it knocked him out cold and I was able to tuck him safely in his crate. I stood back and surveyed the two sleeping bazerats that looked so harmless now. But I knew better. I shuddered as I headed for the door. I hoped I never ran into a whole pack of those things.

"Well, I'm happy to see you are still in one piece," grated Celine when I emerged from the building, and I couldn't help but notice that her expression did not match her words.

Except for a few scratches, I was unharmed, and I felt pretty proud of myself for finishing the task. "Piece of cake," I said, moving past her.

"Wait," she barked, and I stopped walking as she opened the door and went into the building. In less than a minute she was back with a scowl on her face. "You're not done. Get back in there and finish them off."

"They are back in their cages where they can't hurt anyone. There is no need to kill them."

Celine took a step toward me, towering over me by at least six inches. "The task was to kill them. So kill them or you fail."

"The task was to *neutralize* them, and they are neutralized. If I have to kill senselessly to pass your test, then you can go ahead and fail me." I tossed the knife on the ground between us and walked over to stand by Michael, who was gawking at me like I'd just sprouted another head. I half expected Celine to come after me, but she had apparently decided to let it drop and was already looking for another trainee to enter the building. First, they had to get another pair of bazerats since mine were out cold. I hid my smile of satisfaction.

"Well, well, the kitten has claws after all," drawled Jordan, who walked over with Olivia to join us.

"What the heck did you do in there, Sara?" Michael wanted to know, forgetting his shyness for once.

"I caught them and put them back in their cages." I conveniently omitted the part where electricity had shot from my fingertips.

Terrence laughed. "Why go through all the trouble when it's easier to kill them?"

I met his mocking gaze and shrugged. "Anyone can kill. Taking them alive is a lot more of a challenge, don't you think?"

He scoffed, but I could see it in his eyes; the gauntlet had been thrown. "I'll go next," he called to Celine before he stalked off.

I watched Celine talking to Terrence. Of course, she looked quite pleasant now that she was talking to someone besides me. If Celine had been human, I might have blamed her attitude toward me on a natural female aversion to undines. But she was Mohiri, so she was supposed to be immune to that. "What is her problem anyway?" I muttered to no one in particular.

"You."

I frowned at Jordan. "Me? I just met her twenty minutes ago."

"She's jealous of you," Olivia said in a voice that wouldn't carry to the trainer. "Supposedly, she and Nikolas Danshov go way back and she's still got it bad for him."

I pictured Nikolas with cold, beautiful Celine and something hardened in my gut. "What does that have to do with me?"

"Let me see." Jordan tapped a finger against her lips. "Could it have something to do with how much time Nikolas spent in Maine protecting a certain pretty little orphan?"

"What? No, it wasn't . . . You don't understand." I felt a blush creeping up my neck. "It wasn't like that. We don't even get along."

Jordan smiled. "Uh-huh."

"No, really. He was just doing his job. I didn't want him around any more than he wanted to be there."

Jordan and Olivia laughed, and it was Olivia who spoke first. "Nikolas is one of the best warriors on the *planet*, and his job does not include babysitting orphans."

I looked from one to the other. "I don't understand. He found me, killed the bad guys, and brought me here. Isn't that what warriors do?"

It was Michael who answered. "Some warriors do, but you're the first orphan Nikolas has ever brought in."

Jordan and Olivia watched me closely while I digested that piece if information. Nikolas had never brought in anyone before me? Well, that certainly explained his lack of patience; he obviously had no experience with orphans. Whatever his reason for doing it, I knew for certain it was not because of any romantic feelings he might have for me as the girls implied. It was more likely his male ego; I'd challenged him and he couldn't handle it. "I know what you're insinuating but trust me, there is nothing going on between me and Nikolas."

Jordan let out a short laugh. "You are probably the only female in existence who would go out of her way to deny having a thing with him."

"God what I wouldn't give . . . " Olivia fanned herself. "Hot doesn't begin to describe that man." She sighed. "Can you imagine what it feels like to have those arms around you?"

There was no way I going to tell them that I knew what it felt like to be in Nikolas's arms. But his embrace had been comforting instead of romantic. I could not understand how he had treated me with such kindness one day and then taken off without a good-bye two days later. I admit I'm not the best at reading people, but how could I have been so wrong about him?

"Booyah! Take that!"

The four of us turned to stare at Terrence, who was emerging from the arena looking like he had just gone a few rounds with an angry badger. His hair was sticking out all over the place, his shirt and jeans were shredded in places, and he had a bloody scratch on one cheek. But he was grinning like he had won the lottery. He walked past Celine and Sahir and came up to me, his hazel eyes shining. "Now *that* was fun."

I glowered at him. "Yes, I'm sure killing is a real blast."

"Who said anything about killing? And if you look at the time, I believe I finished faster than you." He touched his cheek and winced. "Mean little bastards, though."

"You didn't kill them?" Josh asked in disbelief.

Terrence chuckled. "Sara is right; anyone can kill them, but it takes a *real* warrior to take them alive." It wasn't exactly what I had said, but I decided not to correct him.

Celine strode over to us, and her gaze raked across mine. "What the hell has gotten into you people?"

Terrence shot me a grin. "Just mixing it up a bit, making it a little more fun."

"This is not supposed to be fun," Celine bit out. She pointed at me and Terrence. "You two, you're done here. Go cause trouble somewhere else." She spun away from us and yelled, "Is there anyone here who wants to do this thing correctly?"

"Later," I said to the others, glad to get away from Celine and her killing. I set off toward the main building, and Terrence ran to catch up with me.

"Seriously, that was a blast," he panted. "Who would ever have thought not killing demons would be fun?"

I came up short. "The bazerats are demons?"

"Of course. What did you think they were?"

"I don't know – mutant rats?"

He snickered like I'd made a joke. "We covered them in class last year."

"I wasn't here last year." I had learned a lot about the world from Remy, but nothing like the formal education Mohiri kids received. I had years of learning to catch up on.

I resumed walking. The bazerats were demons, and my power made them freak out instead of calming them. Demons fear Fae magic, and it must have hurt them when I touched them. It could also be why my power had reacted to them and zapped them. It still didn't explain the little flare-ups that were happening every day now. Was my elemental side growing stronger as Aine had hoped it would?

My stomach clenched as a scary thought came to me. I was surrounded by people with demons inside them, and I had no control over whatever was happening to me. What if I hurt someone without meaning to? I was half Fae, half demon, and even the Fae admitted they had no idea what powers I would develop. Nikolas had brought me here to keep me safe, but what if *I* was the dangerous one?

* * *

I quietly approached the library. It had been three days since my encounter with Desmund, and even though Tristan had encouraged me to come back, I felt a little apprehensive about seeing Desmund again. I didn't want to upset him and cause some kind of setback, but I had to admit I was more than a little curious about him.

The library door was open, and the room looked much as it had the first time I'd been here. I would have thought the room empty if the slightest rustling of paper behind one of the high backed chairs hadn't alerted me to the presence of someone else. Instead of announcing myself, I moved silently to the bookcases to return the copy of *Jane Eyre* I had borrowed. I almost hated to give it up, but I was excited to see what other treasures were waiting on the shelves.

No way! My eyes lit upon a perfectly preserved copy of *Daniel Deronda*. I slid the book off the shelf and opened the cover to see that it was indeed a first edition. How many people got the opportunity to appreciate classic literature like this? *Oh, Dad, what I wouldn't give for you to be able to see this.*

I debated sitting by the fire, but if it was Desmund in the chair – and I had a suspicion it was – he was keeping to himself and I didn't want to give him a reason to be upset. He was used to having this room to himself, so it was probably best to ease him into the idea of sharing the space. I carried my book to the table near the window where there was a small reading lamp. The chair wasn't as nice as the ones by the fire, but the book provided a happy diversion.

"Oh, it's you again."

I started at the voice a few feet away. He had moved so quietly that I never noticed him approach. He was wearing similar dated clothing to what he'd worn during our last encounter, but I saw that it was clean and pressed. His hair was neater, and I couldn't help but think he cleaned up well. My eyes went to his face, and I was not surprised to find a scowl there. Remembering what Tristan had said about Desmund's bad mood being due to his illness, I ignored his glower and gave him a polite smile. "Hello."

My friendly greeting seemed to throw him, and he stared at me for a moment before his dark gaze fell on the book in my hands. "You have odd taste in literature for one your age."

I lifted a shoulder. "I read a lot of different books – whatever appeals to me." He didn't respond so I asked, "What do you like to read?"

Desmund lifted his hand, and I saw he was holding *Hamlet*, which we'd covered in English lit last spring. It was too dark and violent for my taste, and I didn't think it was good reading material for a man who already seemed slightly unhinged. I kept that observation to myself.

"You don't like Shakespeare?" His tone was chilly, and I wondered how I had offended him so easily.

"I have trouble understanding the English," I replied honestly. "I don't like it when I have to stop and figure out what every word means."

He turned and walked across the room to a tall cabinet built into the wall. Opening the door, he retrieved a remote control and fiddled with it for a minute before soft strains of classical violin music filled the room. It was not something I'd normally listen to, but it wasn't unpleasant either.

"You don't like Vivaldi?"

"I'm not familiar with him." I assumed Vivaldi was the composer and not a type of music.

He made a scoffing sound. "Not surprising. Young people today have horrid taste in music. What do you call it . . . pop?"

"Just because I don't know every piece of classical music doesn't mean I don't like any of it." I waved at the bookshelves lining the walls. "I bet you haven't read every book that's been published."

His eyes narrowed. "Oh, and pray tell me, which of the great composers do you prefer then?"

A week ago, I couldn't have answered that question. Before I came here, I listened mostly to classic rock, but that was before I discovered the vast selection of classical music in the common rooms. I'd sampled music from different composers and discovered a few I liked. I still couldn't tell Bach from Brahms, but there was one that stood out for me. "Tchaikovsky."

"And what is your favorite *Tchaikovsky* piece?" he asked scornfully as if he didn't believe me. His attitude annoyed the hell out of me. I obviously didn't know as much about classical music as he did – hell, he and Mozart could have been buddies for all I knew – but he didn't have to be such a snob about it.

I reminded myself that he was ill and tempered my response. "I don't know what it's called; it's some kind of waltz. I listened to it a bunch of times in the common room."

At first I thought he was going to insult me again, but instead he hit a few buttons on his remote and the waltz began to play.

"That's it!"

The beautiful sweeping melody filled the room for almost a minute before he turned back to me with a bemused expression. "*Serenade for Strings in C major*. It is one of my favorites as well."

"Oh no, we actually have something in common? How dreadful." My tone was teasing, but with him it was impossible to know how he'd take it.

One corner of his mouth twitched. "Tragic indeed," he retorted, but some of the edge had left his voice. "Well, since you are determined to make yourself at home here, I suppose I should know your name."

"Sara Grey."

He gave a shaky but elegant bow. "Desmund Ashworth, seventh Earl of Dorsey."

"Aha! I knew you were some kind of English lord." He arched an eyebrow, and I said, "You've got aristocrat written all over you."

He seemed inordinately pleased by my remark, and a smug smile tugged at his lips. For the first time since I'd met him, the wildness left his eyes. "You have good taste in books and music so there is some hope for you," he stated as if he was appraising my worth. "What else do you like?"

"I draw, but it's nothing like the art on the walls here. You probably wouldn't like it."

"Probably not," he agreed, and I had the urge to stick out my tongue at him. He could at least pretend to be courteous. "Do you play chess by chance?"

"No. I can play checkers, though." Roland's uncle Brendan had taught me to play checkers, and we used to have a game whenever I stayed over at the farm. I'd even beaten Brendan a few times, and that was no easy feat.

He scoffed. "Anyone can play draughts. It requires a much more organized mind to master chess."

Something told me that Desmund's mind was about as organized as my closet, but I wisely kept that thought to myself. "It's been a while since I played, but I think I could give you a run for your money in checkers. Too bad we don't have a set."

His eyes lit up, and he spun back to the cabinet where he leaned down and pulled out a dark mahogany box. He carried the box to my table and laid it in front of me, then opened it to reveal a polished checkerboard. Inside the box was another flat box that contained a set of ebony and boxwood checkers. Desmund took the chair across from me and spilled the checkers out onto the board. "Lady's choice."

I hesitated for a moment before laying aside my book, even though his eagerness told me he was probably extremely good at either game. I reached for the boxwood pieces and started to line them up on my side of the board.

We were not long into the game before it was evident that Desmund was in a totally different league from Brendan, and I had to concentrate hard to keep up with his moves. I earned a few scowls when I captured three of his pieces, small victories compared to his dominating play. He didn't gloat as much as I thought he would when he won, but he wasn't all graciousness either.

"You have some potential, but it will probably take us years to polish you up."

"Gee thanks," I replied. "Maybe after a few hundred years, I'll be as good as you."

Desmund pursed his lips. "Doubtful, but you will make a decent opponent."

I shook my head at his cockiness. "How old are you anyway?" The Mohiri didn't have the same hang-ups about age as humans so I saw nothing wrong in asking.

He paused as if he'd forgotten the answer. "I was born in sixteen thirty-eight."

Wow. "I can't imagine living that long. I only found out a few months ago I was Mohiri."

"Ah, you are *that* orphan. I knew there was something different about you."

"That's me." I couldn't help but think that it's probably not good when someone as eccentric as Desmund thinks you're different. "I'm not exactly like the other trainees here; they are all such good fighters. I don't think I'd make a good warrior – or know if I even want to be one."

He gazed out the darkened window. "'It is better to fail in originality than to succeed in imitation.'" When he looked back at me, he wore a little smile. "Melville. Words to live by."

I smiled back. "I'll try to remember that."

"So, shall we have a rematch?" He deftly rolled one of the ebony pieces between his long fingers.

"Not tonight," I said with real regret. Desmund was a little unbalanced, but he was also intelligent and interesting and I couldn't help but like him. I began gathering checkers to put them away. "It's getting late and I have training in the morning."

"Another time then?" His question was casual, but he was not able to hide the glimmer of hope in his eyes. It struck me that he must be lonely up here, even though he drove everyone away.

My smile widened. "Definitely. I need to practice if I'm ever going to beat you."

He let out a short laugh, the first since I'd met him. "You have your work cut out for you." He helped pick up the pieces, placing his in the box and holding it out to me. I reached over to drop mine in and my fingers brushed his hand.

Cold sickness assailed me. My heart fluttered, and my skin felt like there were cold wet things crawling over it. I shuddered and leaned back as sweat broke out on my upper lip and blackness swam before my eyes. Taking a gulp of air, I braced my hand on the edge of the table and fought off the faintness threatening to swallow me.

"Are you unwell?" Desmund's voice sounded worried, and he reached for me.

"I'm fine!" I managed to stand before he could touch me. If this horrible attack was from a brief touch, I did not want to know what longer contact would do. He seemed oblivious to the real reason for my distress, and I didn't want to alarm him. I gave him a shaky smile. "I probably shouldn't have skipped dinner."

His brow furrowed. "I can have food brought up for you if you wish."

"Thanks, but I can grab a muffin from the dining hall on my way." He did not look convinced. "I'm okay, really."

He stood and followed me to the door. "You still look pale. Are you quite certain you don't want to sit and rest a little?"

I gave him what I hoped was a reassuring smile. "I'm starting to feel better already." It was partially true; my body was already recovering from the strange illness even though I was still a bit shaken up. "I'll see you again soon."

I slipped out of the library and hurried toward the stairs. *What the hell was that?* The Mohiri had no special powers – unless they were some kind of half breed like me – but I'd definitely sensed something off when I touched him. Was he something more than a Mohiri, or could this have to do with his illness? I needed to ask Tristan about it as soon as I saw him again. If Desmund was dangerous, it wouldn't be smart to spend time alone with him. It didn't make sense because Tristan had urged me to get to know Desmund. I found myself hoping I was overreacting, because Tristan had been right; I did like Desmund once I got to know him.

Chapter 5

"I HEAR THERE was some excitement in training yesterday." Tristan peered at me over his glass of red wine. It was our first time talking since we met two days ago, and we were having dinner in his apartment. I still wasn't sure how I felt about suddenly having a grandfather – especially Madeline's father – but I was trying to get past my reservations and give us a chance to get to know each other.

I looked up from my salad, prepared to defend my actions. I wasn't surprised that Celine had complained about me. She had made it clear from the first time she opened her mouth that she did not like me. I still stood by my decision not to kill the bazerats, even though they were demons. Being demons did not make them inherently evil like vampires. The world is full of demons and many of them are more of a nuisance than a real threat. I used to live in a house infested with imps, and though they were sometimes annoying, they had never shown any real malice.

Roland hadn't agreed with me when I told him about the bazerats last night. Werewolves have more of a black-and-white view when it comes to demons, even if my friends made an exception for me. Roland thought I should have killed the bazerats, and it rankled me that he seemed to be siding with Celine. We'd argued about it for at least thirty minutes before we agreed to disagree for the sake of peace. He was actually more interested in how I'd zapped the bazerats and knocked them out than whether or not I'd killed them.

"Did you really throw a knife at Celine and urge the other trainees to refuse to complete the task?"

My mouth fell open. "I did not throw a knife at anyone. I tossed it on the ground. And all I said was that I didn't believe in senseless killing. Okay, I might have told Terrence it was easier to kill something than catch it, but that's it, I swear."

Tristan's laugh took me by surprise. "Celine always did have a flair for the dramatic. She is a skilled warrior and a good trainer . . . most of the time."

"I must have gotten her during one of her off times."

"Celine is . . . well, let's just say she has a better rapport with men than other women." He set his glass down. "I can speak to her if you'd like."

"No, I can handle it on my own. She's no worse than some of the girls I knew in high school."

His eyebrows rose. "High school sounds like a rather perilous place."

"You have no idea." I went back to my salad, feeling a little more at ease. Tristan was surprisingly easy to talk to, and it almost felt like I was hanging out with a cousin instead of a grandfather.

"How are your new pets doing? Sahir tells me you named them."

"Hugo and Woolf. They're really smart and already know some commands." I was always happy to talk about the hellhounds. "I just wish they didn't have to stay locked up in that cage all the time. They need fresh air and space to run around."

His brow furrowed. "I'm not sure that is a good idea. We don't know if we can trust them not to kill the first person they see."

"I go in the cage with them every day and they are gentle with me."

"They have imprinted on you and you are their master now. They would never harm you."

"They've stopped growling at Sahir when I'm there." I leaned forward earnestly. "I really believe they just need to get used to being around people. I can't bear to think of them locked up for the rest of their lives."

"I'll talk to Sahir and see what he says. I cannot make any promises."

"Thank you." I was confident that once he saw they could be trusted around others, he would give them more freedom. "You have miles and miles of woods out there, perfect for them to run in. I could take them out every day without bothering anyone."

Tristan laid down his fork. "It is not a good idea for you to be out in the woods alone." I started to protest, and he said, "I know you are unhappy with the restrictions placed upon you, but we are only trying to keep you safe after everything you've been through."

"But everyone thinks I'm dead, including the vampires."

"You will have to forgive me for being a little overprotective. I believe that is a grandsire's right. Just be patient a little longer until we can be certain this Master is not still searching for you. We are monitoring activity around Maine, and so far it is very quiet there."

"I could have told you how quiet it is in Maine." I shrugged at his questioning look. "I have werewolf friends there, remember? Anyway, trust me; no one wants the Master to think I am dead more than I do. I can't even go for a walk without one of the warriors escorting me back in irons."

He laughed. "I'll tell them to lay off the irons. In the meantime, why don't I arrange for a day out for you? How about a day trip to Boise? With supervision, of course."

"Okay," I conceded, excited about the possibility of a change of scenery, even if it was only for a day.

He got up to take away our salad plates, and my eyes wandered around his apartment, which had a decidedly masculine décor. It made sense since he had been a widower for so long. There were some softer touches like a pale-blue throw on the back of the couch and a number of framed photos and paintings on the mantle and walls. One photo in particular caught my eye, and I knew immediately who the blond woman was because I had seen the faded picture of her that my dad used to carry in his wallet. Madeline was stunningly beautiful – even Celine could not compare – and the happy smile she wore did not reconcile with my image of the woman who had hurt me and my dad so much.

Questions that had hovered in the recesses of my mind for weeks finally pushed their way to the forefront. My dad and Madeline met in college, according to Nate, and they'd dated for several years before they married. They were married for two years before they had me, and she left when I was two. In all those years with Madeline, didn't my dad realize she was not aging at all? How did Madeline hide her strength and control her Mori without him ever suspecting she was not human? Or had he known what she was all along? I bit my lip and looked away from the photo. There was no sense pondering over questions that would never be answered.

Another picture got my attention, a painting of the same blond girl from the portrait in Tristan's office. "Is that your sister?" I asked him, and he turned and followed my gaze to the painting in question. "Nikolas once mentioned his friend, Elena, who died a long time ago, and he said she was Madeline's aunt."

He laid a plate of salmon and rice in front of me and took his seat again. "Elena was my younger sister, much younger. I was almost two hundred years old and quite surprised when my parents told me they were having another baby. It is not unusual for Mohiri siblings to have many years between them, but my parents love to travel and they are not what you would call the most affectionate people. They were already here exploring America by then, and I decided to come here to be with them when the child was born. Elena was the most captivating little baby, and of course I adored her immediately and spoiled her excessively. When she was five, my parents decided they wanted to continue their travels, and it didn't take much convincing to get them to leave Elena with me."

"A warrior raising a little girl?"

He cut into his salmon. "My sister, Beatrice, would have taken Elena, but she was in South America at the time. I lived in a family compound in

Virginia back then, and it was more of a community than this one. There were other children for Elena to play with and women to go to when I needed advice. It was a lot more suitable for a child than travelling the world, and Elena had a very happy childhood there."

"Nikolas told me very little about her," I said softly. "But it sounded like he cared about her a lot."

Tristan nodded. "I am not surprised he mentioned her. Nikolas came to our compound when Elena was nine, and he spoiled her like the rest of us did. She was like a little sister to him, and he took her death very hard. He blamed himself even though I and everyone else told him it was not his fault. My sister was beautiful and used to people doting on her. She was precocious and charming, but she was also willful, and I blame myself for that. She never should have left the compound alone, and she died because of it."

"Why did Nikolas blame himself?"

"As I said, Nikolas loved Elena like a sister, but Elena, she adored him and she constantly tried to get his attention. By the time she was sixteen, most of the boys in the compound believed themselves in love with her, but she only had eyes for Nikolas. He knew how she felt and he always deflected her attentions gently, but she was determined to have him and nothing would dissuade her. Her schemes to get him alone grew more creative every day until even I began to tease him about us one day being brothers if he was not careful. If only I had known the lengths she would go to be with him, I might have intervened before her games got out of control. I might have saved her."

"What happened?"

"Elena knew how protective Nikolas was of her. She concocted a plan to sneak away from the compound, and she had her friend Miriam go to Nikolas and tell him Elena had run away. Miriam confessed later that they were hoping the thought of losing Elena would make Nikolas realize his true feelings for her. But Miriam could not get to Nikolas because he was giving a report before the Counsel at the time. By the time she found him, four hours had passed and she was in a panic because it was nearly dark. Nikolas raised the alarm, and a group of us rode out after Elena. We picked up signs of vampires, and we split up to cover the area faster."

Tristan paused, and I saw raw pain on his face as he continued. "It was Nikolas who found her. What they did to her . . . it was beyond inhuman. After they had finished their fun, they burned what was left of her until my beautiful little sister was unrecognizable. They left her horse unharmed and tied to a tree, a message to us that her life meant less than an animal's."

"God . . . " I had seen what vampires left behind of the people they killed. I also knew they took special delight in killing young Mohiri.

"Nikolas took her death as hard as I did, and he blamed himself for not making her understand that there could never be anything romantic between them. He stayed out for months until he had hunted down every vampire in a hundred-mile radius. I tried to convince him that he was not at fault and that no one blamed him for her death, but he would not listen. He was different after that, harder. A year later, I left Virginia and came here to build this place, and he came with me. We both wanted something that did not remind us of Virginia, which is why we made this into a military stronghold instead of a community."

"I'm sorry about your sister," I said, not knowing what to say about someone who'd been dead for so many years. "It's no wonder Nikolas gets so overbearing and angry with me all the time."

"Sara, do not compare yourself to Elena. Don't get me wrong, I loved my sister with all my heart, but I was not blind to her faults. Elena was beautiful and spirited, but she was also spoiled and selfish. You have done some reckless things in the past, but you are also very loyal to your friends and you have a kind heart. Sahir tells me you bring raw meat treats for the wyvern when you visit the hellhounds, even though that creature would likely try to kill you given the chance."

"He can't help what he is, and I know he must get lonely in there, especially not being able to fly. Don't worry, I don't expect him to eat out of my hand or anything, and I'll be keeping my distance. I like my body parts where they are."

We laughed and turned the conversation to other things. He wanted to hear more about my life, so I described what it was like growing up with Roland and Peter. And Remy. I told him about Roland's recent trip to the cave and how much it meant to get the message from Remy.

We were in the middle of our dessert when I remembered something I'd been meaning to talk to him about. "I saw Desmund again last night."

"Did you?" He took a sip from his wine glass. "And how did it go?"

"Better than I expected. We both like books and Tchaikovsky, so he thinks I'm not a total lost cause. We even played a game of checkers."

Tristan's eyes widened. "You got Desmund to play checkers? I haven't seen him play anything but chess since I've known him."

"I don't know how to play chess, so it was checkers or nothing at all." I dabbed my napkin to my mouth then laid it beside my plate. "Honestly, I think the only reason he played with me is because he's lonely. Why does he stay up there all alone like that? I mean, I can tell he's not well, but he's not that bad, is he?"

Tristan settled back in his chair. "You might be the first person in a long time to feel some kind of empathy for Desmund. He goes out of his way to frighten most people away."

"Why? He's obviously intelligent, and he can be nice when he wants to be. Why does he drive everyone away?"

"Desmund is not the same man he was before he became ill. He was charming and outgoing and one of the finest warriors I've ever met."

During my time with Desmund last night, I had seen tiny flashes of the man Tristan described, and it was sad to think of how much he had changed. "What happened to him?"

There was a short pause before he answered. "It was a Hale witch. Desmund and his team were in Algeria hunting a nest of vampires that had wiped out over half a village. The witch took offense to them being in his territory even though they were there to help his people. Desmund confronted him to draw him away from the rest of his team, and he took the brunt of the witch's attack. He spent many years in confinement before he was stable enough to be released. It's a testament to his strength that he has come this far, but I fear he will never be the man he once was."

I couldn't respond because I was reliving my own battle with a Hale witch, remembering the horror of that vile magic burrowing inside my head like a maggot. My throat tightened at the agony Desmund had gone through, and I felt a surge of admiration for him having taken the brunt of the witch's power to save his team.

"Are you okay?"

I summoned a smile I didn't feel. "It just brought up some memories I'd rather forget." Now I understood the cold nausea that had overcome me when I'd touched Desmund's hand and the sensation of things crawling over my skin. It felt like the same abhorrent presence that had invaded my mind. What I couldn't understand was how the witch's magic could still be alive inside Desmund over a century later. I'd thought Hale witches used their magic to damage their victim, but what if it was more than that? What if they were able to leave some of their magic behind?

"It must have been frightening."

"It was. Now that I know their magic doesn't work on me, they don't scare me as much."

He nodded approvingly. "You've become stronger because of your experience. That is one of the marks of a good warrior."

"I don't know about that," I replied wryly. "You do remember seeing me in training, right?"

"I take it your training with Callum is still not going well?"

"No, and I'm pretty sure he's almost fed up with me." My shoulders slumped. "I know what he wants me to do, but I honestly don't know if I can do it. I've spent my whole life keeping my Mori under control. The one time I let it out, it almost destroyed me."

"And now you're afraid of it."

"Yes," I admitted.

He took his time folding his napkin and laying it beside his plate as if he was searching for the right words. "We are taught from an early age how to contain our Mori and to find a balance between ourselves and our demons. It is second nature for us to tap into their power, but even then, we sometimes struggle with control. Your power gives you incredible control over your Mori, and now we are asking you to loosen that control. I can see how that would be very difficult for you, and I've been thinking that we may be going about your training the wrong way. Perhaps we should try some other techniques on you."

"Like what?" I asked hopefully.

"Maybe pair you with a trainer more sensitive to your particular needs. There is one in India who relies heavily on meditation. Janak's had some success with a few troubled orphans we have sent to him." By *troubled*, I knew he meant the orphans were suffering from psychological problems caused by their demons. The older an orphan was before they were found, the more likely it was that their Mori would torment them into insanity.

Tristan smiled and pushed out his chair. "Don't worry. We'll figure something out. For now, why don't we go into the living room and see if I can't teach you a few checker moves to try on our friend Desmund when you see him again?"

*   *   *

Over the next few days, I found myself settling into a familiar routine. After a disappointing morning training with Callum, I visited the menagerie. Hugo and Woolf were always excited to see me, and I spent our time together teaching them to walk beside me properly and to heel when commanded. I was determined to show Tristan that they were well-behaved enough to be trusted out of their cage. I understood Tristan's reservations – they were hellhounds after all, bred and raised to kill – but I also saw gentleness in them and I refused to condemn them to a life of confinement.

Alex continued to crouch in the back of his cage and watch me like I was a juicy steak whenever I passed him. Even the nice chunks of red meat I brought him didn't soften his attitude toward me. Once I forgot to keep an eye on him and I didn't see him move closer to the bars until it was too late. My reward was a blistering four-inch burn on my arm, which required a dose of gunna paste and a trip to the medical ward. Mohiri medicine was very advanced, and by the next morning, the burn was nothing more than a patch of reddened skin that quickly faded. But I had learned my lesson. After that, I was extra careful not to let the wyvern catch me unaware. I still gave him his daily treat, but I made sure to throw it from a safe distance.

I took to spending a lot of time in the main library and accessing the stronghold's vast database, reading up on demons, vampires, witches, shifters, and anything else I would have learned about if I'd had a normal Mohiri education. Remy had taught me a lot, but I was just coming to realize how much about the supernatural world I did not know. It was going to take months to catch up to the other trainees in that area.

I also looked for anything I could find on Hale witches. I knew the likelihood of me finding a way to help Desmund was slim when the Mohiri had tried for centuries to cure people like him. But I felt compelled to try. More than anyone, I understood what Desmund had endured and I could not forget the feel of the terrible sickness inside him. I searched through every article I could find that referenced Hale witches, and I was frustrated that there wasn't a single mention of how their power worked. I despaired of ever finding a way to help Desmund.

Three days after my dinner with Tristan, I got the nerve to go visit Desmund again. I entered the library and let out a gasp. Books were strewn all over the room and an overturned lamp lay on the reading table with pieces of broken lamp shade on the floor. Scattered around the chairs near the cold fireplace were ripped pages. I picked one up and made a sound of dismay when I saw that it was from *Daniel Deronda*, the same book I'd been reading the last time I was here.

My eyes fell on a partially charred piece of wood that had fallen from the fireplace, and I immediately recognized the beautiful antique checkerboard. Tears burned my eyes. Why would Desmund wreck the library he loved and destroy the checkerboard and this particular book? Was he angry at me for some reason, maybe for the way I had run away? With his illness, it was almost impossible to know what went on in his head or what would set him off.

The scene from the library troubled me long into the night. When I entered the dining hall for breakfast, I was tired and barely aware of the people around me until Olivia slid into the chair across from me.

"How can you look so glum? I would have thought you'd be happier than anyone else?"

I frowned at her grinning face. "Happy about what?"

She rested her elbows on the table. "About going to Boise. God, I haven't been to the mall in a dog's age. This whole credit line is awesome, but buying clothes online is just no fun. You know what I mean?"

"Yeah," I replied, though I hadn't used my line of credit yet. But a day in the city? I felt Olivia's enthusiasm infecting me at the thought of getting away from here for a day. My gaze moved around the room until I found Tristan sitting with Celine at his usual table. He smiled at me, and I smiled back before I looked at Olivia again. "When are we leaving?"

Olivia laughed. "That's more like it. You'll have plenty of time to finish your breakfast because we aren't leaving for another hour."

At ten minutes before nine, the trainees who wanted to go to Boise gathered in the common room closest to the main hall. I walked over to Michael who was in his usual spot with his laptop.

"Are you sure you don't want to come with us, Michael? We're going to a movie after the mall."

He looked up, a spark of interest in his eyes. "What movie are you going to see?"

"Mark found a zombie marathon playing at Overland Park Cinemas this afternoon." I beckoned him with a finger. "Come on, you can't honestly tell me that your computer is more fun than that?"

He made a face. "More fun than hanging out with Jordan for a whole day."

I snorted softly. "Listen, I'll be her bosom buddy if it gets me out of this place for a few hours."

"Let's not get carried away," drawled Jordan as she sauntered past the door. "Bus is leaving in five minutes, with or without you losers."

I pulled on my jacket. "Last chance."

Michael went back to his laptop. "I'm good here. You have fun."

I shook my head. If ever there was a boy who needed to get out and have some fun, it was Michael. "Who are you always talking to on that thing anyway?"

"No one," he said almost defensively. "I play *World of Warcraft* with a bunch of guys online. We like to talk strategy."

"Ah." I had never been one for gaming. There was enough craziness in this world already without having to go look for it in a game. But to each his own.

The bus was actually a large black SUV with tinted windows. As I walked toward it, the front passenger window rolled down, and I groaned when I saw the red-headed warrior grinning at me. Seriously? There wasn't a single other warrior they could send to chaperone us besides the two of them? *Tristan, we are so having a talk when I get back.*

Olivia and Mark were in the back seats so I took the middle row with Jordan who promptly popped in a pair of ear buds and ignored me. That was fine by me. I settled back against the headrest, too excited to be going somewhere, anywhere, to let her bother me.

An hour later, Niall pulled up in front of the Boise Town Square mall and Seamus turned in his seat to smile at us. "Okay, kiddies, here is the drill. You have two hours to shop or browse or whatever it is you kids do in these places. Just remember that whatever you buy has to fit in here on the way back and I'm not sharing my leg room. If you behave yourselves and don't go wandering off " – his eyes met mine – "then you get to enjoy a movie and dinner. Any questions?"

Jordan opened her door and slid out. "Nope."

The four of us entered the mall together, but the other three immediately split off, going in their own directions. This obviously wasn't their first time here. I fingered the Visa card in my back pocket and thought about what I needed: a heavier coat, warmer boots, and some new gloves.

Idaho was definitely a lot colder than Maine, and there was no way I was going to stay cooped up inside all winter.

It took me a little over an hour to get everything I was looking for, and I spent the rest of the time wandering around while I waited for the others. It didn't take me long to spot one of the twins following me at a discreet distance, and I gritted my teeth, doing my best to ignore him. I was pretty sure the others didn't have a personal bodyguard tailing them. With my track record, I guess I wasn't surprised they were worried I might give them the slip, but they really had nothing to worry about. I'd promised Nate I would try to lay low and stay out of trouble, and I meant to stay true to my word after what I'd put him through.

I was walking past a jewelry store when an item in the window caught my eye. It was an antique chessboard that looked strikingly similar to the one Desmund and I had played on. The middle-aged salesman eyed me dubiously when I asked to see it, and he watched me like a hawk as I opened the box and examined the playing pieces. It contained a set of checkers and a full chess set.

I reached for my credit card. "I'll take it."

"It's four hundred dollars," he said in a haughty tone.

"Yes, I know." I handed him the Visa card, and his eyes narrowed a little when he saw the name on the card.

"What is the Westhorne Institute?" he asked, peering at me over his glasses.

I tapped my fingers on the glass counter and met his gaze squarely. "It's a special school where they send rich kids with anger management issues and problems with authority."

"Excuse me?"

I stifled a sigh and pointed over my shoulder to the large warrior I knew was visible through the window. "See that red-haired guy out there? He's my chaperone. You want to talk to him instead?"

He glanced behind me and swallowed nervously. "That won't be necessary. Would you like this wrapped?"

I was still smiling when I met the others at the exit. The three of them were lugging multiple shopping bags each, and they eyed my two bags in disbelief.

"I don't need much," I said, earning a scoff from Jordan.

"When you have unlimited credit, you don't buy things you need." She shook her head. "What a waste."

Olivia walked through the door ahead of us. "Don't mind her."

"I don't." I was not going to let Jordan spoil my day out.

The twins dropped us off in front of the movie theater. "You should be able to get enough zombie gore in four hours," said Niall dryly. "We'll pick you up here at five. Decide where you want to go for dinner and remember, we like big juicy steaks."

"You mean you're going to trust us to be on our own that long?" I asked in feigned shock.

"Even you couldn't get into much trouble in a movie theater in the middle of the day," Seamus replied with a snicker. "And we'll be out here waiting for you."

We loaded up on popcorn, candy, and drinks at the concession stand and found four seats in the back row just in time for the start of *28 Days Later*. I'd watched it at Roland's with him and Peter two years ago, but it was way creepier on the big screen in a dark theater. I even jumped once or twice when Olivia did, and we laughed at each other. It felt so good to do something as normal as going to a movie.

It got to the scene where the car breaks down and the girl gets under the car to fix it and you want to yell at her to not be so freaking stupid. All of a sudden there are rats and zombies all over them. Down in one of the front rows a girl shrieked and people twittered. I shook my head. *Please, like you didn't see that coming.*

A man screamed and people laughed even harder. A second man cried out. The laughter died. I leaned forward in my seat to try to see what was going on down front, but it was too dark. People started to stand, and there were more screams.

A few seconds later, pandemonium broke out and people began screaming and shoving and climbing over each other to get to the exits.

"What the fuck?" Mark uttered as the four of us jumped to our feet.

Olivia moved closer to him. "Guys, this doesn't look good."

"No shit, Sherlock," Jordan growled, her eyes wide and glowing with excitement while everyone else screamed in fear. She nudged Mark who was next to her. "Move it! We're sitting ducks here for whatever is down there. We need to get to the aisle where we can fight."

"Fight?" Mark shoved me and Olivia toward the stairs. "We don't even know what it is. And in case you haven't noticed, we didn't exactly come dressed for battle."

"Fucking amateurs." Jordan pulled off her leather jacket to reveal a short thin sword strapped to her back. From her boot she pulled a long silver knife, which she handed to Mark. "Always come prepared," she said with a wicked grin when she saw me trying to figure out how she had hidden that sword under her coat without cutting off something vital.

Even more surprising was the silver-tipped whip that Olivia pulled from her purse and uncoiled with a snap and a practiced flip of her wrist. I watched her move to a spot a few feet from Jordan with her feet apart and the whip in front of her. Mark gripped the knife and stood on Jordan's other side. The three of them were suddenly transformed from teenagers enjoying a day out to young Mohiri warriors prepared to do battle.

I stared helplessly at my empty hands and kicked myself mentally for getting caught without a weapon. It wasn't so long ago that I wouldn't leave home without a knife inside my jacket, a knife that had saved my ass on more than one occasion.

"Stay behind us, Sara," Jordan ordered sharply. "We'll try to get to the exit on this side. Keep your eyes peeled everyone."

None of us questioned her orders and, as one, we moved down the stairs. Below us it was utter chaos, but I was less frightened by the screams than I was by whatever was causing them. What the hell attacks people in a crowded movie theater in the middle of the afternoon? Most supes, even the dangerous ones, hide from humans and don't show themselves in crowded public places like this. Even Eli had pulled me into a dark alley before revealing his true nature to me.

Whatever it was, it was apparently going after anything that moved, so we tried to go as quietly as possible down the stairs. By the time we hit the middle landing, we were the only people on our side of the theater except for two teenage boys who were crouched behind some seats. I motioned for them to come with us, but they just shook their heads and huddled closer to the wall. All I could do was hope they would be safe there until we dealt with the threat or someone came to help.

In a matter of minutes, the theater had all but emptied except for our small group, the two boys, and a few stragglers limping for the door. People yelled outside, but inside the theater the only sounds were the zombie moans from the movie, which in our current situation didn't seem quite so entertaining anymore.

The movie hit a quiet scene, and silence fell over the dark theater.

Somewhere in the lower rows of seats, a popcorn bag rustled. Closer, there was a rattle as a drink cup full of ice tipped over onto the floor. My nails bit into my palms, and my heart sped up like a freight train. *Shit, shit, shit. How do I keep ending up in these situations?*

Olivia cried out, and I jerked my head to the side just as something shot out from beneath the seats on our right and leapt into the air, coming right at our faces. In the flickering light from the movie screen I was able to make out a long, pale gray body and a flash of teeth, just before a blade whistled through the air and cut the thing in two mid-flight. Black blood sprayed, and I almost gagged on the putrid stench that rose up around us as the creature's severed halves landed at Jordan's feet.

"What the hell?" Mark bellowed, jumping back from the writhing parts. "That's a goddamn lamprey demon!"

"Yeah, and they never go anywhere alone." Jordan kicked the top half of the demon down the stairs and brandished her bloody sword again. "Incoming!"

Chapter 6

"OH MY GOD!" Olivia squeaked, and I followed her horrified stare to the two six-foot long bodies slithering up the stairs toward us. I had never seen or heard of a lamprey demon until this moment, but I knew that if I survived this, they would be starring in my nightmares. The creatures advancing on us resembled eels, but they were bigger around than my thigh with large unblinking eyes on either side of their heads. But it was their mouths – round and funnel-shaped with row upon row of curved teeth – that made my bladder feel like it was about to empty.

"You two take the one on the left. I'll deal with this one," Jordan shouted, already moving forward to meet one of the advancing demons, her blade dripping blood from her first kill.

Without a weapon, I was helpless to do anything but watch as Mark and Olivia followed Jordan. The demons struck first, and the air was filled with gurgling hissing sounds and grunts as my companions fought them off. Olivia's whip sailed through the air and wrapped around one of the thrashing bodies while Mark tried to get around it to come at it from behind. Beside them, Jordan was finding her demon a lot harder to kill than the first one. It dodged her blade and struck back with a speed I would not have expected from its thick body, missing her by inches.

Behind me, one of the huddled boys made a mewling sound, and I turned to look back at them just as a demon flew at me from above. I twisted to one side, feeling it brush against my arm as it went by. I stumbled and regained my footing, but not fast enough to jump out of the way as the demon came at me again. A scream ripped from my lips as sharp pain seared through my right calf and I stared in horror at the sucker-like mouth clamped onto my leg. I kicked and pulled frantically at the demon, but its mouth was attached like a leach. The demon convulsed and swallowed and fiery tendrils of pain shot up my leg.

Oh God, it's sucking my blood! It's sucking my blood!

Metal flashed and the thing latched onto my leg jerked and went slack. I reached past the knife protruding from the demon's head to pry its mouth from my calf. It hurt like hell when the dozens of sharp teeth ripped from my flesh, and I was afraid to look at the damage to my leg.

Mark shouted at me, and I looked down to find him and Olivia locked in a struggle with their lamprey demon. "Sara, the knife!" he yelled.

I reached down and yanked the knife from the dead demon then limped down the stairs to the others. Jordan looked like she was getting the upper hand in her fight and the demon in front of her bled from several long gashes. Olivia and Mark were barely holding onto theirs while keeping its mouth from latching onto one of them. Olivia had a cut on her cheek and her right arm hung limp and bloody by her side. If not for the whip around the demon's neck, the thing would have broken free of them. Instead of using his knife on the creature, Mark had thrown it to save me.

"Watch out." Ignoring Mark's reaching hand, I grabbed the knife in both hands and slammed it into the head of the demon. It took three blows to bring the demon down, and Mark and Olivia sagged against each other when it finally hit the floor.

Mark panted, looking around fearfully. "Did we get them all?"

"I think so. I don't see any – " I broke off when noises in the dark theater alerted us to the presence of at least two more demons.

"Where the fuck are they coming from?" He shouted, grabbing the knife and moving between me and the approaching demons. "A little help here, Jordan."

"Let me take care of this bastard first." Jordan brought her sword down in a graceful arc and sliced cleanly through the neck of the demon. She gave a triumphant smile and kicked the dead demon for good measure before turning to meet the new threat. "How many?"

"At least two, it's hard to tell in here," Mark called to her.

I scanned the dark theater. "What should we do?"

Jordan replied without looking back. "We've got this. You get the hell out of here."

"Are you nuts? I'm not leaving you guys in here with those things."

"Sara, you and Olivia are bleeding and neither of you can fight. The last thing I need right now is to be worried about keeping your asses safe."

I looked at Olivia's pained expression, then down at the dead demon on the stairs. Smoke curled from it where the silver tip of the whip touched its sickly gray skin.

"Here they come!" Mark yelled. "Oh Jesus, there are three of them!"

I pushed Olivia aside and grabbed the handle of the whip, yanking hard to unroll it from the dead demon's body and sending the creature thumping down the stairs. Whip in hand, I spun around as Jordan and Mark were attacked. Mark went down, stabbing at one demon that was ferociously trying to latch onto his neck. Jordan moved fast, but the demons were just as fast. No matter how good or fast Jordan was, she was outnumbered this time.

I put my fingers to my lips and let out a sharp whistle. "Hey, you fat ugly worms, come and get me." One of the demons turned my way, and I gripped the whip handle so tight my knuckles turned white. "Yeah, I'm talking to you, you overgrown maggot!"

The demon made a sound somewhere between a hiss and a shriek and came at me. *Oh shit!* This ranked way up there on the list of the stupidest things I had ever done, and that was a pretty big list.

I struck out with the whip and felt it connect with the demon's body, leaving a long smoking gash along its side. It wasn't enough to stop the demon, and I dropped the whip to fend off the thing with my bare hands. The force of its body hitting mine sent us both tumbling down the stairs and knocked the breath out of me when my back hit the bottom landing. The demon recovered fast and struck, and my hands came up just in time to grab it and keep its nightmarish jaws away from my throat. It thrashed its powerful body, and I grunted as I fought to hold it away from me. No way could I fight this thing off alone. I was totally screwed if help didn't come very, very soon.

"Sara! Are you okay?" Jordan bellowed.

"Could . . . really use . . . some help!" I panted.

The demon twisted violently, and I suddenly found my body pinned beneath it. "Argh!" I pushed with all my strength at the head mere inches above me. Drool dripped onto my face and neck, and I nearly choked on the fetid breath invading my nostrils. As I stared into the deep funnel-like mouth with its rows upon rows of undulating teeth, I swore there was no way I was going out this way. I had not survived all I'd been through just to be taken down by an overgrown grub with teeth.

Static sizzled across my skin and crackled through my hair. My whole body felt like there was electricity buzzing just below the surface, building in intensity and looking for a way out. Instead of fearing it, I welcomed it and fed it with more power. Heat spread through my arms and filled my hands until they began to glow like they did for a healing, and the air around me sparked and filled with the thick smell of ozone.

The demon began to writhe and thrash frantically as it tried to tear away from me, but my hands were welded to its head. Tiny bolts of electricity leapt from my fingers, and it felt like I held a lightning storm in my hands. Power surged forward into the demon until the creature began to swell and glowing cracks appeared in its skin. I watched its fishlike eyes bulge in terror a second before it let out a gurgling shriek and exploded, raining me with hot, stinking blood and guts and thousands of demon bits. Stunned, I stared at my raised bloody hands for few seconds before I rolled over onto my side and puked up my popcorn lunch.

Jordan was the first to reach me. "What the fuck?" she swore when she caught sight of me and what was left of the demon. "What happened? What did you do to it?"

I held up my hand and shook my head as Mark and Olivia crowded behind her, staring at me covered from head to toe in demon guts. There was no way to tell them what had happened. Even if I could share my secret, I wasn't even sure what I had done.

The doors below us slammed open, and Niall and Seamus burst into the theater. They came up short when they saw Jordan, Olivia, and Mark standing over me lying on the floor, covered in blood and guts. Their sharp eyes quickly swept the scene and took a count of the dead lamprey demons littering the stairs and the four of us, bloody but standing. Well, most of us were standing.

"Sweet Mother!"

One of the twins crouched beside me. "Are you alive beneath all that, lass?"

I raised an arm and tried to wipe some of the gore from my face. "Yes, but right now I kinda wish I wasn't."

He grinned and held out a hand to me, easily pulling me to my feet. I wasn't the only one who blanched when demon pieces slid off me and slopped onto the carpeted floor. I looked around at the expressions of shock and revulsion and then at the wide area spewed with black demon blood and guts. I had seen a lot of strange and awful things in the last few months but exploding demons definitely beat them all.

I am so glad I don't have to clean up this mess. I imagined the expressions of the theater's cleaning crew when they saw this and a giggle burst from me, earning me confused stares from the two warriors and the three teenagers standing a few steps above me. Something in their expressions struck me as incredibly hilarious and I couldn't help myself, I started to laugh. The harder they stared, the harder I laughed until my stomach hurt and tears ran down my cheeks.

"What's wrong with her?" Olivia asked, her voice quivering.

Jordan narrowed her eyes at me. "I think she's hysterical."

"N-no," I stammered, straightening. "Can you imagine being a janitor here and having to clean up *this*?" I waved at the gore around us. "Talk about a realistic zombie movie."

The twin who had helped me up shook his head at me as he put his phone to his ear. "It's Niall. We need a clean-up crew. Bloody lamprey demons in the movie theater. Hell, your guess is as good as mine." He looked at us. "No, they're all okay, just a little beat up. No, they took out the lot of them on their own. Some civilians were hurt, too, and we'll need to treat them. It's a pretty big mess so put a rush on it."

He gave them directions and hung up. Pursing his lips, he studied the carnage at his feet. "Someone want to tell me what in bloody hell did this?"

I was still fighting back laughter, which probably made me look slightly unhinged, so he addressed the others. Jordan shrugged and pointed at me. "Ask her. I was busy keeping one of those bastards off my ass when she did . . . whatever she did."

"Same here," Mark added.

"All I saw was Sara and the demon falling down the stairs," Olivia supplied. "I saw a white flash and suddenly the demon exploded everywhere."

Niall looked at me, and I shook my head. Whatever he was thinking, he did not push the matter and instead pulled off his coat. "Remove your coat, lass, and try to wipe off your face and hair as best you can. Then put this on. It'll cover the worst of the mess."

I did as he instructed and let him put his much larger coat on me. Jordan, Mark, and Olivia did what they could to clean up as well. All we could do after that was wait for backup. Niall and Seamus managed to lock the doors to keep the civilians out, except for the two boys who were sitting in their seats now and staring at us like we were a satanic cult about to sacrifice them. I didn't know if the Mohiri had something to modify memories. If so, these two were going to need a strong dose of it.

The cleanup crew wasted no time, and fifteen minutes after Niall's call, the employee door to the left of the screen opened and they filed in. The eight-man crew could not hide their surprise as they took in the number of dead demons as well as what was left of the one I had exploded. Their initial reaction passed quickly, and two of them headed for the teenage boys who had witnessed everything while the others began to assess the situation.

"You weren't kidding about the mess. We'll need to bring in another team," one of the men said to Niall. "Paulette is waiting in the van to take the trainees home. Looks like they all could use some medical attention."

"How did they get here so fast?" I asked Seamus, and he told me they kept teams in the major cities in every state. It made it easier to respond to situations like this one.

Before I knew it, we were shuffled outside to a black van where a tall blond woman gawked at my bloody hair and clothes before she started ushering us into the vehicle. I hung back while everyone else climbed in, wishing I could change my clothes before I crowded in with them.

Without warning, coldness slammed into my chest, leaving me almost gasping for breath, and I had to hold onto a stair rail for support. *Not now.*

"You okay?" Seamus asked, and it took me several seconds to nod. He helped me into the van's second row of seats and got in behind me. We had plenty of room because everyone gave me a wide berth.

As soon as the van started Jordan raised the question on everyone's minds.

"What the hell are lamprey demons doing in a movie theater? Don't they live in sewers?"

"Yes," Seamus responded. "I've never heard of them attacking humans in the open like that."

"Do you think they were after us?" In my experience, bad things like this did not happen by coincidence, especially not to me.

"I doubt it," Niall said, but I noticed a slight pause before he spoke. "Lamprey demons are not known for their intelligence. They are more like leeches, and they'll latch onto the nearest warm-blooded creature. They attacked a few humans, too, so I don't think they were targeting you specifically. You were just the last unlucky ones left in the theater."

The ride home was a lot less fun than the one to Boise. When the van pulled up to the main entrance, Tristan came out to meet us. He asked if we were okay and walked with us to the medical ward where a small team of healers waited. One of them ushered me into a room with an attached bathroom where I immediately stripped and showered. I couldn't help but shudder as the water ran off me in black streams until I was clean. I dressed in a hospital gown and lay on a bed while a healer tended to the bite on my leg. She cleaned the wound and applied a special salve that drew the pain from the wound even before she had finished dressing it in a light gauze bandage. Then she gave me some of the dreaded gunna paste and told me to get some rest before she left the room.

Tristan entered the room a minute after she left, and he gave me a quick hug. "How are you feeling?"

"These guys have good drugs. Not even feeling an ounce of pain." He did not look convinced, so I gave him a reassuring smile. "Trust me; I've been hurt a lot worse than this. It takes more than a bloodsucking demon to keep me down."

His expression was serious. "It must have been very frightening."

"Are you kidding me? Have you seen Jordan with a sword? That girl is scarier than a dozen demons worms."

Tristan laughed softly, and some of the tension left his body. "Niall told me about the demon that exploded, and he said no one could tell him what happened. Do you want to tell me about it?"

I started by telling him what I had done to the bazerat a few days ago, followed by my fight with the lamprey demon. "I honestly don't know how I did it," I confessed. "It feels like my healing power – only different if that makes sense. It's like it's amped up on steroids, and I don't think it likes demons."

"Elementals are very powerful beings and natural enemies of demons. It is very likely that you are beginning to come into some of those powers. Unfortunately, we know very little about them."

"Aine said she would visit me. I hope she comes soon because I could really use some answers."

"Well, I doubt she will come tonight, and you need to sleep so your body can heal." He stood and tucked the blanket around me. "I'll come back later to check on you."

I tried to sit up. "Can't I go to my room? I'd sleep much better in my own bed."

He gently pushed me back down. "The healers want to keep you all here overnight for observation. The bacteria in a lamprey demon's mouth are very potent, and we need to watch for signs of infection."

The healer came in then and gave me a glass of sweet smelling liquid to drink. I looked at it warily, and she said, "This is takhi juice. It will help you sleep and fight infection. Drink it all."

I drank it obediently, and Tristan nodded in approval. "Sleep now and we will talk about it tomorrow. Is it okay if I come back to sit with you tonight while you sleep?"

I smiled sluggishly, already feeling the effects of the takhi juice. "Okay."

My dreams were filled with zombies with large round sucking mouths full of teeth. I tossed fitfully and tried to wake up, but the sleeping potion held me in its grasp. First, I felt like I was freezing and warm thick blankets were laid over me. Then my body felt like it was on fire, and I cried out until someone pressed a cool wet cloth to my face. A few times I almost gained wakefulness and heard people talking softly nearby, but I was pulled under again before I could open my eyes.

After what seemed like forever, the flames subsided and all I could feel was the warmth of a hand encasing mine where it lay on the covers. There was comfort and safety in the touch, and I reached for it instinctively until the strong fingers entwined with mine. I sighed as the nightmares were banished, and I sank at last into a deep healing sleep.

*　　*　　*

I awoke slowly, listening to the sounds of people talking and moving around outside my room. My body felt stiff, my throat was parched, and my head pounded with a fierce headache. I moaned and lifted a hand to rub my forehead.

"Here, this will take care of your headache."

I turned my head toward Tristan who sat by my bed, holding a glass of brownish liquid. After the sleeping draft from last night, I was hesitant to take any more medicine.

He smiled as if he read my mind. "You had a bad fever last night from the demon bite, and you are dehydrated now, which is causing your headache. I promise this will only ease your pain."

My head was pounding, and his words were all the reassurance I needed. I accepted the glass and downed the contents, then lay back on the bed. "I heard someone here with me last night. Was that you?"

"I came in a few times. Your fever made you very restless."

"What about the others? Are they okay?"

He took the glass from me and laid it on a table. "Olivia also had a fever from her bite, but Mark and Jordan were okay. They have all been released. Once you are feeling better, you may leave, too."

"I feel better now." I tried to sit up, but he pushed me back down.

"Give it a few more minutes. While we wait, I want to talk to you about your training."

I groaned. "Are you trying to torture me after the night I just had?"

He did not laugh as I expected him to, and his expression grew serious. "You could have been hurt a lot worse than you were or even killed last night. You have to learn to fight and to harness your Mori's power so you will be better prepared the next time you face danger."

"I think I did all right."

"Yes, but we don't know exactly what you did or if you can summon it at will. We live in a dangerous world, and I need to know you can defend yourself before you go out into it. So I am making changes to your training routine."

I fidgeted with the blanket. "What does that mean?"

"Nothing bad, I assure you. We are just going to try you with another trainer and see if a different technique works better for you." He patted my hand. "Don't look so worried. I have a feeling this will be just what you need."

Why didn't I feel as confident as him? "When do I start with the new trainer?"

"Tomorrow. Today, just rest and get your strength back."

It was noon before the healers finally let me leave the medical ward. I was ravenous, which the healers said was normal after such a fever, so I headed straight for the dining hall after I showered and changed. Lunch was over by the time I got there, so I begged a plate from the kitchen staff and ate alone in the dining hall.

"Hey, Sara, what are you doing in here by yourself? Aren't you going to the arena?"

I looked up at Michael who stood in the doorway. "What's going on at the arena?"

"Some of the warriors are dueling." His eyes flashed with excitement.

"Dueling?"

"For fun. They do it every now and then, and it's so awesome to watch. Come on, I heard Tristan is joining in this time."

I carried my plate to a bus tray and followed Michael. I hadn't seen Tristan fight yet, and I was eager to watch him in action. A man who garnered the kind of respect he did had to be more than a good leader. I bet he was an amazing fighter, too.

"Everyone's talking about what happened to you guys last night."

I gave him a sidelong glance. "I bet you're glad you decided not to come with us, huh?"

He nodded quickly. "Yeah. You could have been killed. Why would lamprey demons do something like that?"

"Your guess is as good as mine."

The arena was half full when we entered, and I saw the other trainees sitting and standing together near the door. Looking past them, I caught sight of Niall and Seamus standing with Tristan in the middle of the floor. I felt a surge of pride when I saw Tristan holding a long slender sword and looking every bit the fierce warrior.

We weaved through the crowd to the other trainees. "What did we miss?" I asked them.

"Tristan is wiping the ground with the others," Terrence replied without talking his eyes off the older warriors. "And here comes his next victim."

I watched as a Korean man approached Tristan, carrying a similar sword. Something about him seemed familiar, and it wasn't until he reached Tristan and the twins that I recognized him as one of the warriors I'd met in Portland. His name was Erik, if I remembered correctly, and he was in the unit that had helped clean out the mansion where Remy's cousins had been held. He had also accompanied me here along with Nikolas and Chris, but I hadn't seen him since I arrived.

The twins moved back to give the dueling warriors room, and Tristan and Erik saluted one another. Tristan's eyes gleamed like I had never seen before, and I realized he was looking forward to the fight as much as the spectators.

They came together in a clang of metal, and I caught myself holding my breath more than once as they parried and thrust, dancing around each other with deadly grace. Eric was a skilled swordsman, and once or twice I thought he was going to get the better of Tristan until I realized that Tristan was just toying with him. Tristan might not hunt as much as he used to, but he was as good a warrior as anyone else there, which he proved when he suddenly disarmed his opponent.

I clapped and cheered with everyone else. Tristan's eyes met mine in the crowd, and I gave him two thumbs up. "Wow, he's so good!"

Josh's face glowed with excitement. "You haven't seen anything yet. The main attraction is just about to start."

"What could be better than that?" I asked a second before I felt a soft telltale flutter against my mind. *You have got to be kidding me.* I fumed as the last person I expected to see walked through a doorway at the far end of the room. All eyes were on the commanding figure who strode toward Tristan, muscles rippling beneath his T-shirt and a sword grasped in his right hand. His mouth was curved into a brotherly smile for Tristan.

Around me, the trainees and younger warriors were riveted on Nikolas and Tristan, and their excitement was almost palpable. All I could feel was anger. I couldn't forget how I felt when I found out he'd left after dumping me on someone else like I was their problem now. I shouldn't care what he did, but for some reason it bothered me more than I wanted to admit.

No longer entertained, I turned to push back through the crowd, but Olivia grabbed my arm. "Where are you going? You don't get to see Nikolas fight every day."

"I've seen him fight plenty."

Terrence turned to give me an appreciative look. "That's right. You've seen him in action. Man that must be something."

"It is," I replied grudgingly.

The ring of steel on steel stopped me when I would have taken another step, and I stood there for half a minute, refusing to look until I heard small intakes of breath around me. Unable to help myself, I turned back toward the room.

It was immediately clear which of them was the superior swordsman – not that I was surprised after seeing Nikolas fight more than once. Tristan was a fine fighter, but where he moved with the smooth grace of a fencer, Nikolas's movements were like a lethal dance, so beautifully controlled that you could not take your eyes off him. His long blade glinted in the sun shining through the tall windows as he rained blows on Tristan, keeping his opponent on the defensive and circling him like a lion preparing for a kill. If I didn't know this was a friendly duel, I would have been afraid for my grandfather's life at that moment.

Nikolas saw an opening and moved in, bringing the tip of his sword to Tristan's chest and just like that it was over. Tristan smiled and bowed, then slapped Nikolas on the back as everyone clapped. The two men stepped aside to let the next pair duel, but it was anticlimactic after the thrill of watching them. I couldn't help but notice that my companions were more interested in watching what Nikolas was doing than the current fight.

"Someday, I'm going to be that good," said a worshipful voice beside me.

I turned to face Jordan, who stared at Nikolas like he was a rock star. "Good and when you are, you can kick his ass. In fact, let me know so I can be there to watch." She looked at me like I was nuts, and I shrugged. "Spend a month with him and you'll sing a different tune."

Jordan started to respond but stopped when her eyes went to something behind me. I turned to see Tristan and Nikolas walking through the crowd toward us. My jaw clenched. I had plenty of choice words for Nikolas, but this was not the place to share them. His expression as he approached was neutral, but when our eyes met I saw the familiar arrogant gleam and it fed the angry embers smoldering inside me. Did he really expect me to greet him as if all was well between us?

Tristan stopped to talk to someone, and as soon as he and Nikolas turned their heads away from us, I was out of there. I ducked through the crowded room in an effort to put as much distance as possible between me and Nikolas. If I confronted him now, I might start yelling at him and end up looking like an idiot in front of everyone.

At the door, I looked back and saw Nikolas wearing a surprised scowl as he searched the room. *Not very nice when people just take off like that, is it?* I thought with intense satisfaction and left before he saw me.

If I knew one thing about Nikolas, it was that once he set his mind on something it was almost impossible to shake him. I had seen the look in his eyes, and he was not going to let me give him the slip that easily. He also had an uncanny ability to find me, which was great when I was in danger, but not so much when I wanted to avoid him.

I set off for the main building, hoping that the people in the arena held Nikolas up long enough for me to make my escape. I felt like a sulking child, running away from him, but between last night and the shock of seeing him again, my emotions were all over the map, and I just couldn't deal with him right now.

I took ten steps before I realized the only place I could hide in the main building was my room, and I had no desire to spend the afternoon cooped up inside. Changing direction, I headed to the menagerie instead, and I let out a long breath when the heavy door closed behind me. Hugo and Woolf ran to the front of their cage and began to whine. "Hey, you two," I greeted them as I unlocked the door to their cage with the key Sahir had given me. "Looks like you get me for the whole afternoon."

Chapter 7

HUNGER FINALLY FORCED me to come out of hiding. After I cleaned up, I headed for the dining hall, hoping I wouldn't run into Nikolas there. It was his first day back after a mission, so he and Tristan were probably locked away in Tristan's office.

My anxiety lessened when I entered the dining hall and saw that Tristan was not at his usual table. I let out the breath I hadn't known I was holding and went to get a tray.

I'd always had a healthy appetite – to the envy of the other girls at my high school – and now I knew I could thank my Mohiri genes for my high metabolism. Those girls would positively hate me now if they could see the stack of pizza on my plate.

I was on my second slice of pizza when Jordan pulled out a chair across from me and laid down her tray of burgers and fries.

"What do you want?"

She tucked loose strands of blond hair behind her ears and fixed me with an appraising stare. "I think I may have misjudged you, kitten. You could have left the theater last night, but you stayed even though you had no weapons and a good chance of becoming demon chow. That took guts."

"I don't run away." *Liar. You've been running from Nikolas all day.* "And my name is Sara, not kitten."

"Noted." She picked up one of her burgers and took a huge bite that would have scandalized every teenage girl I knew back home. She took a few minutes to polish off the burger before she spoke again. "You don't scare easily, do you? Too bad you can't fight, because you've definitely got a pair."

"Gee thanks, I guess."

"No, seriously. Olivia's a decent fighter but she still jumps at her own shadow, and the guys wouldn't know what to do if they saw a real monster.

But I saw you last night. You jumped right in even after you were hurt, and you taunted those lampreys to draw them off us. That was kinda badass."

"Or stupid." I picked up my third slice of pizza. "Anyway you were pretty cool yourself. That was some impressive sword work. I probably would have chopped off my own head."

Jordan grinned widely, and her whole face lit up. I'd been right in my assessment of her a few days ago. She was beautiful when she wasn't glaring at everyone. "That was the most fun I've had . . . like *ever!*"

"Too bad you weren't in Maine with me two months ago. You would have had the time of your life."

Her hand paused in lifting a fry to her mouth. "You really did all those things you told the others about, didn't you?" I nodded. "Damn. You really got to see Nikolas in action?"

I waved my slice of pizza. "What is the fascination everyone has with him anyway? So he's good with a sword. Big deal."

Jordan looked at me like I was slow-witted. "Nikolas is better than good, Sara. He's the best. He does whatever he wants, and they let him because he so damn good. Plus, no one could stop him anyway. No one says *no* to Nikolas."

"So everyone keeps telling me. I hate to burst your bubble, but he's just a man who walks on the ground like everyone else." I dropped my uneaten pizza back on my plate and pushed it away. "It's no wonder he's so arrogant with the way everyone here worships him."

"Ha! I dare you to say that to him."

I gave her a small smile. "Wouldn't be the first time."

She plucked a slice of pepperoni from my pizza and ate it. "Yeah, well I'll believe that when I see it. I think – "

I sensed him a second before I saw Jordan blush and look down at her plate in a rare show of timidity. There was barely time to notice that the dining hall had grown oddly quiet before the chair next to me moved and Nikolas laid his tray on the table. "You don't mind if I join you, do you?" he asked then sat before either of us replied.

I turned to glare at him, and I was startled to find his gray eyes inches from mine. "You. . . " I stammered and leaned away from him, causing his mouth to curve into a familiar smirk. "Let me guess, no one else will eat with you."

He gave me a lazy smile that made my stomach do things it definitely should not be doing. "I seem to remember you being a lot nicer the last time we had dinner together."

"Like I had a choice," I retorted, thinking of my last night in New Hastings. "You guys wouldn't let me out of your sight that night."

"Actually, I was thinking about the night of the storm when the power went out."

Images of that night – eating sandwiches by candlelight, sitting by the fire talking – flooded my mind, and the room suddenly felt too warm. I looked away from him. "People change," was all I could think of to say. I could feel Jordan's eyes on us as she listened to our exchange, and the last thing I wanted to do was spar with Nikolas in front of an audience. I reached for my tray.

"I hear you're having some difficulty in training." His statement stilled my hand. "I thought perhaps you might want to talk about it."

He knew more about me than anyone here, but he was the last person I wanted to have a heart-to-heart with. "No thank you."

Nikolas was completely unfazed by my rejection of his offer. He smiled at Jordan. "Jordan, right?" She nodded mutely. "I hear you're pretty lethal with a blade."

I watched her blush and turn from a bold, outspoken warrior-to-be into a flustered teenage girl who had finally met her idol. "She is," I said, not sure why I felt the need to come to her rescue. "You should have seen her last night, taking on those lamprey demons. If it wasn't for her, we probably would have been demon chow. She – "

I stopped when I sensed the tension flowing off Nikolas and I remembered how he used to get whenever I was in danger. Well, I was no longer his responsibility, so he was going to have to get over it.

Apprehension filled Jordan's eyes at his stiffness; she had obviously never witnessed one of Nikolas's dark moods before. I wanted to tell her "I told you so," but instead I elbowed Nikolas in the ribs a little harder than was necessary. "Quit scowling before you scare off my new friend."

His eyes remained narrowed on me for a moment. Then his face relaxed and the tension seeped out of him as he picked up his burger. "I certainly wouldn't want to do that. At least this one doesn't shed."

I started to make a retort when I saw one corner of his mouth lift and I knew he was playing with me. It was a side of him he didn't show much – to me anyway – and I wasn't sure how to respond. He bit into his burger, looking pleased with himself.

"Just ignore him," I said to Jordan, even though I knew how ridiculous it was to expect that of someone who looked at Nikolas with a mix of fear and reverence. "He has to ruin at least one meal for me before he disappears on another one of his missions."

"You didn't hear?" he asked and his smug look gave me a sinking feeling in my stomach. "Maybe you would have if you hadn't *disappeared* this afternoon."

"Hear what?"

"I'm not going anywhere for the next month at least."

"What? Sick of hunting already?"

"No, I just have another job at the moment. I'm your new trainer."

My first thought was that he was joking to get another rise out of me. But then I saw that he was serious, and I shook my head in denial. "I am *not* training with you." Callum suddenly didn't look so awful anymore. I looked around the room for Tristan, to have him set things straight, but he was nowhere to be seen.

"It was Tristan's idea," Nikolas informed me as if he knew who I was looking for. "He thinks it might help you to work with someone you know."

"Since when do you work with trainees, or follow orders for that matter?" I hoped this was his idea of a joke. "Don't you have more orphans to rescue?"

"After you, I have a much greater respect for the people who usually handle those jobs," he drawled. "I agree with Tristan on this. We need to try a different approach with your training."

"A few days ago, Tristan mentioned a guy in India who he thought might be able to help me."

"Janak?" Nikolas chuckled, and I wanted to elbow him again. "Janak's a nice guy, but way too soft for this. One session with you and he'd be on the first plane back to India."

I folded my arms and glowered at him as he dug into his burger again. If he thought he could just show up out of nowhere, push his way back into my life, and throw insults at me, he obviously did not know me as well as he thought he did. "So, what is your brilliant plan, to harass me until I get so pissed off that I sic my demon on you?"

He took time to finish off his burger before replying, and I knew he did it just to provoke me. What really bugged me was that it was working. I wanted to yell at him and run away from him at the same time, but I refused to let him see how much he was able to get to me.

"If that's what it takes, but I think something else will work better for you."

"What?" As much as I wanted to pretend not to care, I couldn't hide my curiosity.

He stood and picked up his tray. "Get some sleep tonight because training starts tomorrow." Before I could argue or ask him again what he meant, he walked away. I stared after him until Jordan exhaled sharply, reminding me I was not alone at the table. I turned back to find her watching me with something akin to awe in her expression.

"You are the luckiest female on the planet right now. You know that, don't you?"

"Really? How do you figure?" I felt decidedly more cursed than lucky and wondered how I was going to get out of this training. Why would Tristan suggest such a thing, knowing how I felt about Nikolas?

"You're shitting me right? Nikolas Danshov is going to give you private lessons. Look at him. Do you really expect me to believe that you aren't the least bit attracted to him?"

I shifted uncomfortably. "I never said he wasn't good looking. It's just that he can be very intense and bossy and he's a lot to take sometimes."

Jordan rested her chin in her palms and let out a gusty sigh. "Yes, please."

"You wouldn't say that if you knew him. Nikolas is like an iceberg." She raised an eyebrow, and I shook my head. "I don't mean he's cold. I mean *you* only see what's above the surface. Underneath there is a lot more to him than you realize, and it's not always pretty."

Jordan gave me a sly smile. "Well, it sounds like you are going to be spending some serious one-on-one time with him. What I wouldn't give to be shut up alone in a room with that man." Her smile widened to a grin. "I can't wait to see Celine's face when she hears about this."

I scowled to hide the heat threatening to fill my face. "I hate to ruin your fantasies, Jordan, but I am not training with Nikolas, privately or otherwise."

"Not what it looks like to me." Her eyes gleamed as she reached for my cold pizza. "I told you no one says *no* to Nikolas."

"Shut up," I snapped, but it only made her grin more.

∗   ∗   ∗

"I can't believe you finished the first draft already. I hope you're not staying up all night working."

Nate laughed into the phone. He was usually stressed toward the end of a first draft, and hearing him sound so relaxed meant the book was going well. "I've discovered I work way too much when I don't have you around to make me stop."

I tapped my pencil against the drawing of Hugo and Woolf I'd been working on when he called. "So, it's been quiet there?" I didn't need to elaborate because Nate knew what I was asking.

"Very quiet. Brendan dropped by two days ago to visit and told me they think it's safe here now. But they are still keeping an eye on things."

"I still hate you being there alone. I wish I knew if the troll ward still worked." The ward I'd put on our building to protect it was supposed to last as long as it was my home. I still considered the apartment home even though I was here, but I didn't know if the spell took the meaning literally or figuratively. It wasn't like we could get someone evil to try to enter the apartment to test it. "You started using the Ptellon nectar though, right?"

There was a short pause. "Not yet. If Brendan thinks it's safe – "

"Nate, you promised!"

"I know. I'm just having trouble with the idea of taking something I know nothing about."

I repressed a sigh of frustration. Nate had accepted the existence of the supernatural world, but he still couldn't handle it all. Every time we spoke, I asked him about the Ptellon blood I gave him to help keep him safe from demons and other nasty things, and every time he said he would start using it. Even knowing the dangers out there, he would rather not ingest something with magical properties.

"*I* know what it is. You have to trust me, please. If you only knew what I went through to get that stuff." I'd never told him about my little adventure at the marina. With everything else going on at the time, I didn't think he needed to hear about a pack of possessed wharf rats. "It will make me feel a lot better if you take it."

I heard his chair squeak as he shifted position. "I'll do it. I just need to talk myself into it."

"Promise me."

"I will, I promise. So, what's been going on with you?"

I opened my mouth to tell him about the demon attack and shut it just as quickly. I couldn't tell him something like that; it would freak him out. The only reason he was okay with me moving here was he thought it would be safer for me. And it was, just not as much as he believed.

"Hugo and Woolf are doing a lot better, and they don't growl as much at people. Did you get the picture I sent of them?"

"Yes, and I thought someone was spamming me until I realized you were using a different email address. That picture's not Photoshopped, is it?"

I chuckled. "Nope."

He let out a low whistle. "When you told me about them, they didn't sound real. Who would believe hellhounds really exist? But then, a few months ago, I didn't think a lot of things were real. Do their eyes always glow like that?"

"Yes, but I think the camera flash makes them look redder than usual."

"They look terrifying. Are you sure it's safe to be around them?"

"Absolutely. Trust me; Tristan wouldn't let me near them if he thought I'd get hurt. He's almost as bad as Nikolas." Nate knew all about Tristan being my grandfather, and he'd said he was glad I had family here. If he found the idea of me having a grandfather who looked almost young enough to be his son strange, he didn't let on.

"Ah, I knew you sounded out of sorts, and I can guess why. No word from Nikolas yet?"

I threw down my pencil and it skidded across the desk. "He's back."

"And?" Nate asked slowly.

"And he showed up out of the blue today to tell me he's going to train me now. Just like that!" I still couldn't believe Tristan was making me do this. I'd tried to track him down after dinner, but he was suspiciously unavailable. I was contemplating not showing up for training tomorrow, but something told me Nikolas would not let me out of it that easily.

"I know you were upset when he left and you missed him, but he probably had a very good reason for leaving."

"I did not miss him." I got up and started pacing. "I just think he could have had the courtesy to say he was leaving. I don't see him for weeks, and now he's back and he thinks he can tell me what to do again. I don't think so. You should see how the others act around him. They talk about him like he's a god or something. As if he needed to be more full of himself."

Nate waited until I finished my rant before he spoke. "I know you don't want to hear this, but I'm glad you'll be working with him. You told me yourself that your training is not going well. Maybe Nikolas can help you. If I learned anything about him during the weeks you were gone, it was how dedicated he is and how much he cares for your wellbeing."

"More likely he wanted to make sure he did his job right," I said bitterly.

"That's your anger talking. You don't really mean that."

"I don't know what to think anymore. He left, Nate."

"And now he's back."

I didn't say anything, and for a long moment there was silence on the line.

"Listen, I have to get back to work. I told my editor I'd let her have the first five chapters this week." I heard the soft whir of his chair and knew he was headed back to his office. "Don't be too mad at Nikolas. I'm sure he had a good reason for being away this long."

"That's easier said than done." Dejected, I sank down in my chair again. "I'll call you in a few days, okay?"

My stomach growled when I hung up, reminding me I hadn't finished my dinner. I went to my small kitchenette to grab the blueberry muffin I'd stashed there earlier. Pulling off the plastic, I nibbled at the muffin as I walked back to my desk. The cooks here were amazing, but their blueberry muffins had nothing on Nate's.

Thinking about Nate's baking made me homesick again. I laid the muffin on my desk and went to my closet to start going through the boxes I hadn't had the heart to open yet. The box containing my grandmother's quilts was ripped on one corner, and I pulled them out to make sure they hadn't been damaged. Nate had collected them from my home in Portland after my dad died, and I treasured them as much as my dad's books. My favorite was a blue one with a different bird beautifully hand-stitched into each square. I shook out the quilt, thinking it would look great on my bed. In fact, it was time I started to add my own touches to the room and make it feel more like mine.

"What the – ?" Something squished between my bare toes. I looked down at the blueberry muffin I had left on the desk. "How the hell did that get there?"

Out of the corner of my eye, I caught a flutter of the bed skirt, and I whipped my head around to see a tiny pale face peering out at me. Imps in a Mohiri home? I almost laughed at the notion of the great demon hunters' stronghold infested with the thieving little demons that were considered vermin in the supernatural world. This one was a bold little fiend too, showing himself to me like that. It had taken years to form an unlikely truce with the imps in our home back in New Hastings. Was I going to have to lock up my things now to keep them safe from these new imps?

I tossed the quilt on the bed and bent to scrape the squashed muffin off the floor. Rising, I moved to throw it in the wastebasket, but a small chattering from under the bed made me look at the imp that had come farther into the open and was watching my hand intently.

"Are you hungry? Do you want this?" I extended my hand toward him, and I was so shocked when he nodded that I almost dropped the muffin. Imps are not the friendliest of creatures and they usually go out of their way to pretend not to understand people. Suspicion filled me. There was no way an imp would reveal itself to someone, let alone communicate with them.

"I know you, don't I? You hitched a ride in my boxes from home." The ripped box made sense now. Sneaky little buggers.

The imp shifted from one foot to the other before he nodded again.

"I know you didn't decide to go off and explore the world on your own. Where are your buddies?" When he did not move, I said, "If you guys want this muffin, you better come clean with me." I had no intention of withholding the food from him, but he didn't know that.

A long moment passed before two more faces appeared around the edge of the bed skirt. I held back a groan. What was I going to do with three stowaway imps? And what would Tristan say if he discovered I'd infested his home with the little demons?

"I hope you guys didn't come here to get away from Oscar, because if so, I have bad news for you. Nate's bringing him when he comes for Thanksgiving." *Which reminds me I need to buy a litter box and some cat food.* My room was going to get very crowded all too soon.

I broke the flattened muffin into three pieces and laid them on the floor near the bed. Then I backed away so the imps could run out and grab their treats. As they disappeared under the bed again, I wondered if they had made a home under there or somewhere in the walls like they had back home. "Hey, you guys better not go to the bathroom under my bed or I'm going to find some new roommates," I called after them.

Shaking my head, I pulled my grandmother's quilt over the bed, and it immediately made the room feel homier and more like a place I would live in. I replaced the expensive rug with my faded blue-and-yellow one and installed my dad's old stereo on a table in the sitting area along with my stack of CDs. A soft red throw blanket lay across the couch, and a framed drawing I'd done of my dad a long time ago took the place of honor on the mantel. Against one wall I stacked a few drawings and framed photos of Nate, Roland, and Peter to hang when I found some tools. When I finally stood back and looked around my transformed room, I felt at home in it for the first time.

There was one more thing I wanted to do tonight. I reached under my desk and pulled out the bag containing the antique chessboard I'd bought at the jewelry store to replace the one that had been burned.

I hadn't seen Desmund since the night we played checkers, and I felt a mix of eagerness and trepidation as I approached the library. Had he noticed my reaction when I touched his skin? Was my sudden hurry to leave what made him angry enough to rip apart the book I'd been reading and burn the chessboard? It was impossible to know how much pain he endured or how that affected his mind. It had hurt to see the destroyed book, and I had to remind myself that Desmund was not well and not responsible for his behavior.

When I entered the library, I was happy to see it had been restored to its previous state. The fire burning low in the hearth and the empty brandy glass on the table by Desmund's chair told me he had been there recently, and it surprised me how disappointed I was that I'd missed him. I told myself that I just wanted to check on him and make sure he was okay, but the truth was that despite his volatile moods, Desmund was interesting and unlike anyone I'd ever met. When he turned on the charm he was almost endearing – in a Mad-Hatter-meets-Mr.-Darcy kind of way.

Even if I did not see him tonight, I could at least leave the chessboard. *And hope he doesn't torch this one, too.* I laid it on the table by the window where we'd played and looked around for some paper to leave a note with the board. I found some stationary supplies in a small desk and scrawled a quick message: *Looking forward to our rematch. Sara.*

I left the room and started back toward the stairs but stopped when I heard music coming from somewhere at the far end of the hallway. The haunting melody called to me, and I found myself walking toward it until I stopped in front of a half-open door with soft light spilling into the hallway. I stood there for several minutes listening to the music before I quietly entered the room to find a man sitting at a grand piano, his long fingers moving deftly over the keys. His back was to the door, but I recognized Desmund immediately. I stood in the doorway as still as a mouse for fear of disturbing him and causing him to stop playing. As moody and reclusive as he was, he might not like an audience, but I couldn't tear myself away from the achingly beautiful music.

The piece came to an end and Desmund sat bent over the keys, unmoving. I watched him for a moment then moved to quietly slip away.

"Did you like it?"

I turned back to find him watching me with an unreadable expression. "It was beautiful. I've never heard anything like it."

His expression did not change, and I wondered if he was angry at me for intruding on him again. "I'm sorry; I didn't mean to bother you."

"I have not seen you in days." Something like anger or hurt edged his voice, but I could not be sure which one.

"It's been kind of crazy lately." I winced inwardly at my thoughtless choice of words. "I went to the library to see you and I heard the music."

"You came to see me?" I nodded, and his eyes softened. He patted the piano bench. "Come, sit with me."

I hesitated for a moment before I walked over to the piano. The thought of sitting in such close proximity to him after my last experience unnerved me, but I had a feeling it would upset him if I refused. He shifted over to make room for me, and when his sleeve brushed harmlessly against my bare arm, I let out the breath I'd been holding.

"What were you playing when I came in?"

Desmund played a few notes, and I noticed that his long hands were perfect for playing piano. "That was Beethoven. I like to play him when the mood strikes me. Would you like to hear another one?"

"Play one of your favorites for me."

He started to play again, and I was immediately mesmerized by his fingers dancing across the keys and the captivating music that filled the air around us. Before I'd come here, I'd never given a second thought to classical music, but listening to Desmund play made me feel like I had been granted a rare privilege. It amazed me that he could play with such precision and beauty while struggling with the sickness and instability inside him.

My research on Hale witches had turned up nothing to help me understand Desmund's affliction, and I knew the only way to learn more was first hand. I really did not want to experience that horrible sickness again, but I also couldn't bear the thought of him suffering it alone. I would have gone mad a long time ago if our roles were reversed, and it spoke volumes about his strength that he was able to function at the level he did.

I wasn't sure I could handle direct contact so soon after the last time I touched him, so I tried for something passive first. I let my power infuse the air around us, like I did when calming an animal, and pushed it toward Desmund. He never faltered in his playing and looked completely unaffected so I turned it up. Nothing. *Well, it was worth a try.* I looked down at where our arms touched, separated by his sleeve. Time for a more direct approach.

I let my power flow to the arm touching Desmund's, but I hesitated before I attempted to push it into him. I had to prepare myself mentally to face what might come. Even if I could not help him, there was still the chance that this would open me up to his illness even more than touching his skin. I remembered the cold, vileness of the Hale witch in my mind and suppressed a shudder. Steeling myself, I sent my power into him. I felt the warmth of his body as I pushed inside, then I felt a heartbeat, and the unmistakable glow of life that every living creature possesses.

My exultation at feeling his life force was quickly drowned by the cold wave of nausea that swept over me and left me silently gasping for breath. *God, how does he bear it?* I had to force myself to not pull away, to stay and endure the feel of the repulsive magic living inside him. Any uncertainty I had about how Hale witches hurt their victims was swept away and replaced by outrage. Instead of simply striking at someone in battle, they actually left a piece of their magic behind to fester and torment their victims. What made a person's soul so dark they would inflict endless suffering on another?

Desmund's arm jerked slightly, and I felt another presence stir inside him. *Shit!* I pulled my power back until it barely touched him. I had completely forgotten about his Mori. I doubted it would like my power any more than other demons did. The fact that I had my own demon was not lost on me, but I'd have to sort out how that worked later. Right now, I needed to figure out how to reach the witch's magic without upsetting Desmund's Mori, and that was easier said than done.

If the mountain won't come to Muhammad...

As soon as the idea formed in my head, I knew it was the right one, even if it freaked me out more than a little. I almost shuddered at the thought of that horrible magic inside me again, but it made sense to try to pull it into me where I could fight it with my power. If it was even possible to draw it out of Desmund. I had no idea how the magic would behave if it had access to another host, and confronting it wouldn't be the same as battling a Hale witch because there was no sentient presence to fight against. This magic had lived inside Desmund for a very long time, saturating every cell like a cancer. I wasn't foolish enough to believe I could eradicate it as easily as I'd defeated the Hale witch, but maybe I could weaken it a little and ease some of Desmund's suffering. *There's only one way to find out.*

I tried to steel myself for what was to come, but I knew it would not be enough. Even though I had told Tristan I wasn't afraid of Hale witches, I still abhorred their magic, and I already felt unclean just being near it. I pushed my power toward Desmund just enough to touch the swirling coldness inside him, and instead of putting up a barrier to protect me, I opened myself to the magic, calling it to me. It did not take long for the dark magic to begin moving toward a new potential host. I had to force myself not to jerk away and to clamp my lips together so I did not cry out when it trickled from Desmund into me like a cold slimy sludge. My heart sped up and sweat broke out on my upper lip as the magic invaded my body. It took every ounce of my strength to keep my power back except for the small tendril that lured the foul magic into me. Nausea twisted my stomach until I knew I was going to throw up if I endured it for one second longer.

My body trembled as I closed the connection between me and Desmund and pulled back until an inch separated us. I fought the urge to retch and opened my power, letting it sweep through me like a cleansing fire. There was no scream like the time I fought the witch, and the magic didn't even fight as my power burned it away to nothing. My power receded leaving me only slightly nauseous, which all things considered, was a vast improvement over how I felt a moment ago.

Desmund finished the piece with a flourish and smiled at me. I had not been able to take all the magic from him, but it had to have helped him a little. Was I imagining it, or did he look more relaxed than he had when I arrived?

"That was pretty," I said, searching his handsome face for any changes. He did look a little happier, but that could just be the joy he got from his music.

"*Pretty*? You don't call Schubert *pretty*." He sighed in mock aggravation. "I see I have my work cut out with you, little one."

His playful words made hope spark inside me. The Desmund from a few days ago would have scowled at me and even showed disdain over my ignorance. Was it possible that I really had lessened his pain?

"You keep playing like that and you will spoil me for other music." I touched the cool keys, still amazed that he could draw such incredible notes from them.

"Would you like to learn to play? I can teach you."

I laughed, touched by his offer. "God, no. I tried to play the flute back in elementary school before I discovered I'm tone deaf. I'd much rather spend the time listening to you play."

"As you wish." His eyes sparkled with pleasure, and he began to play another piece. We spent the next hour like that, with him playing and me listening. There was no need for conversation, and an easy companionship grew between us. For a while I was able to forget my homesickness and my dread of tomorrow.

It took me a few minutes to realize I felt only slightly tired from my healing. Considering the amount of power I had used, I should have felt more drained than I did. It confirmed my suspicions that my elemental power was growing as Aine said it would. I didn't know what that meant for me, but if it gave me more healing power, then it couldn't be a bad thing.

"It is late, you should be in bed," Desmund said, interrupting my thoughts. "Tristan will not be pleased with me if I keep you up all night and you fall asleep in training tomorrow."

I made a face. "Don't remind me."

"You don't like training?"

"Do the words 'I suck at it' mean anything to you? And now Tristan has decided to torture me by making me train with Nikolas."

Desmund smiled. "Ah, Nikolas."

"Do you know him?"

He chuckled. "Nikolas and I go way back." His tone told me the two of them were not exactly friends. "Most women would be happy to spend time with him."

"Not me. He's always trying to tell me what to do, and I swear he does things just to bug me." I tapped one of the keys and an angry note resonated. "He acts like I'm totally helpless, and he gets all uptight if there is the slightest hint of danger. Okay, maybe he had reason to worry a month ago, but not since I came here."

"Nikolas always did take this vocation very seriously."

"I'd say. He got so mad one time when I got hurt by a crocotta that he went into some kind of rage. At least that's what Chris called it."

Desmund's eye widened. "A rage? Is that so?"

"Yes," I said with a moan. "How am I supposed to train with someone like that?"

He was quiet for a long moment, and his next words surprised me. "I think you just have to trust that Tristan knows what he is doing."

"How can you say that? Tristan knows how I feel about Nikolas, and I bet he knows what Nikolas thinks of me, too."

"I'm sure he does." He stood and held his arm out like a gentleman. I took his arm, and he led me to the top of the stairs. "As much as I enjoy your delightful company, you need to get your rest for tomorrow."

"You know, this is so not what I signed up for."

Desmund laughed softly. "If I know my old friend Nikolas, you are not what he was expecting either."

"Gosh, thanks for the pep talk, Desmund."

His eyes flashed with amusement as he turned away. "Anytime, little one."

Chapter 8

"IS IT TRUE? Are you really going to train with Nikolas?"

I quit pushing my scrambled eggs around and looked up at Olivia as she slid her breakfast tray onto the table. A few feet behind her, Jordan followed with her own tray. Just a few days ago, I was eating alone. I wasn't sure how I felt about my new popularity, especially since all anyone wanted to talk about around here was how awesome Nikolas was.

"Yes."

Olivia gave a very un-warrior-like squeal that made me wince.

"Do you have to do that?" snapped Jordan. She obviously wasn't a morning person.

"How the hell did you swing that?" Olivia went on, ignoring Jordan. "No one trains with Nikolas. What I wouldn't give . . . "

I gave up pretending to eat and pushed my plate away. "You know, just because he's like some kind of warrior god around here doesn't mean he's all sunshine and roses to be around. If you think training with him will be easy or fun, you are delusional and welcome to take my place."

"And deprive us all of the enjoyment of watching you and Nikolas?" drawled a familiar male voice.

I smiled up at Chris, whom I had not seen since my first day here. The blond warrior was the kind of gorgeous that made women forget their names, and he was a lot more easygoing than Nikolas. "Hello, Dimples. Shouldn't you be out breaking hearts or something?"

Chris grinned and the dimples I'd nicknamed him for appeared. I heard Olivia let out a soft sigh. "You and Nikolas training together – I wouldn't miss that for the world. And this time when you tell him to kiss your behind, I won't intervene."

"I thought you were supposed to be the nice one."

Laughing, he turned away. "I'll be seeing you . . . if you two don't kill each other."

Olivia stared after him with cow eyes. "Okay, Sara, what is your secret?"

"My secret?"

"You're training with Nikolas and flirting with Chris?"

"I was not flirting with Chris. We're friends, sort of."

"If you say so. Any more super-hot guys you have stashed away that we don't know about?"

I decided not to mention Desmund who could probably fit into Olivia's "hot" category even if he was just a little insane. "The girls back home think my friend, Roland, is pretty hot, but I don't think he's your type."

"Why, is he gay?"

"Nope, werewolf," I smothered a laugh at her look of mingled disbelief and distaste, which to her credit, she tried to hide.

Jordan leaned over to nudge Olivia with her shoulder. "It's that whole waif look she has going on. Men can't resist it."

"I am not a waif," I shot back. "I can take care of myself."

Jordan chuckled. "I didn't say you *were* a waif; I said you look like one. Did you happen to notice that you're way shorter than everyone else here?"

I had noticed that fact soon after I arrived. Mohiri men were all over six feet tall, and the women were close to six. At five-five, I definitely stood out. I supposed I had my Fae heritage to thank for that. Aine was around my height and build. But being shorter did not make me weaker, and I said as much to Jordan.

"You won't hear me argue with you." She toyed with her pancakes and gave me a sly grin to let me know she had been trying to get a rise out of me. "So, do you know what kind of training you'll be doing with Nikolas?"

"No idea, but you can bet it won't be exciting enough for you." Knowing Nikolas, he wouldn't let me do anything even remotely dangerous. "He'll probably make me run in place until I pass out."

She snorted. "That man doesn't strike me as the type to do anything boring. Just be prepared to tell us *everything* tonight."

"Yes, take pity on the rest of us." Olivia let out a groan. "While you get to hang out with Nikolas, we have to spend the morning nursing stupid kark eggs for Sahir."

"What are kark eggs?"

"Karks are ugly little bat-like things, and they hatch from eggs that smell like they've been rotting for six months," Jordan said with a grimace. "This batch was supposed to go to Mexico, but someone screwed up and sent it here by mistake. They're close to hatching, and Sahir says we have to turn and spray the eggs or they'll lose the whole batch before they get to Mexico. For some reason, he thinks this would be a great educational experience for us."

Jordan wasn't happy about handling Kark eggs, but to me it sounded a lot more appealing than training with Nikolas. "Are karks dangerous?"

"No, they eat bugs and stuff, but scarab demons are their favorite treat. If you've never seen a scarab demon, think of that flesh-eating beetle in *The Mummy*."

"Well, look at the upside; at least you don't have to feed them."

Olivia made a face. "Says the girl who will be spending her morning with Nikolas."

"Look I told you – " I sensed Nikolas the second he entered the dining hall. Even if there hadn't been a tell-tale touch against my mind, I still would have known he was there by the sudden lack of conversation from the other trainees and the way Jordan and Olivia stared at him as he approached. My body tensed as a shadow fell across our table.

"Ready to start training?" His curt tone told me he was in warrior mode, no playful Nikolas today. He was dressed casually in jeans and a dark-blue sweater, but he carried a sword on his back and a sheathed knife on his hip. It wasn't fair that he looked so at ease and I was a bundle of nerves.

I nodded reluctantly.

"Come with me then."

Standing, I picked up my tray of uneaten food, carried it to one of the bus bins, and followed him to the door. As I passed Chris's table, he raised his cup to me with a grin. Good to know at least one person was enjoying this.

Nikolas was waiting for me in the hallway, and we walked without speaking to the front entrance.

"We're not using a training room?"

"I thought we'd go outdoors. Would you rather stay inside?"

"No."

We left the building and walked across the lawn without him saying a word about where we were headed. When we entered the trees, I asked, "Where are we going?"

"For a walk," was all he said.

"I think I should tell you that when I go for walks, I usually end up brought back in chains."

He shot me a look that said he wasn't sure if I was kidding or not. "I think we'll be fine."

Of course. Who would dare stop Nikolas from doing what he wanted?

Nikolas slowed his pace so I could keep up with him, and we walked side-by-side through the woods. He didn't seem inclined to speak, and I didn't know what to say to him. Most of the time I'd spent with him back in New Hastings had been full of tension or danger or both. I'd thought after all we'd been through that we had started to become friends, but then he'd left me here and I'd spent the weeks since then angry at him. Last night at dinner, he'd thrown me with his teasing and his announcement that he would be my new trainer. Now I was confused and I didn't know how to act around him anymore.

We walked for a good ten minutes before he finally spoke. "Other than the problem with your training, how are you doing here?"

"It's not home," I replied a little more harshly than I meant to.

I felt him look at me, but I didn't meet his gaze. "I know you miss Nate and your friends, but it's not like you won't see them again. And you aren't alone here. You've made some new friends and you have Tristan and Chris and me."

"Until you go off on one of your missions again."

"Are you trying to tell me that you missed me?" The change in his voice told me he was smiling, but I refused to look at him.

"No." As soon as the words were out of my mouth I knew I was lying. But I would bite my tongue off before I would admit anything to him.

"I have no plans to go anywhere for the next month so you are stuck with me for a while."

"Lucky me," I muttered, and I heard him laugh softly. "Where did you go?"

His laughter died. "It was a job, clearing out some nests. Nothing you want to hear about."

"You were looking for the Master, weren't you?"

"You don't need to worry about him anymore."

I stopped abruptly. "I'm not a child, Nikolas, and I deserve to know what is going on. If you can't be open with me, you can go find someone else to train."

I spun back toward the stronghold, but he grabbed my arm and let out an aggravated sigh. "I see you are still the same pain in the ass."

I kept my face turned away from him as a smile played around the corners of my mouth. "Takes one to know one."

"We found where we believe Eli was staying in Portland, and there were signs that the Master could be in Nevada. It's not surprising since Vegas is the perfect place for vampires to blend in and hunt. We hit a nest in Henderson and that led us to two more nests near Vegas, but none of them gave us anything useful about the Master. Whoever he is, he is well hidden and his followers have no idea where he is."

I faced him again. "So, what happens now?"

His smile returned. "Now we train while someone else looks for him. A Master is no small matter, and the Council has made it a priority to find him. They've already sent extra teams to the US dedicated to hunting him. It is only a matter of time before he is found." He didn't say it, but I knew he would join the hunt again if the Master was not found. As upset as I was with him, I didn't want to think of him out there facing such a powerful vampire.

We resumed walking and a few minutes later, I saw a glimmer through the trees and knew exactly where we were going. I ran ahead and burst out of the trees onto the rocky shore of the lake I had been trying to get to for weeks. It was bigger than it looked on the map and, except for the water lapping gently at the shore, not a ripple marred its glassy surface. The woods around the lake teamed with life, and I could hear birds and frogs and insects. A ways down the shore, a doe stood alert, watching us for signs of a threat. It was just as serene and lovely as I'd imagined it would be.

"This is incredible," I said as Nikolas caught up to me. "I can't believe people don't come here all the time."

"Not everyone loves the woods as much as you do."

I looked back at him. "Then why did you bring me here?"

"Because I'm not like everyone else." He sat on a large rock and waved at another rock near him. "Let's talk."

I hesitated for a long moment before I took a seat on the rock. "I thought we were going to train."

"We will, but first I want to talk about your training. Callum told me you don't seem to want to use your Mori strength or speed."

"You talked to him about me?" I wasn't sure why it bothered me, but I did not like the idea of them discussing me.

"Of course. I needed to understand the problem so we can fix it."

The problem was that I did not want to be fixed, but I didn't say that. Nikolas, like the rest of the Mohiri, had some mysterious connection with their Mori that I couldn't comprehend and he would not understand why I didn't have or want the same thing. "You think you know what my problem is?"

"I have several theories. The first is that you are so used to suppressing your Mori that you don't know how to do anything else. Demons are afraid of Fae magic, which explains why your Mori doesn't fight for control like mine would if I kept it locked away. You need to learn to loosen your control just as you would exercise any muscle. It takes practice."

I loosened my hands which I had unconsciously clenched in my lap. "That's it then?"

"That is one theory." Nikolas rested his elbows on his knees bringing him closer to me, and his eyes held mine as if he was reading my thoughts. "My other theory is that you are afraid."

I swallowed hard and tried to look away but couldn't. "Why . . . would I be afraid?"

"I was there in the wine cellar, Sara, and I saw what happened when you let your demon out. I also saw the fear on your face when I asked you about it the next day. It terrified you how close the demon came to controlling you. But that would never have happened."

A shudder ran through me, and I tried to block the memory of the demon moving beneath my skin, controlling my body and filling my mind. "You're wrong," I whispered hoarsely. "It almost did."

"No, it didn't. Look at me," he commanded. "I would not have let it take you."

"But if you hadn't gotten there when you did, I – "

"You would have done it on your own. You're a lot stronger than you give yourself credit for. The demon might have gained control for a short time, but you would not have let it stay that way."

My breath bottled up in my chest. "How can you know that?"

His gaze did not waver. "Because I know you. You are one of the most willful people I've ever met, and it would take a lot more than a demon to control you." His mouth curved into a smile, and I felt an answering warmth in my belly. "That I know from experience."

"Are you going to train me to fight without my demon?"

"Today we are going to start with the basics. You will learn to open yourself to your Mori safely."

A cold knot formed in my chest. "I can't – "

"Yes, you can. This is something every one of us learns to do, and you will, too. You are a lot stronger than the rest of us were when we started." His voice was firm but reassuring and I wanted to believe him, but I could not get the memory of that night in the cellar out of my head.

He must have seen my fear because he reached out unexpectedly to take my hand in his, sending a warm tingle up my arm. "Do you trust me?"

I bit my lip and nodded slowly.

"And you know that I would never let anything harm you, right?"

"Yes."

"Good." He smiled, and his eyes softened. He released my hand and sat back. "It might be easier if you tell me how it is that you are able to control your demon. How do you keep your Mori separate from your Fae power?"

I thought for a minute about the best way to answer because I'd never had to explain my power to anyone before now. "It's hard to explain. I can feel the demon in my head and sense its thoughts, or rather its emotions, if that makes sense."

He nodded.

"When I was little I used to hear its voice whispering in my mind, kind of like a song you get stuck in your head and it won't go away no matter what you think about. I think I was five or six when it first tried to come out, and it scared me so much that I accidentally released my power, which I had no idea about until that day. The beast – that's what I used to call my demon before you told me what it was – was afraid of my power and it pulled into the back of my mind to get away from it. I was scared to death and I had no idea what was going on with me, but I knew I'd done something to make the creepy voice in my head quiet. It wasn't until I found an injured robin and the power burst out of me to heal the bird's wing that I realized what I could really do. After that, I had to learn to keep my power locked away and only call on it when I needed it and also how to tap into it to keep the beast – I mean the demon – caged in the back of my mind. The only times the demon seemed to wake up was when I did a healing and drained my power. That used to happen all the time in the beginning, but it doesn't happen anymore."

He was quiet for a moment, and his expression was impossible to read. *He must think I'm a total freak now.*

"I don't know if I am more amazed by your level of control or that you learned it at such a young age with no guidance or training. Are you consciously doing it?"

There was none of the disgust I feared I would hear in his voice, and some of my anxiety left me. "In the beginning I did, and it was hard as hell. I lost control of my power all the time because I had to focus on keeping the beast – demon – quiet. Now, it's like breathing. I don't have to think about it unless I use too much power and get weak. Then the demon starts to move and I have to use force with it. How do you do it?"

"Not like that." He laughed and ran a hand through his hair, and I couldn't help but notice how the black waves shone in the sun. "You talk about your Mori and your Fae power like they are parts of you that you move as easily as an arm or a leg. For the rest of us, there is no real separation between us and our demons. My Mori and I are joined completely, and I feel its thoughts and emotions as easily as my own."

"How can you control it if it's that much a part of you?" I could not imagine constantly sharing my mind with another consciousness. It was already noisy enough in my head with my own thoughts. I would go crazy if I was bombarded with the demon's thoughts all the time.

"I learned from a young age to suppress the demon's natural urges just like you would any craving. But unlike you, I can't block it completely, and I'm always aware of my Mori because together we make one person."

"I don't think I could live like that."

"And I couldn't live any other way," he said with a smile. "Now I understand why it's so difficult for you tap into your Mori's strength. You keep it bound so tightly you aren't even aware of its presence half the time. We need to show you how to get to know it."

My hands twisted in the bottom of my hoodie. "How do we do that?"

"You said you keep it locked in a part of your mind, right? You need to loosen your hold on it and connect with it."

I jumped to my feet. "I can't do that. You don't understand how it felt when I let it out before."

Nikolas did not move from his rock. "It won't be like that this time because we won't let it." He looked calm and sounded so confident that I wanted to believe him. He was strong but could he protect me from what was inside me? He extended a hand toward me. "Trust me."

My hand had a mind of its own, slipping into his so he could he pull me down gently to sit on the rock again. Fear chilled me, and the only warm part of me was the hand he held.

"Take it slowly. Just open up a little and remember that you are the stronger one."

"I thought the whole purpose of this is to tap into the demon because it has all the strength and speed."

His gaze did not waver. "Physically yes, but mentally you are stronger, and your Mori knows that."

I closed my eyes and reached for the wall between me and my Mori. With one thought the barrier began to lower, and I immediately felt excitement from the demon huddled behind it. The demon shifted restlessly and fear shot through me, sending the wall back up again. I took a deep breath and tried again. The wall lowered, the demon surged forward, and the wall slammed up. Two more times I tried it with the same result. I gritted my teeth as frustration filled me.

Strong fingers squeezed my hand gently. *I'm safe with Nikolas. I can do this.* Resolve filled me, and I let the wall fall before I could stop myself. The demon rushed forward, and this time it made it past the barrier. I cried out as it pressed forward eagerly against my mind and pressure started to build inside my head.

"Look at me," Nikolas ordered, his warm hands moving up to frame my cold face. I opened my eyes to meet his. "I know this feels wrong and frightening to you, but that is only because you aren't used to it. Don't run from it, and don't push it away. Feel your Mori, get to know it, and let it get to know you."

I grabbed a thread of my power and held onto it like a lifeline as I faced the Mori. *Stop!* I told it sharply, but it ignored me and surged forward again. I brandished my power like a weapon. *Stop!*

The Mori froze, and I sensed it watching me warily. We faced off for what seemed like forever before it slowly pulled back in a reluctant act of submission. I pulled back my power, and we studied one another for the first time without a wall between us. The Mori was a small blob of brooding darkness that broadcast a myriad of emotions and jumbled thoughts I could not understand. We were like familiar strangers, two people who had shared the same house for a long time without ever speaking.

Hello, I said before I realized how stupid that sounded. You did not talk to the demon in your head. *Yeah, because having a demon in your head is so normal. They have hospitals for this kind of thing.*

The Mori shifted position slightly, reminding me of a dog tilting its head when you speak to it. *Do you understand me?* I asked it.

It did not speak, but I sensed something that felt like recognition – and resentment. I'd be resentful too if I had been locked up for years. Still, I couldn't help the spark of excitement that flared in my chest. *Don't you want to talk to me?*

Talk? The word filled my mind, and I recognized the voice I had heard in my head my whole life.

Yes, you know – get to know each other, I guess.

The Mori did not respond, and I wondered if I had imagined it speaking. I reached toward it, and it shrunk back suddenly, making a sound like a growl. It took me several seconds to realize it was scared of me, or more likely of the power I held. Taking a huge leap of faith, I dropped the power and let it sink back into my core. *I won't hurt you,* I said the same way I would talk to a feral animal.

Glow burns, it snarled.

Glow? What was it talking about? Then I looked down inside myself and saw the shimmering well of my power. I gave myself a mental head slap. My Fae power hurt it because it was a demon.

I'm sorry. I didn't know it burned you. I won't hurt you anymore.

The Mori appeared to understand, and it relaxed but did not move closer. It studied me quietly as if it was trying to figure out why I was talking to it all of a sudden.

Nikolas says we –

Solmi! the Mori cried, and a wave of emotions blasted me and left me gasping. I was dimly aware of someone speaking to me, and it took me a few seconds to recognize Nikolas's voice. I opened my eyes and looked into his worried ones.

"Are you okay?"

"Yes," I replied, trying to focus on him and watch the demon at the same time. "This is so weird and kind of intense."

"I imagine it is. I think that's enough for now."

"But I just started."

His eyebrows lifted a fraction. "You've been at it for over an hour."

Disbelief rippled through me. "I have?"

"Yes, and you don't want to overdue it."

"Okay." I closed my eyes and looked at the demon that had not moved. *I hate to do this when we are just getting to know each other, but I have to put you back now.*

Back? it asked, and I felt its fear and sadness.

For now. I actually felt guilty about forcing it back, but I was not ready to have a demon running free in my head. I didn't know if I would ever be ready for that.

The Mori surprised me by retreating of its own accord back into its prison, but its anger and pain touched me even after the wall went back up.

I opened my eyes and was shocked to find them welling with tears.

"Sara?"

I pulled away from Nikolas and wiped my eyes with my sleeve. "I'm fine. It was just . . . not what I expected."

"What happened?"

"We talked a little. Well, I did most of the talking." I stood and walked to the water's edge, too full of nervous energy to sit. Nikolas was still sitting when I turned to face him again. "I can't describe it. What is it like for you?"

"I feel my Mori's thoughts, but they are almost like my own thoughts. I don't talk to it like I would to another person."

"Oh." I felt a little deflated at his answer. Why did everything have to be so different for me? Why couldn't I be like everyone else for once?

"Don't do that." His voice was firm as he walked to where I stood. "You've made great progress, considering your fear when we started."

"I know. It's just . . . never mind."

"Tell me," he ordered gently.

I picked up some small stones and started tossing them into the lake so I wouldn't have to look at him. "Nothing about me is normal. I'm probably the only one of my kind in existence, and I don't fit in here like the other trainees. I can't fight, and I hate killing. What kind of warrior doesn't like killing? I don't even connect with my Mori the way the rest of you do."

He took one of the stones from my hand and sent it skipping far across the surface of the lake. "Your Fae blood does make you different, but that doesn't mean you are not as much a Mohiri as the rest of us. And there is nothing wrong with not wanting to kill."

"My Mori is afraid of me. I bet you don't have to worry about that with yours."

Nikolas shook his head. "No, and that will change for you once you and your Mori learn to join. Trust me; all it wants is to be one with you. Without that, it has no purpose."

"It said my power burns it. I promised not to hurt it again, but what if my Fae power keeps getting stronger?"

My question took him off guard, and he stared at me for several seconds. "*Is* your power getting stronger?"

"Yes." I told him about the strange bursts of power I'd been experiencing and the coldness I'd felt in my chest twice. His eyes widened when I explained what I'd done to the bazerats and the lamprey demon, and he was silent for a good minute after I finished talking.

"Have you told anyone else about this?"

"Only Tristan and Roland."

He nodded. "Good. Keep it between us for now and let me know if it happens again."

"You didn't answer my question." Fear crept into my voice. "Will my Fae power hurt my Mori? Could I hurt another Mohiri?"

"Honestly, I don't know," he said uncertainly, and my anxiety grew. "The way I see it, you've had the two of them inside you your whole life and if you were going to hurt your Mori, you would have done it by now. Did you feel like your demon was in danger when you had these flare-ups?"

I thought about it and realized I hadn't felt any fear or pain from my Mori either time. "No."

"There's your answer then." He gave me a reassuring smile. "Let's not worry about that unless we need to."

His confidence eased my fears, and I took a deep breath to relax. "What now?"

A gleam entered his eyes. "Now we do some other training."

"What kind of training?" I gave him a wary look as he pulled off his sword and thin sweater and tossed them on the rock he'd been sitting on. I got a good view of a ripped stomach before he tugged his black T-shirt down past the waistband of his jeans. Heat unfurled in my stomach and I looked away quickly before he caught me staring.

"Nothing difficult," he said, showing no sign he noticed my pink cheeks. "How about we go for a run?"

I couldn't help the laugh that escaped me. "You expect me to keep up with you?" I was a good runner, but Nikolas was as fast as a vampire.

A corner of his mouth lifted. "I'll try to dial it back a bit."

"Gee, I feel so special," I retorted and began to stretch my legs. "How long will it take me to be as fast as you?"

"About a hundred years or so."

I straightened and stared at him. "A hundred years?"

"Give or take a few. Your Mori will give you strength, but it'll be a long time before you develop that kind of speed. Didn't anyone explain that to you?"

I shook my head, trying to figure out if he was kidding me. "I think Callum was too busy trying to get me to use my Mori to go over that stuff. But what you're saying doesn't make sense. How can warriors fight vampires if they can't keep up with them?"

Nikolas crossed his arms looking displeased. "Apparently there is a lot they haven't told you. How much do you know about vampires and how they are made?"

"I know a vampire drinks from someone and forces the person to drink their blood and that's how the demon is passed into the new host. It takes three or four days for the new demon to grow strong enough to take control of the person. Oh, and only mature vampires can make another vampire."

He nodded. "That's all true, but did you also know that new vampires are weak and their strength grows over time. They are stronger than a human, but no match for a trained warrior, and it takes them almost as long as it does us to develop the kind of speed you've seen. Most of the vampires we saw in Maine were mature, and it's unusual to see that many mature vampires together. Many of the vampires warriors deal with don't have that kind of strength or speed."

"I knew baby vamps were weak, but I thought that only lasted a few months." His explanation surprised me, but it also filled me with a sense of relief to learn not every vampire was as fast or as strong as Eli had been. It was another reminder of the holes in my education and how much I had to catch up on.

"We're going to need to add some studies to your training," he said as if he'd read my mind. "We'll start this afternoon."

Oh yay. All day training with Nikolas.

"But right now, how about that run?"

Part of me was still mad at him for taking off the way he had, but the thought of running free through the trees again like I used to at home was too tempting to resist. And it was hard to stay angry after he'd been so supportive in training. "Okay."

"Follow me."

We set off around the lake, and it wasn't until we were at the halfway point that I realized the lake was bigger than it looked. There was no trail so I had to dodge rocks and jump over fallen trees, but that hardly took away from the pleasure of just running. True to his word, Nikolas slowed down so I could keep a few feet behind him, and unlike me, he showed no signs of tiring by the time we got back to our starting point.

I didn't say much on the walk back to the stronghold, and Nikolas seemed content to leave me to my thoughts. I felt different, changed somehow from the experience with my Mori. I had never really thought of my Mori as a sentient being with thoughts and emotions, but after today, I could never think of it as the beast again, either. I knew it was still a demon with demon urges, but it was also a part of me.

"Get some lunch and rest for a bit," Nikolas said as he opened the door for me and I entered the main hall ahead of him. "We'll meet up again at two."

"Okay."

"Here. This is to replace the knife you lost." He unclipped the sheath on his hip and passed it to me. I pulled the knife free and saw that it looked identical to the last one he'd given me.

I slipped it in the pocket of my hoodie, touched by the gift.

"You did great today."

"Thanks," I turned away before he could see me flush with pleasure at the unexpected praise.

Shouting and pounding feet interrupted us, and we both turned as Mark came tearing around a corner. "Shut the door! Shut the door before they get out!"

"What the – ?" I uttered before a small white object whipped past Mark's head. Nikolas slammed the door shut before the creature reached us, and it veered away sharply to spiral upward toward the massive chandelier hanging from the arched ceiling.

"What is it?" I asked as I tried to follow the creature with my eyes.

"Goddamn kark eggs hatched while we were . . . " Mark's voice was drowned out by squeaks and flapping wings, and my eyes went wide as hundreds of the tiny creatures zoomed around the corner and headed straight for us.

Chapter 9

NIKOLAS REACHED FOR me and drew me behind him. As soon as the karks saw that there was no way out, they swerved away from us and began to zoom frantically around the hall, looking for another means of escape. By the time Sahir, Jordan, and Olivia showed up, followed by Terrence and Josh, there were karks everywhere. The small white bodies careened up the large curved staircase, through open doorways and down every hallway, swerving around people with amazing agility and speed.

"Don't hurt them!" yelled Sahir, grabbing Josh's arm to stop him from swiping at the creatures with a long thin sword. Sahir need not have worried. The karks were so tiny and fast that they were almost impossible to hit.

"Do you realize how long it takes to breed karks?" Sahir ducked as one of the creatures shot toward him. "We can't kill them."

"What the hell are we supposed to do with them?" Josh yelled back.

"We have to round them up somehow."

I looked at the mass of white bodies whipping around us and shook my head. I couldn't see how on earth anyone was going to catch these things. Pulling away from Nikolas, I ran over to Sahir. "How do you catch them?"

"Normally you'd use a spray made from scarab demon pheromone. Karks can't resist it. Unfortunately, this batch was not supposed to hatch yet and I didn't see a bottle of spray in the crates."

I put a hand over my head when a Kark flew close enough to hook my hair with its tiny clawed wings. "So, what do we do about them?"

Sahir studied the situation. "I have a sedative that might help slow them down. I'll go get it, and you try to keep these people from killing them."

"Me? How am I supposed to stop them?" I asked, but Sahir was already running away.

Someone squealed, and I whirled around to see Olivia batting at two Karks that were zipping around her head while Jordan was bent over, holding her sides and laughing. Mark, Terrence, and Josh were running around the hall chasing after the creatures as a dozen warriors burst into the hall and stopped short at the pandemonium before them. I saw Chris among them, and his eyebrows shot up when he spotted me in the middle of the hall. I shook my head to let him know this one was not my doing.

"What in God's name is going on here?" Tristan bellowed, and I looked up to see him on the second floor landing with Celine. Celine looked down on me with a sneer on her beautiful face as if I was somehow responsible for the whole thing. Why the hell did everyone assume I had something to do with this?

Tristan started down the stairs with Celine on his heels, and twice they had to stop as Karks fluttered around them like large white moths. I couldn't contain my smirk as I watched Celine swipe at them.

"Who is responsible for this?" Tristan demanded in a commanding voice that carried through the main hall. "Where is Sahir?"

"He went to get some kind of sedative to knock them out," I told him when no one else answered.

Tristan stared in displeasure at the scene before him. "How did this happen?"

"Ask them." I pointed at the other trainees. "I was with Nikolas."

Behind Tristan, Celine's eyes narrowed on me, but she said nothing. Her hand went to her pocket, and for a few seconds I half expected her to pull out a knife and come after me with it.

"It was an accident," Jordan said. "We laid all the eggs out after breakfast and turned them as Sahir instructed. We just went back to turn them again and they were all hatched."

Shaking his head, Tristan strode into the center of the chaos. "I want these things caged before they make an even bigger mess." To punctuate his words, a splatter of white landed in Celine's straight black hair, and the female warrior shrieked as if it was acid instead of poop. I almost laughed before I got a whiff of the kark dung. I immediately slapped a hand over my mouth and nose at the noxious odor that was a mix of rotten eggs and dead skunk. If we didn't round the karks up soon, this place would reek of it for a month.

My first thought was to use my power to calm the karks, but common sense told me there was no way I could handle this many at once. Still, it might work on some of them and that was better than nothing. At least they weren't demons, so I could not hurt them or cause them to go nuts.

Opening my power, I let it saturate the air around me. After a few minutes, I noticed the karks closest to me were moving slower than the rest before they began to flutter down drunkenly to perch on the stair banister, the chandelier, or any surface nearby. I walked over and picked up one to get a closer look at it. Its snow white fur was downy soft, and I stroked it with one finger as I studied the small bat-like ears and teeth and soft white leathery wings that looked almost fragile enough to tear.

"They must be getting tired," Mark said. "Should we try to catch them now?"

Glancing up, I caught knowing looks from Nikolas and Tristan. Thankfully, no one else seemed to notice. "Go find some crates or boxes or whatever you can to put them in," Tristan told Mark and Josh, who immediately ran off to do as ordered.

Nikolas came over to stand by me and spoke so no one else could hear him. "Are you doing this?"

"Yes, but I'm not sure how long it will work on them. I hope Sahir gets here soon."

Tristan walked up to us, followed by Celine who was still trying to get the sticky kark dung out of her hair. "Someone needs to be reprimanded for this disaster." I ignored her pointed glares in my direction. No matter how much she disliked me, there was no way she could blame this mess on me.

"Here, we can put some in these." Michael ran into the hall carrying two of the mesh equipment bags from the training rooms. He spotted Tristan and headed for us. "Will these do?"

"Good idea," I told him as he opened one of the bags and I laid the kark inside. "Come on," I called to the other trainees. "Help us out here."

With the help of Olivia, Jordan, and Terrance we managed to round up at least three dozen karks that were close enough to reach, but there were still over two hundred of them whipping around the room with no signs of slowing down. To make matters worse, more of the creatures decided they had to go potty, and soon we were all dodging their little stink bombs like we were in an eighties arcade game. If my nose hadn't been burning from the stench, I probably would have burst out laughing at the ridiculousness of the situation.

"Watch where you're going," Celine snapped when I backed into her to avoid getting hit by a white glob of poo. Unfortunately, Michael chose that same moment to slip on the stuff and come barreling into us, sending the three of us tumbling to the hard marble floor. Lucky for me, Celine broke my fall, but she was not as happy about that as I was, and I was pretty sure the elbow she jabbed sharply in my ribs was not by accident. I grunted and rolled off her and right onto poor Michael, who let out a moan when the back of my head butted his nose.

"Ah hell," I muttered when I sat up and saw the white streaks on my jeans. My eyes watered at the smell. It was going to take all day to get rid of this stench, and my clothes were ruined for sure. I spotted a small streak of yellow on my sleeve and hoped it was not urine. I rolled my eyes. Like a little spot of pee would make a difference now.

"Need a hand up?" Chris's voice quivered with amusement, and I scowled up at him, which only made him burst out laughing. Tristan joined in, and I glared at both of them before they each grabbed an arm and pulled me to my feet.

"Ugh!" I groaned when I looked down at myself. I really didn't want to know what my hair looked like right now.

Nikolas helped Celine up, and she clung to his arm. How was it possible for her to be even filthier than me and still look ridiculously gorgeous?

"If anyone needs me, I'll be soaking in my tub for the next two hours," Celine declared, and I couldn't help but notice the meaningful look she gave Nikolas. I couldn't see his face, but I heard his soft chuckle at her blatant invitation. Annoyance stiffened my limbs, and I stalked away from them. We were covered in poop with no idea how we were going to bag the two hundred or so karks whipping around, and those two were flirting with each other like they were at a cocktail party.

The door opened and Sahir slipped inside with a respirator mask hanging from his neck and carrying a foot-long metal canister with a rubber hose attached. On the other end of the hose was a spray nozzle. "Sorry it took so long. I had to dilute the sedative and transfer it to a spray canister so it will reach them." He lifted the nozzle and sprayed a couple of karks as they flew by him. At first it appeared to have no effect on them, but after a minute or so they fluttered to the floor.

I immediately picked them up to make sure they were still alive, and I smiled at Sahir when I felt their strong heartbeats. "It worked."

He turned to Tristan. "I diluted this, but it still might knock people out if they breathe too much of it. We should clear the hall before I spray more of it."

Tristan nodded and ordered everyone to head to the common areas until Sahir said it was safe to come out. All I wanted was to find the nearest shower and scrub myself clean, but as soon as Sahir knocked out all the karks, we'd be needed to bag them before they woke up again. Dutifully, I trailed behind the others instead.

"Ouch!" I jerked my head to one side when a kark flew at my face and nicked my ear with its sharp little teeth. I put my hand to my ear and frowned when my fingers came away red. "The little bugger bit me!"

"It must have scratched you by accident. Karks don't bite people," Sahir said, fitting his mask over his mouth and nose as he waited for everyone to clear out.

Needles of pain stung my forearm, and I gasped at the white creature latched onto my sleeve, its pointed teeth digging into my skin. I let out a yelp and grabbed the little body to yank it from my arm. It squeaked and twisted, frantically trying to break free from my hand. "What is up with this thing?"

No sooner had the words left my mouth when another kark flew into my chest. I batted it away, but it did a one eighty and came at me again. I snatched it up in my other hand, and it went nuts like the first one. My first thought was that these things really were demons and no one had bothered to tell me. Why else would they be acting so bizarre around me? But if that was the case, my power would have freaked them out a few minutes ago instead of putting them to sleep.

"Ow! What the hell?" I yelled as, from out of nowhere, five or six karks dive-bombed me, and I had to throw up my arms to protect my head. "Sahir, will you spray these things before they try to eat me."

"I told you, karks don't – " Sahir broke off when dozens of the creatures flew at me from every direction like a swarm of angry hornets. I cried out and tried to run for cover, but I could not see past the mass of white bodies around me. Over the squeaking and flapping wings, I heard Sahir yelling, but I was too busy fending off his *harmless* karks to pay much attention to what he was saying.

A few seconds later, something large collided with me and I flew backward. Instead of hitting the floor, I found myself circled by a pair of arms and pulled against a hard body, bracing me from the impact. My rescuer and I rolled over once, ending with me on the floor and his body covering mine. I didn't need the flutter in my head to tell me who was holding me tight against him and shielding my body from attack with his own. I suddenly found it hard to breathe, and to my dismay I was pretty sure it wasn't from the fall.

"I don't give a damn. Just do it," Nikolas barked at someone, and I felt the angry rumble deep in his chest. He lowered his head, and his warm breath fanned my cheek. "Cover your mouth and nose. Sahir is going to spray around us."

I pressed my face into the crook of his shoulder, acutely aware of his body against mine and the fact that I had never been *this* close to a man before. Unless you counted that time I healed Roland, but I didn't think holding a half-crazed werewolf fell into the same category.

"There are too many of them," Sahir said a minute later in a muffled voice.

"Keep spraying us," Nikolas ordered.

"I can't. It'll poison you two if I spray more around you." I heard Sahir move away. "I'll do what I can to reduce their numbers. What the hell is wrong with them? Why are they only going after her?"

"I don't know." Nikolas shifted his weight and surprised me by leaning in and sniffing at my hair first and then my hoodie. How he expected to smell anything over the stench was beyond me. "Something smells off here."

I could not contain my snort. "You think?"

Instead of smiling like I expected him to, he reached down and grabbed the bottom of my hoodie. "What are you doing?" I demanded in a panic when he started to lift it up.

"I think something on your clothes is making the karks behave like this," he explained without stopping. "I can detect something that doesn't smell like you or their droppings."

He knows my scent? That revelation shocked me so much I forgot to protest further, and Nikolas used that opportunity to quickly yank the hoodie over my head and fling it away from us. Despite his body heat, I shivered as cold from the marble floor seeped through the back of my T-shirt. A few karks used the opportunity to squeeze beneath him and latch onto my hoodie, but as soon as the piece of clothing flew away, they followed it.

"Jesus, look at that." Buried beneath Nikolas, I couldn't see what Sahir was referring to, but his tone sent another chill through me. "They're still trying to get to her. Whatever it is, it has to be on her T-shirt, too."

"I know." Nikolas lifted his head again, and his eyes were dark and apologetic when they met mine. "Sara – "

"No way! Forget it." There was no way in hell I was stripping in front of him and everyone else. "We can make a run for it."

"There are too many of them. As soon as I get off you, they'll attack you."

"I don't care. I am not taking off my clothes." The very thought of it made my stomach clench.

Nikolas sighed roughly. "I'm sorry but this is no time for modesty. It's just your shirt, and I'll cover you."

That's supposed to make me feel better? My throat was dry, and I averted my eyes from his as my trembling hands pushed between us to reach the hem of my T-shirt. Why did this shit keep happening to me?

"Stand back, boys. Time for the girls to show you how it's done," Jordan yelled above the racket. "Let her rip, Liv."

I barely had time to wonder what the girls were up to before Nikolas and I were hit with a blast of cold water that soaked the two of us within seconds. Coughing, I turned my face into his chest to keep from drowning in the onslaught. A minute later, a deep rumbling started in his chest and I pulled away when I realized he was laughing.

"I'm glad you're enjoying yourself," I grumbled, still upset about how close I'd come to stripping in front of him and everyone else.

"Immensely." He raised his head and looked around, then rolled off me and to his feet in one easy movement. Before I had time to move, he reached down and pulled me up to stand beside him.

All around us, white bodies littered the floor and stairs while the few karks still moving desperately tried to evade the powerful jet of water from the fire hose Jordan was holding. Jordan wore a devilish smile as she swung the hose back on us for several seconds before going back to taking down anything with wings.

"Hey!" I sputtered as water ran off me in rivulets. I pushed wet hair from my face to shoot her a dirty look.

"Sorry, had to make sure I didn't miss any of it," she said, but her smirk belied her apology. "Hey, it worked, didn't it?"

She was right; there wasn't a single kark interested in me anymore. I looked around for my hoodie and spotted a splash of blue beneath a pile of unmoving bodies. Sahir must have dosed them with his sedative.

"I think that's enough, Jordan." Tristan wore a serious expression as he surveyed the mess in the main hall. He waited for Jordan to shut off the hose then he started toward us, followed by Chris and the other warriors. "Are you two okay?" he asked me and Nikolas. I nodded, and he turned to Sahir who was the resident creature expert. "Sahir, what could have caused this?"

Sahir removed his mask and shook his head. "I've never seen karks behave this way. They didn't go after anyone but Sara."

"Something on her clothes attracted them." Nikolas strode over to the pile of white bodies and yanked my hoodie out from under them. "Look at this."

I barely held back a gasp when I saw the tattered remains of what I had been wearing a few minutes ago. The karks' sharp teeth had literally shredded it before Sahir could knock them out. Coldness spread through me when it hit me what would have happened if Nikolas hadn't gotten to me when he did.

Tristan's face hardened. It was the first time I had ever seen him this angry. "Have that garment examined. I want to know exactly what happened here." He addressed one of the younger warriors I only knew as Ben. "Get something to put these things in before they wake up. And we're going to need the cleanup crew in here."

"Yes, sir," Ben said before rushing to follow his orders.

"Are you sure you're okay?" Tristan asked me again. Concern colored his voice after seeing the damage to my hoodie.

"I'm fine." Or I would be after a very, very long hot shower.

Jordan had abandoned her fire hose and walked over to join us. "Sara, you look like you just won a wet T-shirt contest," she announced, causing more than one male head turned my way.

"What?" I croaked and looked down at the pale yellow V-neck clinging to me in a way that left absolutely nothing to the imagination. Heat enflamed my cheeks, and I yanked the wet material away from my chest.

Nikolas stepped in front of me, and I stared at his broad back as he blocked me from the others in the room. A surge of gratitude wiped out my annoyance at him from a few minutes ago. I would never understand him. One minute he did or said something that made me want to hit him, and the next he did something nice like this.

Once I had arranged my T-shirt so it no longer looked like a second skin, I stepped out from behind him, hoping my face wasn't as red as it felt. The first face I saw was Chris's, and he quirked one corner of his mouth at me but wisely kept his thoughts to himself.

"Nikolas, we need to talk when you have a minute," Tristan said, and Nikolas nodded tersely. There was an undercurrent in their communication that I couldn't read, but it sounded serious.

"If you don't need me, I'd like to get cleaned up," I said to Tristan, who glanced at Nikolas and told me to take the rest of the day off. I wasted no time escaping to my room where I spent half an hour showering kark poop out of my hair and skin and mourning the loss of my St. Patrick's hoodie and my favorite jeans. I stood in front of my bathroom mirror drying my hair and wondering if Roland could score another hoodie for me. I hadn't really been involved in much at high school, but now that I was no longer there, I found myself holding onto the things that reminded me of that part of my old life.

I felt immeasurably better once I was clean, and I was trying to decide how to spend the afternoon when my stomach growled loudly. It was lunchtime, and I'd barely touched my breakfast, but I was loath to go down to the dining hall. I was pretty sure that by now, the whole place knew what had happened and everyone was asking the same question. Why had the karks attacked only me?

It was a question I had avoided thinking about since I left the main hall. If karks did not attack people, someone had to have done something to send them after me. And if Nikolas was right and something on my clothing had attracted them, then how did it get there? Or more importantly, who put it there? It had to be someone in the hall, or at least someone I'd come into contact with today. I made a mental list of everyone I had been near this morning and quickly dismissed it. Nikolas and Chris would never harm me, and I found it difficult to believe Jordan or Olivia would either. Besides, the two girls had sat across the table from me at breakfast and neither of them got close enough to touch me. There was too much chaos in the main hall to remember who had been near me. The only people I recalled touching me were Nikolas, Tristan, Chris, Michael, and Celine.

The last name gave me pause. Celine obviously disliked me, and we had been in very close contact when I fell on top of her, which would have given her ample opportunity to mark my clothes with something that would attract the karks. And she had taken off right after that. I stared out my window without seeing anything. Could jealousy really have driven her to try to hurt me?

I couldn't help but laugh out loud at that thought. Celine jealous of me? Hardly. She was stunningly gorgeous and could have any man she desired. There was no need for her to do something so drastic when she could easily have Nikolas if she wanted him. And if he wanted someone like her then . . . oh, what did it matter to me anyway?

Snatching up the phone, I dialed Roland's number. He should be just now getting home from school and I needed to hear his voice.

"Hey," he answered breathlessly like he had been scrambling for his phone. "Everything okay?"

I carried the phone over to my bed where I flopped down on my back. "Why do you think something is wrong?"

"Well, because you never call this early and I haven't heard from you in two days."

My free hand slapped my forehead. Crap. Nikolas's sudden return threw me off so much yesterday that I'd forgotten to call Roland. Now I had to tell him about the karks *and* the lamprey demons all at once. "It's been kind of nuts here the last few days. Nikolas came back yesterday."

"Ah." It was amazing how one syllable could hold so much meaning.

"That's not all." I filled him in on the disastrous trip to Boise, deliberately making the whole demon attack sound a lot less scary than it had been. No need worrying him when he could do nothing about it. I did include the part where I blew up the demon.

"Whoa! You weren't kidding about your power getting stronger."

"Yeah, well I could have done without the shower of blood and guts."

He brushed off my revulsion in typical male fashion. "I think it rocks. I'm just surprised Nikolas let you go off to Boise in the first place. You know, with him being the way he is."

"He wasn't here, and even if he had been, he doesn't tell me what to do," I declared irritably.

Roland chuckled. "Uh-oh. What did he do now?"

"He didn't do anything. It's just been a crazy few days. First the lamprey demons, then Nikolas shows up and tells me he is training me, and then – "

"Hold up. Nikolas is training you?" Roland burst into laughter.

I scowled at the ceiling. "Remind me again why I call you."

"S-sorry. I just can't help picturing him trying to teach you how to use one of those swords. Can the Mohiri re-grow limbs?"

"Oh shut up," I retorted, but a smile crept across my face because I was pretty sure Nikolas wasn't foolhardy enough to put a sword in my hand.

"Well, at least it's not boring there." He sighed heavily, and it was my turn to ask him what was wrong.

"I hate this. It's our senior year; we should be hanging together: you, me, and Pete. School totally sucks without you."

"It can't be that bad."

"No?" Roland groaned. "Do you know how hard it is to pretend to be sad over your best friend's death when you know she is still alive and well?"

I tried to put myself in his shoes and couldn't. "That'll get easier soon. I bet people have already started to forget about me."

"You still don't get how much people noticed you, do you? People at school talk about you all the time."

"They do?" That shocked me, considering how few friends I'd had at St. Patrick's. Other than Roland and Peter, I could only think of one other, a boy name Jeffrey who I'd sat with at lunch every day.

"I told you it's not the same here. Even Scott is different since you disappeared. Pete thinks he misses you."

"Ha! Now I know you're messing with me."

"Seriously, he is not the same guy. He doesn't say much anymore, and he's even nicer to people. I heard he broke up with Faith two days ago."

I didn't know what to say to that. There had been animosity between me and Scott for years, and it was strange to think he might be affected by my death. It was more likely that he had changed because he no longer had the negative emotions my undine side brought out in him. Maybe not having me around was actually making him a better person. Wow. Now that was a depressing thought.

A knock at the door stopped me from delving further into that line of thinking. "Hold on, Roland, someone's at my door."

I didn't try to hide my surprise when I opened the door to find Jordan, cleaned up and holding a plate of sandwiches and two bottles of water.

"I figured you were avoiding the dining hall and might be hungry," she explained, breezing past me to lay the plate and bottles on my desk.

"I'll call you back later, Roland," I told him, and we said good-bye.

Jordan walked around the room, studying my photos and drawings. "Nice. Did you draw these?"

"Um, yes."

"Is that your uncle?"

"Yes."

"He's hot for an old guy." She finished her little tour and flopped down on my bed as if she'd done it a hundred times before.

I hadn't moved from the door. "What do you want, Jordan?" In my experience, other girls did not visit me to hang out. They usually went out of their way to avoid me. I reminded myself it was only human girls who were naturally repulsed by my undine side, but after years of being shunned, it was hard to believe otherwise.

She actually looked a little hurt by my question, and I regretted my curt tone. "Sorry, that came out wrong. I'm just surprised to see you here."

"Me too. I don't usually like many people. Olivia is nice but she is such a girl, if you know what I mean. I didn't care for you either when you first got here, but you've changed my mind."

I closed the door and went to sit in my desk chair. "Thanks, I think."

Jordan sat up and ran her finger along the outline of one of the birds on my grandmother's quilt. "This is nice. Did your mom make it?"

I laughed harshly. "My mother took off when I was two, and if she had made anything I would have burned it before I brought it here with me. My grandmother made it."

"Ouch! Someone has serious mommy issues."

"If you came here to make fun of me, you know where the door is."

"Geez, chill, will you? I get the whole anger thing. You aren't the only orphan here with a sad story." She got up and came over to grab a sandwich and a bottle of water. "Why don't we eat and you can tell me again how there is absolutely nothing between you and Nikolas Danshov?"

"I told you, there is nothing going on between us. He's my trainer and that is all."

She laid her food and water on my nightstand and sat on the bed again. "Uh-huh. That's why he threw himself over you like a living shield."

I chuckled. "You really don't know Nikolas. That's what he does – he protects people, and he would have done it for anyone."

Jordan let out a burst of laughter. "As much as I wish Nikolas would want to come running to my rescue – not that I need any man to rescue me – it will never happen. You didn't see his face when he saw you getting attacked. I've never seen *anyone* move that fast."

"I wish someone would tell Nikolas and Tristan I don't need a man to protect me," I grumbled.

"Males are just wired that way," Jordan explained through a mouthful of food. "You're tough but you have this whole vulnerable look going on that gets their testosterone in a twist. Of course, I'm pretty sure it's more than that with Nikolas after seeing him downstairs. When you were standing there all wet and he moved in front of you – the look he gave those other guys . . . brrrrr. He did everything but pee a circle around you to mark his territory."

"That is totally absurd. And thanks for that disgusting visual by the way."

She gave me a long searching stare. "You simply cannot be that clueless. Anyone with eyes can see the sparks between you two."

I looked away from her and unwrapped my sandwich. Before I could take a bite, Jordan let out a squeal. "Oh my God! You really have no idea, do you?" When I didn't answer, she jumped off the bed and bounced up and down on her feet like she had just won a prize.

"What?" I asked defensively.

She fell on the bed, howling with laughter, and I watched her with growing irritation. After a few minutes, she pulled herself together and sat up, wiping her eyes. "I love it! Celine's been throwing herself at Nikolas for years and he chose a sweet little orphan over her. She must be positively *insane* with jealousy. Oh how I wish she had stayed around to see him go all caveman on the other guys over you."

"He did not choose me, and I certainly don't want him." I slumped in my chair, wondering why I'd ever thought it might be nice to have a girlfriend to discuss girl matters with. I was sure my face must be glowing like an ember now. "Can we please talk about something else?"

Jordan took a drink from her water bottle then made a face. "Sure, but it won't be nearly as fun as talking about Nikolas."

Anything would be better than *that* subject. "I get why Celine might not like me." Jordan snorted at my choice of words, but I ignored her. "But why do you dislike her so much?"

"Are you kidding? Unless you have a penis, that woman is a total bitch to you. She always favors the boys in training. Thank God she is only here a few times a year."

"So, she would have disliked me anyway just for being a girl?"

Her eyes sparkled. "Yes, but you are an extra special case."

"How long have you lived here?" I already knew that all of the trainees here except for Terrence were orphans. Other than Michael, I didn't know anyone else's story. Jordan was brash and fearless and different from the others, and I wondered if she had been like that in her old life.

A shadow passed over her face. "My mother dumped me when I was four and I started telling people about the little person in my head. I guess it didn't help that I was also beating up kids twice my size. No one else in her family wanted to take me, so I ended up in our wonderful foster-care system. I got passed around a lot. No one wants a kid with voices in her head who has to see a shrink twice a week for anger issues."

She flicked her blond hair back, and her eyes filled with pride. "But I always knew I was different for a reason. When I was ten, I ran away from the last shithole they dumped me in. I was living on the street for three weeks before Paulette ran across me by accident. As soon as she spoke to me, I knew she was like me, and she didn't have to ask me twice to go with her. She took me to Valstrom, which is their compound in northern California, and I lived there until I came here two years ago. Do you know I was the oldest orphan ever reclaimed . . . until you?"

"Nikolas mentioned that." Jordan's coldness toward me in the beginning made sense now. Her old life had been pretty rotten, and then she came here where she felt loved and special and, according to Michael, number one in everything she did. Then I came along and everyone was talking about the orphan who survived out there for seventeen years. I stole her spotlight, and even if it was unwilling on my part, she had resented me for it. At least she seemed to have gotten past that now.

Her eyes widened. "Nikolas mentioned me?"

"He told me you were ten when they found you and all the other orphans were no older than seven." Seeing her expression at hearing that Nikolas had spoken of her, I omitted the fact that he hadn't said her name, just that the orphan had been a girl. The smile that lit up her face was worth the tiny omission.

"How did Nikolas find you anyway?" she asked around a mouthful of food.

"I was at a club in Portland with my friends," I said vaguely. "A few days later, he tracked me down and told me what I was. I wasn't too happy about it."

She tossed me an incredulous look. "Why not?"

"It totally freaked me out to learn I had a demon inside me. Didn't it bother you?"

"Are you kidding? I found out that not only was I not crazy like everyone said I was, I was immortal and had superpowers. I was like, 'Hell yeah, where do I sign up?'"

I chewed thoughtfully own my sandwich. She and I had such different pasts. I'd had my dad and then Nate to love and care for me, not to mention my friends. Growing up in foster care and living on the street at age ten, it was no wonder she had embraced her Mohiri heritage. I never realized how fortunate I was compared to people like her and Michael who had it a lot rougher than I did.

Jordan laid her half-eaten sandwich on the nightstand and stood. "I think you and I are going to be great friends. And to show what an awesome friend I am, I'm going to prove to you that I am right about your warrior."

"What do you mean?"

She walked into my closet. "You hide yourself under those awful hoodies, but I saw you in that wet T-shirt and it is a shame to cover that up all the time."

"I am not hiding, and there is nothing wrong with the way I look. I happen to like my clothes because they are comfortable and practical."

"Boring," she sang from the depths of my closet. "Don't you have anything in here besides these ratty jeans and tennis shoes?"

"Hey, I like those jeans."

She emerged from the closet. "Let me guess, you had all male friends back home and not one girlfriend."

"So?"

"So a girlfriend would have made sure you had at least a couple of decent outfits so you could dress like a female from time to time. Thank

God you have me now."

"I thought you liked me because I wasn't too girlie."

Jordan swept a hand up and down her body, which was clad in jeans that probably cost more than three of mine and a pretty black top with a Grecian-style yoke neck. "Do I look girlie to you? No, I look hot. Trust me, there's a difference."

I crossed my arms over my chest. "That is your style, not mine. And if he . . . any guy doesn't like me for who I am, then he's not worth my time."

"Ha! You *do* like him."

"No, that was just an example. Don't turn my words around."

She gave me a sly grin. "You look awfully flustered for a girl who doesn't care."

I turned to pick up my water bottle as an excuse not to look at her smirk. "I'm flustered because you have a special talent for driving people nuts."

She started to laugh then yelled, "Hey!" I spun around in my chair to find her on her hands and knees, peering under my bed. She looked up at me and made a face. "I hate to tell you this, but you have an imp infestation. Little bastards just stole my sandwich."

I put a hand to my forehead. "Shoot, I forgot bring them something to eat today. They must be hungry."

Her mouth fell open. "You feed them? You do know they are thieving little rodents who would steal your mother if they could lift her."

From under the bed I heard outraged chattering. "I don't think they like to be called rodents. And if they wanted to steal my mother, they are welcome to her if she ever shows up." I tore a chunk from my own sandwich and went over to lay it under the bed. "They're partial to blueberry muffins, but they'll eat anything if they're hungry."

Jordan sat back on her haunches and stared at me. "You treat them like pets? You are one strange girl, Sara."

I grinned because she didn't know the half of it. "You wanna see pets? Come with me and I'll introduce you to Hugo and Woolf."

Chapter 10

"SARA, YOU LOOK very nice tonight."

I tugged at the hem of my borrowed top as I stepped into Tristan's suite. "Jordan tried to go all Professor Higgins on me." My new friend was a lot bossier than my friends back home, and it was hard to say no to her when she got an idea into her head. Tonight, she had somehow convinced me to wear one of her tops – a pale pink one with a pretty floral lace overlay that was the least revealing of the ones she'd forced me to try on – and leave my hair down for once. At least the top wasn't as form fitting on me as it was on her. I'd drawn the line at the heels she wanted me to wear and opted for comfortable flats instead.

Tristan laughed and shut the door behind me. "Well, you look lovely and none the worse for wear from your little ordeal this morning."

"That was nothing compared to some of the other scrapes I've been in." I sat on the couch, and he sat across from me, sporting a furrowed brow. "Seriously, I'm fine," I assured him.

His face relaxed into a smile. When I'd first met him, I wasn't sure how I felt about him, especially with him being Madeline's father. Tristan was an easy person to like, and it wasn't hard to see that he cared about me.

"I have a surprise for you."

I made a face. "I don't really like surprises. They tend to try to eat me or do some other awful thing to me."

His blue eyes sparkled with humor. "I promise you'll like this one. How would you like to meet your cousin?"

"He's back?" I tried to remember if I'd seen any new faces today, but I couldn't think of one.

"He got back a few days ago. We talked today and decided it was time you knew who he was. I thought it would be nice if the three of us had dinner together – if you are ready for that."

"O-okay." It took me less than ten seconds to figure out who had returned to Westhorne a few days ago. My mouth suddenly felt very dry and a pit opened in my stomach. Cousins?

Someone rapped firmly on the door, and my stomach dipped.

"Ah, perfect timing." Tristan went to the door. I stood, my hand nervously touching my hair.

"Hope I'm not late. I wouldn't have missed this little family get together for the world."

My mouth fell open as Chris sauntered into the room, his grin aimed at me. He strode over and pulled me into a hug. "My little cousin."

Recovering from my shock, I pushed him away, which only made him snicker.

"*You're* my cousin?"

"Yep."

I burst into laughter.

After a minute, I was in tears and holding my sides, and Chris was starting to look affronted. I honestly didn't know if I was laughing so hard because out of all the Mohiri in the world Chris was my cousin, or because I was relieved it had been him and not someone else on the other side of the door. If I hadn't been so anxious, I would have realized that I hadn't sensed Nikolas nearby.

"Sorry," I said, composing myself. Looking from Chris to Tristan I saw a resemblance I couldn't believe I had not noticed before. Chris's eyes were green whereas Tristan's were blue, but their hair color was almost identical and they had similar facial features, especially around the nose and mouth. "So, you are Tristan's nephew?"

"We call each other kinsmen. He and my mother are brother and sister."

"Did you know we were related when you were in New Hastings?"

Chris made a face. "Not at first. And once I did, you have no idea how many times I wanted to take you over my knee for your little antics."

"Ha! You could have tried. If I recall correctly, you were too busy fending off girls to do much else."

"Human girls are a lot more aggressive than Mohiri women, and you were no help at all. In fact, I think you encouraged some of them."

I couldn't hold back a smirk. "I use any weapon on hand to get the job done."

Tristan smiled at both of us. "Well, at least I don't have to worry about breaking the ice between you two."

I helped him carry roast chicken and salad to the table and filled the water glasses. Tristan's suite had its own kitchen, and he had confided to me on my last visit that he liked to cook but rarely had anyone to do it for. Now that I was here, he was enjoying using his stove again.

It was the first time Chris and I had ever eaten together – or spent any amount of time together when I was not in danger – and I found myself enjoying his company immensely. I already knew he was charming and had a great sense of humor, and over dinner I learned a lot more about him. He was born in eighteen seventy-six, and he told me all about growing up at a compound in Oregon. He was an only child, and he didn't see his parents much because they lived in Germany now. Not long after he became a warrior, he came to Westhorne to serve under Tristan and had been there ever since. It was clear that Chris was very loyal to Tristan and not just because he was family. Tristan had a way of commanding the respect of the people under him. Watching my cousin and my grandfather together, I saw the closeness that Nikolas had told me existed in Mohiri families. If only Nate was here, my family would be complete.

After dinner, Chris and I cleared the table and tidied the kitchen together, and I couldn't help but think that a few weeks ago, the last thing I'd expected to be doing was having dinner with family or washing dishes with my cousin. They were such normal family activities, and they made me smile to myself as I put the dishes away.

When the dishes were done, Tristan poured drinks for him and Chris and we went into the living room where they told me more of my family history. They mentioned a lot of people, some living and some dead, and it was hard to keep up with the conversation at times. Inevitably, Madeline's name came up, and I tensed when Tristan asked me about her.

"You've not asked me anything about your mother or what her childhood was like. Do you ever wonder about her?"

"No," I said more abruptly than I'd meant to. "I know Madeline is your daughter and you'll love her no matter what, but she means nothing to me. I'm sorry if that sounds cold."

Tristan nodded sadly and I regretted hurting him, but I would not lie to him or let him harbor any false hopes of reconciliation between Madeline and me. All she was to me now was a means of finding the Master, and once we had him, she could disappear again for all I cared.

Chris swirled the amber liquid in his glass. "So, Sara, I hear you've actually named those two monsters of yours. And you have them eating out of your hands, just like Nikolas said you would."

"Nikolas?"

"He tracked them down at one of our holding facilities in Minneapolis and had them sent here." Chris smiled wryly at my look of surprise. "He said you would be upset if they were locked away. I told him they were going to eat someone, and he bet me you'd have them eating out of your hands in no time. You, little cousin, cost me my favorite set of throwing knives."

"Sorry," I replied absently, shocked by the news that Nikolas had found Hugo and Woolf and sent them here for me. First, he takes off without a word and I don't hear from him for weeks. And now I learn that he went out of his way to do something he knew would make me happy. I would never figure him out.

"About the hellhounds." Tristan leaned forward, smiling again. "Sahir thinks it'll be safe to let them out for short walks with you as long as we keep everyone else away at first."

"Really? When can we start?"

"Tomorrow."

I let out an excited squeal that would have made Olivia envious.

Chris and Tristan were still laughing when someone knocked on the door. I felt the telltale flutter before Tristan opened the door to invite Nikolas in. I was still embarrassed about that morning, and as much as I had argued with Jordan about him, all her words came rushing back to me now.

Nikolas entered the apartment and stopped as if he was surprised to see me there. His gaze lingered on me for several seconds before it shifted to Chris and then Tristan. I could see no sign that he was happy to see me. So much for Jordan's theories.

"I'll leave so you guys can take care of business," I said to Tristan.

He shook his head. "No, this concerns you. Nikolas has been investigating the kark attack." He looked at Nikolas. "I assume you have something for us."

Nikolas sat on the other end of the couch, and I immediately sensed the stiffness in his bearing even though I was trying to look anywhere but at him. His dark mood confused me, and I tried not to fidget when I felt his eyes on me.

"We examined Sara's shirt. The karks destroyed one side of it, so we focused on the scraps of fabric left there and found traces of what looks like scarab pheromone." Nikolas glanced at me. "The only way Sara could have gotten it on her clothes is if someone put it there."

Tristan's smile faded. "I cannot believe anyone inside these walls would try to hurt one of our own."

"I find it hard to believe as well, but the evidence speaks for itself. Sahir said he found it odd there was no pheromone spray in the crates with the shipment of eggs. It's likely someone took it out before he searched them."

"Why would anyone here target Sara?" Chris mused. He gave me a sidelong look. "Your beasties didn't snack on someone, did they?"

"Ha, ha," I retorted. "It's not like I don't have enemies out there."

Tristan shook his head. "Out there, yes, but not in here, and we've found nothing to indicate the vampires believe you are still alive. Even if they did, there is no way a Mohiri would betray one of their own people for a vampire."

"I agree." Nikolas's tone was clipped but full of conviction. "There must be another motive." He looked at me like he thought I was keeping something back, but I had no reason to hide anything.

"Trainees have been known to prank each other. They were brutal back in my day. Perhaps one of them did this as a practical joke and it got out of hand," Chris suggested.

"I don't know any of them that well, but they've all been nice to me. I really can't see one of them doing something that could hurt me."

Chris's eyebrows went up. "Jordan? Nice?"

"She has her moments." *Even if she did make me wear this stupid top.* "I like her actually. I took her to meet Hugo and Woolf today, and they didn't go all growly on her so she must be okay."

"Jordan will make a great warrior one day," Nikolas commented, and I knew she would be ecstatic to hear such praise from him. "You could learn a lot from her."

"She is already teaching me a lot." I wondered what he would say if I told him that Jordan's education centered on what to wear to attract guys instead of how to use a sword.

I stood and turned to Tristan. "I should get going. I need to call Nate because I forgot to ask him yesterday if he's still coming for Thanksgiving."

Tristan chuckled. "I doubt you could keep him away. I've already arranged for the plane to pick him up in Portland in two weeks."

I thought about the small private jet that had flown me to Boise, and I wished I could see Nate's face when he saw it. I never asked about finances, but the jet was evidence that the Mohiri must have a sizeable fortune at their disposal.

"I can't wait for you guys to meet each other."

He walked me to the door. "I'm looking forward to it, too. He sounds like a nice person on the phone."

I stopped short to stare at him. "You talked to Nate?"

Tristan looked surprised by my reaction. "We speak at least once a week. You didn't know?"

"No." Why hadn't Nate mentioned it to me? "What do you talk about? You don't even know each other."

"We are getting to know each other. He wants to make sure you are happy here; he knows how much you miss your friends back home. The last time we spoke he wanted to know if you'd started dating anyone yet. Apparently, the boys back home were not to your liking."

I cringed inwardly. The absolute last thing I wanted anyone – especially my uncle and my grandfather – discussing was my nonexistent love life. "Excuse me while I go kill my uncle."

"I will see you tomorrow." Tristan opened the door, not hiding his amusement. I turned to say good-bye to the others, only to find Nikolas standing a few feet away from us wearing a scowl. What did he have to be annoyed about? I was the one who was embarrassed.

"I'll walk with you so we can talk about tomorrow's training," Nikolas said. He had been cool toward me since he arrived, and I hoped he would get over it by tomorrow. I did not want to train with him like this.

Tristan put up a hand when Nikolas moved toward the door. "Actually, I need to speak with you, Nikolas, if you don't mind."

Nikolas looked as if he was going to refuse, but he merely nodded instead. I was pretty sure they were going to continue their discussion about the karks, and I was done with that conversation. Chris was probably right about it being a prank gone astray, and even if it turned out that Celine was behind it, I found it hard to believe she would want to cause me serious harm.

"I will walk my sweet little cousin out," Chris announced. He came up behind me to tug on my hair and laughed when I smacked his hand away. "Just trying to make up for all the years I missed out on."

"Before you get any ideas, Dimples, I should remind you my best friends are boys and I know many forms of retaliation. I even picked up a few tricks from Remy."

He winked as he slipped past me. "I've learned to never underestimate a girl with troll friends."

"I'll see you later," I said to Tristan and Nikolas. Then I followed Chris. His apartment was two doors down, and I said good-bye at his door to head back to my own room. Away from Nikolas's brooding stare, I breathed a little easier. I had expected him to be less intense now that I was finally safe inside a Mohiri stronghold, but if anything, his moods were more mercurial than ever. Didn't the guy ever loosen up and let go of the whole warrior thing? I thought back to the night we had sat by the fire and talked during the storm. That was probably the most relaxed I had ever seen Nikolas. Why couldn't he be that way again?

Gah! Two months ago I was running from vampires and rescuing trolls, and now I was reduced to obsessing about some guy's moods. It figured that I had to find out I was immortal only to start behaving like a normal teenage girl. I was sure there was some great irony in this and someday I'd laugh at it, but I was too annoyed with myself to look for it now. *God, do not let me turn into one of* those *girls.*

I was still frowning when I picked up the phone and called Nate, who answered on the second ring.

"Is everything okay?" he asked with a note of concern in his voice.

"Everything is great. Why?"

"Because you usually call every few days and we talked last night. You're sure you are okay?"

I stretched out on the bed. "I'm sure Tristan would have told you if anything was wrong."

There was a short pause before he cleared his throat. "So he told you. I thought I should know what kind of people are taking care of you out there. Your . . . grandfather sounds like a nice, responsible person, and he cares about you very much."

"I'm not mad at you, Nate. I think it's kind of sweet actually. I just don't know why you didn't tell me you two were becoming long-distance pals."

"I didn't want you to think I don't trust you or that I'm checking up on you. If you don't want me talking to him, I won't."

"No, I think it's great that you two are getting to know each other. Just do me one favor and please, please don't talk about my love life with him ever again. Do you know how awkward it is to find out that your uncle and your grandfather have been discussing your boyfriend situation?"

Nate laughed. "Okay, I promise no more of that. Is there a boyfriend situation?"

"Nate!"

"You can't blame me for trying."

I let out a loud, exaggerated sigh. "No, there is no boyfriend. I think I made a friend, though."

"You *think* you made a friend?"

"Well, with Jordan it's hard to tell. She can be a bit prickly, and she's not really a people person."

"Hmmm. Sounds a bit like a girl who used to live here for a while."

"My uncle, the comedian," I quipped, earning another laugh from him. "Anyway, you'll meet her when you get here. You *are* still coming for Thanksgiving, right?"

"Wouldn't miss it."

"Tristan told me he's sending the jet. Wait'll you see this thing; it's like the whole rock star treatment."

"I can't wait."

"And don't forget Oscar." I couldn't wait to see him again, although the imps probably wouldn't be as happy about his arrival. I still needed to pick up a litter box and food for him, and I made a note to ask Tristan if I could go shopping in town. Terrence and Josh went into Butler Falls all the time and no one seemed to have a problem with it.

"Don't worry; he is at the top of my list."

"List? What else are you bringing?"

There was a noticeable pause before he answered. "A box of things from your old house."

I felt my brow crease. "What things? I have all my dad's stuff."

Another pause. "These are some things your father kept of your mother's. I held onto them because I thought you might want them someday."

"I don't," I replied stiffly, too shocked by his revelation to say more. I'd always assumed Madeline had taken everything of hers when she left us. Now to find out that Nate had kept some of her belongings all this time . . .

"I know but I thought Tristan might like to have them. It's just some old books and photo albums and a few letters, but they may be of sentimental value to him."

I started to say something not so nice and stopped myself. I felt nothing but animosity for Madeline, but she was still Tristan's daughter and it was clear he cared about her. I saw the pain he tried to hide whenever I refused to talk about her. Madeline's belongings meant nothing to me, but they might mean a great deal to him.

"I'm sure he will appreciate that, Nate."

We talked for another ten minutes, mostly about his book. He told me that a reporter from a New York literary magazine had contacted him yesterday about doing an interview. The woman was coming up from New York next week to meet with him, and I could tell Nate was pretty excited about it. He promised to tell me all about it when he came to visit.

I hung up and started to log into my computer when I heard a soft knock on the door. Glancing at my clock, I saw it was after nine thirty, and I wondered who was visiting me this late. I was surprised to find the hallway empty, except for a small flat box on the floor in front of my door. Who would leave me a package? I picked it up and shook it, but it didn't make any noise.

Closing the door, I carried the box to my desk and lifted the top to reveal a folded sheet of heavy linen stationary lying on top of the tissue paper that concealed the contents of the box. I opened the note and felt a second jolt of surprise when I saw who had penned it.

I hope you will come to love these as I do. Desmund.

The handwriting was elegant and precise with a slight flourish in the D at the beginning of his name, just how I would expect an English lord to write. I sat there for a full minute, staring at the note and marveling that Desmund had actually sent me a gift, before I pushed aside the tissue paper to see two CDs of Beethoven's and Shubert's greatest hits.

Touched by his gift, I popped in the Shubert CD before I sat down at my computer again. My good mood lasted as long as it took me to log into my favorite message board and see the flurry of activity there. The vampire watchers were out in full force tonight, exchanging stories of suspected vampire-related disappearances all over the country. Something was up and everyone was on edge. People went missing all the time, but vampires were usually discreet about their involvement, taking care not to hunt openly and attract too much attention. But according to the stories I was reading, missing persons cases had almost doubled in Los Angeles, Vegas, Houston, and a number of other large cities. I chewed my lower lip as I read each disturbing post. Could vampires really be responsible for all those disappearances? If so, why weren't they being more careful to hide their tracks? Weren't they worried at all about bringing the Mohiri down on their heads?

An email from David arrived as I was about to log off for the night. It was brief like most of his correspondence, just a note to tell me he thought one of his new leads might pan out and he'd let me know if anything turned up. He also mentioned the increase in vampire activity and told me to make sure I kept my head down. I rolled my eyes as I signed off. *As if I need to be reminded of* that.

Later, as I lay in bed trying to still my racing thoughts, I felt the softest brush against my mind. It made me think of Nikolas, and a feeling of security settled over me. It was strange how he was still the only Mohiri I could sense that way.

Maybe if I learned to connect with my Mori I would be more attuned to others. *What do you think, demon?* I asked it as I drifted deeper into sleep. *You ready to make some other friends?*

It could have been my imagination, but I swear it said, *No.*

Chapter 11

"WE'RE NOT GOING back to the lake?"

"Not today."

I followed Nikolas around the corner of the main building, waiting for an explanation that did not come. Scowling at his back, I hurried to keep up with his long strides as I wondered what the hell was eating at him this morning. He'd barely said a word to me since he had shown up in the dining hall five minutes ago, and his stormy expression was even worse to deal with than his mood last night. I'd been laughing at something Terrence had said when Nikolas arrived and glared at us so hard that poor Terrence and Josh had actually cringed and hurried off to their own table. Even Jordan had refrained from teasing me about Nikolas when she caught sight of his expression. I had no idea what was up with him, but surely he wasn't still upset about the kark incident. We'd been through a lot worse situations and I'd never seen him in such a black mood after any of them.

"Will you slow down? I'm not going to chase you all over creation because you're too cranky to walk like a normal person."

I did not expect him to stop and turn so suddenly, and I ran right into him. Stepping back, I rubbed my nose and met his steel gaze squarely. This – whatever it was – might scare everyone else, but I'd felt the brunt of Nikolas's moods too many times to be cowed by them.

"I don't get cranky," he declared as if I had insulted him.

"Really? Could have fooled me."

He started walking again, but slower this time, and I was able to keep abreast of him.

"So where are we going?"

"The arena."

"You're not going to make me fight bazerats, are you? Because I have to say that was not one of my favorite experiences."

"You are going to work with your Mori some more."

"Oh, okay." A small thrill passed through me at the thought of talking to the Mori again after our first conversation – if you could call it that.

When we got to the arena, Nikolas opened the door and I entered the building ahead of him. He flipped a switch, turning on the overhead lights, and casting a bright glow over the large room, which looked a lot less creepy with the lights on.

The center of the arena was bare except for some thick chains and weights on the floor, and I eyed the chains, wondering what they were for. But Nikolas ignored them and led me over to the bottom row of the bleachers. I sat and he took the seat beside me, putting us so close our shoulders touched. Needing a little more space, I moved down one seat and turned sideways to find him watching me with an almost bemused expression.

"What?"

He looked at me for several more seconds. "How do you feel after yesterday?"

"Do you mean training or the kark thing?"

"Both."

"Talking to my Mori was not what I expected. I'm really not sure how I feel about it."

"And the kark attack?"

I lifted a shoulder. "I don't know; I haven't really thought much about it. Compared to some of the other stuff I've been through, that was nothing."

His face lost some of its hardness. "That is true."

"Well, you did call me a danger magnet once."

A small smile hovered at the corners of his mouth. "I believe I said *disaster* magnet."

"The kark incident could hardly be called a disaster, so I think my luck is improving."

"Maybe it is, but let's work on training you so you don't need luck. Do you think you can talk to your Mori like you did yesterday?" I nodded. "Start with that, and then I'll tell you what I want you to do next."

I closed my eyes, because it felt more natural that way, and opened my thoughts to the demon crouching inside its cage. Even before I started to lower the wall, I felt the demon's mixture of anticipation and fear. *Come out,* I said as the wall disappeared. *I won't hurt you.*

The Mori did not need more encouragement than that. Instead of rushing out like it had the first time, it emerged from its cage cautiously, and I could feel it searching for *the glow* as it called it. When it realized that my power was still locked away, it relaxed, reminding me of a cat sitting back on its haunches. It was hard to believe this small, seemingly timid blob of darkness was the same one that had tried to fill me with violent urges and could give me strength and speed to match a vampire's.

Now that we're here, I'm not sure what we are supposed to do, I told it. *I don't suppose you would know.*

The demon looked at me with its featureless face but said nothing. Great, neither one of us was a conversationalist. This should be interesting.

Nikolas's voice cut through the silence between us. "How are you doing?"

Solmi? The demon asked eagerly, and I wondered if maybe it sensed the other Mori nearby.

"I'm good," I replied without opening my eyes. "What should I be doing?"

"Touch it."

My eyes flew open. "Touch it?"

He smiled at my reaction. "Yes. If you ever want to tap into all of its powers, you will have to learn to merge with it. Touching it is the first step."

Merge with the demon? Fuse our minds together the way he'd described yesterday? I wasn't sure if I would ever be able to do that.

"We will take this as slow as you need to."

I shut my eyes again and looked at the demon that hadn't moved at all while I was talking to Nikolas.

I'm not going to hurt you. I'm just going to touch you. I reached toward it slowly, and it shrank back at the last moment.

Look, Nikolas says we have to do this if we're ever going to work together.

The demon perked up. *Solmi?*

Yes, Solmi. Maybe if my Mori thought the other demon wanted us to do this, then it would be okay with it. It was worth a try.

It worked. The demon started to lean toward me as I reached for it. This time, it did not flinch away and my mind made contact with the dark shapeless blob.

There is no way to describe the sensations that flowed into me through that single touch. Colors, sounds, and smells bombarded me along with a wave of emotions: fear, love, rage, joy, loneliness, and so many more. It was how I imagined a prisoner would feel, emerging into the sunlight after a lifetime of solitary, a blind man seeing for the first time, a deaf man hearing music. It was the joy of freedom, the fear of losing it again, and an overwhelming need to connect with another living creature.

I absorbed every one of the Mori's emotions and felt how much I had been hurting it by imprisoning it all these years. It was a demon, but it was also a sentient being and as much a part of me as my heart or lungs. I'd treated imps and bazerats with more compassion and kindness than I had the demon living inside me.

I didn't know I was crying until a hand touched my face. "Sara, what is it?"

"It hurts so much."

"You're in pain?"

I shook my head without opening my eyes. "Not me, my Mori. It's so lonely and sad."

"You're crying for your demon?" There was surprise in his voice along with something else I could not identify.

Pulling back, I turned my face away from him. "You wouldn't understand."

It took him a moment to answer. "Do you want to tell me what is happening?"

"I feel so many things it's almost too much." I swallowed past the lump in my throat. "I don't know how you do it, how you live with this all the time."

"This is your first time opening yourself to your demon. The more you do this, the easier it will be." He sounded like a trainer again. "Give yourself a few minutes to adjust, and then I want you to tell me what else you feel."

I faced the onslaught from the Mori until I could take it no longer. *Please, it's too much*, I pleaded, about to pull away. The Mori shifted, and the flow of sensations began to lessen until they became a trickle. We were still touching, but I was no longer overwhelmed by its emotions, which allowed me to start exploring our connection. The first thing I discovered was the intelligence of the demon. It had always felt like a mindless beast, lacking rational thought, and even when I had spoken to it yesterday, its halting speech had made me see it as less intelligent than I was. But I realized now that its lack of communication was due to it just not knowing how to talk to me, since I had shut it away for most of my life.

The second thing I found was a pulsing energy I had never felt before. Dark and coiled, it was almost frightening in its intensity and so different than my other power. Whereas my Fae power healed, this power felt angry, destructive. I knew instinctively that this was the essence of the Mori demon and the place from which all Mohiri drew their strength. Curiously, I opened our connection more to draw a delicate thread of it toward me, and the demon let it go willingly. I felt a rush of energy like pure adrenaline, and I took a deep breath, marveling at the strength coursing through me. If this was from our thin connection, I could not imagine what it felt like to become one with the demon the way Nikolas did.

"This is . . . incredible." For the first time I understood how Nikolas was able to fight all those vampires at once.

"What do you feel?"

I opened my eyes, beaming. "I feel strong, like I could lift a car."

He smirked. "I think we should start with something a bit smaller. See that small weight over there? It weighs forty pounds. Do you think you can lift that?"

"Do you think I'm that weak? I can lift forty pounds."

"Yes, but how easily? Can you do it with one hand?"

I stood and walked over to the weights, stopping by the smallest one, a cast-iron kettlebell. Bending at the knees, I grasped the handle in my right hand and straightened up. The weight lifted about a foot off the floor before I lowered it back down with a grunt. "I don't get it. I feel like I should be able to pick it up."

"You are feeling your Mori's power, but you aren't actually tapped into it yet. In order to do that, you have to work with the Mori instead of trying to take from it."

"You mean merge with it like you do?" I asked, hearing fear slip into my voice.

"Eventually you'll do that, but it's not necessary for this exercise. Right now, I want you to stop touching the Mori and let it reach out to you instead. Open yourself a little, and your Mori will know what to do. You already know you can control the demon, so don't be afraid of it. Let it in."

Sure, easy for him to say. I pulled away from the Mori and immediately my mind felt quieter and calmer without all the extra emotions of the demon's energy. *Okay, let's do this,* I said to the Mori that seemed more at ease with me now. It appeared to know what I wanted, but it moved toward me slowly as if it was unsure of what to do. The moment it reached me, its natural instinct seemed to kick in, and it began to stretch and press itself against my mind. I could hear it asking me to let it in, and taking a deep breath, I opened to it.

Tendrils of the demon's power reached into my mind while others stretched along my spine and down my arms and legs, fusing with my muscles and strengthening my bones. I fought the urge to push it away and concentrated on studying it instead, observing how different it was from my scorching Fae power. This power made me feel physically strong and agile, and it was a heady sensation.

My hand reached for the weight again, and this time I lifted it with more ease. It was still heavier than I'd expected it to be, but the fact that I stood there holding a forty-pound weight in one hand awed me. I let it drop and jumped in the air. "Yes!"

I spun to grin at Nikolas. "Did you see that? That was awesome!"

"Very good. You learn fast." He had his trainer face on, but I could hear a note of pride in his voice. "Now, I want you to do that again five more times, with each hand."

I did as he asked, and by the time I finished, a fine sheen of sweat covered my brow. I wiped it away with my sleeve and looked at him triumphantly.

He nodded in approval. "Tired yet?"

"A little," I lied.

He got up and walked over to me, then bent and lifted a larger kettlebell as if it weighed nothing. "This one is sixty pounds. Think you can lift it?"

I chewed on my lip. "I don't know."

He laid the weight on the floor again. "If you need more strength, you just need to ask your Mori to give you more."

"More?" My body hummed with the strange power filling it. I didn't know if I could handle more than that.

"If you're not up to it, it's okay."

I knew what he was doing, and still I let myself be goaded. "No, I can do it," I said to him as I told the demon what I needed. Within seconds, I felt more power flowing into my body. I bent and gripped the handle of the heavier weight and tried to lift it off the ground. It might as well have been welded to the floor. I huffed and tried two more times, barely moving it each time. "I can't," I finally admitted, straightening to look at him.

"Lesson number one, demon strength is expendable. You use it up and you will need to let it replenish, just like your own energy."

"But you never get tired."

One corner of his mouth lifted. "I do, but it takes a lot more than lifting weights, and I have been doing this a long time." He went to the largest weight, which judging by its size was at least one hundred and fifty pounds, and hefted it in one hand. "Lesson number two, using your demon strength takes practice. Don't expect to lift cars any time soon."

"Show off," I muttered, and he chuckled.

"You'll get there. It just takes time." He laid the weight on the floor again. "You've already come a long way for your second lesson."

"Really?"

His eyes were sincere. "Yes."

I looked at the sixty-pound weight. "I want to try it again."

"You've done enough for now."

"You don't think I can do it."

"I know you can't." He let out a small laugh. I opened my mouth to argue, but he shook his head. "You might not realize it yet, but this is more strenuous than it seems and you'll feel it later. You don't want to overdo it."

"So, are we done training for now?"

He sat and pointed at the seats next to him. "We'll take a short break, and then I want to try something new."

I joined him, not sure if I wanted to know what he had in store for me. So far he had been careful not to push me too hard, but we had definitely moved out of my comfort zone. Still, I'd had more progress with my Mori after two days training with Nikolas than weeks with Callum. Despite Nikolas's mood changes, I was more comfortable talking to him, and it felt like I'd known him a lot longer than three months.

"Can I ask you something?" I said after several minutes of quiet. "You know all about my life, but you never talk about yours. What was it like where you grew up? Where is your family now?"

He leaned back and rested his arms on the backs of the seats on either side of him. "I grew up in a military stronghold just outside Saint Petersburg. Miroslav Fortress is nothing like Westhorne. It's surrounded by high stone walls and run more like a military base, although there were a number of families like mine there. My parents were advisors to the Council and very involved in planning military operations, so it was necessary for us to live there instead of in one of the family compounds."

"It doesn't sound like a fun place to live." I couldn't imagine spending my life confined by walls that blocked everything but the sky. The picture in my mind matched the one I had of the Mohiri when I first heard about them, of living in barracks focused on nothing but hunting.

"It was actually a very good life, and we had a lot more luxuries and conveniences than most people had at the time. Back then, even the wealthy didn't have running water, indoor plumbing, or indoor gas lighting, just to name a few." His eyes took on a faraway look as he recalled the details of his childhood. "My parents were busy and travelled a lot, but they were very loving, and one of them always stayed home while the other travelled. They pushed me hard in my training and schoolwork, but I knew they were preparing me for the dangers I would face when I became a warrior."

"So, you're an only child?"

"Yes."

"Well, that explains a lot." I smirked, earning a playful scowl. "Did you have many friends? What did you do for fun?"

"I had a few good friends over the years. Most families moved when the parents were transferred to other strongholds and others moved in. I don't think I was ever lonely. I liked to watch the warriors train, and I spent a lot of time hanging around the training grounds. They all taught me how to fight and use weapons. By the time I started formal training, I was so advanced they had to place me with the senior trainees."

Why did that not surprise me? "I bet your parents were very proud of you."

His eyes shone with affection. "They were; they still are."

"You said you were in Russia until you were sixteen and then your family moved to England. Why did you move if you all loved the compound in Russia?"

He looked surprised that I had remembered that detail, which he had shared with me back in Maine. "My sire was asked to assume leadership of a key military compound outside London when its leader was killed in a raid. We lived there for eight years before my parents were asked to help establish several new strongholds in North America. By then, I was a full warrior and I found the wildness of this continent appealing, so I tagged along."

"Where are your parents now?"

"They went back to Russia about fifty years ago. My sire is the leader of Miroslav Fortress now. My mother was offered leadership of another stronghold, but she did not want to be separated from him. I see them at least once a year."

"So, um, what do you do for fun besides killing vampires and bossing people around?"

His eyebrows rose, and I gave him what I thought was my most innocent look. "Come on, you have to do something for fun. Do you read? Watch TV? Knit?"

"I read sometimes." He named a few books by Hemmingway, Vonnegut, and Scott, and it was no surprise they were all about war. He did not care for television or movies, and according to him the best decade for music was the sixties. I laughed when he admitted that he and Chris had been at Woodstock and I tried to imagine them in the bohemian clothes popular at the time. He said he was there because the event attracted a lot of vampires, and most of the attendees were too stoned or drunk or high on love to pay attention to them. I found it impossible to believe that Nikolas or Chris could go anywhere unnoticed, but I kept that observation to myself.

"By the way, why didn't you tell me Chris was my cousin? What if I'd started crushing on him like every other girl back home?" Ugh.

The look he shot me was indecipherable. "You were spooked when you learned what you were, and I thought it was too soon to introduce you to your Mohiri family. If it makes you feel better, Chris didn't know at first either."

"Just promise, no more keeping things from me."

"Ask me anything and I'll give you an honest answer," he said after a short pause, and it made me feel like there were important questions I didn't know to ask.

"You ready to try something different?" he asked after we had been sitting for twenty minutes.

"Like what?"

He turned more toward me. "I've been thinking about what you told me yesterday about your power getting stronger. You were worried it might hurt your demon or another Mohiri, but I don't think it will, at least not intentionally. The bazerats and lamprey demons were in their true form, which made them more vulnerable to your power." He reached over and took my hand in his. "Our demons live inside us and are shielded by our bodies. I think *that*, and the fact that you also have a Mori inside you, is why your power is not flaring up right now."

I held my breath as the truth of his words sank in. He was right; my power was not reacting to him at all. The only thing stirring in me were the tiny butterflies in my stomach from him holding my hand. Tugging my hand from his, I tucked it into my pocket. "Was that what you wanted to try?"

One corner of his mouth quirked. "Not quite. We know your power doesn't react instinctively toward me, but I want to find out if you can use it against me consciously."

"What?" I jumped to my feet and backed away from him. "Are you crazy? I could kill you."

"You won't."

"You don't know that!" An image surfaced of what had been left of the lamprey demon, and I shook my head. "You didn't see what I did to that demon in Boise. If you had, you wouldn't even suggest this."

He stood but didn't move toward me. "I saw the pictures our guys took before they cleaned it up."

I took another step back. "Then why the hell would you ask me to try to do that to you?"

"I'm not asking you to do that." He held up his hands. "Listen to me. I think your power reacts when you are frightened or in danger, and you don't believe it, but you *can* control it. You were in mortal danger when the lamprey demon attacked you and you knew you had to kill or be killed, so you did what you had to do to survive. You may have been afraid when you were in here with the bazerats, but you never really felt like you were in real danger, did you? Not with everyone outside."

I thought about how I'd felt when the bazerat had leapt at me. I'd been scared yes, but afraid for my life? No. All I'd wanted was to subdue them, and I didn't even know they were demons until after the task was complete.

"You've been using your power to heal creatures most of your life and you know how to manipulate it and how to release it in controlled bursts, right?" I nodded. "It's the same power; you just used it offensively with the demons. I think you can learn to use your power as a weapon if you start thinking of it as one and the same."

I chewed the inside of my cheek. I was pretty sure he was right about the power all coming from the same source, and I was excited about the possibility of learning to use it to protect myself. After all, what would be better than a weapon you could carry inside you?

But what if I tried to use it on Nikolas and I couldn't control it? What if I hurt him or worse? The thought of him dying left me cold; the thought of me being the one to end his life sucked the air from my lungs, and I had to remind myself to breathe. "I can't . . . I can't do it . . . " I wheezed, close to hyperventilating.

Nikolas moved so fast he was gripping my shoulders before I could react. His eyes softened to a smoky gray as they captured mine. "This really frightens you, doesn't it?"

I could only nod.

"All the more reason for you to learn to master it. If you don't, it will control you instead, and we both know how much you hate being controlled." His lips curved into a small smile. "You trust me, right?"

I looked past his shoulder, wondering how he could ask that after everything we had been through. "Yes."

"And I trust you with my life."

My eyes snapped back to his and met his unwavering gaze.

"I trust you, Sara, and I know you won't hurt me."

"Yes, but – "

"You were afraid to connect with your Mori at first, but you did it and now you no longer fear it. This is no different." His hands left my shoulders and ran down my arms to take my hands and lay my palms against his chest. I could feel his slow steady heartbeat under my fingers, telling me with more than words how confident he was in me. "Start slow and see what happens. You can pull away anytime you need to."

"Okay," I agreed shakily. "But not here." I was not going to take a chance of something going wrong so close to his heart. Lifting my hands from his chest, I took one of his hands in both of mine, acutely aware of the rough texture of his palm against mine. I opened my power and let it slowly fill my hands but didn't try to push into him. He stood, unmoving, showing no signs he felt anything out of the ordinary.

"Do you feel anything?" I asked him, and he shook his head. I turned it up a notch and asked him again. Still nothing. More power pooled in my hands and they began to emit a soft glow. It was enough power to mend a dog's broken leg yet Nikolas didn't even twitch a muscle.

"Your hands feel warmer. What are you doing?" he asked, and I explained how I was directing power to them as I would for a healing.

I released his hand. "I don't think this is going to work. I only know how to heal things, and I don't know what I did to those demons."

"Hmmm." He stared over my head for a moment before he gave me a smile that made me wary. "Your offensive power only surfaces when there is a demon nearby, but it doesn't sense my Mori."

"That's a good thing though, right?" At least I could rest knowing I wouldn't hurt another Mohiri.

"It is as long as we keep our demons restrained, but what happens if we allow them closer to the surface." Something in his voice made me nervous and I tried to pull away, but he grabbed my hands again

"Nikolas, whatever you are thinking is a really bad idea." I gasped as his eyes began to shimmer like pools of liquid silver. I stared into them like a moth mesmerized by flame, and it wasn't until my Mori came roaring awake and straining against its walls that I was able to break free of their spell. It was all I could do to restrain my own demon that fought to get closer to Nikolas's.

It wasn't until I had wrangled my Mori back under control that I realized it wasn't the only thing that had awakened. *No, no, no,* I wailed silently as the first sparks of static crackled through my hair. I reached for the runaway magic and pulled it back inside me with more ease than I had expected. It felt wild and exhilarating compared to the tame healing power I knew so well, and for several seconds I was tempted to let it go free, to see what it could do.

Strength I didn't know I possessed filled me, and I tore my hands from Nikolas's and backed away from him. Surprise flickered on his face before he began to stalk me silently, his intent clear in his eyes. What the hell was wrong with him? Didn't he realize how much I could hurt him right now?

"Nikolas, please stop," I pleaded as he continued to advance on me. "I don't want to do this. I don't want to hurt you."

Instead of answering, he blurred out of sight. A second later, I screamed as hands gripped my shoulders from behind. I knew it was him, but instinct took over and the power I had just reigned in lashed out at him. The Mori surged forward, and I cried out as I latched onto my power at the last second to keep the brunt of it from hitting him. I smelled ozone a split second before there was a crackling pop, followed by something crashing into the wooden seats behind me.

I spun around, and my heart stuttered when I saw Nikolas sprawled unmoving on the floor. "Nikolas!"

In seconds, I was at kneeling at his side, shaking him roughly. "Nikolas, wake up! Oh God, please don't be dead." He didn't move, and I pressed my ear to his chest, swallowing back a sob when I heard his heartbeat and felt his chest rise and fall. I rose over him and peered at his closed eyes and slightly parted lips that made him look like he was merely sleeping. He was alive, but I had no idea what my power had done to him. My chest squeezed painfully until I could barely breathe.

His lids flickered open and his smoky gaze locked with mine, making the breath catch in my throat. Before I could find my voice, he gave me a lazy smile. "I said you could do it."

"You jerk! You . . . you asshole!" I punched his chest hard and scrambled to my feet. Angry tears burned the back of my throat as I ran toward the door. To think I had been worried about hurting him. If I wasn't afraid I'd actually kill him this time, I'd turn around and give him a real dose of my power.

"Umph!" I grunted when I ran smack into his chest. Too angry to speak or look at him, I tried to move around him, but he grabbed me before I could get past him.

"Sara, we needed to test your power to see if you can use it at will, and now we know."

"At will?" I blazed at him. "I almost fried your ass! If I hadn't pulled it back in time, you'd be singing a different tune. No, actually, you'd probably be dead."

"But you did control it, as I knew you would. You want to know how I knew that?"

He let go of my arms, and I crossed them to keep from throttling him. "Please, educate me."

"I know because if there is one thing I have learned about you it's that you are incapable of hurting someone – unless they are trying to hurt you or someone you care about." He gave me one of his infuriating smiles. "Then all bets are off."

Feeling my anger abate under the force of his smile, I looked away from him. I used to watch Roland and some of the other boys back home using sweet words and boyish grins to charm girls, but Nikolas was in a whole different league. "You scared the hell out of me," I said, unable to keep a note of hurt out of my voice. "I thought . . . "

"I'm sorry. I didn't want to frighten you, but the only way to get you to show your power was to expose you to a demon and to put you on the defensive. Now we know what you can do and we can work with that, and teach you to call on it when you need it."

I shook my head fervently. "I am *never* doing that again."

"Not that, no," he replied calmly, ignoring my outburst. "We won't have to try anything that drastic next time."

"Next time? What part of *never* do you not understand?" I practically shouted at him.

His eyebrows rose. "So you refuse to use your power on me again, no matter what I do?"

"That's right."

"And how will you stop it?"

I knew he was trying to trick me somehow, but I couldn't stop from asking, "What do you mean?"

"If I bring my Mori out again and come after you, what's to stop your power from attacking me again?"

"*I* will stop it."

"How?"

So much for his faith in me. "I just will, okay? I know what it is now, and I won't let it get away from me again."

He did not respond, and my words hung in the silence between us until the full meaning of what I'd said hit me. That sneaky bastard! He had planned this all along.

"So now that we have that settled, why don't we try something easy that doesn't involve throwing me across the room?" He looked entirely too self-satisfied for someone who had just gotten his butt kicked. "If you are up for it, that is."

Damn him. He knew I would not back down from a challenge like that. I turned and stomped back to the center of the arena. "Fine, but don't blame me if I knock you on your butt again. And you owe me for making me believe I killed you."

Nikolas's husky laughter followed me. "Okay. What do you want?"

I watched him walk toward me and smiled. "I need to go into town this week to pick up a bunch of stuff for Oscar before he gets here." I had a suspicion Nikolas had never been inside a pet store, let alone picked out kitty litter. Maybe those muscles would come in handy.

His brows drew together. "Oscar?"

"My cat. Nate is bringing him when he comes for Thanksgiving."

"Oh." I could tell by his expression he had expected me to ask for something bigger than a ride to the pet store. Maybe next time I'd think up something more impressive.

We spent the next hour working on my ability to summon my defensive power. It wasn't easy to stimulate it without a demon nearby, and I flatly refused to let Nikolas use his as bait again. After forty minutes, I started to get a feel for it and managed to send a few sparks flying from my fingertips. Nikolas made me concentrate on that until I started to tire and my stomach began to growl. I didn't admit it, but I was pleased by my progress by the time we broke for lunch.

"When do you want to go into town?" Nikolas asked, opening the door for me.

"Can we go this weekend?" I asked eagerly. I had plans this afternoon.

"I think we can arrange that."

Thinking of my afternoon plans reminded me I hadn't thanked him for what he had done for the hellhounds. "Chris told me you were the one who had Hugo and Woolf sent here. Thank you for doing that."

"You don't have to thank me. They belong with you."

A companionable silence settled over us as we walked across the grounds, but it was broken when Nikolas muttered, "That boy is going to cut his own head off."

I followed his gaze to Michael who was swinging a slender sword in an unsteady arc as he practiced some moves near the edge of the trees. As if he sensed our eyes on him, Michael stopped mid-swing and stared at Nikolas in awe before he looked away shyly.

I watched Michael thoughtfully and let out a quiet sigh. "Can I exchange the trip into town for something else?"

Nikolas stopped walking and gave me a questioning look. "You don't want to go into town?"

"I do, but I want something more now."

Interest sparkled in his eyes. "All right, let's have it."

"I want you to teach Michael not to cut off his head." Nikolas gave me a puzzled look, and I shrugged. "He needs a lesson in sword fighting a lot more than I need a ride to town. Besides, you have no idea how much this will mean to him. He looks up to you a lot."

Nikolas looked at Michael, and his gaze was unreadable when it returned to me. For a moment, I thought he was going to say no. "If that's what you want."

"It is," I replied, and I meant it.

"Okay, I'll see what I can do for him, but no promises. And I'll still take you into town."

I imagined Michael's excitement when Nikolas offered to work with him, and I couldn't restrain myself. I threw my arms around Nikolas's waist and gave him a quick hug. "Thanks!" Shocked by my actions, I pulled away from him and hurried toward the main building before he could see the hot blush creeping across my cheeks.

*   *   *

"You're serious? You are actually going to take those two monsters for a walk?"

"Don't call them that, Jordan. You saw how good they are with me. They're like big puppies."

Water sprayed across the table and a few drops landed on my face. I wiped them away as Jordan grabbed a napkin to clean herself up. "You have one twisted imagination if you think those mons – er – brutes are like puppies. I'm starting to think there is something way off about you, Sara"

"Scared?"

"Not." Her lips curved into a pretty smirk. "Despite your weirdness, your cluelessness when it comes to men, and your complete lack of fashion sense, I still believe there is hope for you. Besides, you are the only other female here I can actually be around for more than an hour."

I plucked a grape from my fruit bowl and threw it at her. "You keep insulting me and you can find someone else to play dress up with." Not that I had any intention of allowing her to turn me into her life-sized doll.

"Speaking of dressing up, did your warrior boy see you all prettied up last night?"

I rolled my eyes. "He is not my warrior, and you were totally wrong about him. I might as well have been wearing a pillow case."

"I am never wrong about these things. He is a temperamental one so he was probably in a bad mood. Hell, I thought he was going to rip someone's head off this morning. I almost pitied you having to train with him, but it looks like you survived in one piece."

"Barely."

Chris chose that moment to walk in for lunch, and he smiled and waved at me as he passed us. Jordan's eyes followed him appreciatively for a moment before she looked back at me with a sly smile. "So, Nikolas has some competition, does he?"

The girl never quit. "Chris is my cousin, Jordan."

Her eyes grew round. "Cousin? Why didn't you say something before?"

"I found out last night."

It took her a less than thirty seconds to make the connection. "But he is Tristan's kinsman. Does that mean . . . ?"

"Tristan is my grandfather. His daughter, Madeline, is my mother."

Her eyes grew round. "Holy hell! That is crazy! You found out all of that last night?"

"Tristan told me who he was almost weeks ago. I didn't want people to make a big deal of it, so I asked him to keep it between us for now. I guess it won't be a secret much longer."

"No shit. Talking about winning the orphan lottery."

"I would have settled for not being abandoned by my mother in the first place."

"Mommy issues. Gotcha." Jordan leaned across the table with a gleam in her eyes. "If you are *Lord* Tristan's granddaughter, does that make you a lady or something?"

"God no, or at least I hope not. I'm having trouble just getting used to the idea of having a grandfather who looks a few years older than me."

"Especially one so hot."

"Ugh! Do not even go there."

She burst out laughing, drawing the attention of some of the people around us. It was obvious by their stares that Jordan's laughter was not an everyday occurrence, and they were probably wondering if I had spiked her water or something.

She pursed her lips and studied Chris who was sitting with Seamus and Niall. "Hmm. You know, I've always liked blondes."

I ducked my head to hide my smile. Poor Chris, he thought human girls were aggressive.

"Just the two ladies I wanted to talk to." Terrence stopped at our table carrying his lunch tray. "You girls up for a party Saturday night?"

"A party?" Jordan's eyes lit up. "Will it be better than that one you guys threw last month, where you all got drunk and passed out by midnight?"

"A lot better." He ignored her barb and laid his tray on the table so he could lean down to say in a low voice, "A townie party."

"I'm in," Jordan declared without asking for details.

"Wait. Are we even allowed to go?" After our trip to Boise, I wasn't sure Tristan would let me go anywhere without a bodyguard. A party wouldn't be much fun with one or both of the twins looming in the background.

Terrence smiled. "Josh and I go to Butler Falls all the time, so I doubt anyone would have a problem with it."

"And they can't say no if you don't ask," Jordan added. "That usually works pretty well for me."

"You mean sneak out?" Tristan said they believed the Master thought I was dead so I was safe from that threat, but he was feeling overly protective after the demon attack and I didn't want to worry him.

Jordan snorted. "You so don't strike me as the type to ask permission before you do something."

"It's not that simple. I did some really stupid things before I came here, and I almost got my friends and my uncle killed. I promised Nate I would be more careful."

"Well, it's gonna be a hell of a party," Terrence said. "Our friend, Derek, has a killer pad and he keeps his bar well stocked."

Jordan swung her gaze from me to Terrence. "I'm still in. Anything is better than Saturday night hanging out here."

Terrence straightened and picked up his tray. "Cool, and maybe Sara will change her mind by then."

I watched him walk over to join Josh before I turned to Jordan. "I thought you two couldn't stand each other."

She shrugged one shoulder. "Na, Terrence just knows how to flip my bitch switch and I know how to get a rise out of him. We hooked up once last year, but we both realized that was a huge mistake."

Jordan and Terrance? I speared a piece of pineapple with my fork and chewed it, trying to figure her out. Hanging out with her was like having a friend with multiple personalities; you never knew who was going to show up next.

"Anyway, whether or not you go to the party is probably moot."

"Why?" I asked her.

She gave me a cheeky grin. "Because those two *puppies* of yours are most likely going to eat you today."

Chapter 12

"WHO IS READY for a walk?"

Hugo and Woolf began to whine and run in circles when I unlocked their gate. In their excitement, they looked so much like dogs that I let out a laugh. When the door slid open, they plunked their behinds on the floor as I'd trained them to do whenever I entered their cage. Instead of stepping inside as I always did, I pointed at my feet and said, "Come." The hounds looked confused, so I issued the command again. This time they stood and sauntered toward me, and when they realized they were leaving their cage, their tails began to wag and their mouths opened wide in doggie grins.

"They look like they are about to eat someone," Sahir said over the security intercom from the safety of his office.

I rolled my eyes at the closest camera. "They can't help how they look." With their enormous teeth and red-black eyes, the hellhounds did look anything but harmless, but looks were deceiving. Everyone thought trolls were bloodthirsty creatures, but I'd been friends with Remy for ten years and he was one of the gentlest people I had ever met.

"Tristan had everyone clear away from this area as a precaution, so you are good to go."

"Thanks. Come on, boys." I walked to the exit, and the hounds followed at my heels until I threw open the door and stepped outside into the sunshine. I looked back to find them watching me uncertainly, and I tapped my thigh. "Let's go."

It was all the urging they needed, and I was almost bowled over when they leapt toward me eagerly. They circled me and pushed against me, unable to believe they were free, and I let them have a few minutes of play before I ordered them to stand on either side of me like we had practiced. When we set off across the lawn toward the woods, I was aware of the people watching us from the windows of the main building and I resisted the urge to look at them. Word of the hellhounds had finally spread. Now everyone was watching to see how this would play out, and I was sure that more than one of them expected a bad outcome. We'd show them.

Despite my determination to prove everyone wrong, it felt good to walk under the canopy of trees and escape the curious stares. Once we were out of sight of the building, I broke into a jog and whistled for the hounds to follow me. It felt amazing to run free, and I enjoyed it as much as they did. For such large animals, they weaved through trees and leapt over large rocks with incredible ease, running ahead of me and circling back when I lagged behind. Once Hugo caught the scent of a fox and set after it, braying like a bloodhound and scaring every creature within a mile. Luckily, the fox escaped. I did not like to see an animal hurt, but I also didn't want to deny the hounds the joy of hunting. They were predators after all, and hunting was a part of their nature.

I had no trouble finding the lake, and I ran down to the rocky shore with the hounds at my heels. They lapped nosily at the cold water, sending ripples across the mirror-like surface. When they were done, they looked at me and began to sniff along the shore. "Don't go too far," I told them, pretty sure they wouldn't let me out of their sights. I let them explore, and I found a dry flat area to lie back on and soak up the sun. The woods were unusually hushed as the birds and small animals hid from the larger threat invading their territory. I missed their calls and scurrying, but it was still very peaceful here.

I had almost dozed off when it struck me that I could no longer hear the hounds moving about. Sitting up, I scanned the shore until I found them a few hundred yards away, sitting side-by-side and staring out over the lake. I whistled but neither of them moved or even looked in my direction. *Strange.* They rarely liked to sit still, even when I commanded them to do it, and I couldn't believe they would do it now with so many things to explore. Unease stole over me, and I got to my feet. Something was not right.

"They are quite safe and content," said a musical voice behind me, and I whirled to face a barefoot red-haired girl in a flowing yellow dress. My mouth fell open, and a smile lit up her angelic face. "Hello, little sister."

"Aine!" I ran the short distance between us and threw my arms around my sylph friend. She laughed softly and hugged me, enveloping me in the incredibly alluring scent of Faerie she carried with her. If you spend any amount of time in that place, its sweet perfume begins to cling to you, something I discovered after my own stay there. The first thing Roland and Peter had said to me when they saw me again was that I smelled like sunshine and something else that even their sharp werewolf noses couldn't identify.

"Sara, it is good to see you, too. You have been making new friends since I last saw you."

I pulled away laughing, still unable to believe she was here. I looked behind me at the hellhounds that were as still as statues. "Are they asleep?"

"They are in a waking dream. In their minds, they are running through the forest, chasing deer. They are quite happy, I assure you." Her eyes twinkled mischievously. "And as for the two red-haired warriors who followed you, they have momentarily forgotten their mission and are guarding the woods as they always do."

"Seamus and Niall followed me?" I should have known Tristan wouldn't let me come out here alone even with two hellhounds to protect me. "They are okay though, right?"

"I have not altered them in any way, and they will remember you again once I lift my magic."

"Okay." I faced her again. "I missed you. I wasn't sure when you would come to see me again."

She smiled and took my hand to lead me over to sit on the grassy bank. "I am sorry. Our kind do not interfere much in the human world anymore. But I am here now, and I want to hear all about you. Are you happy here?"

"It's a lot to get used to, but I'm trying. The people are nice and I have family here. I miss Nate and my friends, but we talk all the time and it's getting easier."

"I am pleased to hear that. Coming to live with your people was the right decision, but I worried that you would not be happy."

I plucked a blade of grass and twisted it around my thumb. "It's certainly not how I expected my life would be. I always thought I would graduate school with my friends and go to college and all that. It's hard letting go of that life, but I'm starting to see the good things in this one, too."

Aine laid a slender arm around my shoulders and gave me a squeeze. "Sometimes it is difficult to see the goodness in your life when you are in turmoil. Just remember that even during a storm, the sun is shining. You may not see it, but it is always there above the clouds, waiting to warm you again."

I cocked an eyebrow at her. "Is that some Faerie proverb?"

Her laugh made me think of wind chimes. "Just some sisterly wisdom. Now tell me about your magic. I can feel that it has grown since we last parted."

I'd been longing to see Aine for weeks to ask her about my new ability. Telling her about it now was like lifting a huge weight from my shoulders. She listened intently as I described the strange power surges and my experiences with the demons. She nodded in approval when I told her about my earlier training with Nikolas.

A smile broke over her face when I finished. "This is exciting and wonderful news, sister! Your elemental magic is growing, which I suspected it would. Do not fear this. It is a good thing."

I almost slumped in relief. "Why is it suddenly acting up now? Did being in Seelie trigger something in me?"

"That is part of it, but it has accelerated because of the demons. You are surrounded by them here, and even though they reside inside a host, their nearness is causing your magic to emerge. The more contact you have with demons, the more your power will grow."

I stared at her in alarm. "What does that mean? My power already killed one demon, and it would have hurt Nikolas if I hadn't stopped it. I don't want to hurt any of the Mohiri. And what about my own demon? Will my power kill it, too?" There had been a time when I would have been happy to be free of the beast in my head, but I didn't feel that way anymore. I felt a swell of protectiveness for my Mori.

Aine's red curls bounced when she gave a delicate shake of her head. "I have not met another like you, so I honestly cannot say what will happen. But I do believe that being half Mohiri, you pose no real danger to your people. As for your own demon, it has lived with your Fae magic its whole life so it may be safe. Only time will tell."

Her words did not give me the assurance I was looking for. "Nikolas said those other demons were in their true forms so my power affected them more. But I healed an imp last year when it got caught in a mouse trap, and it didn't flip out when it got near me."

"Your power was very weak then, but it has grown a lot since I last saw you. You would not be able to touch one of them now without killing it, until you learn to control your power."

"So I'll be able to control it and only use it when I want to?"

"Yes."

"I'm so glad to hear that." I would have to be very careful with the imps until it was safe to go near them. Maybe I should find them a new home. They wouldn't like it, but it wasn't like they would be happy there once Oscar arrived. My cat's favorite pastime was trying to catch the little fiends.

I brushed pieces of grass off my legs. "What about the cold feeling in my chest? Is that caused by my elemental power?"

"That I do not know." She pursed her lips in thought for a moment. "We were unsure of how your body would react to the vampire blood it absorbed. This might be a side effect."

"Great. I just hope I don't wake up one of these mornings with a little vampire demon bursting out of my chest."

"That is not how vampires are made."

I shook my head and smiled at her bemused expression. "It was a joke."

Aine scrunched up her nose and still somehow managed to look angelic. "Humor in this world is very strange." She smoothed out the folds of her dress then laid her hands in her lap. "I did not come only to visit you, sister. If you had been raised among us, you would have learned all you needed to know about your magic by now. It is my duty to teach you what you need to know."

My breath hitched in anticipation. "Like what?"

She stood and beckoned for me to follow her. We walked to the water's edge, and she told me to wade into the lake. I did not question her; I pulled off my hiking boots and socks and rolled my jeans up to my knees. Then I stepped into the frigid water until it was halfway up my calves.

"I am a sylph so I can control the air and draw on its power. You are undine, which means you can do the same with water in any form. You can also communicate with any creature that lives in water. "

"What kind of creatures?" I peered at the glassy surface of the lake and tried to imagine what sorts of things could be down there. If Aine had not been with me, my overactive imagination would have sent me scrambling out of the water.

Aine smiled as if she had read my mind. "I promise you, you have nothing to fear from anything in this lake. Call to them and I will prove it to you."

Curiosity overcame my nervousness. "How do I call them?"

"Send your magic out into the water and use it the way you would to summon an animal."

"I don't summon animals; I use my power to calm them."

"It is the same thing."

"Oh." I called on my power, but instead of releasing it into the air, I let it flow from my feet into the water. Looking down, I gasped at the sparkling golden cloud spreading outwards through the water. It was like looking into a beautiful snow globe. "Wow! Do you see that?"

"Water not only strengthens you and deepens your magic, it also shows your magic's true form," Aine said softly.

I wiggled my toes and found the water around my feet to be a few degrees warmer than it had been when I stepped into the lake. I raised my eyes to Aine's amused ones. "This is incredible!"

Something tickled my foot, and I stared down in surprise at the long speckled trout nibbling on my toes. It was joined by a second trout, then a third, and within a minute there were dozens of them swimming around my feet.

The water began to ripple a few yards away, and the trout darted away as something big approached. I stared in shock as it broke the surface and a long black head emerged from the water. *Kelpie!* I wanted to run, but my feet were rooted to the spot as the horse-like creature rose up to tower over me. It was midnight black with a long flowing mane and tail. My breath caught, and I took a step back when the kelpie looked me in the eye and began moving toward me.

"Do not be afraid, sister; you have nothing to fear. This is Feeorin. He and his brother, Fiannar, are guardians of the lakes and rivers in this valley, and they have watched over you since you moved here. Feeorin is very curious about you, and he comes to greet you."

The kelpie stopped when its muzzle was inches from my head, and I could feel its hot breath on my face. Despite Aine's assurances, I tensed, waiting for it to grab me and try to pull me beneath the surface and drown me, because that is what kelpies supposedly do. Seconds passed like hours until Feeorin bowed his head and nudged my shoulder gently. I looked back at Aine, who nodded at me. Then I reached up to touch his wide forehead. The kelpie snorted softly and butted me again until I began to stroke its face and neck.

"Hello, Feeorin." My voice trembled in awe. I could not believe I was touching a real live kelpie. Two years ago, I'd helped Remy find medicine for a sick kelpie, but I hadn't gone near the creature because of how dangerous they are to humans. Now I was standing here petting one.

Feeorin raised his head, and his large black eyes stared into mine for a long moment before he bowed again and returned to the lake. When the water reached his back, he gave a soft ninny and sank beneath the surface. I watched the spot where he had disappeared until the ripples stopped moving along the surface of the water.

"Kelpies do not linger long above water. That Feeorin stayed as long as he did is a sign of the esteem he has for you." Aine practically glowed. "He recognized you as an undine, which means I was right; your Fae side is definitely stronger than your demon side."

I did not ask her what would have happened if the kelpie hadn't recognized me as Fae.

"Now it is time for you to learn to control water." I must have made a face because she laughed. "Do not fret; we will start with something easy. I will show you how I make the air move, and then you can try it with the water."

She went to stand beneath the trees, facing me. Then she raised a hand and moved it in a small circular motion. On the ground, leaves and twigs began to flutter and dance, forming a column that stretched upward toward her hand. "To do this you do not need to release your magic like you did to summon the water creatures. Water is your element so you simply draw on its power and then command it to do your bidding."

Oh, is that all? "How do I do that?"

"Everything in nature has a life force, an energy that flows through it, and it is the same power you have inside you. If you look for that power outside instead of within yourself, you will find it."

I did as she instructed and felt around outside my body for a power like mine. I knew what I was looking for and what it should feel like, but either I was doing it wrong or I could not draw on the power like she could. After a few minutes, I looked at her in defeat. "It's not working."

Aine pursed her lips and thought for a moment before her green eyes lit up. "You need more contact with the water. Sit in the lake and try again."

"Sit in it? This water is freaking cold!"

"It is the only way," she said, brushing aside my objections. "Once you do it a few times, you will need only to use a finger, but for now more of your body must touch the water."

I just had to be a water elemental. I pulled off my hoodie and threw it on dry land – not that a dry hoodie was going to help much when my bottom half was soaked. Grimacing, I lowered my body until I was sitting in the cold lake with water lapping at my stomach. "C-can an undine g-get hypothermia?" I asked through chattering teeth.

Aine let out one of her musical laughs. "No, and the sooner you learn to draw on the water magic, the sooner it will warm you."

That was all the motivation I needed. I laid my hands on my thighs beneath the water and began feeling for magic around me. It was hard not to reach for my own power, and to ignore the cold seeping into my bones. I pictured glowing energy infused with each water molecule, and then I imagined pulling all that warm energy toward me. I concentrated on only that, and after a few minutes, my imaginings grew so vivid that I no longer felt the cold.

"Look, sister!"

I didn't realize I had closed my eyes until Aine spoke, and when I opened them, my gaze was drawn immediately to the soft glow outlining my body beneath the surface. My first thought was that I had accidently released my power – until I saw what had to be thousands of golden sparkles drifting through the water toward me like tiny underwater fireflies. Mesmerized, I watched the particles join the ones clinging to me and the golden aura around me grow brighter. I waved my right hand slowly through the water and saw with delight that the magic followed it. I also noticed that the water offered little resistance, and my hand might as well have been moving through the air. Mimicking Aine's actions, I started moving my hand in a circular motion, and a dazzling spiral of magic formed in the water. I picked up speed until I had made a mini whirlpool, and then I lifted my hand from the water, still moving it in a circle. My eyes widened and I sucked in a sharp breath as a spinning column of water formed between my hand and the surface of the lake. *I'm dreaming. I can't really be doing this.*

Clapping broke my concentration, and the tiny waterspout collapsed with a small splash. I looked over my shoulder at Aine, grinning so wide that my cheeks hurt. "Did I really do that?"

"Yes." She walked to the water's edge where I could see her better, and her face glowed with pride. "You are indeed Sahine's progeny, and she would be so proud of you."

"That was awesome! Can I do it again?"

"You may do it as many times as you wish" – her eyes gleamed with mischief – "if you are not too cold to continue."

"Nope, I'm nice and toasty." It was true. The water around me felt as warm as bathwater now, and I could sit in it all day.

Aine settled down on the shore and spread her skirts around her. "I'll be here as long as you want to do this."

For the next two hours, I played with the water, making bigger and bigger spouts and whirlpools, small waves that broke against the shore, and even a plume of water that rose ten feet in the air and sprinkled down on us like rain. I marveled over each new trick, still unable to believe that I was the one doing it. The best part was that I never tired because I was using the water's power instead of my own. If only my Mori powers came to me as naturally as this.

It was with great reluctance that I finally stood and released the power around me. My hands were wrinkled and white from being in the water so long, and my dripping clothes clung to me as I joined Aine on the shore. It was going to be a cold walk home, but I didn't care because I'd just had the most amazing afternoon and I was happier than I had been in a long time.

Aine came over to take my hands in hers. "You did very well today, sister."

"It was unbelievable," I said, struggling to come up with a better word to describe the experience.

"I am glad you enjoyed it. Now let's take care of this." She waved a hand and my clothes were instantly dry.

"That is a cool trick." I sat down to pull on my socks and boots and saw that the sun had started dipping toward the west. "I wish I didn't have to leave yet, but they will come looking for me if I don't get back soon. When will I see you again?"

"When you have mastered your water magic, I will come back. I do not like to stay long in this world anymore."

"You could visit me at home," I said hopefully.

She smiled and shook her head. "It is safe for you to walk among the Mohiri because you are half demon. I am a full Fae, and it would cause chaos if I appeared among so many Mori demons."

"What would happen?"

"They would be confused, afraid, and very angry. Most Mohiri go their entire lives without meeting a Fae, and they would not be able to handle their demons' reaction to one. I do not think your people would be too happy about that."

I winced at the thought of dozens of Mohiri warriors thrown into a Fae-induced rage. "No, definitely not."

She hugged me. "I will see you soon, little sister," she said stepping back. She smiled and waved, and just like that, she was gone.

The next time I see her, I gotta ask how she does that.

Running feet alerted me to the hounds approach. They were panting and happy like they had spent the afternoon running around instead of sitting by the lake. I felt a stab of guilt for having so much fun while they were in a dream state, but they did not look any worse for it. To make up for some of it, we spent another fifteen minutes at the lake before I told them it was time to go home. It was very unlikely we'd encounter anything this close to a Mohiri stronghold that two hellhounds could not handle.

When we walked out of the woods just before dusk, I spotted Nikolas and Chris standing near the main building, facing the woods, and I knew they were watching for my return. I was pretty sure that if I'd waited ten minutes longer before coming back, I would have met the two of them in the woods.

I was changing for dinner an hour later when I heard someone outside my door. When I went to see who it was, I found an envelope that had been slipped under the door. As soon as I picked it up, I recognized the stationary. Smiling, I unfolded the paper inside and read the message written in his elegant handwriting.

I would be pleased if you would join me for dinner at seven this evening in the library. Desmund.

I stared at the note for a long moment. Desmund was inviting me to dinner? The same Desmund who had thrown a fit when I trespassed in his library less than two weeks ago? It amazed me how much he had changed in such a short time. The night we met, I thought he was the most unreasonable person ever, and now I looked forward to spending time with him.

Music greeted me as I approached the library, and I recognized it from the Beethoven CD Desmund had sent me. Inside, there was no sign of him, but I found a small table set for two near the hearth and a side table holding several covered dishes that smelled amazing and made my stomach growl.

"Sara, I am glad you could make it. I was not sure if you had already made plans for this evening."

I turned to greet Desmund, and I was so surprised by the change in his appearance that I almost forgot to speak. He was impeccably groomed and wearing brown trousers and a beige jacket, looking every bit the English noble. But it was not his attire that shocked me; it was the color in his complexion and the warm easy smile he gave me. He still looked ill but so much improved since the last time I'd seen him. Was it possible that the small healing a few nights ago had affected him like this?

"Well, I did have to turn down all my other invitations, but they'll get over it," I said when I had found my voice again.

His smile faltered. "Oh, I did not mean to make you cancel your plans for me."

"Desmund, I'm kidding. If you hadn't invited me to dinner, I would have come to see you tonight anyway. You owe me a checkers rematch, remember?"

I knew I'd said exactly the right thing when his mouth curved smugly and a gleam entered his dark eyes. "Indeed I do. Let us enjoy the meal the kitchen prepared for us, and then we shall have our rematch."

He pulled out a chair for me, insisting that I sit while he served us since he was the host. He seemed to be enjoying himself so I obliged him even though I felt a little silly being catered to. I started to say he shouldn't have gone through any trouble for me, but then I realized that he must have all his meals brought to him since he did not venture downstairs. I guessed that Tristan visited him sometimes, but still it had to be lonely eating alone up here most of the time.

"Here we are." He laid a plate of lamb chops, rosemary potatoes, and vinaigrette salad in front of me then sat across from me with his own meal. It was a lot fancier than the food I normally ate, but I had a feeling it was standard fare for Desmund.

"Wine?" He held up a bottle of red wine, and I politely declined. "How are lessons with your new trainer?" he asked as he cut into his lamb chops.

"Better than I expected. I used my Mori strength to pick up a forty-pound weight with one hand this morning. I've never been able to do anything like that." Desmund didn't know anything about my Fae heritage, so I couldn't tell him about the rest of my training.

"So working with Nikolas is not as bad as you had feared?"

"I guess not," I admitted reluctantly. "He is helping me, even if I do still feel like clobbering him half the time."

He laughed, and I was struck again by how different he seemed, relaxed and confident. I wished I could tell him about my incredible afternoon at the lake, but I still didn't know him well enough to trust him with such a secret.

"Desmund, the last time I was here, you mentioned that you and Nikolas go way back and I got the impression you don't like each other. Can I ask why?"

His expression became shuttered and I thought he was not going to answer. Then the ghost of a smile settled on his face. "Nikolas is one of the greatest warriors of this age, but there was a time when I held that distinction. I led hundreds of missions across Europe, and my kill rate was unmatched by anyone.

"I was leading a team to deal with a vampire problem in Glasgow when we encountered another team led by this upstart young Russian warrior, barely out of training. I told him we had the situation under control and he could turn around and go home, but young Nikolas did not take kindly to my words." Desmund's smile turned into a smirk. "Perhaps I said something about him not being old enough to leave his mother's teat. Needless to say, we did not sit down to a drink together after the job was done."

In the short time I had known Desmund I had already formed a picture of the arrogant and sardonic man he had been before the Hale witch attack. I could only just imagine the fireworks when he and Nikolas had butted heads, having had some firsthand experience with Nikolas.

"You two never got along because of that?"

Desmund chuckled. "Oh, that was nothing. We had a few other clashes over the next few years that were even better. It actually got quite boring over there when he decided to travel to America."

I shook my head. "Somehow I doubt it ever got boring where you were."

"True," he replied with a cocky shrug. He took a sip of wine, and we ate quietly for a minute before he said he had heard about the excitement downstairs yesterday. After that I had to describe the whole kark incident in detail for him.

"I found out last night that I have a cousin here. Do you know Chris . . . Christian . . . um . . . shoot, I don't even know his last name."

"It is Kent, same as Tristan," he supplied.

"I thought Tristan's last name was Croix – like Madeline's."

Desmund scowled lightly. "Ah, Madeline. Never cared much for that one. I cannot conceive how a good man like Tristan could have sired a child as selfish and troublesome as her. Croix was her mother's maiden name, and Madeline took it when she left here."

"She hurt Tristan a lot when she left." It was not a question; I saw flashes of hurt in Tristan's eyes every time he mentioned her.

"Madeline was a fine warrior, but she thought that having Tristan as a father meant she was entitled to certain privileges and that she was above following the rules set down for everyone else. Tristan finally set her straight, and she ran off rather than change her ways. Too much like Elena, that one."

"You knew Elena? Tristan told me what happened to her."

There was no warmth in his laugh. "Tristan remembers Elena with the love of a brother and to him, she was spoiled and spirited, but good at heart. I remember her differently. Even at sixteen, Elena was a manipulative little thing, always scheming and trying to wrap every male she knew around her finger. Fortunately, her wiles did not work on me."

"Why not?"

"She wasn't my type." He wore his usual smirk when he picked up his wine glass. I sensed there was a story behind that statement, but he wasn't going to share it. I tried to imagine what he was like before he was attacked by the Hale witch. With his good looks and the charm I saw glimpses of, he must have been quite the ladies' man.

"Have you ever been in love?" As soon as the question left my lips I wanted to take it back. He had suffered so much, and the last thing I wanted to do was remind him of a past love. "I'm sorry; I shouldn't have asked you that."

He set his wine glass on the table and stared at it like he was seeing into his past. "I was in love once or twice, or I thought I was. It was so long ago that I really can't say anymore. What about you? Have you been in love?"

"No. I had a crush on a boy once but nothing happened. And there was a guy I liked a few months ago but . . . "

"He did not return your affection?"

I toyed with my fork. "We had one date – if you could call it that – and he wanted to go out again, but I'd just found out what I was and I didn't think it was right to start a relationship with a human."

Desmund nodded in understanding and thankfully did not push the subject. He laid his utensils across his plate. "I am sorry that I forgot to ask for a dessert. I don't usually eat them myself."

"That's okay. I probably couldn't eat much more anyway." I pushed back my chair and stood. "Why don't we have that rematch instead?"

A familiar gleam entered his eyes. "With pleasure."

We walked over to the small table by the window, and I found a game already set up on the board I had left for him the last time I was here. We sat across from each other, neither of us saying anything about the new board or the fate of the old one. There was a lot I still didn't know about Desmund's illness, and it was possible that he did not remember thrashing the library. He was doing so well tonight, and the last thing I wanted to do was upset him by bringing up something so unpleasant.

Two games later, three things were very clear to me. The first was that I would never defeat Desmund in checkers. The second was that the more I got to know him, the happier I was to have him as a friend. The third was that his health had not improved as much as I'd thought. After several hours together, he began to show signs of strain: his eyes grew overly bright, and though he kept smiling, he could not hide the tremble in his hands when he reached for his checkers. I realized what an effort it must be for him to hide his constant pain and inner turmoil for so long. He chose to stay up here, shut off from almost everyone else, not because he did not like people, but because it was too hard to conceal his condition. He was a proud man who had once been a great warrior, and it must be agony for him to endure this weakness of his mind and body.

I had no way to know if my healing had done him any good, but I wanted to try it again. The problem was that I couldn't just reach over and take his hand or touch his arm without giving him the wrong idea. All I needed was for Desmund to think I was hitting on him. Talk about the last person who should be getting mixed signals.

"Another match?"

"Actually, I'd love to hear you play the piano again – if you want to, that is." He'd gotten so wrapped up in his music the last time that I'd been able to do a healing without his being any the wiser. Maybe I could do it again.

Some of the weariness left his face. "What would you like to hear?"

"Surprise me."

He stood and held out his arm. I took it, and we went down the hall to the music room. We sat together on the bench, and Desmund began to play a darker piece full of dramatic sweeps that seemed to echo his emotional state. It wasn't anything I'd heard before and I found it a bit depressing, but he lost himself in the music, which made it possible for me to do my thing.

This time when I opened myself to the Hale witch's magic, I was ready for the cold blast of nausea that hit me. Gritting my teeth, I braced myself and drew the dark magic into me until sweat trickled down my back and I was fighting the shivers that tried to wrack my body. When I could take no more, I discreetly pulled away and let my power burn away the witch's magic.

Desmund finished the piece and started another, oblivious to the silent battle being fought beside him. As soon as my heart rate slowed to normal, I formed the connection between us again and siphoned more magic from him. At first, the magic flowed in a steady stream that seemed never-ending, but it eventually began to slow until it was little more than a trickle. Using so much of my power to destroy the foul magic should have exhausted me, but I felt strangely invigorated after my afternoon in the lake.

Desmund played two more pieces before I saw that he was tiring. There was definitely more color in his cheeks again, but it occurred to me he was probably beginning to feel the same lethargy that most creatures experience after a big healing. Not that he would ever admit to being tired.

I put up my hand to cover a fake yawn, and he stopped playing. "Sleepy, little one?"

"Sorry, all this training has me beat."

"Then you should retire and get some rest. We can continue this another time." He stood and smiled down at me. "Come. You must get plenty of rest if you are going to keep up with your new trainer."

We parted at the landing as usual, and I took a detour to the dining hall for a blueberry muffin before heading to my room. As I passed the tall windows, I spotted Nikolas and Celine walking across the well-lit lawn. They stopped and Celine gazed up at Nikolas with a sultry smile. He said something to her and her lips parted in what I knew was a throaty laugh, making me feel like I was intruding on a private moment. Seeing them like this, I couldn't help but notice how good they looked together, and I wasn't surprised that Nikolas would want to be with the beautiful woman. She might be a bitch to other females, but obviously males were very attracted to her.

Celine reached up and put her hand intimately on Nikolas's shoulder, and I felt like someone had socked me in the gut. I pulled back out of sight before either of them could see me and ran from the room, embarrassed and confused by a host of strange emotions. Why did it bother me to see them together? It wasn't as if there was anything between me and Nikolas; he was probably the last person I could picture myself with. Yes, he was gorgeous, and okay, maybe I was a little attracted to him. Who wouldn't be? He was good to me, but he was also arrogant and bossy and moody.

I just couldn't stand the thought of that awful woman getting her claws into him. *He can do so much better than Celine.*

What do you care? my inner voice asked. *You don't even like him, remember?*

I do like him, I argued back. *He's my friend, and I wouldn't want one of my friends with someone like that.*

Who the hell are you trying to kid? You have never thought of Nikolas as just a friend.

"No, you're wrong," I whispered as I opened my door. "I don't care about him that way."

Liar.

I closed the door and pressed my forehead weakly against it. "This is not happening."

The voice did not say a word.

Chapter 13

THE NEXT MORNING when I stumbled out of bed, my head felt like it was in a vise, and I was sporting dark shadows under my eyes. I wanted nothing more than to crawl back under the covers and hide there all day, anything to avoid seeing Nikolas. How was I going to train with him, to be alone with him after realizing last night that I had feelings for him? I still didn't know exactly what they were, but they scared the hell out of me. I honestly didn't know if I could deal with any more complications in my life. Nikolas was my trainer and my friend, and he was nothing, if not complicated.

Despite Jordan's assertions, I knew Nikolas wasn't attracted to me, especially after seeing him with Celine last night. Anyway, it wasn't like I wanted him to like me that way, did I? No, of course not. We didn't even get along half the time. Although, I had to admit that the last few days he had been patient and understanding. He was different here, more relaxed than he'd been in Maine, and it was throwing me off. That had to be it. We were spending a lot of time together and this nicer side of him was confusing me.

Right?

I wrung my head in my hands. "God, I don't need this right now." My throat felt tight and my voice sounded hoarse. My sleepless night was screwing with my emotions, and I would be a total wreck if I didn't get it together. I'd slept better than this when I'd had a psycho vampire hunting me. How messed up was that?

There was only one way to fix this. I had to act as if nothing had changed and put as much distance as possible between me and Nikolas until these stupid feelings went away. I wasn't sure how that was going to work with him being my trainer, but I would have to make the best of it. Outside of training, I had to avoid him at all costs.

Feeling slightly better now that I had a course of action, I dressed and headed down to breakfast. I passed Olivia on the stairs, and the questioning glance she shot me was enough to tell me how awful I looked. My head felt like it was full of cotton, and I wasn't sure if the queasiness in my stomach was from hunger or lack of sleep. If there ever was a day I needed Starbucks, this was it. A venti Mocha could do wonders for me right now.

All thoughts of coffee flew out of my head when I entered the dining hall and the first two people I spotted were Nikolas and Celine having breakfast together. They were not alone – Tristan and Chris sat with them – but that did not stop me from remembering the intimate scene between Nikolas and Celine the night before. As if she heard my thoughts, Celine leaned to one side to say something to Nikolas, laying her hand possessively over his. Anger burned through me, pounding in my ears and filling me with the urge to go over there and rip her hand away from him and let her know that he was . . .

He is what? I came up short, and my irrational anger immediately dissolved, leaving me confused and hot with embarrassment. Suddenly, the thought of food made me want to throw up. I spun on my heel and walked out as fast as I could without drawing attention to me. I sucked in a deep breath but it wasn't enough; the air felt stifling and heavy. Outside – I needed to be outside, to breathe fresh air or I would suffocate.

I exited by the nearest door and stood still, breathing deeply of the crisp air, and letting the morning chill cool my heated face and calm my frazzled emotions. What was wrong with me? Had I really almost gone over to their table? The thought of how close I had come to total humiliation sent me striding across the lawn, searching for a place to pull myself together. A few people waved to me as I passed them, but to my relief, no one tried to talk to me. I found myself at the river, where the deep rushing water drowned out every other sound and slowly began to draw the tension from my body.

Sitting on the grassy bank with my knees drawn up to my chest, I stared the fast-moving water without really seeing it. What had just happened back there? It was like I had no control over my emotions anymore, and that scared me more than I could say. I was fine before I'd started training with Nikolas. Had connecting with my Mori somehow made me more susceptible to its emotions and urges? Maybe it was my demon's rage I'd felt a little while ago and not my own.

I folded my arms across my knees and rested my forehead on them, wishing there was someone I could talk to about this. My first thought was Roland, but I quickly dismissed it. He never let himself develop feelings for a girl, so he wouldn't understand. Jordan might be able to explain the Mori emotions, but as soon as I mentioned Nikolas she would probably start planning my wedding. Hell would freeze over before I confided in my grandfather about my sudden attraction to a guy who happened to be his friend. That was just too weird, and I'd probably need therapy after.

Remy would know exactly what to say, but he was the one person I could not talk to. I took a deep shuddering breath. It looked like I was on my own for this one.

"Are you okay?"

My body tensed and my head jerked up when Nikolas spoke from a few feet behind me. I'd been so consumed by my thoughts that I hadn't heard or sensed him approach.

"You left without eating and you can't train on an empty stomach." He came to stand near me. "These are your favorite, right?"

I looked up to see him holding a wrapped blueberry muffin, and I stared at it for several seconds before I took it. "Thanks," I said thickly without meeting his eyes.

"Are you going to tell me what is wrong with you?"

"I'm fine."

"I think I know you well enough to know that is not true." He sat on the grass beside me, and I became hyperaware of his scent and his arm almost touching mine. I tried to swallow, but my mouth was dry.

"I didn't sleep last night and I'm tired," I managed to say. I picked at the muffin's plastic wrap and hoped my explanation would satisfy him.

"Is that all? You sound upset." The concern lacing his voice made me want to cry on his shoulder and run away from him at the same time. Why couldn't he be overbearing, annoying Nikolas right now instead of the nice one?

I stared at the foaming water; half wishing it could take me away from his perceptive gaze and unsettling kindness. "Not getting any sleep messes me up."

He was quiet for a long moment, and I felt his eyes on me. "Perhaps we overdid it yesterday in training."

"Maybe you're right."

"We'll skip training today," he said to my surprise. "Is there anything else you want to do instead? We could take that trip to town."

My pulse quickened at the idea. But then I remembered my resolve to put some distance between us. "I think I'll eat my muffin and then I'll go take Hugo and Woolf for a walk."

"Just as long as you don't do anything to tire yourself too much." He stood, and I felt his presence towering over me before he turned to walk away. "I'll see you later."

"See you, and thanks again for the muffin," I called after him.

"Anytime."

I didn't talk to Nikolas again that day, a feat I accomplished by eating lunch with Sahir in his office and then by grabbing a sandwich to take to my room for dinner.

The next morning, as luck would have it, Nikolas was called away on Mohiri business. I was actually glad to train with Callum again, something that surprised both of us. I surprised my old trainer by demonstrating my new ability to use my Mori's strength to pick up heavy objects. It was the first time I'd ever received a nod of approval from him. We worked on my reflexes after that, and though I managed to avoid being pummeled only once, he admitted I was finally making progress.

It wasn't until that evening at dinner that I saw Nikolas again and only in passing. He entered the dining hall as I was leaving, and I was immensely relieved that none of the crazy feelings resurfaced. I couldn't imagine how awkward it would have been living under the same roof with someone, having to see them every day while harboring unrequited feelings for them. We were both immortal and forever is a long time to try to avoid someone. But now things could go back to normal – as normal as my life could be.

I was in the common room after dinner watching an awful sci-fi movie with Michael when a flustered-looking Sahir found me. "Sara, there you are. Can you come with me? I need your help."

"Sure. What's up?" I got up from the couch and joined him by the door.

"We got a new creature in today and it is . . . " He exited by the main door. "Come on, it's easier if I just show you."

A new creature? Bursting with curiosity, I hurried to catch up with him. "What kind of creature, and what to you expect me to do with it?"

"She's a griffin, and she is – "

"Whoa!" My feet skidded to a stop on the grass. "A . . . a griffin?"

Sahir stopped a few feet ahead and looked soberly at me. "A young griffin. From what I can tell she is little more than a child."

My mouth refused to close so I slapped a hand over it. "Oh my God." If there was one race more elusive and protective of their children than trolls, it was griffins, and they were just as vicious when one of their young was threatened. Not that I'd ever seen a real live griffin or had dreamed of doing so. Griffins are not native to North America; they live in the most remote mountains of southern Africa. Capturing one, especially a young one, was almost unheard of.

"Some of our people raided a warlock in Los Angeles who was raising demons, and they found her locked up in a cage. Griffins have powerful blood, and we believe he was using hers to create a protective spell against the demons." Sahir shook his head in disgust and started walking again. "He refused to say how he got his hands on her, so we have to try to track down her flock. It won't be easy; griffins don't like to deal with outsiders."

"What can I do?"

"She flew up to the rafters before we could shut her cage door, and she's been throwing herself at the windows. You obviously have a way with Hugo and Woolf, and I'm hoping you can help calm her before she hurts herself."

We were almost at the menagerie when the door to the arena opened and Nikolas and Chris stepped outside. Judging by the swords they carried, they had just finished sparring.

"Where's the fire?" Chris asked.

"The young griffin we got in today is in distress, and Sara is going to help me with her," Sahir told them.

Chris gave me a lopsided smile. "Griffin wrangling? Another one of your talents, cousin?"

Nikolas strode toward us. "Griffins can be very dangerous when they are cornered. Sara is not going in there unprotected."

Ah, now there's the old Nikolas I know and – I let the thought die a quick death. "She's just a child, Nikolas."

He stepped in front of me. "That child could easily rip a grizzly bear apart with her claws."

"So could the troll you thought was going to kill me," I said, reminding him of the night he met Remy.

Sahir stared at us. "Troll?"

"I'll tell you about him later. Let's take care of your griffin first." Excitement curled in my stomach. I was about to meet a real live griffin.

Nikolas didn't move. "Not without us."

I let out an aggravated sigh and moved around him. "Fine, but you better not frighten her. You two can stay by the door unless the *vicious* griffin attacks me."

"I think she's gotten bossy since she came here," Chris said to Nikolas in a stage whisper. "What have you been teaching her?"

Nikolas muttered something in Russian. I knew he was just being . . . Nikolas, but it wasn't like we were going to face a pack of crocotta for heaven's sake. This was a frightened child who had been stolen from her family, and she needed compassion, not force.

We entered the menagerie, and Nikolas and Chris stayed just inside the door while Sahir and I walked toward the cages. Hugo and Woolf started to whine as soon as I drew near them, and I had to stop and pet them, then order them to go lie down so they did not upset the griffin.

Alex was crouched in the back of his cage as usual, and I called softly to him while giving him a wide berth. He watched us with that unblinking stare of his that never failed to give me the willies. People who trained wyverns must be either the bravest or the most insane people on earth.

A golden feather floated in front of my face, and I looked up at the ceiling. "Wow, oh, wow." I stared at the creature perched on the highest rafter at the center of the glass roof. She was as big as a Golden Retriever with a leonine body, the head of an eagle, and wings folded against her sides. Even from this distance, I could see that her feathers were ruffled and dirty, an unusual state for a creature known for its preening and cleanliness. At the sound of my voice, she tilted her head and peered down at me with a sadness that tore at my heart.

"Sara, this is Minuet."

I couldn't take my eyes off her. "She's incredible," I breathed.

"She won't be that way for long if we don't get her down from there and get her to eat something," Sahir said, reminding me why I was there.

"Right, sorry. I've just never seen anything like her." I studied the griffin a minute longer, then looked around for a place to sit. This might take a while – if it worked at all. I settled for a spot on the floor with my back against the cage across from Minuet's. "Sahir, could you stand with the others so you don't frighten her?"

"What are you going to do?"

"I'm just going to talk to her for a bit."

He walked over to join Nikolas and Chris, and I felt their eyes on me as I began to release my power into the air. Trying my best to ignore my audience, I spoke to the young griffin.

"I hope you don't mind me keeping you company, Minuet. I bet it's pretty scary and lonely for you here." She blinked and turned her head away. My chest tightened. "I know how you feel. I miss my family, too."

She did not make any sounds, but I saw her shift from one foot to another. Another feather drifted toward me. According to Remy, griffins are very intelligent, and they can understand every spoken language. I wasn't sure if young griffins had the ability, but I hoped my soothing tone would put her at ease – that, and the power rising through the air toward her.

"Minuet, would you like to hear a story about a girl who got lost far away from her family? Kind of like you, I guess. It has a happy ending, I promise.

"The girl's name was . . . um . . . Mary, and one day she disappeared and none of her friends or family knew where she'd gone. They all thought she was lost to them forever. But what they didn't know was that Mary was very sick, so sick she almost died, and some good faeries had taken Mary home with them to heal her. For a long time, Mary lay in a deep sleep while the faeries worked their magic on her. And then one day, she woke up and found herself in the most amazing place she had ever seen."

I looked up the griffin and caught the slight tilt of her head toward me. Hiding my smile, I continued with my story. "Mary was lying in the softest bed you could ever imagine surrounded by walls made of vines and pretty flowers. Then the vines moved and in walked the most beautiful red-haired sylph who told Mary they had healed her. Then she shocked Mary by telling her that she was actually half faerie, which was why the faeries had saved her. She took Mary outside and gave her the most delicious food and drink, then took her on a walk to show her a place so beautiful it brought tears to Mary's eyes." I described a glassy lake, lush greenery, a brilliant blue sky, and the birds and creatures living there.

"Mary and her new friend talked for a long time, and the sylph told her this was her home now if she chose to stay. Mary looked around her and knew she might never feel as safe or as content as she did at that moment. She could have that forever if she gave up her life in the human world and stayed in Faerie."

I stopped when I heard a scratching above me, and I looked up to see Minuet sidling along the rafter. I held my breath when she ruffled her wings as if she was going to take flight, but she stopped moving as soon as she caught me looking at her. I quickly lowered my gaze until I was looking straight ahead.

"Most people would never want to leave Seelie once they saw it. But Mary thought about her family and how they must be worried about her and – " I froze as a gust of air lifted my hair and four paws landed on the floor less than five feet from me. Slowly, my eyes travelled up the feathered body until they met Minuet's golden eyes. A sound near the door drew her attention away from me, and I knew Nikolas had drawn his sword.

I looked away from her and continued my story. "Mary knew that, even though the human world can be dangerous and scary, she could never leave her family and friends behind. So she asked the sylph to bring her home. The sylph was very sad because she had been so happy to find Mary and thought of her as a sister. But she did as Mary asked and brought her right to her front door. Mary was overjoyed to be home, and soon she was reunited with her family and friends, who could not believe she was alive and well. And they were grateful to the Faeries for taking care of Mary until she could come home again."

Minuet made a small squawk, and I met her sharp, intelligent eyes. "I know it's scary being away from home. I don't know if you can understand me, but I promise you're safe here with us until we find your family."

She stared at me for another long moment. Then she walked forward until she stood over me and all I could see was a wide feathered chest. I held my breath as her head lowered until it was beside mine, and then she began to slowly rub her beak and face against my hair. After a minute, she pulled away and walked into her cage where she began to tear at the whole raw salmon in her food dish.

No one said anything as I got up from the floor and shut her cage door. I turned to face the others and saw that their shocked expressions mirrored my own.

Chris was the first to speak. "I thought I'd seen it all when I met the troll, but this . . . "

"Sara, do you realize what just happened?" Sahir asked with some difficulty, and I shook my head. "She marked you with her scent. To her you are one of her flock now. I-I have never seen anything like it."

"So, I'm like an honorary griffin? Cool." I smiled as I walked toward them, still dazed from the experience. My eyes met Nikolas's. "See, piece of cake."

The words had barely left my mouth when I heard a rustling to my left. I realized too late that I had been so distracted by my success with Minuet I hadn't noticed how close I was to Alex's cage. I turned my head to see the wyvern rushing toward me, flames already shooting from his mouth.

The flames seared my arm a split second before I was snatched away from the cage and out of the wyvern's range. Nikolas brought us to a stop and put out the fire on my sleeve, but already I could feel the agonizing pain from my wrist to my elbow. Tears welled in my eyes, and I cried out when my charred sleeve touched the skin that was already blistering.

"Sara, are you okay?" Sahir cried, running toward us.

Nikolas turned on him, eyes blazing. "Goddamnit, Sahir, I told you it wasn't safe in here for her. That thing could have killed her."

"It's not his fault," I said between clenched teeth. "I was careless. I got too close."

"The hell it's not," Nikolas raged, still holding me. "He should never have allowed you in here."

"Nikolas," Chris said sharply. A look I could not decipher passed between them, and Nikolas's hold on me loosened a little.

I tried to pull away from him, but his arm was still like a steel band around my waist. "D-don't blame Sahir for this. I'm old enough to make my own decisions." I tried again to move away from him to no avail. "Let me go."

Nikolas glared down at me, totally ignoring my request. "You can't keep taking risks like this."

His condescending tone drove all thoughts of pain from my mind. "Would you just get the hell over yourself?" I shouted, pulling until he finally released me. I rounded on him. "You don't get to say where I can go or how I spend my time. And I'm not some weakling you need to jump in and save all the time."

He cocked an eyebrow at me, and it only made me madder. "Okay, you just did and I'm grateful, but that doesn't give you the right to yell at everyone or treat me like I'm useless. If that's all you think of me, I wish you'd just stayed away."

He took a step toward me. "I didn't say you were – "

"Just forget it." I put up a hand, and my sleeve chafed painfully against my burnt arm. Biting my lip did not stop the whimper of pain that escaped me.

Concern replaced the anger in Nikolas's eyes. "We need to get you to the medical ward."

I turned for the door. "I don't need your help. I can get there on my own."

"I'm coming with you."

I pushed open the door. "No, you're not. Just leave me alone."

I could barely see through my tears as I hurried to the main building, and I didn't know if they were tears of pain, anger, or hurt. I felt miserable on too many levels to try to separate my emotions, and all I wanted was to put some distance between me and Nikolas.

The healer on duty was the same one who had tended to me the first time I'd been burned by Alex, and she shook her head when she saw my charred sleeve. Before she looked at my arm, she gave me some gunna paste, and for once, I took it without complaint. Within minutes, the pain receded, and as soon as I relaxed she set to work removing my shirt and coating the burn with the same cool salve she had used the last time. Then she wrapped my numb arm in a soft gauze bandage and helped me back into my shirt, ordering me to lie still for a few minutes.

When the door opened a few minutes later, I turned my head, expecting to see the healer, but saw Nikolas instead. His expression was unreadable, and I turned my head to look up at the ceiling. "I'm really not up to arguing with you again, Nikolas."

"I wanted to make sure you were okay."

"I'm fine. I've had worse injuries, remember?"

"I remember," he said in a gruff voice.

Neither of us spoke for a minute, and the silence in the room quickly unsettled me. Feeling vulnerable in my current position, I sat up, letting my legs dangle over the side of the exam table. I held up my bandaged arm. "Look, all taken care of. I'll be as good as new in no time."

He did not smile, still wound up from the incident. I didn't understand why he got so angry over these things. No one else had made a big deal of it.

"You don't have to stay with me. The healer said I'm fine."

"I'm sorry for yelling at you."

My jaw dropped. *Did I hear that right? Did Nikolas just apologize to me?*

"I never meant to make you feel useless. It just angers me to see you taking risks like that."

I tried not to let my own anger resurface. "What do you expect me to do – hide out in my room so I don't get hurt? I can't be safe all the time. You have to realize that I will get hurt sometimes, especially if I become a warrior."

The glint in his eyes told me I had said the wrong thing again. "I thought you didn't want to be a warrior."

I threw up my good arm. "What am I training for, if not to become one?

Isn't that what we do?"

He started walking toward me. "I'm teaching you to defend yourself if you ever need it, not to go out looking for trouble."

"I'm not looking for trouble, and that thing with Alex was a freak accident. It could have happened to anyone." I looked away from him and hugged my stomach with my uninjured arm. After all the progress I'd made in training this week, did he think I was totally useless? "Why is it so hard for you to believe I can take care of myself? I'm not a child, you know."

He stopped two feet away, and I discovered that my seat on the exam table put our gazes at the same level for once. Unfortunately, that meant I had nowhere to look but into his eyes.

"No, you are not a child." His husky words made my mouth dry up like the Sahara. The air in the room grew warm and thick, and I suddenly found it hard to breathe.

Another step and he stood between my knees, close enough for me to feel his body heat and smell his warm, spicy scent. My heart pounded in my ears; I tried to swallow and failed. In my stomach a troupe of acrobats were having the performance of their lives.

Nikolas's stormy gaze refused to release mine. His hand rose, and his thumb traced my jaw in a featherlike caress that turned my limbs to noodles. Dimly, I felt my Mori stirring. "Sara," he said in a strained voice as he touched his forehead to mine. I sat very still, battling the onslaught of emotions that threatened to push my heart from my chest. "Yell at me. Tell me to go," he whispered.

I brought my hands up between us and laid them flat against his chest to push him away, until I felt the strong rapid beat of his heart beneath my fingers. I closed my eyes and swallowed hard. "Nikolas, I . . . "

He pulled back, and I felt like I'd been set adrift until his fingers curled under my chin, lifting my face to his. My eyes moved over his sensual lips, and all I could think about was what it would be like to taste them. Shocked by my sudden boldness, I raised my eyes to his and was lost in their smoky depths. Something tugged at my chest, a vaguely familiar sensation that drew me toward him. I read the intention in his eyes before they lowered to my mouth.

Then I forgot how to breathe.

Chapter 14

CONSCIOUS THOUGHT FLED when Nikolas's lips brushed mine. Warm and firm, his mouth explored mine with aching slowness and infinite tenderness as his hands framed my face, holding me against him. As if I had the strength to pull away. Sensations I had never felt before blossomed in my chest, and instead of trying to understand them, I leaned in and kissed him back tentatively. I sensed something indecipherable shift between us – like two repelling magnets that flip and are suddenly drawn to each other – and my lips parted to let my breath escape in a soft sigh. He pulled me closer, if that was possible, deepening the kiss, and I surrendered to it, exhilarated and terrified at the same time and never wanting it to end.

Seconds, or maybe a lifetime later, Nikolas made a sound deep in his chest and pulled back. Trembling, I took a breath and met his dark, smoldering gaze that told me I was not the only one affected by the kiss. A storm of emotions assailed me: wonder, bewilderment, elation, but they soon gave way to shock as it hit me what I had just done.

Oh my God, I kissed Nikolas.

Neither of us spoke for a long moment, and I was acutely aware of his hands still cradling my face and his lips only inches from mine. Was he going to kiss me again? Did I want him to?

Before I could answer that question, his eyes became flat and unreadable and he dropped his hands to take a step back. "I'm sorry. I did not mean to . . ."

His hoarse words hung in the air between us for a second before they hit me like a bucket of ice water. *He didn't mean to?* I tore my eyes from his, but not before I saw regret creep into his expression. My stomach dropped, and my body grew warm as humiliation washed over me.

"Sara – "

"No." I didn't want to hear him to explain or tell me it had been a mistake; his reaction said that loud and clear. It didn't matter why he'd kissed me. It was done and we couldn't change it. I did not want to talk about it, either. Tears pricked my eyes, making me angry that I should let a simple kiss bother me so much, even if it had been my first kiss.

A heavy silence stretched between us. I refused to look at him, but I had never been so aware of another person. *Please, just go,* I begged silently.

Nikolas sighed. "I'm sorry," he said again. Then he turned and walked away.

* * *

I knocked on Tristan's office door, and he looked up from his computer and motioned for me to come in. He pressed the mute button on his phone. "I just have to finish this call and I'll be with you."

"I can come back."

"No, take a seat. It won't be more than another five minutes."

I sat on the couch and stared out the window, trying not to listen to his conversation, although bits and pieces of it reached me anyway.

" . . . That's seven people in Nevada this week that we know of . . . How many in California? . . . No, he didn't find any leads in Vegas . . . It seems to be mostly the western half . . . "

My mind began to wander as it did a lot lately, and soon my thoughts drowned out Tristan's voice completely. I found myself going back, as I did way too often, to that night in the medical ward three days ago. My fingers came up to touch my lips the way they did every time I remembered the kiss. Before that night, I had convinced myself that the stirrings I felt for Nikolas weren't real. But his kiss had not only reawakened them, it had brought them back so strong that they'd sent me into an emotional tailspin. Something had shifted inside me that night, and I didn't know how to put it back the way it used to be.

The embarrassment I'd felt after Nikolas walked away was nothing compared to the burning rejection that hit me the next morning when I found out he had left very early on business and was not expected back for three or four days. Last week, he'd said he wasn't going anywhere for at least a month and yet he was already gone. Did he regret kissing me so much that he had left so he didn't have to see me?

In his absence, I'd gone back to training with Callum in the mornings. Now that I was doing better we didn't clash as much, and it was a far better than training with someone who couldn't even bear to face me.

"I'm sorry, I know I've been buried in work the last few days," Tristan said, pulling me from my thoughts. He sat in the chair across from me and gave me a warm smile. No matter how busy he was, he always looked happy to see me.

I returned his smile. "I understand. Comes with the job, right?"

"It is a part of the job, but I will always have time for you." He studied my face for a moment. "You seem troubled."

"No, I'm good," I said, because there was no way I could tell him the truth. I could only handle so much humiliation in one week. "I actually came to ask you something. Well, two things. Terrence and Josh are going to a party in town tonight and they asked me and Jordan to go. I wanted to run it by you and see if it's okay."

"You are asking my permission to go?"

"Yes. I'd really like to go, but I know you have all those restrictions for new orphans, even though I *am* a lot older than most orphans." I could probably sneak out if I tried hard enough, but I wasn't going to do that.

To my surprise, he nodded. "Butler Falls is safe, especially with the others. I might worry about those town boys, though."

Nikolas's look of regret flashed through my mind. "Trust me; the last thing I want is to get involved with anyone right now." *Or ever.*

Tristan smiled, and his eyes seemed a little too shrewd for my liking. Did he know what had happened between me and Nikolas? God, I hoped not.

"What else did you want to ask me? You said there were two things."

I shifted uncomfortably because my second request was a lot harder to make. "My training is coming along a lot better now. I've been working with Callum the last few days and it's going pretty good, so I wanted to ask if I could go back to training with him." With Nikolas due back any day, I knew I had to get my trainer situation settled before I had to see him again.

I could tell he was not expecting me to say that. "You want to work with Callum again?"

"If he's available, or someone else."

"Not Nikolas? But you have been doing so well with him."

I fumbled my answer even though I had prepared for the question. "Nikolas helped me get started, but I've really only trained with him twice. And you need him for warrior business. This will free him up for that."

Tristan frowned. "I'm not sure how Nikolas will feel about this. Have you told him?"

"No, but why should he mind? He's only training me because you asked him to."

He let out a chuckle. "I'd like to think I have more compassion for my trainees than to appoint Nikolas as a teacher. He asked to train you, and I thought it was a good idea, considering your history."

Nikolas had asked to train me? "You wouldn't let him train the others, but you let him work with me?"

"I was pretty confident you could hold your own against him."

Until he kissed me.

"So about Callum?"

Tristan nodded, but he did not look happy. "If you really want to go back to him, you can." He glanced at his watch. "And if you are going to a party in a few hours, you probably should go get ready. I haven't spent much time around teenage girls, but I hear it takes a while to prepare to go out."

I laughed. "It doesn't take long to find a pair of jeans to wear. Although, Jordan might be another story."

"Have fun, but not too much fun."

"Now you sound like Nate," I chided, and he looked pleased by the comparison.

I started to rise from the couch. "I guess I *should* go tell Jordan the good news."

"Wait. Before you go, I'd like to ask you something."

"Okay." I sank slowly back to the couch. *He can't know about me and Nikolas. Can he?*

"I had dinner with Desmund last night. We try to visit every week for a drink and a game of chess. Did I tell you that?"

"No." I knew they were friends with the way they spoke of each other, but I'd assumed Desmund kept pretty much to himself. I wasn't sure why Tristan was bringing him up now, and it worried me. Desmund was unpredictable. Had he told Tristan he no longer wanted me to visit him?

"Desmund usually likes to talk about the past, about his life before his affliction." He leaned forward slightly in his chair. "Do you know what we talked about last night?"

I shook my head, and a small knot formed in my stomach.

"You."

"Me?" I squeaked.

Tristan's smile caught me off guard. "He is quite taken with you. I haven't seen him warm to someone in a very long time. He is like a different person since you started visiting him."

"Oh." My body relaxed. "I like him, too. He took a little getting used to, but he's really sweet when he wants to be. I wish I could go back and meet him before he got sick."

"That's the thing. The Desmund I saw last night was very much like the one I used to know. When I say he's a different person, I mean he is almost like his old self again. It's as if he has been miraculously cured." Tristan's shrewd stare made me fidget. "*You* did this, didn't you?"

"I – " I broke off, uncertain how to proceed. If I told him what I'd done, would he be angry with me? I'd healed hundreds of creatures over the years, but using my power on a person was not the same and neither was dealing with magic. No one had ever healed a Hale witch victim, and here I was thinking I could do it because I'd battled a single witch and won. Just because I succeeded did not mean I'd had the right to take that risk with Desmund in the first place.

"I'll take that as a yes." He ran his hand through his hair. "You don't have to talk about it now, but we will have to discuss it soon. What you've done . . . do you know what it could mean for others like Desmund?"

Until that moment, all I'd cared about was helping Desmund; I never thought about what it would mean if it actually worked. The idea that I could help other warriors suffering from the same fate made me feel like I might have a purpose here after all.

Tristan stood and waved at the door. "Go on; get ready for your party. We'll talk more about this later."

"Okay," I said, relieved he was not angry with me.

"Sara," he called as I opened the door. "I don't think Desmund realizes what has happened or what you've done for him. I want to thank you on his behalf."

Tears pricked my eyes. "You don't have to thank me. He's my friend, too."

*   *   *

I tugged on the hem of the borrowed white shirt that hugged my body a little tighter than I was used to. Maybe *borrowed* was not the right word. *Coerced* was probably a better one. I almost shook my head in disgust. I could command hellhounds, but I could not stand up to a teenage girl when she got it into her head that I needed a party outfit. The jeans weren't too bad though, even if they hung a bit low on my hips. I still couldn't believe Jordan had ordered them online for me days ago along with the cute brown leather boots I was wearing. She was pushy *and* sneaky. I wished I could take her to New Hastings and introduce her to Faith Perry and the other mean girls at my old school. They wouldn't know what hit them.

"Any of you girls want a beer?" called our host, Derek, over the music as he approached with two unopened beers in his hands.

I held up my bottle of water. "I'm good, thanks." When we got here two hours ago, I'd had a couple of beers, but I wasn't much of a drinker.

"I'll have one of those." Jordan took one of the offered beers with a smile that made the good-looking twenty-three-year-old grin like a teenage boy. I hid my smile behind my water bottle. I had been a little worried about being around human men again, especially now that my elemental powers were growing. At first, some of the guys, including Derek, showed interest, but after I gently deflected their flirting, they moved on. They didn't go too far. Half of them were falling over themselves for Jordan who looked amazing and had a sexy, confident air men couldn't resist. She loved their attention, and I was happy to stay back in the shadows and enjoy the party.

"How about you?" Derek offered the second beer to Olivia.

"Mark is getting me something," she told him, pointing at Mark, who was talking to Terrence and Josh on the other side of the room.

Jordan said something to Derek, and I took the opportunity to nudge Olivia and confirm a suspicion I'd had all evening. "Hey, what's up with you and Mark? You two have barely left each other's sight tonight." I knew they had been best friends for years, but it was obvious there was something else going on between them.

Olivia blushed and her eyes sparkled. "We finally decided to start going out. We've been joking about it for a while and last night we just . . . kissed. My first kiss and it was amazing. I've been crazy about him forever, and I never realized he felt the same way."

"That's awesome, Olivia."

She sighed blissfully, her eyes following Mark. "I still can't believe it."

When Mark joined us a minute later, I watched the warm looks that passed between them as he pulled her out for a dance. An ache formed in my chest. It wasn't that I was jealous of them or even wanted a boyfriend right now. I just couldn't help thinking how different my first kiss was from Olivia's and how happy she was, while I was . . . I wasn't quite sure how I felt. Rejected? Confused? Hurt?

Geez, it was just a stupid kiss. Get over it already.

"You girls having fun?" Derek asked, and I nodded. The crowd here was a little older than the high school set, but they seemed nice enough and not too wild.

"Your place is great," I told him. "Did you really do all this yourself?"

Derek's face lit up when I mentioned his beautifully restored turn-of-the-century farmhouse. He had inherited the place on the outskirts of town from his grandmother three years ago, and he had turned the old house into a modern home that still retained its country charm.

"Yep, with help from a few of my buddies. I'm not done yet. I'm working on the barn now, gonna make it into garage and a workshop. You want a tour?"

"Sure." I looked at Jordan, who nodded. We went to grab our coats and followed Derek through the back door. As soon as the door closed behind us, the noise level dropped considerably, and I let out a sigh. I was never going to be a partier. God knows Roland had tried to make me into one. I preferred fresh air to the cloying heat of a crowded room.

The barn was a good fifty yards from the house, but the full moon made the night so bright it was easy to make it out. As Derek pointed out his planned renovations, he told us he had studied art in college and, luckily, his grandmother had left him enough money to pursue art instead of having to get a nine-to-five job to support himself. His other passion was classic cars, and he was currently restoring a nineteen sixty-nine GTO in his friend's garage until he got his own garage finished. I thought about Roland, who would die for a GTO and didn't even have his old Chevy truck anymore because of me.

"I already have a room at the house for my art, but I can't wait to finish the studio," Derek was saying, and my ears perked up at the mention of an art studio.

"Sara draws, but she keeps her sketches hidden in her room," Jordan said, and Derek looked at me with new interest.

"What do you like to draw? Do you paint, too?"

"Mostly people and animals. I tried painting a few years ago, but I like drawing more, and it's a lot less mess."

Derek laughed. "My parents said the same thing when I lived with them. If you want I'll show you some of my work when we go back to the house. But right now I want to show you the loft. That's where my new studio is going."

Derek grabbed a battery operated lantern from a hook by the door and led us to a ladder at the back of the barn. "My buddy, Seth, is going to help me build the studio; he said it only seems right since it was our fort when we were kids. He and his girlfriend, Dana, are in Vegas now, but when he gets back we might do some work on it before it gets too cold."

"Lead the way," I told him and started following him up the ladder with Jordan behind me. At the top, I stepped into the loft that was wide enough that the beam from Derek's lantern barely reached the dark corners. The loft smelled faintly of old hay, and it was empty except for a few crates and a small square table with some rolled-up papers on top.

Derek hung the lantern on a post in the middle of the room and went to push open the wide shutters at the front of the barn. Moonlight and crisp night air flowed in along with the distant sounds of the party. He went to the table and unrolled one of the papers to reveal a detailed blueprint of the barn.

"It pays to have a best friend who's studying to become an architect," he confided with a wink. "Seth drew these up for me at school." He pointed to some long rectangular markings on the walls and explained that they were going to put in windows on all sides for maximum natural light. "Plus the view up here in the daytime is amazing."

"This is pretty cool," Jordan said, walking around the loft. "You'll have to show us when it's finished."

"Absolutely," Derek declared, and I raised an eyebrow at Jordan, who gave me a small shrug when Derek wasn't looking. Was she more interested in him than she let on? "You girls are welcome whenever you want to come over. Maybe Sara and I can draw together sometime?"

"Maybe." I'd never had someone to draw with before, and it might be fun, especially in a real studio.

"I guess we should be getting back to the party before Terrence and Josh come looking for us." Derek held up the lantern and waved at the hatch. "After you. I'll hold the light while you climb down."

I barely took a step before coldness punched through my chest, making me double over. *Not now!* If my elemental powers started acting up here, there was no way I'd be able to explain it away. Derek, I might be able to fool, but Jordan was way too sharp to fall for a simple explanation, especially after what I'd done to the lamprey demon.

"Sara, are you okay?" Jordan rushed to my side and laid her hand on my back.

"Is she sick?" Derek asked. "I didn't see her drink much."

It took some effort, but I straightened up and smiled to let them know I was okay. The cold was still there, worse than it had ever been, but it was more uncomfortable than painful. And thankfully, there was no sign of the strange static power to give away my secret. "I'm fine. I felt a bit woozy there for a second. Probably should have eaten more at dinner."

Derek smiled in relief. "I can fix that. I have plenty of food at the house." He held the lantern out to Jordan. "Jordan, why don't you take this and I'll help Sara down the ladder."

I almost laughed at the look on Jordan's face as she took the lantern. We both knew she was stronger than three men and could carry me down on her back, but we couldn't tell Derek that.

"A damsel in distress? Looks like I got here just in time."

The three of us swung around to the man stepping off the ladder. Jordan raised the lantern and illuminated a smiling blond man who looked to be Derek's age.

"Seth!" Derek smiled broadly. "When did you get back?"

"Got in a few hours ago. We had to take care of some things at home and thought we'd check out the action here tonight. I figured you'd have a bash going on and lots of goodies here to eat." Seth's eyes slid slowly over me, and the hair rose up on the back of my neck. How could someone as nice as Derek have a creep for a best friend?

"We were just heading back to the house. I have enough beer and food to keep even you happy. Is Dana with you?"

"She's on her way with a friend we brought back with us. We can have our own little party out here."

Something about Seth's leering smile seemed eerily familiar, and my mind suddenly conjured an image of Eli staring at me with the same hungry expression. Alarm bells went off in my head. *It can't be,* I thought even as my hand slowly reached for the dagger tucked in the inside pocket of my coat. After Boise, I'd decided to err on the side of caution and start carrying a weapon again. I *really* hoped I did not have to use it.

Derek laughed. "Stay here? Dude, what are you talking about? All the booze and food is at the house."

Seth laid a hand on the top of the ladder. "Oh, I think the real party is gonna happen here, my friend."

My eyes were drawn to the movement of his hand the second it began to change. I pulled my dagger free as his fingernails became long black claws. "Vampire!"

"What?" Jordan cried as she whipped out two lethal knives with lightning fast reflexes.

"What's this?" Seth sniffed the air and his smile widened, showing off his glistening fangs. "Oh, I've heard all you juicy little morsels from that Westhorne Institute."

"Seth, what the fuck man!" Derek yelled as horror settled on his face. "What's wrong with you?"

"Wrong?" Chilling laughter burst from Seth. "I've never felt so great in my life, buddy, and it's about to get a whole lot better."

The moment Seth moved, Jordan threw Derek behind us so hard he hit the wall and crumpled to the floor. She and I took up fighting stances against the vampire who used to be Derek's friend. Jesus, what were the odds of going to a party where the host's best friend returned from vacation as a vampire? And this close to a Mohiri stronghold? I really was a disaster magnet.

"How cute. The little girls think they can take me." Seth rolled his shoulders. "I know all about you Mohiri children and how there is nothing sweeter than your blood." His eyes narrowed, and he swallowed like an alcoholic looking at a glass of whiskey.

"We know about you, too," I said with a lot more bravado than I felt. "You're a baby vamp, less than a week old, which means you're not as good as you think you are. And my friend Jordan here is the best warrior you'll ever meet. In fact, she's the *last* warrior you'll ever meet."

Jordan recovered from the shock of meeting her first vampire and shot me her signature smirk before deftly twirling the knife in her right hand. Seth's eyes followed the weapon, and I caught the hesitation in his eyes. The fact that he was a new vampire was the one thing we had going for us. That, and Jordan really was as good as I'd said she was.

"Are you going eat us or what?" Jordan taunted, and I saw Seth's nostrils flare. New vampires are also rash and quick to temper, and if anyone could piss one off, it was Jordan. "I'm thirsty and I could be having a beer instead of wasting time with you."

If we hadn't been in mortal danger at that moment, I would have laughed at her sheer brass.

Seth did not find it as funny. "If anyone will drink here, it will be me," he spat, leaping forward. He was faster than I'd expected, but he did not have the blurring speed of the other vampires I'd seen. Jordan met him halfway and delivered a blow to his chest that just missed his heart. He spun away with a shriek of pain and wisps of smoke rose from his chest when he turned for a second attack. "You'll die for that, bitch."

"Yeah, yeah, you're the big bad sucker. Shut up and kill me already."

When this was over, Jordan and I had to have a talk about how *not* to talk to a vampire.

Seth made a sound somewhere between a growl and a scream and went for Jordan again. I guess he thought I was less of a threat than the girl with two knives so he'd take her out first. For an architect, he was pretty stupid. His claws went for Jordan's throat when he should have been paying attention to the two silver blades she wielded with deadly ease. One blade slashed across his midsection, opening a deep smoking gash there, and as soon as he dropped his hands to keep his guts from spilling out, the second blade found its mark. The vampire's eyes flew wide with shock as Jordan pulled her knife free. Then he crumpled to the floor with a heavy thud.

"God I love this job!" Jordan crowed as she bent to wipe her bloody blades on the dead vampire's sleeve. When she stood, I saw that she didn't have a speck of blood on her. How was that even possible?

"We should get back to – " Cold blossomed in my chest again and dread filled me as it finally dawned on me what was happening to me. I whirled to the ladder as a female vampire about my height with long dark hair flew through the hole. Her appearance did not shock me nearly as much as the revelation that my episodes were not random bursts of elemental power.

I had developed my very own vampire radar.

"Seth!" the female vampire shrieked when she saw him on the floor, and I knew she was his girlfriend, Dana, whom Derek had mentioned.

I realized how quiet Derek was, and I glanced behind me to see him out cold against the wall. Damn, Jordan didn't know her own strength. I hoped he wasn't hurt too bad, but there was no time to check on him now. We had Dana to deal with, and if Seth had been telling the truth, there was a third vampire here somewhere. All I could do was hope he was as new as these two.

"What have you done with Seth?" Dana screamed, advancing on us.

Jordan smiled and raised her weapons again. "Seth's gone to hell, but don't worry, you'll see him again very soon."

"Brent!" Dana screeched and bared her fangs at Jordan. "I am going to kill you slowly, bitch."

I almost groaned when Jordan replied, "You go ahead and take your time, but just so you know, I plan to kill you quickly."

Up until that moment, I thought we had a chance to get out of here alive. But when a second male vampire appeared at the top of the ladder, I knew we were in trouble. Jordan could probably take one of them, but I wasn't a fighter. My only strength was my elemental power, and it wasn't reliable. I had a feeling these vampires weren't going to stand still while I tried to summon it.

My Mori stirred at the approaching threat, and I felt a spark of hope. I wasn't as strong or as fast as Jordan, but I wasn't completely helpless either. Fear for my life overshadowed the fear of my demon, and I dropped the wall between us. *Help me.*

I suppressed a shudder as the Mori's consciousness touched mine, and I felt its power rush through my body a second later. When Brent flew at me, I shocked us both by sidestepping his attack so fast it would have made Callum proud. The vampire recovered quickly and came at me again, his fangs and claws bared. There was no time to think or to worry about how Jordan was faring in her own fight. My demon's instinct took over and I swung the dagger in an upward arc, ripping it across Brent's hands. He screamed, and I gagged as a clawed pinky bounced off my boot.

Enraged, Brent lunged at me again, and this time he hit me so hard I flew into the wall. My dagger went skidding across the floor, but not before I landed a good blow to his neck. He stepped back to put his hands over the gushing wound, giving me time to get to my feet again. My demon strength was already fading. It had saved me from his first attack, but I couldn't take another blow like that, and I had lost my weapon.

I flexed my fingers in frustration. Where was all the power that had flared up around the other demons? Vampires are demons too – or at least they have a demon inside them – so there was no reason I couldn't call on my power like I had with Nikolas. Vamhir demons are a lot closer to the surface than Mori demons. My power should be freaking out already being this close to two vampires. Maybe it just needed a little push.

My eyes did not leave the vampire as I pushed my Mori back and threw up a wall to protect it before I opened my power. The comforting heat flowed through me and I reached for it, trying to shape it into the weapon I had used on Nikolas and the demons. Nothing. What was I doing wrong?

There was a shout to my right, and Brent turned to see Jordan deliver a killing blow to his female friend. His eyes widened in fear at the sight of the other vampire falling. It was the opening I needed. Using the last of my borrowed strength, I launched myself at his back and wrapped my hands around his neck and face. All I had to do was hold him long enough for Jordan to finish with the female.

As soon as my bare skin made contact with his, a surge of electricity ripped through me, making all the hair on my body stand on end. Static crackled up my arms and sparks flew from my fingertips. The vampire jerked and stiffened like he'd been electrocuted and dropped to the floor.

I lay on top of him in shock as the sickly smell of burnt flesh filled my nose. Was he dead? I got my answer when he moaned and tried to push himself up before collapsing back to the floor. Whatever I'd done to him, he was down for now, but vampires healed quickly. I looked around for my dagger and saw it on the other side of the loft.

"Here." Jordan held out one of her blades. I didn't hesitate; I took the knife and plunged it into the vampire's heart.

Chapter 15

THE VAMPIRE SHUDDERED violently and went still. For several seconds, I sat still and stared at the grisly scene around me.

"Holy fuck!"

Jordan's voice snapped me out of my trance, and I realized I was sitting atop a dead vampire. I rolled off the body and onto my hands and knees, panting and trying not to vomit.

"You okay?" she asked, and I nodded slowly. To prove it, I got unsteadily to my feet.

Jordan stared at me. "What did you do to him?"

I glanced at the corpse lying face down on the floor, the burns on his face hidden from view. "I – "

"Sara? Jordan?"

Trembling, I went to the window and saw at least half a dozen people below. "Tristan?"

"Is Jordan with you? Are you girls okay?"

I looked behind me at Jordan, the three dead vampires, and Derek who was still out cold. "We're fine, but we could use some help. We had a, um, situation, and there's an unconscious man up here who probably needs a doctor."

"We're coming up," he called back.

"Just don't freak out, okay?" I said as he started up the ladder. I stood back and took in the bloody scene again, and my only thought was thank God Nikolas wasn't here to see this.

Great, we take down three vampires and the first thing I think about is him.

Tristan was the first one through the hatch, followed by Chris and Callum. The three men stared at the carnage in shocked silence.

"You two killed three vampires by yourselves?" Tristan asked, looking at me. I felt an absurd rush of pleasure that he didn't assume Jordan had done all the work.

"Baby vampires." I knelt to check on Derek and heaved a sigh when I found a strong pulse. "He's alive," I told Jordan.

Callum joined me and did a quick exam of Derek's head. He pulled out some gunna paste and winked at me as he put some in the unconscious man's mouth. "He likely has a concussion, but the gunna paste will take care of that. He'll still need medical attention."

"Young vampires?" Tristan murmured.

"He knew them." I pointed to Derek's dead friends. "They're from town. Their names are Seth and Dana, and according to Derek they were supposed to be on vacation in Vegas. I don't know who the other guy was. She called him Brent."

The three men exchanged grim looks, and I could tell they knew more than they were saying. "What are you not telling us?"

Tristan shifted as if he was carrying a great weight. "We've had reports of an increase in missing persons in certain areas the last month. Las Vegas has been the worst."

I didn't say that I had also heard about the missing people. "Vampires."

He nodded silently.

"Young vampires are still strong. How did you girls manage to take out three at once?" The look Callum gave me said he still didn't think much of my fighting skills even though my training was going better.

I let Jordan tell the story, and her narration was a lot more colorful than mine would have been. She was pretty psyched about her first vampire kills. When she got to mine, she paused like she didn't know how to continue, and I took it from there.

"He came at me and I got him good in the throat, but I lost my knife. He had to cover his throat because blood was going everywhere." I waved a hand at my blood-splattered clothes for emphasis. "I jumped on his back and knocked him down, and then Jordan gave me her knife to finish him off."

My explanation sounded normal and straight forward even to my ears, but out of the corner of my eye I saw Jordan give me a puzzled look. I hoped she was not going to question my story, because I couldn't tell her the truth. Not yet anyway.

"How did you guys know we were in trouble anyway?" I asked to change the subject.

"We monitor the police bands in town, and we heard a call about a residential homicide," Tristan told us. "Chris came to check it out, and he said a neighbor told the police he saw the victim's son enter the house several hours ago. The neighbor thought it was strange because the son was supposed to be in Las Vegas. With all the reports out of Vegas, I didn't want to take any chances."

"How did you know where we were?"

Chris showed his dimples. "You of all people should know that we have GPS trackers on all our vehicles. We went to the house, and Terrence said you girls had gone outside with his friend, Derek."

I made a face at him. "Well you missed all the fun."

"Are you girls sure you aren't hurt?" Tristan asked again. "You're covered in blood."

Jordan looked down and noticed her blood splattered legs for the first time. Her two kills were clean so there was no doubt where the blood had come from. "Damn it, Sara, I just bought these jeans."

I let out a strangled laugh. "Sorry."

Chris shook his head. "The two of them sound okay to me."

I looked down at my shirt, which was now more red than white, and grimaced. "I hate to tell you this, Jordan, but I don't think your shirt is going to make it."

Tristan started issuing orders. "Callum, you carry the young man down. Chris, call for a cleanup crew. We need to keep everyone at the party away from the barn." He looked at me. "Now, let's get you girls out of here."

We waited for Callum to descend the ladder with Derek over his shoulder before Jordan and I climbed down. As soon as my feet hit the floor, my legs wobbled a little, but Tristan was right behind me to keep me steady. "I'm just a little tired," I assured him when he looked worried.

Tristan kept his arm around me as we walked to the barn entrance. "Can you walk to the SUV? I can carry you."

"Thanks, but I can make it on my own." There was no way I wasn't walking out of here under my own steam.

"All right, let's – " Tristan looked at something outside the barn and froze, his hand tightening on my arm.

What now? I peered around him, not sure what I'd find. I saw Terrence, Josh, Seamus, and Niall standing to one side and Olivia, Mark, Callum, and Jordan to the other. Between them stood Nikolas. My stomach fluttered wildly at seeing him for the first time since the kiss. It was impossible to see his expression, so I had no idea what he was thinking or how he felt about seeing me.

Does it matter? He made his feelings perfectly clear.

I pulled away from Tristan and walked away from the barn, intending to go around Nikolas. He was the last person I wanted to talk to right now. I was done with his whole hot-and-cold attitude, and I was not in the mood to be yelled at for what had happened here. He could go find someone else to be his emotional punching bag.

Nikolas made a sound deep in his chest, and everyone but Tristan and I took a step back. I came up short and narrowed my eyes at him. "Did you just growl at me?"

"Nikolas, she is okay," Tristan said behind me in a calm voice. Too calm.

I took a closer look at Nikolas and saw that he was standing rigidly with his hands clenched into fists at his sides. His eyes were so dark they looked black, and his face could have been chiseled out of stone. I had seen him furious before, but never like this. He looked like he was about to explode.

And he was staring right at me.

"Sara, listen to me," Tristan said slowly. "You need to walk toward him, talk to him, and let him know you are okay."

"I don't understand," I said without taking my eyes off Nikolas.

Tristan's exhale was loud in the silence. "I know and I will explain it to you later. Right now, you need to do what I tell you. Nikolas's Mori is upset, and the only thing that will calm him is to see that you are unhurt."

Nikolas was about to lose it and Tristan wanted me to go to him? Was he nuts? "Can't he see that from here?"

"No. You need to get a lot closer. He won't hurt you. If there is anyone here who is safe from him, it is you."

My breath caught. What the hell did that mean? Was Nikolas going to hurt the others if he lost control? Why was I the only safe one? I darted a glance at Terrence and Josh who looked like they were too terrified to move. *Ah hell.* I really hoped Tristan knew what he was doing.

I took a gulp of air and approached Nikolas. A few feet from him I could feel hot waves of fury rolling off his body. "Look, Nikolas, I'm perfectly fine, see? Okay, I've looked better, but that's beside the point."

He didn't respond or move, and I could see something feral, something savage behind his eyes as they locked with mine. Cold fingers tickled the back of my neck, and my Mori stirred restlessly. *What am I supposed to do now?*

"Touch him," Tristan called softly, and I had to stop myself from spinning around to gape at him.

"What?"

"Take his hand. Trust me."

My stomach twisted nervously as I moved until no more than a foot separated us. Without taking my eyes from Nikolas's, I reached out and placed my hand inside his. The instant we touched, my fingers twitched as a warm tingle ran through them. Then they were crushed as his hand closed around them in a painful grip.

"Ow!" Tears sprang into my eyes, and I smacked him hard in the chest with my free hand. "Let go!" When he didn't respond, I reached up and slapped his cheek. "Nikolas, snap out of it! You're breaking my hand."

He released my hand, but before I could nurse my bruised fingers, he pulled me against him and wrapped his arms around me so tightly I could scarcely breathe. His whole body trembled, and I could feel his heart thumping furiously beneath my cheek. My fear was swept aside by an overwhelming need to comfort him, and I wriggled my arms free to wrap them around his waist. "Hey, it's okay. I'm here," I whispered, rubbing my hands against his back. My own traitorous heart sped up at his nearness, and I could not help thinking about the last time I touched him. *This is not the same.* There would be no repeat of the other night.

Minutes passed, during which his trembling faded and his heart rate slowly returned to normal. I was about to ask him again if he was okay when his arms loosened and fell to his sides. I took a cautious step back and looked up at him. His face was still hard, but at least he no longer had that crazed look in his eyes. The anger seemed to have burned itself out.

Tristan came up behind me. "Nikolas, we need to get Sara and the others home."

Nikolas looked at him over my head and nodded.

I looked from him to Tristan, waiting for one of them to explain what had just happened. Tristan gave a slight shake of his head, and Nikolas did not seem inclined to speak to me at all. My gaze fell on Terrence, who still looked half scared to death, and then on Jordan, who watched us with more curiosity than fear. What the hell was going on, and why was I the only one who seemed confused?

This time when I moved to go around Nikolas, he did not try to stop me. I didn't look at anyone else; I just started walking toward the driveway where our SUVs were. Physically I was fine, but my emotions were a wreck. I needed answers, but right now I needed some space.

I heard footsteps behind me and knew it was him, but I didn't stop until I reached the two black SUVs parked at the end of the driveway. I tried the back door on one and it was unlocked, so I got in and sank wearily onto the leather seat, not caring about the vampire blood I was getting all over it. I rested my head against the headrest and closed my eyes while I waited for someone to come and drive me home.

Muffled voices carried to me from outside, and it sounded like people were arguing. I tuned them out until the door across from me opened and Tristan got in. At the same time, Seamus and Niall took the front seats and Seamus started the vehicle. I turned my head toward Tristan, who looked tired for the first time since I'd met him.

"Where is Jordan?" I asked him.

"She'll follow in the other vehicle. Do you want me to get her?"

"No, that's okay." Jordan was most likely having the time of her life bragging to the others about her vampire kills, and I wouldn't ruin her fun. I wished I could join them, but I was too freaked out by whatever it was that had just happened with Nikolas.

Tristan placed a hand over mine on the seat. "I'll explain it to you at home."

No one spoke on the drive back to the stronghold, which told me that whatever Tristan was going to tell me was probably something I was not going to like. When we got there, the first person I saw was Nikolas, standing outside the main entrance, waiting for us. He didn't say anything, but he wore a scowl and I could feel his eyes on me as we passed him.

Inside, Tristan tried to bring me to the medical ward, and I refused, insisting I was not hurt. All I wanted was a shower and some answers, in that order. But when I started for my room, Tristan said it was best if I came with him to his apartment instead. Something in his expression told me it was best not to fight him on this one.

Tristan's apartment had a guestroom, and I closed myself in there as soon as we arrived. I pulled off my blood-soaked clothes and stuffed them in a garbage bag, sure that Jordan would not want her top back. She'd probably love the excuse to order more clothes for both of us.

When I emerged from the bathroom wrapped in a thick robe, I was surprised to see some of my clothes laid out on the bed. Whoever had gotten them from my room had also remembered to get a fresh bra and panties. Normally I would be embarrassed by the thought of one of the warriors going through my underwear drawer, but I couldn't bring myself to care about it.

Tristan was waiting for me in the living room when I finally emerged from the guestroom. "What's wrong?" he asked, and I realized I was frowning.

"Every time I go out, I come back looking like Carrie after the prom." I heaved a sigh. "At least this time I didn't need a doctor. I guess my luck is improving."

"I would not call what happened tonight luck. You and Jordan should be very proud of yourselves."

I took a seat on the couch. "I am, and I know she is. She's probably telling anyone who will listen about it."

Tristan chuckled. "I'm sure she is. She is one of the finest young warriors I've ever seen. I am glad you have become friends."

"Me too."

Neither of us spoke for a moment. It was easy to see that he had something on his mind and he was not sure how to start. When he did speak, it was the absolute last thing I had expected to hear from him. "Sara, before I explain things, I need to ask you something. The last thing I want to do is invade your privacy, but I have to ask this. Have you and Nikolas been intimate?"

"What? No!" I sputtered. Heat flooded my face. "Why would you ask me that?"

He looked as uncomfortable as I felt. "I don't mean sex. I mean, has there been any physical contact between you . . . outside of training?"

I stared down at my clenched hands. "A few nights ago . . . we kissed. It was just one kiss and don't worry, Nikolas made it crystal clear that it was a mistake. That was the last time I saw him until tonight."

"I see."

"See what?" I looked at him again. "What does that have to do with anything?"

He put a hand through his blond hair and sighed. "I was hoping to have a little more time before I explained this to you. If you had grown up among the Mohiri, you would have learned about these things by now." He paused. "What I'm going to tell you might be a bit hard for you to understand at first, given your human upbringing, but it is very natural among our people. Please, let me tell you everything and then you can ask all the questions you need to.

I nodded mutely and pulled my knees up to my chest, wrapping my arms around them as if they could shield me from whatever he was about to reveal to me. The last time someone had spoken to me in this tone, it was Nikolas telling me I was Mohiri. I didn't think I was ready for another revelation like that one.

Tristan paused a moment before he launched into his story. "We are like humans in many respects, except for the obvious differences. We have relationships, and we date and form emotional connections. Couples can remain together for many years, but most don't form unions like human marriages. In order for us to join with another, they must be our, *solmi*, our life mate. Most of us go many years before we meet a potential mate, but when we do, our Mori recognize each other immediately from the first touch."

Solmi? That's what my Mori called . . .

"Males usually feel the bond first, and it is stronger for us. Our first instinct is to become very protective of our female. As you have seen, Mohiri females are strong and most do not want to be protected, so the courtship can be a bit volatile in the beginning. As deeper feelings form, the bond begins to grow between them and it strengthens the more they spend time together, particularly if they are . . . intimate in any way. Eventually, they complete the bond and become life mates. It is a very deep and profound experience."

I tried to swallow, but my mouth was too dry. My insides felt like they were on a rollercoaster, and my emotions were along for the ride. "I-I think I know what you are trying to say, but you're wrong. I would know if I . . . if we . . . " Anxiety gripped me. "He doesn't want . . . "

"Nikolas called and told me about your bond a few days after you disappeared in Maine. He knew you weren't dead because the bond was still there." Tristan paused to let that sink in, and I remembered Nate telling me

184

how Nikolas had been sure I was still alive and he had refused to give up looking for me.

"Another Mohiri female would have recognized the bond between her and a male, but you don't have a normal connection with your Mori. Otherwise, you would sense Nikolas when he is near, as he does with you. That is why I asked Nikolas to give you time to become accustomed to our way of life before telling you about the bond. You're young and you've been through so much recently. You were upset about leaving home, and I didn't think you were ready to hear this. Nikolas didn't want to upset you or confuse you more than you were. He didn't like it, but he agreed to go away for a while and give you space and some time to adjust. He refused to stay away any longer when he heard about the lamprey attack. He came back that night."

I chewed on my lower lip and tried to calm my stomach. It just couldn't be true. Yes, I could feel Nikolas when he was close, but that didn't prove anything. I'd seen him with Celine, and the way he looked at me after we had kissed, there was no mistaking the regret in his eyes. Those were not the actions of a man enamored with me. "But I saw him . . . with Celine. And he told me the kiss was a mistake."

"Nikolas and Celine were together for a period a long time ago, but I can assure you there is nothing between them now. As for the kiss, Nikolas is an honorable man and he knew I didn't want him to pursue a deeper relationship with you until you understood what was happening between you."

"I . . . I'm having trouble believing this. It's not that I don't trust you. It's just that you haven't really seen us together. We argue all the time, and he's always trying to tell me what to do. He gets so uptight every time I – "

"Every time you are hurt or in danger?" Tristan supplied and the bottom dropped out of my stomach. "As I said, males can be very protective, and the relationship between the male and female is usually stormy at first. When a male senses his female is in real danger or distress, his Mori can go into what we call a rage."

"A rage?" Something Chris had said to me once came back to me. *He's worked himself into a bit of a rage . . . It's a Mori thing . . . You'll learn about that stuff soon.*

"It happens when a male warrior and his Mori become too agitated to control their emotions," Tristan explained. "It's easily restrained if the bond is new or weak, but the stronger the connection, the deeper his instincts are to protect you. Tonight, when Nikolas saw you covered in blood, he went into a full rage, and one wrong move from any of us would have set him off. I've seen it before. The only way to calm him was to assure him you were safe. That was why I told you to talk to him and touch him. You were the only one who could get through to him. The bond between you is much stronger than I had suspected, which is why I asked if you and he had been intimate."

I laid my forehead on my knees and squeezed my eyes shut. It was all too much. I cared for Nikolas. He infuriated me half the time, but I'd be lying if I said there was nothing between us, at least on my part. I'd had plenty of time since our kiss to analyze my emotions and realize that my feelings for him had begun to change before I even left New Hastings. The kiss had just made me admit what I had been trying to deny all this time.

But love? Not just love but the deep soul mate kind of love that Tristan spoke of? I wasn't ready for that. The thought of committing to a lifelong relationship with anyone at this point, even if I did have strong feelings for him, was too much to think about right now.

How did Nikolas really feel about all of this? Had he been driven to kiss me only because his demon felt a connection to mine? What if he felt trapped by this bond and that was why he had looked unhappy after he kissed me. How would I ever know if it was he and not his demon who wanted to be with me?

"You are very quiet."

I rubbed my eyes. "Sorry. I'm really trying to understand all this. What exactly does it mean to be bonded?"

Tristan hesitated as if he was thinking of the best way to explain it. "A bonded couple share what I can only describe as a spiritual connection. They can always sense one another when they are near, and after they complete the bond, they can communicate through the bond and feel each other's emotions when they are together. Bonded mates can also share their Mori power to comfort each other and aid in healing if one is sick or hurt. It is a very intimate connection and something an unmated Mohiri cannot do."

The first time Nikolas came to see me in New Hastings, he had tried to push into my mind to prove to me I was Mohiri. He'd known even then about the connection between us. What had it been like for him all this time, knowing about it when I had no idea?

"You said people meet their potential mates. Does that mean a person can have more than one life mate? Can a bond be broken?"

My question seemed to trouble him, and it took him a moment to answer. "Finding a mate can take a long time, but I have known several people who rejected the bond and found other mates. Your Mori may be compatible with several others, and if you choose not to pursue a relationship with one, that bond will not grow. Once a bond has formed – like the one between you and Nikolas – it can be broken, but the separation can be painful. Not physically" – he rushed to say when I sucked in a sharp breath – "but emotionally. It depends on how deep the bond is. Once a couple completes their bond, it is for life and cannot be broken."

I swallowed hard. "How do you break it before it's complete?"

Tristan looked even unhappier by that question than my last one. "First, you tell the other person you want to break it. Then you sever all contact with them. No communication and absolutely no physical contact. Over time, the bond will grow weaker until it eventually dissolves. Only then, can you see each other again."

Sever all ties with Nikolas? Say good-bye to him and maybe never see him again? A heavy weight settled in my chest. After all we'd been through he was more to me than a protector and a trainer. He was more than a friend even if I didn't know exactly what. I didn't want to be forced into a relationship, but I couldn't imagine him not being in my life.

"You don't have to decide anything now. Give yourself some time to think about it," Tristan said as if I'd spoken my thoughts aloud. "No one will try to make you do anything you don't want to do."

My lungs stopped squeezing like I was under water, and I took a deep breath. "How does the couple complete the bond? Is there a ceremony?"

Tristan cleared his throat. "No. When the couple is ready, they declare their love in private and join physically."

"Physically? You mean . . . ?" He nodded, and my stomach took another tumble at the thought of Nikolas and me . . . My face heated up again because I could not believe I'd just had that thought – and in front of my grandfather. "If everyone knows about this bond stuff, they'll know about me and Nikolas." *And after his reaction tonight they'll think we do a lot more than train together.*

"Yes. Does that upset you?"

"How am I going to face them?" I hid my face in my knees again with a groan. "How am I going to face Nikolas?"

"Nikolas understands how difficult this is for you. It has not been easy for him either."

I raised my head at this surprising news. "I didn't think anything bothered him."

"Nikolas has focused on being a warrior his whole life, and he's never had anything more than casual relationships. After almost two centuries of never meeting a potential match, I doubt he ever expected to find one." Tristan smiled warmly. "He certainly never expected you; you turned his world upside-down, and he had no idea how to deal with it. Imagine how it was for him. He is on a routine mission when he stumbles across an orphan in a bar of all places, and suddenly his Mori is telling him that she is the one. I doubt he took it well."

"He was a bit rude." *Rude* was a mild description of Nikolas's hostile first reaction to me, but I didn't want to say that to Tristan.

Tristan let out a rich laugh. "You forget I have known Nikolas for a long time. I can well imagine how he behaved." He leaned forward, resting his elbows on his knees. "He only wants the best for you, Sara. You should talk to him and let him tell you himself how he feels."

Panic flared in me at the thought of seeing Nikolas. "Now? I-I can't . . . "

"Not tonight and not until you are ready."

I sagged against the couch, suddenly mentally and physically burned out. All I wanted to do was sleep. Maybe I'd wake up tomorrow and find out that this was all some crazy dream.

"I'm sorry you had to find out about everything this way. I know you must be very confused and overwhelmed."

Confused couldn't come close to describing how I felt in that moment. "One of you should have told me. All the time I spent with him, I never knew what was happening between us. If I had, I might have decided to stop it before it went any further, before we got any closer."

"Are you saying you want to break the bond?"

"No . . . I don't know," I answered honestly. I did have feelings for Nikolas. If I walked away without exploring them, would I regret it for the rest of my life? "I need some time to process all of this before I do anything."

Tristan stood and waved at the guest room. "You've had a lot to deal with tonight. Why don't you try to get some sleep and we'll talk again tomorrow?"

"Okay." I really wanted to crawl into my own bed, but the possibility of running into anyone – especially Nikolas – on the way to my room made me accept Tristan's invitation. I said good night to him and burrowed beneath the covers in the guest bed, waiting for exhaustion to overtake me. But as tired as my body was, my mind refused to shut down. It kept running through my conversation with Tristan and reliving every moment I'd ever spent with Nikolas, looking for evidence of the things Tristan had told me. Since I'd met Nikolas, his overprotective, overbearing ways had chafed me and led to most of the arguments between us. But there was no denying that I had always felt safe with him and I'd trusted him with my life from the beginning. Why would I place such faith in a total stranger? I delved deeper and remembered the flash of recognition I'd felt the first moment I saw him. Had that been my imagination or my Mori recognizing its mate?

Groaning, I rolled over and punched my pillow. Tristan was right. It was no use trying to deny there was some kind of connection between me and Nikolas, and it had been there since the first moment we met. I wasn't romantic enough to call it love at first sight because I didn't believe that existed no matter what people said. But there was something between us nonetheless, and I had to decide what I was going to do about it.

Me and Nikolas? *Nikolas!* How was I going to talk to him, knowing what

I did? It wasn't that I blamed him or anything; he'd been caught up in this, too. I thought about seeing him at the barn, the way his eyes had never left me and how he'd trembled as he held me tight against him. It was the first time I'd ever seen him not in control, and it had scared me.

The last thing I wanted to do was hurt him, but I'd never dealt with anything remotely like this. Part of me was scared to death, while another part of me wanted to go to him and . . . do what? Tell him it would be okay? Tell him I cared about him, too?

I curled up miserably under the covers and prayed for sleep. Pink streaks appeared in the sky outside my window before my body finally succumbed and let me slip into a temporary oblivion.

Chapter 16

THE SUN WAS high in the sky when I opened my eyes, letting me know I had slept straight through the morning. But it wasn't the bright sunlight spilling into the room that woke me; it was the soft touch of butterfly wings against my mind followed by the sound of men's voices in the other room.

"She is not ready to see you," Tristan said in a firm voice. "Last night was a shock to her, and she needs some time to process it."

"I frightened her. I need to talk to her, to explain." Nikolas's gruff voice made my stomach do a little flip, and I couldn't tell if it was from nervousness or excitement.

Tristan's tone turned conciliatory. "Sara knows you would never harm her, and she's the only one who wasn't afraid of you last night. You and I both knew she would be upset when she learned about the bond, which is why we agreed to wait to tell her."

"I did wait," Nikolas replied, a note of impatience slipping into his voice. "I left for almost three weeks."

"When you returned and asked to train her, you said you could keep your distance. Kissing her is not what I'd call *keeping your distance*."

Oh God! My face burned, and I pulled a pillow over my head to block out the rest of their conversation. As curious as I was to hear what Nikolas had to say about the kiss, I did not want to hear him talking to my grandfather about it. Did these people have no concept of boundaries?

I waited a good five minutes before I lifted the pillow to hear silence in the other room. I waited another ten minutes before I dressed in the same clothes I'd worn after my shower last night. I cracked the door open to make sure Tristan was alone before I left the bedroom.

He looked up from some papers he was going over at the table, and I realized he had stayed here with me instead of going to his office today.

"Good morning."

"Morning," I replied weakly, remembering what I'd heard of his conversation with Nikolas. "You didn't have to stay with me."

"I wanted to be here when you woke up. Are you hungry?"

My stomach growled in response, and we both laughed.

He got up and took a carton of eggs from the refrigerator. I tried to argue that I could feed myself, but he ignored my protest and ordered me to sit. "I like cooking for someone again, and I'm going to make you the best omelet you've ever had."

I took a seat at the table and watched him chop vegetables and crack eggs into a bowl. I waited for him to say something about Nikolas's visit or last night, but he seemed content to focus on cooking. I figured it was as good a time as any to tell him what I had discovered last night.

"Tristan, when those vampires showed up I sensed them before I saw them."

He stopped beating eggs to peer at me. "What do you mean?"

"I got this cold feeling in my chest just before the first one arrived, and it happened again when the other two came." I saw his look of incredulity, and I didn't blame him because I knew how it must sound. "It's happened a couple of times before, only I didn't put it together until last night."

"It happened back in Maine?"

"No, only since I came here. The first time, I was out in the woods. It was the day Hugo and Woolf got loose. The other time was outside the movie theater in Boise."

"We have twenty-four hour patrols in the woods around Westhorne. It is unlikely that a vampire would risk getting that close to us."

"But it's not impossible."

He studied me for a moment before he shook his head. "No, not impossible. If not for the three dead vampires I saw last night, I would say the possibility of a vampire showing up in town was slim as well. I'll have someone check the woods, and we'll add another patrol to be safe." He went back to preparing the omelet. "You said you felt the same thing in Boise?"

I told him about the cold sensation in my chest as we were leaving the movie theater. "I'm not suggesting the vampire I sensed had anything to do with the lamprey attack, but I am positive there was a vampire nearby."

Tristan nodded, but he looked troubled as he poured the egg mixture into the skillet. "Boise is normally very quiet. We see some lower demon activity – like lampreys in the sewers – but rarely vampires. I'll ask Chris to assemble a team and investigate. If there was a vampire, it might have been passing through, but I don't believe in coincidences."

His belief in me and his readiness to take action was both gratifying and reassuring. "Me either."

"Tell me, why do you think you can sense vampires now?"

"Aine thinks it could have something do with the vampire blood on the knife I was stabbed with."

This time he turned to face me. "You saw the sylph? Here?"

"No, at the lake a few days ago. She said she couldn't come here because it would upset everyone."

"Did she come to ask you to go to Faerie with her again?" His voice held an edge of worry, and I rushed to reassure him.

"No, she just wanted to catch up and make sure I'm doing okay."

Tristan finished making the omelet and slid it onto a plate. He laid it in front of me with a glass of orange juice and sat across from me as I took a bite.

"This is amazing." I moaned through a mouthful of food, earning a smile from him.

"I'm glad you like it." He clasped his hands together on the table. "So, you believe you can actually sense a vampire's presence? If that is so, it would be an incredible ability to have."

"Yeah, and it's a lot better than having to sniff them."

"Sniff them?"

"You know – that awful odor vampires have. Of course, you can only smell it when you get really close to them."

His brow furrowed. "Vampires don't smell any different from humans."

"You must have been too busy killing them to smell them because, trust me, they reek like road kill when you get up-close-and-personal with them. I only got that close to Eli, but I'll never forget that smell." I laid down my fork and shuddered at the memory.

Tristan stroked his chin. "It must be an elemental trait that allows you to smell them. Interesting."

"You wouldn't find it interesting if you were the one gagging on vampire BO."

"No, I guess not."

I took a few more bites of food. "Hey, we could always test my vampire radar. You could take me somewhere like Vegas and I can find them for you."

To my surprise, he did not dismiss my idea. "We could do that once you get some more training under your belt."

"Great, I'd like that. By the way, was Derek okay? Jordan threw him pretty hard."

"We treated him and took him to the hospital. He has a mild concussion and as far as he knows, he fell trying to climb up to the barn loft while he was intoxicated."

"How do you do that – make people forget seeing a vampire?"

"We manufacture a drug from several plant extracts that allows us to modify short-term memory in humans. We've found that most humans are happier not knowing about the supernatural."

I nodded in agreement as I took a drink of orange juice to wash down the last of my omelet. Back when I thought I was human, I'd spent half my time learning about the supernatural world. But would I have been the same if my dad hadn't been killed? I might have lived in blissful ignorance until vampires came looking for Madeline's daughter or until I discovered I'd had stopped aging.

"Sara, Nikolas was here before you woke up. He wants to see you. I told him you weren't ready, but you should consider talking to him soon."

My stomach tightened. "I don't know what to say to him. Can I have a few days?"

Tristan nodded. "No one is going to rush you, but don't leave him hanging long. This has not been easy for him either."

"I won't. I just . . . I need a little time." The last thing I wanted to do was hurt Nikolas, but I couldn't face him yet. I certainly wasn't ready to talk about our future or this bond between us. I carried my dishes to the sink and washed them. "Does Nikolas know that I'm going back to training with Callum?"

"I haven't told him yet." Tristan crossed his arms over his chest. "Did you ask to switch because of what happened between you?"

"Yes, but I really don't want to talk about that."

"You know that despite everything, Nikolas is the best trainer for you."

I hung up the dish towel and leaned back against the counter, chewing my lip. I knew Tristan had my best interests at heart, but I was not going to discuss my feelings for Nikolas with him.

After a moment, he let out an unhappy sigh. "I'll tell him today."

*   *   *

I stayed in my room for the rest of the afternoon and while everyone else was at dinner I snuck out and went to the menagerie. Sahir brought me a covered tray of food, and I suspected Tristan had asked him to keep an eye on me. I sat across from Minuet's cage and told her about everything while I ate. Since the night she had scented me, she sat on the floor of her cage facing me every time I came to see her, and every now and then, she cocked her head as if I'd said something of particular interest. Sahir kept shaking his head and muttering that he'd never seen anything like it.

When I finished my dinner, I noticed that Alex had crept closer to the front of his cage and sat listening to me talk to Minuet. The thing about a wyvern is that their expression never really changes so you can't tell if they are just curious or planning to try to fry you. I decided to keep my distance, throwing him pieces of the steak I hadn't finished. Although he preferred raw meat, he gobbled up the food I tossed him.

Back in my room, I picked up the phone to call Roland, but I couldn't dial the number. I shared almost everything with him, but how did I explain something I had trouble grasping myself? I hadn't told Roland yet about kissing Nikolas or my confusing new feelings for him. I loved Roland, but there were some things you just couldn't share with a boy.

Thoroughly depressed, I reached for my sketchbook. I'd started a new one two weeks ago, and it was already filled with drawings of Hugo, Woolf, Alex, and Minuet. Who would have thought a few months ago that I would be drawing hellhounds, a wyvern, and a griffin from life?

I opened to a new page and picked up my pencil. I thought for a minute about the scene I wanted to capture, and then my pencil began to move deftly over the paper. As I drew, I relived every detail of the bloody encounter in the barn. Jordan and I had won the fight, but I knew it could have gone very badly for us. If the three vampires had arrived together, we would not have been able to take them all at once. If I hadn't recognized what Seth was in time or if I'd been with someone less skilled than Jordan – like Olivia – we'd be dead now. If my power hadn't done what I'd hoped it would do, that vampire would have killed me.

The sad truth was that I was a terrible fighter and I didn't even know basic self-defense. I was years behind the other trainees, and if it wasn't for good luck and my sporadic bursts of power, I could have been killed last night. Not to mention surviving the lamprey demons. Having power was great when it worked, but what I really needed was to learn to fight.

I was putting the finishing touches on the drawing when there was a knock at the door. When I answered it, Jordan flashed a small smile and slipped past me without waiting for an invitation.

"Hello, Jordan, would you like to come in?" I asked dryly, closing the door behind her.

"Why thank you, Sara. I think I will." She plopped down in my desk chair, and I went back to sitting on the bed. "So, what excitement do we have planned for tonight?"

I made a face and picked up my sketchbook again. "Last night wasn't enough for you?"

Her face glowed. "That was the best party I've *ever* been to. You should have seen Terrence and Josh when they found out they missed all the action. They were so bummed."

"I'm sure you gave them a complete play-by-play, didn't you?"

"Of course." She grinned and looked around. "You want to do something?"

"Like what?" I was surprised she hadn't already brought up Nikolas, but I was in no hurry to discuss him if she wasn't.

"Let's go for a walk."

I looked up from my drawing. "It's too dark to go for a walk. And since when do you walk anyway?"

She snorted. "Since I met you I've killed demons in a movie theater and vampires at a party. Who knows what we'd run into out there in the woods."

"I've seen the kind of creatures that hide in the woods at night; trust me, you don't want to meet them."

"Fine, then we'll walk inside. God knows this place is big enough."

No place was big enough when you were trying to avoid someone who lived under the same roof. "Or we could just stay here."

"He's not here, you know."

I pretended to be interested in my drawing. "Who?"

"Olivia saw Nikolas and Tristan talking outside this afternoon, and she said Nikolas looked mad about something. Then Nikolas tore off on his motorcycle. Last I heard, he wasn't back yet."

"Oh."

"*So* . . . you and Nikolas, huh?"

I laid my sketchbook on the bed. "It's not like that. Not like you think anyway."

Jordan let out a laugh. "Oh, I know exactly what it is. I just don't get why you didn't tell me about the bond. It's not like I wouldn't have found out soon."

"I didn't know about it until last night."

She made a scoffing sound, but when my expression did not change, her eyes widened. "You're serious?"

I nodded, and she frowned. "How is that possible? A blind person could tell there is something between you two. And last night . . . " She let out a low whistle. "I've heard about bonding males going into a rage, but that was scary."

"I'm sorry." I wasn't sure why I apologized because it wasn't like I had caused it. Had I?

She leaned forward in the chair. "I'll tell you something else; males don't get worked up like that over a casual friendship." Her eyes took on a knowing gleam. "Miss Grey, I do believe you've been keeping secrets. Those must be *some* training sessions."

I crossed my arms over my chest. "I told you it's not . . . we haven't been . . . "

She raised an eyebrow.

"One kiss, okay, we kissed one time." I fell back on the bed and pulled a pillow over my face. "I really don't want to talk about it."

"Oh, hell no!" Jordan pulled the pillow out of my hands and bounced on the bed beside me. "You do not get to say you kissed Nikolas Danshov and then leave me hanging. I want details."

"What details? It wasn't a date, Jordan. It was just one kiss."

She huffed and lightly punched my shoulder. "You are a piece of work. It's never *just* a kiss with a man like Nikolas. So tell me, when did it happen? What did he say? Was it as good as I think it was? Duh, never mind. Of course it was mind-blowing. Just tell me, was he wearing his sword?"

I opened an eye to stare at her. "Sword?"

"What? I have a thing for men with swords." She wagged her eyebrows. "The bigger the sword, the better."

I groaned and rolled away from her. There was no way I was going to tell her that Nikolas *had* been wearing his sword at the time. Thanks to her, I'd never look at it the same way again. Why had I ever thought it might be nice to have a girlfriend to share things with?

"Well, are you going to tell me about it?"

"Okay." I heaved a sigh. "But don't blame me if you're disappointed." I told her how Alex had burned me and Nikolas had followed me to the medical ward. "We had an argument and before I knew it, he kissed me. Then he stopped and said he didn't mean to do it. He left and I didn't see him again until last night."

Jordan flopped down on her back beside me. "He kissed you in a fit of passion? That's even better. Don't you dare tell me you didn't like it."

The memory of Nikolas's hands cradling my face as his mouth covered mine made my stomach do those funny little somersaults again. I'd never understood why other girls made such a big deal over kissing, but now I got it. Just thinking about it made my pulse jump and my breath catch in my throat. Were all kisses that amazing, or was that one special because of Nikolas?

"I did like it," I admitted. *A lot.* "But I'm not sure if he did."

"Uh, his behavior last night would suggest otherwise."

"Tristan told me people have no control over who they bond with and that males feel it a lot stronger. What if the bond made Nikolas kiss me when he didn't want to?"

She made a sound somewhere between a laugh and a snort. "I don't think anything can make that man do something he doesn't want to do. The bond gets stronger only if the two people have feelings for each other. That much was pretty clear last night. So fess up."

"I do care about him, but he drives me nuts always telling me what to do." I rolled onto my back and looked over at her. "This is really freaking me out. I've never even been on a real date, and now all of a sudden I have a life mate? I mean, I could have one."

"Whoa, you've never dated anyone?"

"I had coffee with a guy once. Does that count?"

She shrugged. "I guess. But Nikolas was your first kiss?"

"Yes."

"Excuse me while I hate you for a minute."

I rolled my eyes. "Oh, please."

Jordan smacked her forehead. "Ah, this explains why he almost went nuclear last night."

"Because of one kiss?"

"Because you're a virgin. Didn't Tristan tell you about that?"

My cheeks grew warm. "We didn't talk about *that*."

"Men." Jordan turned on her side and cradled her head in her hand. "Most people go a long time before they meet a mate, and they don't exactly live like monks while they wait. From what I've heard, a male's protective instincts can go a bit haywire if their mate is a virgin."

"Great," I muttered weakly, wishing the floor would swallow me up.

"Don't worry. They say the male calms down once you complete the bond."

"What if I don't complete the bond?" What I felt for Nikolas, it was definitely stronger than friendship, but was it enough to commit to him forever?

"You can choose not to, but then I'd have to smack some sense into you. This is *Nikolas* we're talking about."

I rubbed my temples. "Can we talk about something else?"

"All right. How about you tell me what you did to that vampire last night?"

I pasted an innocent expression on my face. "What do you mean?"

She gave me a pointed look. "I was there, remember? I saw you take him down, and I heard him scream."

He screamed?

"And I'm pretty sure I smelled something burning, too."

"I had a silver knife," I said weakly.

Jordan shook her head. "Your knife was across the room. Listen, I know you did . . . something, just like you did something to that lamprey demon. You're different from the rest of us, aren't you? I mean, look at you. You're a seventeen-year-old orphan and you're totally sane. You don't even act like you have a demon inside you, and the rest of us have to meditate every morning just to control ours. And who the heck owns a pair of hellhounds?"

"You meditate?"

"Don't try to change the topic. If it wasn't for your bond with Nikolas I'd wonder if you were actually a Mohiri."

I should have known Jordan would put it together. I wanted to confide in her, to tell her everything, but something held me back. It wasn't that I didn't trust her. It wasn't easy for me to open up to people, especially about this.

"You're right. I am different. I wish I could tell you how, but I can't yet. Only a few people know about me, and they think we should keep it between us for now."

"Tristan and Nikolas, right?" I nodded, and she pursed her lips. "Is that why Nikolas is training you?"

"Yes." There was no point in denying it.

"Okay."

Okay? "That's it? You're not going to try to figure out what it is?"

Jordan tugged at a loose thread on my sleeve. "If Tristan and Nikolas think you need to keep it a secret then it must be important. I'll just have to wait until you can tell me." Her eyes gleamed. "Or until I can figure it out myself."

"Good luck with that," I said confidently. No matter how smart she was, she would never in a million years guess this one.

She rolled off the bed. "How about that walk?"

"Sure."

"Inside or out?"

"Inside." If Nikolas was out on his motorcycle, there was no chance of me running into him.

It was almost ten o'clock so we didn't run into many people as we wandered from one wing to the next. In one of the common rooms, Olivia and Mark were snuggling on a couch watching a movie, and they both eyed me curiously when we passed by. I couldn't hide from everyone forever, but I wasn't ready for the stares and the questions.

It was different with Jordan. There was something about her bluntness and sense of humor that made it easy to talk to her. I couldn't help but wonder what it would have been like if I'd had a girlfriend like her back home.

We were finishing our walk through the south wing when we spotted Tristan and Celine coming out of his office. We were not close enough to hear what they were saying, but it was obvious that Celine was angry about something. I didn't need to be a mind reader to know what had her out of sorts.

"Poor Celine. She never had a chance," Jordan said in a low voice as we headed back to our rooms. "You should have seen her at dinner. She was like a grizzly bear with a sore tooth."

"She is never pleasant to me, so I probably wouldn't know the difference," I replied, not wanting to talk about the other woman. I still wasn't convinced that Nikolas didn't feel some attraction for her, especially after seeing them together.

Why do you care if you aren't even sure you want him? The annoying little voice in my head asked. Instead of answering, I wondered where Nikolas was now and what he really thought about all of this. Was he angry with me for not wanting to talk to him today? How did he truly feel about this bond between us? It wasn't as if he'd had a choice either, right? Maybe he didn't want this at all and he was waiting for me to reject the bond and set him free.

Why didn't I break the bond? What was I waiting for? If I'd found out I had a bond with any other male here, I would have freaked and ended it on the spot. I was confused and scared and okay, a little freaked out, but not averse to the idea of being with Nikolas. I mean, it was Nikolas. I did care about him a lot, even if he made me want to clobber him sometimes, and I'd have to be comatose not to be attracted to him. And that kiss. I got butterflies just thinking about it. I had nothing to compare it to, but that couldn't be a normal reaction to a kiss.

The truth was I didn't doubt my feelings for Nikolas. I'd tried to bury them, but they refused to go away no matter how upset or angry I got at him. But Tristan said the bond was a forever thing, and I just couldn't see me committing to anyone for eternity after a few months and one kiss. And I'd be surprised if Nikolas was ready to jump into anything either no matter what his Mori was telling him. I wasn't ready to say good-bye to him forever either. Every time I thought about that possibility, my stomach felt like it had been filled with lead. I needed time – we needed time – to get to know each other more and figure this out.

Right now though, what I really needed was space to clear my head and wrap my mind around all of it. I wasn't ready to talk to Nikolas about any of this, and I didn't know how I'd feel when I had to face him again. I was glad I'd asked Tristan to switch me back to training with Callum. Nikolas might not be happy about it at first, but I was sure that once he thought about it, he would agree that this was best for both of us.

Chapter 17

I STRETCHED AND did my warm-up while I waited for Callum in his usual training room. After the last two days, I had a lot of restless energy stored up and I was looking forward to burning it off. If there was one thing I could count on Callum for, it was to work the hell out of me. Today I was going to ask him if he could start teaching me some kicks and punches. My Mori strength would be a lot more effective once I learned how to channel it properly.

When the door opened, I turned to greet my trainer and my smile faltered when Nikolas, not Callum, entered the room. Seeing him so unexpectedly for the first time since the night of the party, my stomach fluttered and my heart sped up. His closed expression made it impossible to tell what he was thinking or feeling.

"I'm waiting for Callum," I said lamely.

He shut the door. "Callum and I talked, and we agreed that I will continue to train you." The determined set of his jaw when he faced me again made me look at the door and think of escape.

"I didn't agree to that. I'd rather work with – " I broke off and took a step back when he moved forward.

He stopped and regret flashed in his eyes. "Don't do that. I would never hurt you."

"I know." Things might be weird between us, but I would never let him believe I was afraid of him. "I just think it would be best if I trained with some other people."

"No one here can teach you anything I can't."

I didn't respond because I knew he was right. I couldn't tell him that what I really needed was to work with someone who didn't tie my stomach in knots and make me so confused I couldn't think straight.

He ran a hand through his dark hair. "We both know what this is about."

"I don't want to talk about it."

"We have to talk about it sometime," he said in an infuriatingly calm voice. How could he be so composed when I was a nervous wreck?

"But not now." My eyes pleaded with him as I fought to hide my panic. "Please."

He exhaled slowly. "Let's train then."

"Okay." If I had to train with him, I would, but I couldn't deal with more than that. Not yet.

"What do you want to work on?" he asked, and I was surprised he was going to let me choose.

"I want you to teach me how to fight. I can have all the demon strength I want, but it's totally useless if I don't even know how to throw a punch correctly."

He started to shake his head, but I cut him off before he could argue. "Listen, I have to learn to protect myself. I'm supposed to train to be a warrior, right? If you're going to get mad every time I mention it, this is not going to work. I'd rather not waste my time."

"You need to condition your body and spend more time getting used to working with your demon before you learn fighting techniques."

I shrugged. "Can't I do both? The bad guys aren't going to wait for me to catch up with everyone else. Couldn't I learn some moves and do that other stuff at the same time?"

A muscle in his jaw twitched, and I groaned, "See, there you go again. Callum wouldn't think twice about teaching me to fight. He'd have no problem giving me a few bruises and throwing me across a room."

"He throws you around?"

"Gah!" I threw up my hands and headed for the door.

"I'll teach you a few strikes and blocks, and then we will put you through a workout to see how much work we have to do. We'll spend time on your fighting technique and your workouts every day. Once you have mastered the basics, we'll move on to more difficult moves." He walked to the center of the room and motioned for me to join him.

I hesitated for a moment before I went to stand before him. Being this close to him made me more than a little jittery, not out of fear but out of a deeper awareness of him. I took a steadying breath and tried to focus on what he was saying and not our complicated relationship. It was the only way I was going to get through this.

"The only rule you need to understand about combat is that there are no rules. We fight to neutralize a threat and to survive, and we do whatever is necessary to win. We use techniques from almost every martial art, and combined with our strength and speed, we can turn our bodies into weapons."

"It sounds like Krav Maga," I said, intrigued and nervous at the same time. "My friend, Greg, used to talk about wanting to learn it."

He gave a small smile for the first time since entering the room. "Where do you think the principles of Krav Maga originated?"

"Oh."

"In a fight, you have to be on the offensive at all times. You never stop moving and every movement counts. You never give your opponent an opening. To do this, you must master every possible strike, every hold and block, until you can do them as naturally as breathing. There is no room for hesitation when you are facing an opponent who is faster and stronger than you. You fight dirty because they will. And remember, a vampire is strong but the body still has human weaknesses. A well-aimed punch or kick to the groin hurts them, too."

I nodded, thinking about how fast he had moved when he fought and killed three vampires at once. His movements had looked so effortless, almost like a dance. "Where do we start?"

"The first strike we're going to work on is the straight punch. There are two types of straight punches." He demonstrated punching with his fist and then with the heel of his hand, and his movements were so fast I could barely make them out. He repeated the strikes several times, but much slower, each time explaining how to stand, how to hold my shoulders, my head, and my arms. Then he stepped back. "Show me what I did."

I positioned my body like he had instructed and punched the air with my fist. Then I repeated the action with my open hand. My movements were slow and sloppy compared to his, but that didn't bother me because I knew that, starting from this moment, everything I learned would make me a better fighter.

Nikolas's face was impassive, his words matter-of-fact as he explained what I had done wrong. When he came to stand beside me and show me how to stand correctly, I was able to concentrate on his instructions despite the slight tremble in my body. If he felt it when he used his hands to position my shoulders and arms, he did not show it. His candid, almost detached manner made it easier for me to put aside everything else between us, at least for the moment, and focus on training.

After I'd done countless air punches to his satisfaction, he stood in front of me. "Hit me."

"What?"

"Strike me."

I frowned. "I'm not going to hit you."

One corner of his mouth lifted. "Trust me, you won't hurt me."

"But – "

"If you want to learn to fight, you'll have to get used to hitting people."

He raised his hands in front of his chest, palms toward me. "Now hit me."

"Don't temp me," I muttered. I got into position and struck out with my right hand. It hit his open hands with a small smacking sound.

"Shoulders forward. Now hit me again."

My fist tapped his palm a second time.

"Relax those arms. Again."

Over and over, he had me strike at him as he barked instructions like a drill sergeant. First we practiced my right arm, and when he was finally satisfied, he made me start the same drills with my left one. I lost count of the number of punches I threw, but I was sweating and my arms ached by the time he put his hands down and told me to take a short breather.

Barely five minutes passed before he handed me a set of dumbbells. "Now we work on strength training and conditioning. We'll stop when you can't go anymore." I narrowed my eyes at his barely concealed smirk. He was enjoying this.

Two hours later, I dropped the skipping rope in my hand and leaned, panting, against the wall. It was all I could do not to face-plant on one of the exercise mats, and the only thing that kept me upright was my determination not to collapse and concede defeat to Nikolas.

He picked up the rope and hung it on a hook. "Ready to call it quits for today?"

"No, just catching my breath." I stepped away from the wall and my exhausted legs quivered, but I stayed on my feet. "What's next?"

Admiration flashed in his eyes, and I felt a ridiculous burst of pleasure. He had pushed me hard for hours, and I think we were both surprised I was still on my feet.

He turned away and began stacking weights on the rack in the corner. "I think that's enough for now. You don't want to overdo it in your first session."

"Okay." I was not going to argue with him. I'd proven myself, and now the healing baths called to me like a siren's song. I couldn't believe I'd thought Callum's lessons were tough. I would be lucky to walk tomorrow . . . if I didn't fall asleep in the bath and drown myself.

"Tomorrow we'll start working with the bag," he said as if it was some kind of reward.

Holding back a groan, I opened the door. "Yay."

I could have sworn I heard a soft laugh as the door shut behind me.

* * *

"Hey, Sara, mind if I sit with you?"

"Huh?" My head jerked up from where it had been resting on my hand, and I squinted at the blond boy standing in front of me holding a lunch tray. "Oh, hi, Michael. Sure, have a seat."

I sat up straighter and surreptitiously wiped my chin in case I'd drooled when I dozed off. A quick glance around the room assured me that Nikolas was not there to see me falling asleep over my lunch. Not even a long soak in the baths had helped me after training with him all morning.

"Thanks." Michael sat across from me and started eating his sandwich. After a few bites, he laid it down and pressed his lips together like he wanted to say something. I didn't press him because I figured he would spit it out if he wanted to.

"I heard what happened in town," he said at last. "Everyone's been talking about it. Did you and Jordan really kill three vamps all by yourselves?"

"Yes, but they were baby vamps and Jordan took out two of them." I told him the story although I knew he'd heard Jordan's version already.

His blue eyes shone with excitement. "Wow! That's totally awesome."

I couldn't help but smile. "Yep, I guess it was."

"I'm glad you're okay." He picked at his food. "You didn't come down at all yesterday, and I wondered how you were doing."

"I was just chilling." Michael was way too sweet to be a warrior. He should be a healer or something like that because I could not picture him killing anything, not even a vampire.

He nodded and took another bite of sandwich, chewing slowly before he spoke again. "Can I ask you, is it true about you and Nikolas?" As soon the question was out, his face reddened. "Sorry. I know it's none of my business."

"No, it's okay. It's not like it's a big secret." I refrained from sighing because I knew I was going to have to face the questions and comments sometime.

"You don't look happy about it."

I took a sip from my room temperature water and wrinkled my nose. "I'm just getting used to it all, I guess. It was a bit of a shock, and I'm not sure what's going to happen now."

"You guys argue a lot," he stated artlessly, and I heard the question behind his words.

I lifted a shoulder. "Well, I guess it wouldn't be boring."

"It's crazy that the first Mohiri you met was your mate, and it's Nikolas Danshov of all people. People go ages without finding one and you're not even eighteen."

"We're not mates yet," I said absently, my mind still trying to process the thought of a life with Nikolas. It was hard to focus when my stomach got all fluttery every time I thought about him.

"They say it hurts at first if you reject a mating bond, but it gets better."

"What?" My mind came out of its fog. "What do you mean?"

Michael looked unfazed by my abruptness. "You said it wasn't final, so I figured you were thinking about breaking the bond. I just meant that Nikolas would be okay if you did."

"That's good to know." Michael idolized Nikolas so it made sense he was concerned about Nikolas's welfare. Still, I was uncomfortable having a conversation about something so deeply personal. I cast about for something else to talk about. "So, do they make a big deal about Thanksgiving here? I'm looking forward to turkey and stuffing next week. And my uncle, Nate, is coming to spend the holiday."

I wanted to kick myself when I saw the fleeting sadness in his eyes. How could I be so insensitive, knowing that he spent half his time searching for a brother who had to be dead? Thanksgiving must be very difficult for someone who missed his family so much that he could not accept they were gone. If anyone should understand the need to hold onto the past, it was me. I also knew when it was time to let go.

"Michael, I know you're still looking for your brother," I started, and he seemed to recoil from me. "No, wait," I said when he pushed his chair back. "I just wanted to offer my help." That stopped him, and he stared at me like he didn't know if I was being sincere or not. I took his hesitation as a good sign and plunged forward. "I never told you about my dad, did I?"

"Your father?" He shook his head and continued to stare at me like he was trying to figure out my angle.

I lowered my voice so no one else in the dining room could overhear me. It also forced him to move closer. "When I was eight, my dad was murdered by vampires." I swallowed the small lump that always formed when I spoke about my past. "I didn't find out until a year later that it was vampires who killed him."

"What does that have to do with my brother? Your father is dead, and Matthew is still alive."

"Let me finish. I knew my dad was dead, but I couldn't understand why vampires would go after him. I spent years trying to find answers, and I got a bit obsessed about it. It almost got me killed. But during the years I was looking, I made a lot of contacts online, people who know things. What I'm trying to say is that I know people out there who might be able to help you. I even know a hacker and a few guys who deal in the underworld black market. If anyone can help us find Mathew, it's them. If they can't find any sign of him, then he is nowhere to be found." I had no hope of finding his brother, but maybe what Michael needed was for someone else to tell him Matthew was dead before he would finally accept it.

The wariness left his face, and in its place I saw a vulnerable little boy who just wanted someone to tell him things would be okay. "You'd do that for me?"

"Of course, what are friends for?"

He fiddled with his napkin, but his eyes shone with conviction.

"Everyone thinks I'm crazy, but I know Matthew is alive. I'd feel it if he was dead."

My chest squeezed when I thought about the pain Michael was going to suffer when he finally had to accept that his brother was gone. "There's something else you need to think about. Even if we do find Matthew, he might not be the same. It's very likely he ended up like the other orphans that weren't found in time."

"You didn't," he said brightly as if he'd already thought about that possibility.

I didn't respond because I could not tell him the truth about me, and why I was different from other orphans. If by some miracle Matthew was still alive, his demon had driven him mad by now. I didn't know what would be worse: finding out your brother is dead or finding out that he is insane and beyond help. It was obvious that Michael was not ready to deal with either of those outcomes, so I decided to keep those thoughts to myself.

The conversation turned to training after that, and Michael wanted to know all about training with Nikolas. It occurred to me that what he and the other trainees needed to cure them of their hero worship of Nikolas was a couple of days training under him. I'd love to see how they handled his boot-camp style workout. If I wasn't so tired, I would have laughed at the idea.

*   *   *

"I can't believe you knew about it, too, and you didn't tell me. Was I the last person to find out?"

"It was not my place to tell you, little one. The mating bond is a very intimate experience between two people, and one does not interfere in such matters."

I scowled at Desmund over our game of checkers. "How did you know anyway? Did Tristan tell you?"

"Of course not. Tristan would not share something so private." He gave me a look of mild reproof. "I knew when you told me Nikolas went into a rage once when you were hurt. I must say it took me by surprise at first."

"You're not the only one." I captured one of his pieces, and he swiftly retaliated by taking two of mine. "We have to be the worst match in Mohiri history. Half the time we don't even get along."

"You both have strong personalities. You will be a worthy mate for him because you will challenge him." His eyes sparkled mischievously. "At the very least, it will be entertaining for the rest of us."

I scowled at the board. "I hate to kill your fun, but I don't even know if that's what I want."

He leaned forward. "Really? What does Nikolas think of that?"

"We haven't talked about it. I told him I'll train with him, but I am not ready to talk about any of this. I'm still upset with him and Tristan for letting me find out the way I did."

"Yes, I can imagine that was something of a shock. But don't be too hard on him. I dare say this has not been easy for him either."

"I thought you didn't like him. Now you are defending him?"

Desmund winked. "How can I not defend a man who has the good sense to care about you?"

"You are such a sweet talker," I scolded, and he gave me a look of mock innocence. "I certainly know how to pick my friends."

His hand stopped in mid-air over the board, and his expression was indecipherable. "Friends?"

"Of course. We are, aren't we?" I asked before I stopped to think. Desmund was eccentric and suffering from a long mental illness. He had come a long way in the time I'd known him, but it was still hard to know how he would react to a situation. It was possible he did not want a friend, as strange as that sounded.

A smile lit up his face. "Most definitely."

"Good." I looked down at my decimated checkers. "I'd hate to see how hard you would play someone who wasn't your friend." At his innocent look I laughed. "Don't think I don't know you go easy on me."

He shrugged, and I knew he would never admit to it. "Did I tell you my uncle, Nate, is coming next week to spend Thanksgiving?"

"You must be excited to see him."

"I can't wait. He's staying for a whole week." The thought of seeing Nate every day for a week made me almost giddy. I couldn't wait to show him around and introduce him to everyone. Just picturing his expression when he saw Alex and Minuet made me grin.

"I have never seen you look this happy," Desmund said. "Your uncle must be a good man."

"He is. I hope . . . " I hesitated, not sure how to say what I wanted to say to him. "I'd like for you to meet him . . . if you want to, that is."

"I'd be honored." His smile changed to a playful smirk. "How often do you introduce young men to your uncle?"

I let out a snort. "Young? Didn't you tell me that you and Tchaikovsky were friends?"

He touched his chin. "Hmmm, so you think your uncle will have a problem with the age difference?"

"Age difference?" My mouth fell open, and I stared at him. Did he mean . . . ? I thought about his reaction a few minutes ago when I said he was a friend. Did Desmund feel something more than friendship for me? But he'd just told me I'd make a good mate for Nikolas. Was he saying that just to be nice?

"Is something wrong?"

I rubbed my suddenly sweaty palms against my thighs. "Desmund, you know that we are only friends, right? I mean, I like you, but I can't – "

His burst of laughter cut me off and made me forget whatever it was I had been about to say. It was the first time I'd ever heard him laugh this hard, and I had no idea what had set him off. I didn't know whether to be worried or relieved.

It took him a minute to compose himself. He wiped his eyes. "You are an absolute delight. I have not enjoyed myself this much in a very long time."

"What's so funny?" I asked, starting to feel a little insulted.

He smiled affectionately. "If I was going to fall for a young lady, you would be at the top of my list. In fact, you would be the list. But alas, you and I have too much in common for that to ever happen."

"I don't understand."

"That is one of your most endearing qualities, little one." He stunned me by leaning across the small table and kissing my forehead. "And if you were a man, I would fall madly in love with you this instant."

If I was a . . . oh. "Oh!"

"Let's just say I did not spend time with Pyotr Tchaikovsky for his musical genius alone."

Heat flooded my face. I couldn't believe I'd suggested Desmund had a thing for me. God I was such a moron. I had always been stupid when it came to guys, but this took the cake.

"I did not mean to make you uncomfortable."

I gave him a reassuring smile. "It's not you. I just can't believe what an idiot I am sometimes."

He shook his head. "I find your innocence charming."

"That's because you are a gentleman," I replied, feeling a little less embarrassed.

"And because I am a gentleman I am very glad I am not enamored of you."

My eyebrows rose. "Why?"

He chuckled. "Because then I would have to fight Nikolas Danshov for you and I like my head right where it is."

Chapter 18

THE NEXT DAY, Nikolas showed me how to execute an uppercut punch and a front kick. Then he put me to work on the punching bag for an hour before he switched over to a grueling workout on the weights. The entire time we were together, he was all business and did not try to talk about the night at the barn or anything about us. In fact, he did not say much at all unless it was directly related to my training. As soon as our session ended, he left and I did not see him again that day.

It wasn't until that night, as I was creating magical whirlpools in my bubble bath, that I remembered I hadn't told Nikolas about seeing Aine or about using my power on the vampire at the barn. The last thing I wanted to do was bring up that night, but it was Nikolas who had helped me learn to call on that power and he was still my trainer.

I waited until after we'd practiced my punches and kicks the next morning to bring it up. I wiped my face with a towel and took a long drink from my water bottle before I blurted it out.

"I zapped a vampire at the barn."

Nikolas set down the pair of dumbbells he was holding and turned to face me. It took me several seconds to realize he was not surprised by my announcement.

"Tristan told you."

"Yes."

I tried to guess what he was thinking, but his tone and expression gave nothing away. "Why didn't you say something?"

He leaned against the wall with his arms folded across his chest. "I figured you would tell me when you were ready, and when you felt like you could trust me again."

"I never stopped trusting you." I flushed but refused to look away from him because he needed to know I was sincere. If there was anyone I would trust with my life it was Nikolas. My heart I wasn't as sure about.

"Do you want to tell me what happened? Tristan said you were able to sense them."

I told him everything as I had described it to Tristan. Nikolas's eyes flashed with suppressed fury as the story unfolded, but he merely nodded when I explained the cold in my chest and how I was able to take down the vampire. I could tell he was fighting his demon for control. His angry outbursts whenever I was in danger made sense now. What I didn't understand was why the bond made him react so strongly, or why I felt a growing need to go to him and soothe away the furrows in his brow and the hard line of his mouth.

Clenching my hands behind my back, I focused on my story instead. "I tried to call on the power like we practiced, but it wouldn't come until I touched him. Then it just jumped out of me like it did with the other demons. I don't understand why it burned him, but it didn't burn you."

Nikolas gave me a tight smile. "A vamhir demon is always close to the surface because it controls the body. You couldn't feel my demon until I called it forth." He stared at the window for a long moment, and his face betrayed the battle going on inside him. He wanted to train me, to help me become strong enough to protect myself. But at the same time, he didn't want me anywhere near a vampire.

To my relief, his pragmatic side won. "This is good. It means you have a built-in defense against vampires, young ones at least. We need to keep working on it to make sure it is reliable."

"What about my vampire radar? Can we go somewhere and test it?" I knew he was going to refuse, but it was worth a shot.

"Not until we spend a lot more time on your training. There will be plenty of time to test your other abilities."

"Okay." I was willing to wait if he was willing to accept that I would have to fight vampires someday. It was a small step forward for both of us. "When can we work on my power again?"

He picked up a jump rope and held it out to me. "Let's finish your workout and we'll meet up after lunch for your other training."

I groaned as I took the jump rope. I had a feeling my days were about to get a lot more exhausting.

Over the next week, Nikolas and I fell into a pattern. Each morning, he taught me a new strike or kick, and then he put me through another punishing workout. After lunch, we spent two hours working with my power. For this he enlisted Chris's help since he was the only other person here besides Nikolas and Tristan who knew my secret.

I could feel my power growing stronger the more I used it, but it was impossible to test its full strength without a demon. I refused to give Nikolas or Chris anything more than a mild shock no matter how much they provoked me. I would not take a chance of hurting either of them even if they made it difficult to resist at times.

My control grew as well, and I was soon able to call as much or as little power as I needed. I demonstrated that one day when Chris began amusing himself by zipping by and tugging on my hair. He got too close and I caught hold of his hand. The little jolt I gave him made his blond hair stand on end and his knees buckle. When he was able to speak a few minutes later, he said it was like being paralyzed. He didn't pull my hair again after that.

Even though we spent hours training together, Nikolas and I barely spoke, and a polite distance grew between us until I began to miss the way things used to be. If the quiet tension between us bothered him, he gave no indication of it, and I wondered if he even cared about it. The more time that passed, the more I was convinced that he didn't want the bond.

I began to dread the day he would show up and tell me he was breaking the bond and leaving. The thought of never seeing him again hurt more than I wanted to admit, and I threw myself into training to avoid thinking about it. After my training, I would take the hounds and go to the lake, hoping to see Aine again. She didn't come, but I thought I caught a glimpse of Feeorin in the water twice. I wanted to practice my water magic in the lake, but it was impossible with warriors watching over me the whole time. After I'd told Tristan about sensing a vampire in the woods, and he'd told Nikolas, they made it clear that I was not to go out alone, even with two ferocious hellhounds at my side. I didn't argue even if it meant I was limited to practicing my magic in my bath tub. It amazed me how quickly I was able to master elemental magic when none of my Mohiri abilities came easily to me. I could make mini waves and water spouts with ease and raise the temperature of the water when it began to cool, but I doubted I would ever feel the same connection to my Mori that other Mohiri shared with theirs.

I ended up asking Chris to take me to town to pick up supplies and food for Oscar. I could hardly ask Nikolas to do it when we were barely talking. As Chris and I loaded my purchases into the SUV I felt a pang when I remembered the light banter between Nikolas and me the day I'd asked him to take me to the pet store. Would it ever be that easy between us again, or was it gone forever?

David emailed me twice that week to say he and his friends were closing in on Madeline. His excitement was infectious. As soon as he found her, I would let Tristan know so he could swoop in and pick her up, if she didn't slip away again. My mother was proving to be very adept at evading everyone, especially her own people.

After my talk with Michael, I'd also asked David to see what he could dig up about Matthew. I gave him every detail I could find on Michael's family in Atlanta and the circumstances around his mother's death and his brother's disappearance. I wasn't hopeful but I had to try for Michael's sake. David confirmed what I already knew – Michael had been to hundreds of sites and message boards, searching for his brother – and he told me he was unable to find a single bit of evidence that Matthew was alive. He would keep searching, but I already knew the truth, even if I didn't know how to make Michael accept it.

My spirits shot up when I woke up on the Tuesday of Thanksgiving week and my first thought was that Nate would be here tomorrow. I grinned to myself in the shower, and I could barely sit still at breakfast. I even smiled at Nikolas when I walked into the training room. It didn't make him ease up on my workout, but I was too happy to care. Nothing was going to bring me down this week.

When my phone rang that evening, I saw Nate's number and laughed. Nate was such a creature of habit. He called me every Tuesday night without fail, and he wasn't going to miss a night, even if he would see me tomorrow.

"Hey, Nate!"

"Hey, yourself. How are things going?" He sounded tired, and I hoped he wasn't overworking himself.

"Oh you know . . . the same." Lightning was probably going to strike me for that whopper, but I couldn't tell Nate about everything over the phone. "So, you all packed for tomorrow?"

"That's actually what I'm calling about." He coughed, and I listened to him wheeze with a growing sense of dread. "I have some bad news. I haven't been feeling too good the last few days so I went to my doctor today. He says I have pneumonia and I can't travel this week."

A pit opened in my stomach. "What? No! They have all kinds of medicines here. They can treat your pneumonia in no time." I was already calculating how long it would take to bring the medicine to him.

He coughed again. "Sara, you know how I feel about that. My doctor prescribed something, and I just need to take it easy for a few days."

And miss Thanksgiving? I started for my closet to find my suitcase. "Then I'll come to you."

"No," he said sharply, and I stopped halfway across the room.

"Nate?"

"Sorry, I didn't mean to bark at you. It's just that you're supposed to be hiding and we can't risk someone seeing you. I won't be good company for you anyway. I'd rather you stay there and I'll come later."

"But you'll be alone for Thanksgiving." The happiness that had carried me all day drained away.

"Don't worry about me. I'll be fine," he rasped. "I'll come as soon as I can travel. I wouldn't miss seeing you for the world."

"It won't be the same without you."

"I know, but we'll see each other soon." He breathed deeply, and I could hear the rattle in his chest. "I need to take my meds and get some rest so I can get rid of this. I'll talk to you in a few days, okay?"

"Okay," I said, even though I was anything but okay. Ever since I got here, I had been counting down the days until Thanksgiving when I would see Nate again. Disappointment cut through me deeply, and I just wanted to curl up in my bed and cry.

God, I am an awful person. Here I was wallowing in self-pity and Nate was suffering from pneumonia. He'd be all alone for the holiday and I was thinking only of myself. I couldn't even call Roland or Peter and asked them to drop in and check on Nate because the family was leaving tomorrow to spend the holiday with their grandmother up near Bangor.

The urge to go to home despite his arguments was so strong that I grabbed a backpack and had it full of clothes before my common sense took over. Nate was right; it wasn't safe for me in New Hastings right now. All I'd be doing was putting both of us in danger, and I couldn't forgive myself if he was hurt because of me again.

It was a long sleepless night, and it left me tired and cross the next morning. Less than ten minutes into training, Nikolas stepped back and asked me what was wrong.

"Nothing," I mumbled, trying unsuccessfully to kick the heavy bag like he'd taught me yesterday.

"You are obviously upset about something."

"I'm fine," I lied. Tears threatened and I punched the bag angrily. I wanted to tell him what was wrong, but things were so weird between us that I didn't know how to talk to him. And I didn't want to run to him whenever things didn't go right. I wanted to prove to both of us that I could stand on my own. "Can we get back to work?"

He moved forward to grab the bag again, and when he spoke his voice had lost some of the coolness that had been present the last few days. "Just know I'm here if you want to talk."

Neither of us spoke much for the remainder of the session, but Nikolas's words played over and over in my head all afternoon. The longer I thought about it, the more guilt I felt for brushing him off like I had. None of this was his fault, and when he had reached out to me, I'd behaved like a brat. Was it because I wanted to be strong, or was it really because I was afraid to open up to him, afraid of where that might lead? The two of us were in a strange limbo right now because I could not deal with *us* and because he wouldn't press me. It was unfair to him, and it was time I stopped behaving like I was the only one with feelings.

By the time dinner rolled around, I had gathered my courage and made up my mind to talk to Nikolas. I spent the meal watching for him, and I barely tasted my food or heard what Jordan and Olivia were saying next to me. When he didn't show, I almost ground my teeth in frustration. I finally wanted to talk, and he had decided to dine somewhere else.

"Hello, cousin, you look like you're lost," Chris said when I ran into him in the main hall after dinner. I knew he and Nikolas worked and sparred together a lot. If anyone knew where to find him, it was Chris

"Actually, I'm looking for Nikolas. Do you know if he's around?"

He cocked an eyebrow. "You're looking for Nikolas? That's a switch."

"Yeah, it's like *Bizarro World*," I retorted and watched his brow furrow in confusion.

"*Bizarro World?*"

"You know, from the Superman comics?" He shook his head, and I sighed. "How can you live forever and not know about Superman?"

He made a face. "I know who Superman is; I just don't read comics. As for Nikolas, I believe he and Tristan had a meeting. They should be almost done now."

"Thanks." I headed for Tristan's office, hoping to catch Nikolas before he left or before my newfound courage deserted me.

Tristan's door opened as I walked down the hallway, and I heard muffled male voices inside. The closer I got I was able to pick out snatches of conversation, and I stopped in my tracks when I heard Nikolas's deep voice. " . . . not what I wanted . . . miserable . . . break the bond."

I flinched as if I'd been slapped. Nikolas wanted to break the bond? I knew I shouldn't be surprised after the last week, but it still shocked me to hear him say it. I wasn't prepared for the sharp pain in my chest. My throat tightened, and I spun to leave before one of them came out and saw me.

My escape was blocked by the last person I wanted to see. Celine tossed her long black hair over her shoulder and speared me with a pitying look that was ten times worse than her usual sneer. "So now you know," she said in a low voice so Nikolas and Tristan could not hear her. "If you care about Nikolas at all you will release him."

I pushed past her. "Like you care. You just want him for yourself."

She kept pace with me easily. "I'm not going to lie; I do want him and he wants me. Nikolas and I had something very special once, and we would be together now if this ridiculous mating bond wasn't messing with his head. Males are so susceptible to these things."

I pretended to ignore her, but she kept talking. "You are a lovely girl, Sara, but Nikolas is a man. I understand why you might fancy yourself in love with him; you wouldn't be the first young girl to lose her heart to him. But he wants a woman, not a girl."

"Why doesn't he break the bond then?" My voice cracked and I walked faster, trying to get away from her.

"He is too honorable. You've known him long enough to see how chivalrous he can be. He doesn't want to hurt you."

Her words were painful barbs, and I had no defense against them because they were true. Hadn't I thought the same things since I'd learned about the bond? Nikolas was no monk, and he'd probably been with many beautiful women like Celine in his lifetime. What could he possibly want with a girl who came unglued by a simple kiss and was so stupid when it came to men that she'd thought a gay man was flirting with her?

We reached the main floor and Celine grabbed my elbow before I could leave. "You can still be friends with him if that is what you want, but it is cruel of you to hold him to this when he is obviously unhappy." She let go of my arm and turned to leave. "Think about it and you will see I am right."

"Just who I was looking for." Jordan bounded down the stairs from our wing and scowled when she spotted Celine's retreating back. "What did *she* want?"

I forced a smile. "The usual; you know Celine."

"Unfortunately." She linked her arm with mine. "Forget her. We have a party to go to."

"Jordan, we can't go to a party after what happened at the last one." Not to mention, Tristan and Nikolas would probably lock me in my room if I even mentioned it.

She snickered and tugged on my arm. "Who said anything about leaving the stronghold? We're going to have our own little holiday party right here."

"That's great, but I don't think I'm in the mood to party tonight."

"Listen, I get that you're bummed about your uncle not coming, but what good is it to hide out in your room all night and be depressed about it?" She fixed me with a determined stare. "Wouldn't you rather hang out with us and have some fun? We have beer, and Terrence got his hands on some Gran Patron."

I had no idea what Gran Patron was, but I assumed it was some kind of alcohol. I wasn't into liquor, but I could handle a beer or two. I looked up the stairs and realized the last thing I wanted right now was to be alone.

"Come on," Jordan cajoled, mistaking my hesitance for reluctance. "Don't make me drink with those losers alone."

"Okay."

"Sweet. Let's go."

I expected us to go to one of the common rooms, so I was surprised when she headed for the main entrance. "Where are we going?"

"The arena," she said once we were outside.

The temperature had dropped a lot since that afternoon, and I shivered in my sweater. I raised my face and breathed deeply of the cold air. If my nose was not mistaken, we might be having a white Thanksgiving.

"What are you doing?" Jordan asked.

"Smelling the air. I think it's going to snow."

She sniffed at the air. "You can smell snow in the air? Seriously?"

"Can't you?"

"No."

"Oh."

She gave me a sidelong look. "You're strange, you know that?"

It felt good to smile. "You have no idea."

The door to the arena opened before we reached it, and light spilled outside. "About time you two got here," Terrence called. "Thought we were going to have to start without you."

Jordan laughed. "Like you lightweights could have a party without us."

He stepped aside, and we entered the arena where the other trainees sat together near a large cooler. Even Michael was there, and it surprised me to see him away from his laptop.

"Time to get this party started," Terrence sang. He went to the cooler and began handing beers to everyone. When all of us held one, he raised his bottle and said, "To us."

"To us." We all drank. Josh turned on a small portable stereo and Coldplay filled the room. The seven of us sat and drank and talked about training and when we would go on our first mission. Everyone had heard Jordan's story of our adventure at the party and they wanted to hear my side of the story. I told them everything I could without revealing my secrets. Jordan beamed when I described how easily she had dispatched two vampires. Human girls bonded over things like boys and music; we bonded over kicking demon ass. It was no wonder I never had any human girlfriends.

"So, you and Danshov, huh?" Josh asked. It was the first time one of them besides Jordan had mentioned the bond, and all I did was shrug and keep my face blank. Inside, my stomach hurt as I replayed Nikolas's words to Tristan.

Jordan set her bottle down. "Hey, Terrence, where is that Gran Patron you were bragging about? I think it's time for a shot."

"Hell, yeah." Terrence reached under his seat and pulled out a bottle of clear liquor and a stack of shot glasses. "Tequila time!"

I tried to pass when Terrence handed a shot to me. "I don't really like liquor."

"That's because you haven't had the good stuff. You have to try it once."

Jordan nudged me with her shoulder. "Come on, you have to do one shot with us."

I made a face but accepted the glass. "Haven't you guys ever heard of peer pressure?"

"That's a human thing." Josh grinned and held up his glass. "Warriors call it a challenge, and we never turn down a good challenge."

Everyone but Michael took a glass and when Terrence said "go" we downed the contents. The tequila was warm and smooth, and it burned its way down to pool in my stomach. A minute later, a pleasant tingle spread through my limbs.

"See, I knew you'd like it," Terrence said when I smiled. "You want another one?"

"Maybe later." I picked up my beer again and sipped it as the buzz from the tequila hit me. *Whoa, I need to slow down.*

I took my time with my second beer but everyone else, except Michael, seemed to be in a contest to see who could drink the most. Jordan wasn't kidding when she called them lightweights because she put away more than any of them and barely seemed to have a buzz going.

By the time I started my third beer, Olivia and Jordan convinced me to do another shot. Although in truth, they didn't have to do much convincing because I'd discovered that the more I drank, the less I thought about Nikolas and Celine and how much I missed Nate. Someone fiddled with the stereo, and I found myself dancing with Jordan and Olivia, singing and laughing and having a blast. So this was what it felt like to let go and have fun. I imagined Roland's face if he saw me now and more laughter bubbled out of me.

By the time I finished my beer, I felt like I could do almost anything, and I was seized by the urge to find Nikolas and tell him he was free to go be with Celine or whoever he wanted. I ignored the sharp pain in my heart as I stood. He had made it clear what he wanted and it wasn't me, so why wait to break the bond? The more I thought about it, the stronger the urge became to seek him out and just get it over with.

"Hey, where are you off to?" Jordan called when I headed for the door.

"I have to take care of something."

"But we're having fun."

"I'll be back in a bit." I opened the door and the icy air felt like a balm to my heated face. Outside, the night was quiet, and heavy clouds hung in the sky. My legs were a little unsteady as I walked to the main building, but that was not going to deter me from my mission. I was going to find Nikolas, give him the happy news, and then go back to the party and celebrate my freedom.

After the freezing temperature outside, the main hall felt like a sauna, and I had to cling to the banister when I climbed the stairs to the second floor of the north wing. Only the most senior warriors lived in this wing so Nikolas had to be here somewhere. *If he's not with Celine,* a niggling voice said, and I shook my head to banish the ugly thought.

Standing at the end of the second-floor hallway, I looked at the row of closed doors and realized the flaw in my plan. I had no idea which door was Nikolas's and I couldn't very well knock on all of them. "Damn it," I muttered, wandering down the empty hallway. Now I was going to have to wait until tomorrow to talk to him, and I had a suspicion I would not feel as courageous in the morning.

"Sara?"

Startled, I whirled and stumbled into a hard body. Hands reached out to steady me, and I looked up into Nikolas's curious eyes.

He released me and stepped back. "What are you doing here? Were you looking for me?"

Seeing him set off a maelstrom of emotions in me and sent my courage flying out the nearest window. "N-no." I moved to go around him, but I was going too fast and I staggered sideways. He caught me and turned me to face him again.

"What is wrong with you? Are you drunk?"

"No," I retorted, and I couldn't help but remember the last time he had accused me of being intoxicated. This time he was probably right. As if on cue, the hallway started to spin, and I knew I needed to get out of there before I did something to humiliate myself. I pulled my arms out of his grasp, but the jerky movements were too much and my stomach began to roll. I clapped a hand over my mouth. "Oh, I don't feel good," I moaned through my fingers.

I heard him sigh before an arm went around my back and another slipped behind my knees to cradle me against his chest. Shock rippled through me, and I would have tried to get free if I wasn't struggling not to throw up on both of us. He hurried to the last door and managed to open it without releasing me. I barely got a glimpse of a living room done in dark woods and muted greens and browns before we entered a large bathroom. He set my feet on the tiled floor, and I threw myself at the toilet where I began to retch violently.

"Oh God, I'm dying," I sobbed between vomiting tequila and beer. I'd barely been ill a day in my life, and the few times I had been sick were nothing compared to how wretched I felt now.

It took a few minutes for me to realize Nikolas had been behind me the whole time, holding my hair out of my face. Humiliation added to my misery. "Please, go away and let me die in peace," I whispered hoarsely before another bout of vomiting came on.

He let go of my hair and I thought he left the bathroom. Then I heard water running in the sink and he was back again, lifting my hair to lay a cool, wet cloth across the back of my neck. It felt so good that I couldn't bring myself to ask him to leave again. I had no idea how long I hung over the toilet throwing up, but he stayed with me the entire time, quietly pressing wet cloths to my neck. When my stomach finally finished expelling every drop of vile liquor, I flushed the toilet and sagged against the blessedly cold porcelain tub, too exhausted to move. I heard the water running again before Nikolas lifted my chin to wash my face with the cloth.

"Do you need to throw up again?"

I shook my head weakly, too tired and embarrassed to look at him. I drew my knees up against my chest and rested my head on them. I wasn't sure where I was going to get the energy to stand and walk back to my room, and all I wanted to do was curl up in a ball and go to sleep right there on his bathroom floor.

"Here." I smelled the gunna paste before it touched my lips, and I raised a hand to push it away.

"Trust me; you'll be glad for it tomorrow."

It took only the suggestion of the whopping hangover I was going to have in the morning to make me open my mouth and take the horrid paste. I shuddered as I swallowed it. I thought I heard a soft chuckle, but I was too wrapped up in my misery to care.

"Okay, let's get you off this floor." Before I could say anything, he picked me up like I weighed nothing and carried me into the other room where he set me down on a soft leather couch. I huddled with my head on the armrest, and I felt the couch dip when he sat at the other end. For several minutes, neither of us spoke and I tried to come up with something to say to him.

"Were you coming to see me?"

I nodded mutely without looking at him.

"And you had to get drunk first?" Was that amusement in his tone? I wanted to make a retort, but I couldn't after the way he had taken care of me.

"The trainees had a party," I rasped. My throat was raw from throwing up.

"Were you coming to invite me?" There was no mistaking the humor this time.

"No, I – " Now that I was here in front of him, I had no idea how to say what needed to be said. More than that, I didn't want to say it. I couldn't bear the thought of never seeing him again.

"Take your time."

I couldn't take my time because then I'd never get it out and he deserved better than that. *Be strong and just spit it out. It's the least you can do for him.* "I wanted to let you know that . . . that you're free. I'm going to break the bond."

"What?"

I looked up at the shock and anger I heard in his voice. His mouth was set in a straight line, and for several seconds raw hurt glittered in his eyes before he looked away. I bit my lip in confusion. Why was he upset? I was giving him what he wanted.

"I'm sorry. I know I'm handling this all wrong."

"Don't apologize," he said stiffly. "I don't think there is an easy way to do something like this."

My throat tightened so painfully I thought I was going to suffocate. Why hadn't Tristan warned me how much it hurt to break the bond? How your lungs constricted until you could barely breathe, or about the ice that filled your veins until you knew you'd never be warm again. If Nikolas felt half the pain I did right now, it was no wonder he could not look at me.

"This is why you were upset in training today."

"No, that was something else." I couldn't talk about Nate now, not unless I wanted to totally lose it. There was only so much pain I could handle at one time.

He was quiet for a long moment, and when he spoke, his voice sounded cool, distant. "What made you wait until now to tell me? We see each other every day."

I decided to tell him the truth even if it killed me to say it. "I-I overheard you talking to Tristan tonight. You said you wanted to break the bond."

His head whipped toward me and his eyes narrowed. "What are you talking about?"

"You told Tristan you were miserable and that you didn't want this to happen." I swallowed painfully. "I didn't mean to listen, and I only heard bits of it. And then Celine said . . . "

His voice grew hard again. "What did Celine say?"

"She said it wasn't fair to hold you to a bond you didn't want, and that you were too honorable to break it." A fresh wave of misery swept through me and hot tears spilled down my cheeks. I buried my face in my hands, unable to look at him anymore. "I'm s-sorry. I never meant to h-hurt you."

"Damn it." Nikolas slid across the couch and pulled me to him, and I went willingly into the comfort of his arms. "Celine had no right to say that to you. And you misunderstood what you heard me say to Tristan. I told him I never wanted you to find out the way you did, and that I would rather you break the bond than see you unhappy because of it."

"You don't want to break the bond?" I asked, more confused than ever. "No."

My breath caught. What was he saying? "You don't?"

I felt his body tense slightly. "Do you?"

How did I answer that question? Did I want to explore whatever this was between us? Yes. Was I ready for a forever thing? No. How did I say yes to one and not the other?

"You don't have to answer right now," he said tenderly. He was protecting me again, putting my feelings before his own, and his selflessness brought on a fresh bout of tears. His arms tightened around me. "I'm sorry you had to learn about it all this way. The last thing I wanted was for you to get hurt."

Minutes passed before I could compose myself to speak again. "Why didn't you tell me about the bond back in New Hastings?"

"If I'd told you the truth back then, you never would have come here, and I needed you to be safe." His voice was thick with emotion, making him sound vulnerable for the first time since I met him.

"Tristan told me the bond makes you overprotective. Maybe you would feel different if we broke it. You wouldn't have to worry about me all the time." I didn't want to suggest it, but I didn't want to be his weakness either.

He pulled me closer until my head was tucked under his chin and his warmth chased away the chill that had invaded my body. I closed my eyes and let his familiar scent fill my nose. "I'll always care about you. Don't you know that by now?"

I nodded against his chest.

"What are you thinking?" he pressed gently. "Talk to me."

"I don't know what to think anymore," I whispered hoarsely. "I mean, we've been fighting since we met, and I know you weren't exactly happy to meet me in the first place. My life is a mess and I'll never be a warrior like . . . Celine." The other woman's name left a sour taste in my mouth, but I had to put it out there. I would never be glamorous or sultry or whatever it was that men liked about Celine. I didn't want to be any of those things. I might be confused about a lot of things in my life but I was also happy with who I was. What if Nikolas wanted something I wasn't and he didn't realize it until it was too late?

"Sara, I don't want you to be like Celine."

"But how do you know what you want? How do you know if what you feel comes from you or from a Mori thing you have no control over?" I wanted to ask him what the bond felt like to him, to help me understand my own emotions, but I couldn't put the question into words.

I felt him sigh. "My Mori and I share our minds and emotions, but I always know the difference."

"I'm so confused. I don't understand any of this. It's like I have no control over my life anymore. I'm scared." How did I explain that it wasn't being with him that frightened me? That the bond would change us and I was afraid of losing me, who I was?

His hand began to stroke my hair. "I felt the same way at first."

"You were scared?" I couldn't keep the disbelief from my voice.

He chuckled softly. "It scared the hell out of me when I saw you in that club and felt something between us. I'd never experienced anything like it, and I wasn't prepared to feel that way for anyone, let alone an orphan I found in a bar. I wanted to stay with you and get far away from you at the same time. I tried to leave, but I couldn't. And when I saw you in the hands of that vampire . . . "

A small shudder passed through him, and I laid a hand against his chest. After a minute, I felt him relax again.

"You said you were confused and scared at first. You aren't anymore?" I held my breath while I waited for his answer. I desperately wanted to know what he was feeling, where he saw this thing between us going.

"No, I'm not. Yes, it started with my Mori in that bar, but it wasn't long before I realized there was more to you than you let people see. You drove me nuts when you were so stubborn and reckless, and you have an uncanny ability to find trouble. At the same time, I couldn't help but admire your independent spirit and how fiercely protective you were of your friends. You were an untrained orphan with no apparent abilities, standing your own against a Mohiri warrior while defending two werewolves and a troll. You were something to behold. I didn't want to feel anything more than responsibility for you, but you made it impossible not to."

His admission left me reeling. Nikolas had never opened himself up to me this way, and his words rang with sincerity. He was telling me that it was me and not my Mori he had been drawn to, and he didn't sound like a man who was being pulled into something against his will. My world shifted to fit this new reality where Nikolas and I were more than friends. We were past that place now, and there would be no going back. I didn't want to go back.

"I felt something too when we met. It was like I knew you somehow even though we'd never met. My life was turned upside-down that night in more ways than one. Then you came to see me and I resented you for telling me what I was and for changing everything. I did some pretty stupid things and I hated that you were right about them. I hated that you wouldn't go away and let me be the way I used to be. I thought you were arrogant and bossy and determined to drive me insane."

He leaned down to say in a husky voice, "If this is a declaration of love, I'm not getting a warm fuzzy feeling about it."

"I'm not finished," I blurted, totally flustered. He just *had* to use the L-word. I was so not ready to go there yet. "Even when I was angry at you, I knew everything you did was to protect me and I always felt safe with you. It was strange. I didn't trust people easily, but I trusted you almost immediately. But I don't think it was until that day at the cliff, before you showed up, that I realized I felt something more. I was alone and expecting to die, and all I could think about was the people I'd never see again. I thought about you. I took a deep breath. "And . . . I did miss you when you left me here, and it hurt because I thought you were glad to be free of me."

"I shouldn't have left the way I did. I should have waited a few days for you to settle in and told you I was leaving for a while."

"What do we do now . . . about this, us?"

"What do you want to do?"

"I don't know. I mean . . . " I took a minute to think about what I wanted to say. "When Tristan told me about the bond, I was upset that you kept it from me, and I admit I kind of freaked. Don't take this the wrong way after what we just shared, but we've only known each other for a few months. I like you a lot, but how are we supposed to know if we want to spend forever together. Forever is a long time." I groaned inwardly. *God, how lame am I?*

"You like me a lot?" he asked in a teasing voice.

My faced burned, and I was glad it was hidden in his shirt. "Sometimes."

He stroked my hair again. "Forever *is* a long time, but we don't have to think about that right now. Let's just take it slow and see what happens. Just promise you'll talk to me if you have questions or doubts instead of listening to other people."

"I promise," I said hoarsely.

"Good. Now, do you want to tell me what was bothering you in training today if it wasn't this?"

"Nate can't come for Thanksgiving." I told him about my call from Nate yesterday, and his hand moved down to rub my back comfortingly.

"I'm sorry. I know how much you were looking forward to his visit."

"It won't be the same without him." I sniffed back another round of tears. "God, I can't stop crying tonight."

"Then it's a good thing my shirts don't shrink when they get wet," he said, making me smile.

I hiccupped and Nikolas laughed softly. He shifted slightly, and his lips brushed the top of my head. My heart swelled and I wrapped my arms around him. For the first time in a long time, I felt no anxiety or fear. I had no idea what was going to happen tomorrow or next week, but right now I felt warm and happy. My Mori sighed softly, and I realized I had never sensed it being this quiet and content.

"Do you feel better?" Nikolas asked, his hand rubbing my back in soothing circles that were making me sleepy.

"Yes, but I'm never touching tequila again."

His chest rumbled with laughter. "If I'd known you were going on a drinking binge, I would have told you that Faeries have very little tolerance for human alcohol, unlike the rest of us. Looks like you inherited that trait from your Fae family."

"Great, now you tell me. Some trainer you are."

"Actually a good trainer lets you make mistakes at first so you learn never to repeat them."

I made a face even though he couldn't see it. "Then you are the best trainer ever."

Nikolas chuckled. "How did you ever get by without me?"

"I have no idea."

Chapter 19

I AWOKE SLOWLY inside a deliciously warm cocoon that I never wanted to leave. Blissfully happy, I sighed and snuggled against the source of the warmth.

"Good morning."

It took several seconds for the voice to register in my brain. My eyes shot open and the first thing I saw was sunlight pouring through a window. The second thing was the wide chest beneath my cheek. I blinked a few times, trying to clear my muddled head, and I soon wished I hadn't when I realized where I was and, more importantly, whom I was sprawled across.

"Morning," I mumbled, too embarrassed to move.

A hand moved against my back. "How do you feel?" Nikolas asked in a husky morning voice that made my stomach quiver.

Last night came rushing back, and I remembered every humiliating detail of my time on his bathroom floor, followed by our conversation and him holding me on the couch. What I did not remember was falling asleep or how I had ended up in my current position.

"Good," I said hoarsely. "Considering."

"Considering the gallon of alcohol you threw up, you mean?" I didn't need to see his face to know he was smiling. I scowled at his chest. Good to know one of us was enjoying this.

"Ugh, don't remind me." I pushed away from him and sat up, unable to meet his eyes. Smoothing my hair back from my face, I wondered how things would be between us now. Emotions had run high last night, and we'd said too much, shared too much, for us to go back to the relationship we'd had a day ago. I was happy with that, but I had no idea how Nikolas felt in the light of day.

"Are you going to look at me?"

"I hadn't planned on it."

He laughed softly and sat up. "You know you can't avoid me forever."

I focused on the blue sky outside the window. "What makes you think I can't?"

"Because you like me . . . *a lot*."

My face grew hot and I turned to glare at him, but whatever I was going to say was forgotten when I took in his tousled hair, warm eyes, and sensual smile. My stomach did a somersault, and my only thought was that I wanted to go back and wake up in his arms all over again.

His smile grew as if he knew exactly what I was thinking. "See, that didn't take long."

"Shut up," I retorted, and he laughed again.

He put a hand through his dark hair, and my insides squeezed again. It was so unfair for him to look this good in the morning when I probably looked like crap, especially after last night. And I didn't even want to think about what my breath must smell like. I could probably take down a vampire just by breathing on him.

"Are you okay?" he asked with more seriousness. "With us?" The uncertainty in his eyes made me want to hug him. God, one night on the couch with him and I was a sentimental mess.

I nodded. "Are you . . . okay with it?"

"Yes." His smile was so tender, I suddenly felt shy.

I got to my feet. "Excuse me; I need to use your bathroom and about a bottle of mouthwash."

He smirked. "Help yourself."

Standing before the bathroom mirror, I grimaced at my tangled hair and puffy eyes. I splashed cold water on my face and did my best to comb through my hair with my fingers. Nikolas's brush lay on a shelf, but it felt too intimate to use his personal things.

Yeah, because using him for a bed wasn't personal at all.

I was gargling my second mouthful of mouthwash when I heard a knock on the outer door, followed by male voices. The last thing I wanted was for someone to know I had spent the night here with Nikolas. I quietly spat out the mouthwash and wiped my mouth with a towel, waiting for his visitor to leave.

I did not expect the knock on the bathroom door. "Sara, do you mind coming out here for a minute?" Nikolas called through the door.

Oh crap! Nikolas wouldn't expose me to gossip so that meant there was only one person who could be out there with him. "Sure," I said nervously and smoothed my hair again before I opened the door.

Tristan stood in the living room, looking equal parts worried and angry as he took in my disheveled appearance. At least my wrinkled clothes were evidence that I had slept in them. I glanced at Nikolas's tousled hair and bare feet that suggested he had just woken up. Seeing us together, I could only imagine what Tristan thought.

"Nothing happened," I blurted out. "I got drunk and Nikolas took care of me. That's it."

He nodded, but his expression did not change. "Nikolas already explained it to me, and I told him he should have brought you back to your own room or to my apartment down the hall."

Nikolas smiled, completely unfazed by Tristan's scolding. "And I told him that whatever transpires between the two of us is no one's business but ours."

"Sara is not yet eighteen, Nikolas, and her uncle trusts me to take care of her. That includes her virtue and – "

"Oh my God, you did not just go there," I croaked in mortification. Nikolas coughed, and I shot him a warning look. If I heard even one snicker out of him, the bond wasn't the only thing he had to worry about me breaking.

Tristan raised his hands. "I'm sorry. I don't mean to embarrass you, but in your situation, you cannot take sex lightly. It would – "

"Gah!" I made a beeline for the door. Both of them called to me, but it would take a legion of demons to keep me in that apartment. I slammed the door behind me and ran down the hallway. Who the hell gets a sex talk from their grandfather, and in front of the guy she spent the night with? Tristan and I were going to have a serious talk about boundaries. At least Nate never tried to step into that territory.

Thinking about Nate reminded me today was Thanksgiving and he wasn't going to be here. I could smell the delicious aromas already coming from the kitchen, but it meant nothing knowing Nate could not enjoy them with me. How could I enjoy dinner knowing he was alone and sick?

"Sara, you missed the rest of the party and . . . Hey, where are your shoes?" Josh said when I passed him on the stairs.

I stared down at my stockinged feet and realized that my shoes were still in Nikolas's living room, where I'd kicked them off last night. "Don't ask," I mumbled and hurried past him to hide the heat rising in my cheeks.

* * *

"Nate, it's me again. Just calling to see how you're feeling. I know you're probably asleep right now, but give me a call when you get this. Okay?"

I laid down the phone and stared at it for a long moment. It was the third time I'd called him today and he hadn't picked up once. Yesterday, I'd spoken to him for a few minutes after lunch and he'd said he was sleeping a lot because of the drugs prescribed by his doctor. He hadn't sounded like himself at all. Worry gnawed at me. Was it normal to sleep this much with pneumonia? Was he eating enough? I decided to call him in another two hours, and if he didn't pick up, I would be on the next plane east whether he wanted me to or not.

I walked over to the window to stare out at the thick blanket of snow sparkling in the last rays of the evening sun. I had never seen snow at Thanksgiving, and I couldn't help but admire the breathtaking picture created by the snow-laden forest with the mountains rising in the distance. It looked like something out of a fairytale.

Turning from the window, I glanced at my alarm clock and saw it was after five. Everyone else was most likely downstairs for the big dinner. I exchanged my T-shirt for a nice top and brushed out my hair. I wasn't feeling the holiday spirit, but Tristan was looking forward to our first Thanksgiving together and he would be hurt if I didn't go. I would not do that to him just because I was down in the dumps about Nate.

It would be my first Thanksgiving with Nikolas too. Warmth filled me when I thought about waking up in his arms. He had been so tender and open last night, and he said we would take our time and figure this out together. What did that mean? Would he kiss me again? My stomach fluttered wildly and I touched my lips, remembering our first kiss, his mouth exploring mine and his heady scent. I definitely hoped he would do that again.

A knock at my door tore me from my daydream, and I blushed at how much one kiss could affect me. "One minute," I called, trying to compose myself. When I'd seen Jordan at lunch, I'd made the mistake of telling her I was not in the mood for Thanksgiving dinner. She'd told me if I didn't show up, she was coming to get me. Apparently, she decided not to wait.

"What are you doing here?" I stammered, staring at the last person I had expected to find at my door.

"I don't think that is the proper way to greet the person escorting you to dinner, little one."

I stepped outside. "Dinner? In the library?"

Desmund smiled with an ease I had never seen in him. "Tristan would not forgive me if I kept you all to myself today. Not to mention a certain warrior who would take umbrage with me as well." He reached around me and shut my door. "Tristan told me how disappointed you were that your uncle could not be here. I know I am a poor replacement for him, but I hope you'll allow me to keep you company in his stead."

A lump formed in my throat. Desmund had left his sanctuary and was willing to go among all those people for me? Was this really the same man I'd met just three short weeks ago? He appeared strong and self-assured, and he looked a lot healthier than he had in weeks. But was he ready to face all those people so soon?

"You are so sweet, but you don't have to do that. I know how much you dislike crowds."

His mouth turned up in an arrogant smirk. "Correction, my dear, I dislike everyone. Present company excluded, of course." He presented his arm to me. "Shall we?"

I took his arm. "Okay, but you have to promise to try to be nice to my friends."

He made a harumph sound. "Let's not push it."

Laughter and the rumble of voices reached us as we neared the first floor. Desmund paused for a moment at the bottom of the stairs and I worried again that this was too much for him to take on all at once.

"You know, I wouldn't mind having dinner upstairs. I'm not that good with crowds."

He patted my arm. "I've dined with kings and czars. A few warriors are nothing. Just follow my lead."

When we entered the dining hall no one seemed to notice us, and I gave a little sigh of relief. It did not last long. Olivia saw us first, and I watched her eyes widen as she forgot what she was saying to Mark. He turned around to see what had distracted her, and his mouth fell open. One by one, people stopped talking and heads turned our way until silence fell over most of the room.

Desmund led me across the floor, and people parted like the Red Sea to let us pass. To avoid their questioning stares, I looked at the tables that were set with nice linens and china for the holiday with candles flickering in pretty centerpieces. At home, Nate and I did the turkey and trimmings, but we didn't make a big deal of decorating or pulling out the good china. This was a lot more festive than any holiday dinner I'd been to.

We stopped at a table at the end of the room. Ignoring our audience, Desmund pulled out a chair for me facing the room. I sat, and he took the one next to me then leaned in close and said, "You see; nothing to it."

Before I could answer, Tristan joined us. "Desmund, I'm glad you decided to dine with us this evening."

"I thought a change of scenery was overdue, my friend." Desmund perused the occupants of the room and I noticed his gaze lingered appreciatively on Terrence. I couldn't blame him; Terrence was gorgeous. I debated whether or not to tell him Terrence was straight, but then I thought, who was I to ruin his fun?

Tristan took the seat on my right. "I'm happy you joined us," he said in a lowered voice. "I know it's not the same for you without Nate."

"No, but I still have family here with me."

He smiled, and then his eyes slid to Desmund. "Did you . . . ?"

I gave the smallest shake of my head. "His idea," I mouthed.

"Well, this should make for a fun evening." Chris pulled out the chair across from Tristan and winked at me like I should be in on some private joke. "I see you're still kicking, Desmund."

Desmund inclined his head. "Christian, it is good to see you again."

Chris looked from Desmund to me, and I ignored the question burning in his eyes. Like everyone else here, he wanted to know what I was doing with Desmund. I had no intention of satisfying their curiosity at the moment.

The noise level in the room began to rise again as people got over their shock and started to talk quietly among themselves. Someone came by and filled our water glasses, and I sipped my water as Desmund and Tristan talked about people they knew from a long time ago. A waving arm caught my eye and I spotted Jordan, who was giving me the "you have some explaining to do" look from the other side of the room. I smiled and shrugged, and she shot me the "don't even think you are getting out of this" look.

One person was noticeably absent. I was wondering if Nikolas was going to join us when he walked into the room. My heart did a little skip when his eyes found mine and he started toward us. Then his gaze shifted to my left and surprise registered on his face when he saw my dinner companion. It was quickly followed by a scowl, and it was obvious he was not happy to see Desmund beside me. I hoped he was not going to make a big deal of it. Bond or no bond, I was still going to pick my own friends whether he liked them or not.

"Hey," I said breathlessly when he sat across from me. I gave him a timid smile, not sure how to act around him now.

"Hey," he replied, his eyes noticeably softer. He greeted Tristan and Chris then looked at Desmund. "I'm surprised to see you here."

Desmund chuckled. "As am I, but I am feeling quite like my old self again of late. It's miraculous really."

"Is that so?" Nikolas gave me a suspicious glance. "I wonder what could have caused it." The look in his eyes promised we would talk later.

"If I could credit it to anything, it would be my charming little friend here." Desmund laid a hand over mine on the table, and Nikolas's eyes narrowed. I could tell by Desmund's tone that he was enjoying himself immensely, and I groaned silently. "I cannot tell you how much I have enjoyed our evenings together."

Nikolas eyes glinted dangerously, and I wanted to kick Desmund for his devilry. Surely Nikolas knew Desmund was gay and only messing with him, right? I gave Chris a helpless look and found him trying to suppress a grin. Now I knew what he'd meant when he said this was going to be fun. At this rate, we weren't going to make it to the first course.

"We play checkers," I clarified, and Nikolas's gaze swung back to me. "One of these days I might actually beat him."

"Checkers. How quaint." Celine slid into the chair next to Nikolas wearing a sapphire blue dress so tight I was surprised she could sit without splitting a seam. She leaned toward him and gave a throaty laugh, her barely covered chest on display. "Although, I can think of much more *entertaining* ways to spend an evening."

Nikolas smiled, and I had a sudden desire to kick him under the table. That, or remind him that I could zap Mohiri, too. The only question was whether to do it to him or Celine first. I would not forget how she had lied to me and tried to manipulate me into breaking the bond with Nikolas.

"Ah, the beautiful Celine," Desmund said, earning a smile from her. "Did I ever tell you that you remind me of a courtesan I knew once in King George's court? She was stunning to look upon and much sought after."

Celine toyed with her hair. "You flatter me, Desmund. Was she someone of noble birth?"

"No, but I believe she serviced a duke or two."

I choked on my water. Tristan reached over to pat my back, while smiling graciously at the outraged woman. "Celine, I have a Beaujolais that would go lovely with this meal. If I remember correctly, you prefer French wines."

She tossed her hair, only slightly mollified. "That would be lovely, Tristan."

Tristan called over a server and requested the wine. While he waited, he stepped in to steer the conversation to safer subjects. He talked about the teams he had sent to Las Vegas after the young couple from town had returned home as vampires. It might just be a coincidence that two local people vacationing in Las Vegas had run into a vampire, but he was not taking any chances. In addition to searching Nevada, he had posted several people in town to keep an eye on things.

"You think they're up to something?" I asked, pleased that he was finally willing to discuss it in front of me.

"Vampires are always up to something," Nikolas replied for him. "It's our job to anticipate what they will do next."

I knew I was safe here, but a shiver passed through me. I had learned firsthand how crafty and resourceful vampires could be – and determined. Eli's Master had enlisted the help of a dying sheik and a Hale witch to get their hands on me. Thank God the Master thought I was dead or who knew what he would come up with next.

The wine arrived, and Tristan poured a glass for Celine then asked me if I would like some. The memory of hanging over Nikolas's toilet made me almost gag at the thought of drinking alcohol. "No thank you," I managed to say. I avoided looking at Nikolas, but out of the corner of my eye I saw his knowing smirk.

While we were talking, everyone else took their seats. Tristan gave the servers the signal to start serving the meal; then he stood and addressed the room.

"My friends, it has been another great year for us. We've had many successful missions and saved countless lives. There is no greater reward for a warrior than to fulfill the destiny we were created for."

"We have a fine group of trainees who will soon be warriors themselves, and I am proud of each and every one of them." He looked down at the people around our table and continued. "I am especially blessed to be spending the first of many Thanksgivings with my granddaughter."

Warmth filled me at the emotion in Tristan's normally calm voice. He wasn't the only one who had been blessed this year. The last few months had been difficult and life-changing for me, but I had gotten so much in return. I had a grandfather and a cousin I hadn't known existed a few months ago and new friends.

And Nikolas.

I looked at him and found him watching me. Our gazes met, and for a moment there was no one in the room but the two of us. The gleam in his eyes told me I wasn't the only one remembering last night and all that had been said between us. It wasn't that long ago that I wished him out of my life, and now I could not imagine my life without him in it.

A server placed a bowl of soup in front of me, breaking the spell between me and Nikolas. Soon everyone at our table, except me and Desmund, was talking about council business. On my left, Desmund was quiet and I figured he found council talk as boring as I did.

"I'm so glad you're here," I said to him. "I wish Nate could have been here, too. I really wanted you to meet him."

He dabbed his mouth with his napkin. "He will come as soon as he is well, correct?" I nodded, and he smiled. "Then he and I will have plenty of time to get to know one another."

Dessert was being served when Ben came to whisper something to Tristan. I could not make out what was said, but Tristan wore a puzzled expression when he stood and excused himself.

"The rest of the world doesn't take a holiday when we do," Nikolas said when I looked at him. His easy manner usually put my mind at rest, but it didn't this time. A tiny knot of anxiety formed in my stomach. Call it intuition or paranoia, or just a history of bad things happening around me, but something did not feel right.

I laid down my napkin and pushed back my chair. "Excuse me."

Nikolas, Desmund, and Chris stood at the same time like perfect gentlemen. "Is everything all right?" Nikolas asked.

"Yes. I just . . . I need to check on something. I'll be back in a little bit."

"She's fine, gentlemen," Celine scoffed, put out by the lack of attention being paid to her. "She doesn't need an escort to go to the ladies room."

For once, I was glad for Celine's presence. "She's right. Please, finish your dessert."

The three men took their seats again. Nikolas was the last to sit, and I saw the doubt in his eyes. I didn't know if it was the bond or our history together, but he was getting way too good at reading me. Soon it would be impossible to keep anything from him.

I exited the room and turned toward the main hall. I didn't know why, but something told me to go that way and intuition was all I had right now. When I rounded the corner, I saw the open front door and my steps picked up. I neared the door and heard male voices outside, one of whom was Tristan. Wintry air hit me when I reached the door, but that did not deter me. The same gut feeling that had made me leave the table, told me I needed to go out there and see who was on the other side of the door.

The cold sucked the air from my lungs when I stepped outside, and I wrapped my arms around me for warmth. The night was dark because the moon had not yet risen, but there was enough light around the entrance to see Tristan standing at the bottom of the steps with Ben, and they were alone and facing the driveway as if they waited for someone. Maybe it was someone from the council. It must be someone important to make Tristan leave dinner and stand out in the cold to wait for them.

The sound of a vehicle reached me before I saw headlights coming up the long driveway. Soon a white van with the name of a Boise airport shuttle service on the side pulled up and stopped a short distance from the steps. I watched as the driver got out and slid open the back door on his side, which faced away from us. There was a murmur of voices and creaking sounds and finally the crunch of feet on snow as he shut the door and came around the front of the van. He was alone and empty-handed, and I stared at him in confusion. What was he doing? Who had he been talking to?

Movement drew my attention from the driver, and I let out a loud gasp at the man coming around the corner of the van in a wheelchair.

"Nate!"

It all made sense now, why he hadn't answered his phone today; he had been flying out here to spend the holiday with us. My heart threatened to explode from happiness.

A wide smile split Nate's face, and he stopped beside the driver. "I hope I'm not too late for dinner."

"You are just in time, my friend," Tristan said graciously. "Why did you not tell me you were coming? I would have sent our plane for you."

I laughed and flew down the stairs. Later, I would scold Nate for travelling against the doctor's orders. Right now, all I wanted to do was hug him. Then he was going to get all the turkey dinner he could eat followed by the biggest piece of pumpkin pie he'd ever seen. I was going to feed him so well he would never want to leave.

It hit me just as my feet touched the bottom step, the sensation that someone had stabbed an icicle into my chest. Gasping, I skidded to a stop beside Tristan and stared in confusion at Nate, and then in dawning horror at the van driver who had stepped behind Nate's wheelchair.

Oh God no.

"Vampire!" I screamed.

Tristan grabbed my arm, and Ben drew his sword. The driver's eyes went wide and he whirled to look behind him. Nate sat calmly in his chair.

The chair creaked as Nate leaned forward. I watched mutely as he put one foot then the other on the ground. His gaze met mine, and his mouth curved upwards in a smile that did not quite reach his eyes.

"No," I uttered, choking on the word.

He stood and my world crumbled around me.

Chapter 20

"WHAT? NO HUG for your uncle?"

Pain obliterated the coldness in my chest, closing my throat and making it impossible to speak. *This is not happening. This is a horrible dream.*

He took a step and threw his arms in the air. "Look, I can walk again. Aren't you happy for me?"

Tristan let go of my arm, and before I knew what was happening, he and Ben had Nate restrained between them. Nate did not struggle, but fangs grew from his mouth as he continued to smile at me. "I have a message for you from the Master. Eli was his favorite and he was very upset to lose him. The Master thinks it's only fair that, since you took one he loved, he should take someone you love."

Roaring filled my ears, and I staggered backward. I did this. I'd brought these monsters into our lives. I'd killed Eli, and now Nate had paid the price for it. Because of my actions, the person who had always loved me, the one I should have kept safe, was gone. Grief suffocated me and I gasped for breath, even as I wished it would kill me so I didn't have to live with this pain.

My legs buckled and someone caught me from behind. "I'm here, *malyutka*," Nikolas said against my hair. I stiffened and tried to pull away from him. Nate was gone because of me; I did not deserve to be held or comforted. Nikolas had warned me I was going to get Nate or one of my friends killed if I wasn't careful. How could he stomach being near me, knowing what I'd done?

Instead of letting me go, he pulled me closer, whispering words I couldn't make out over the pounding of blood in my ears. It was futile to struggle against him, so I stopped and stood woodenly in his arms, waiting for what I knew was to come.

"Nikolas, it's good to see you again," Nate said jovially. Every word was a lash flaying open my soul. I felt tears behind my eyes, but for some reason they did not come.

"I wish I could say the same," Nikolas replied evenly. "I'm sorry this happened to you, Nate."

"Don't be. I've never felt so whole or so strong."

Tristan motioned to someone, and Niall and Seamus strode over to place restraints on Nate. "What . . . will you do with him?" I asked when they started to lead him away.

Nate made a scoffing sound. "What do you think they will do? You are vampire killers, after all."

Tristan walked over to me, and the sympathy in his eyes was almost too much to bear. "We will question him about the Master."

"And then?"

"He will die," he said heavily. "I promise it will be quick and . . . "

I didn't hear the rest. Black dots swam before my eyes and sounds became muffled like I was under water. I swayed in Nikolas's arms. "Let's get you inside," he said gently.

"No, I need . . . I need to be there." No matter what he was now, I couldn't leave Nate to die among strangers. He deserved better than that."

Tristan rubbed his brow. "It won't happen today. It usually takes a few days to get them to talk. He won't hold out long without . . . sustenance." New vampires need to feed daily. Tristan was going to starve Nate until he gave up the information they wanted.

The thought of Nate drinking blood horrified me. But he had done it already, hadn't he? Vampires don't finish the transition until they drink from a live human. Another life lost because of me. When would it stop?

Not until the Master dies . . . or I do.

"You are turning blue from the cold, little one," said Desmund quietly, and I wondered vaguely how long he had been there. "Let Nikolas take you inside, please."

I nodded and let Nikolas turn me toward the building. At the top of the steps, a crowd had gathered as almost everyone from the dining hall spilled outside to see what was going on. I refused to let Nikolas carry me, and I looked straight ahead, trying not to see the looks of shock or pity on the faces I passed. Inside the hall, I spotted Jordan, Olivia, and Michael standing together. Olivia's eyes brimmed with tears and, for once, Jordan wasn't wearing her cocky smile. Michael looked stricken, and I knew he was remembering his lost family. I wished I could offer them words of comfort, but my lips were as frozen as my heart.

Even Celine, who stood alone at the bottom of the stairs, looked at me without her usual sneer. *Imagine that,* I thought numbly. *She might actually have a heart after all.* Not that it mattered, not that anything mattered anymore.

I barely noticed my surroundings as we walked to my room. Nikolas didn't try to talk to me, but he kept my hand in his the whole way. I'd thought of him as my anchor once, and that was what he was to me now. He was the only thing keeping me from coming apart in a million pieces and drifting away.

Later, I would have only a shadowy recollection of entering my room and curling up in a shivering ball on my bed. Voices came and went. I lay there wrapped up in my misery thinking about Nate in a cell below. Only he wasn't Nate anymore. The man who had raised me and loved me was gone, and in his place was a monster. Pain radiated from my chest to every part of me, and I pressed my face into the pillow, praying for the oblivion of sleep.

When I did finally sleep, Nate haunted my dreams. He called to me, begging me to save him, asking me why I let this happen to him. I saw him rising from his wheelchair, his green eyes now red and blood dripping from his lips. At his feet was a blond teenage girl, and I recognized her as one of the girls who had disappeared from Portland months ago. As I stared at him, he became my dad, his face gray and lifeless. *Why, Madeline? Why did you do this to me?* he beseeched in a rattling voice. His face blurred and he was Nate again, clutching the hilt of a dagger protruding from his chest. *You're just like her. She killed my brother and you killed me.*

"Shhh." Nikolas held me while I sobbed against his chest, his hand rubbing my back until I cried myself out. He moved to sit up and I clung to his shirt, but he only tugged a quilt over us and pulled me back into the circle of his arms. Emotionally drained, I fell asleep again to the soothing sound of his breathing and his heartbeat against my cheek.

The next time I awoke, it was morning and I was alone on the bed. I touched the spot beside me and the heat lingering there told me Nikolas had not been gone long.

"How are you feeling?"

I pushed back the quilt and found Jordan sitting by the window. My eyes felt swollen and gritty, and my voice was hoarse when I spoke. "Okay." It was a lie, and we both knew it, but I could not put the truth into words.

"Shit, that was a terrible thing to ask. Sorry." She came over to sit on the edge of my bed, and her tired eyes told me she hadn't gotten much sleep either. "Nikolas had to take care of something, so I said I'd stay with you. You don't mind, do you?"

"No, I'm glad you're here." The last thing I wanted was to be alone.

"Good." She fell silent for a long moment. "I'm really sorry about your uncle."

"Thanks." I pushed myself up to sit against the pillows. My hand rested on the quilt, and I traced the outline of a hummingbird sewn into one of the squares. My grandmother made the quilt to pass on to her children and grandchildren. Nate had never dated much or said anything about wanting children of his own, but he was still young and there'd been plenty of time for him to start a family. Now the Grey name was going to die with him. My throat tightened painfully, and I swallowed hard, fighting tears. How could there be any left to cry after last night?

"Are you hungry? I brought you some food because I figured you wouldn't want to go down to breakfast."

The last thing I wanted to think about was food, but I knew I had to eat. I nodded, and Jordan went to retrieve a covered tray. She laid it across my legs, and I picked up a piece of buttered toast to nibble.

"Here, this came for you." She handed me a cream-colored envelope, and I knew immediately who had sent it. I opened it and read the short note written in Desmund's elegant handwriting.

I am here for you. Desmund.

"It's from Desmund Ashworth, isn't it?" Jordan asked in a hushed tone. "I've heard of him – everyone has – but no one's seen him in like a hundred years. He never comes out of his wing, and no one is stupid enough to go up there. I always heard he was insane and dangerous."

I hated to hear her speak of Desmund that way, but I couldn't fault her for it. Until recently, he had been exactly as she described him. But something told me he would not be going back into seclusion again.

"He was sick for a long time, but I think he's better now."

She helped herself to a strawberry from the fruit bowl on my tray. "You've been here less than a month, and yet you and he looked like old friends at dinner. How did that happen?"

There was no reason to hide my friendship with Desmund, so I told her how we met and how I began to visit him. I left out the parts about his illness and my efforts to heal him. "Everyone stayed away from him because of his reputation, only I didn't know about it. I thought he was a rude person with a bad attitude."

"Never a dull moment with you, is there?" she quipped. Her grin quickly faded. "I'm sorry – "

"It's okay, really." My eyes traveled around the room, and I forced myself to look at the pictures of Nate. I needed to stop feeling sorry for myself and think about what he had lost. He was the victim here, not me. "Have you heard anything about . . . him?"

Jordan bit her lip like she was unsure how much to tell me. "They have him in a holding cell, and I heard Tristan spent half the night down there with him. They are pushing him hard for information about the vampire who changed him, but so far he's not talking."

I didn't want to think about what methods they were using to get Nate to talk. I had to remind myself again it wasn't really Nate in that cell, and Tristan was doing what was necessary to find the vampire who had done this.

Laying aside the tray, I pulled back the covers and got out of bed. I couldn't stay in this room, surrounded by memories of Nate and wondering what was happening to him. I grabbed some clean clothes and went into the bathroom.

"Where are you going? Nikolas said to stay with you until he got back," Jordan called through the bathroom door.

"I don't think he meant for me to stay locked in my room." I was a mess last night, so I didn't blame Nikolas for thinking I shouldn't be alone. But I needed to get outside, breathe fresh air, and clear my mind, or I would go mad.

Freshly showered and changed, I pulled on warm boots and a coat and headed out. "I'm going to the menagerie," I told Jordan when she made to follow me. "Nikolas will know where to find me."

Outside, the air was crisp and it looked like another inch or two of snow had fallen overnight. I stomped snow off my boots at the menagerie door and went inside to find Sahir using a long pole to shove a tray of raw meat into Alex's cage.

"Sara, I didn't expect to see you here today," he said, walking toward me. "I'm sorry about your uncle."

My throat threatened to close off again. "Thank you."

He motioned for me to follow him to his office. Inside, he closed the door and turned to me. "I know there is nothing that will ease your pain right now, but I have news you will be glad to hear. One of our teams may have located Minuet's flock."

"Already? Where?"

"Uganda. They are still trying to verify they have the right flock since it's very difficult to communicate with griffins. Don't say anything to Minuet. I'm not sure how much she understands, and I don't want her to get excited until we know for sure."

I felt myself smile for the first time today. "Thank you for telling me, Sahir."

We left his office, and I stopped by to say hello to Minuet and Alex before I took Hugo and Woolf for a walk. The hounds chased each other around and rolled in the white powder like puppies, blissfully unaware of the grief pressing down on me. I usually loved walking in the snow, but there was no joy in it for me this time. How could I be happy and enjoy this day when Nate had only days left?

We didn't go far from the stronghold. Tristen had extra warriors patrolling the woods, a stark reminder that the Master knew I was alive and living at this stronghold. I wanted to stay close for Nate anyway. I couldn't make myself stop caring, even if he was a demon now. That would be a betrayal of the memory of the wonderful man who had raised and loved me. The vampires had taken him from me, but they would never take that away.

When I came back from my walk, I discovered that as much as I wanted to be close to Nate, I could not bring myself to go back into the building. I spent a few hours at the menagerie and then wandered around the grounds. Maybe if I kept moving, it would keep the terrible pain in my chest from suffocating me.

Nikolas found me walking by the river, and as soon as I saw him, I realized I'd been waiting for him to come for me. Watching him approach, I felt a moment of brilliant clarity and the world fell away until there was only him. Last night when my world fell apart, it was Nikolas I clung to, *him* I needed. I didn't know if my feelings for him had grown deeper because of the night in his apartment or if I was finally seeing what had been there all along.

I love him.

Any other time that revelation might have terrified me, but losing Nate made me see that I could no longer take the people around me for granted. I didn't know if Nikolas loved me or if I was ready to declare my love for him, but whatever this thing was between us, it felt right.

Wordlessly, he wrapped me in his arms, and we stood like that by the rushing water for several minutes before he pulled away and gazed down at me. "How are you holding up?" he asked, brushing my hair back from my face.

"I'm okay."

He smiled sadly at the lie and took my hand. "Come, I have something for you."

"What is it?"

He squeezed my hand as we neared the main building. "I know nothing can take away your pain or undo what's happened. But if you could have anything else right now, what would it be?"

I didn't need to think about it. "I'd want – "

"Sara!"

"Roland!" I let go of Nikolas's hand and threw myself at the dark-haired boy running around the corner of the building. Roland caught me up in his arms and squeezed me until I couldn't breathe. I laughed and cried at the same time.

"Hey, I'm here too."

Roland set me down and Peter swept me up in a hug. I was a blubbering mess by the time he let me go.

I wiped my face on my sleeve. "How did you guys get here?" I asked, though I already knew the answer.

"Nikolas called me last night and told me you needed us. He had a private jet pick us up in Portland this morning." Roland's blue eyes reflected my pain. "He told us about Nate. I'm so sorry, Sara."

I nodded, too choked to speak.

"I'll let you three catch up," Nikolas said, and I grabbed his hand before he could leave.

"Thank you," I whispered, unable to say how deeply moved I was. He knew exactly what I needed, and he'd flown my friends halfway across the country for me.

I lost the battle with the tears again and one scorched a trail down my cold cheek. He reached up and wiped it away with his thumb. "I'll be close if you need me." I nodded, and he left us alone.

Roland watched him go then gave me a crooked smile. "So, you and Nikolas?"

"I . . . it's complicated," I said even though I knew that wasn't true anymore. Watching Nikolas walk away, my aching heart swelled with emotion I could not put into words.

"Took him long enough," Roland quipped, and he and Peter exchanged knowing looks.

I glanced from one to the other. "What do you mean?"

Roland's breath released a thick cloud of steam in the frigid air. "Sara, no one takes their job *that* seriously."

I let his statement sink in. "Why didn't you say something to me?"

"And make it easy for demon boy? Where's the fun in that?"

I was too surprised by his revelation to scold him for the "demon boy" remark. Was I the only person who hadn't seen something between me and Nikolas?

Roland put an arm around my shoulders. "Let's go inside so we can thaw out. Is it always this bloody cold here?"

"It gets this cold in Maine."

"Yeah, but not in November. If I'd known it was like this, I would have brought a heavy coat."

I laughed through my tears as we walked toward the main entrance. "Roland, you're a werewolf. How can you be cold?"

He let out a snort. "Do you see any fur? I'm freezing my butt off right now."

The main hall felt like an oven after being outside so long, and I didn't realize how cold I was until I stepped inside. A few people stared at us when they passed, and at first I thought it was because of Nate, until I remembered that the Mohiri and werewolves didn't exactly care for each other. My friends were probably the first werewolves to ever walk through these doors.

"Are you guys hungry? Lunch is over, but I can get us something to eat." If there was one thing I knew about werewolves, it was that they were always hungry.

"I wouldn't turn down some food," Peter said. "But only if you eat, too."

We entered the dining hall where a few stragglers from lunch watched Roland and Peter with open curiosity. Ignoring them, I went to the door that led to the kitchen to see what I could scrounge up. The kitchen staff must have heard about Nate because they gave me sympathetic looks and told me they would fix something for us. Ten minutes later, two of them carried out three heaping plates of food and set them in front of us before they went back to get us something to drink.

Roland stared at his plate of steak and mashed potatoes. "This is what you have for lunch?"

"Sometimes." I scooped up some of my potatoes. "They have everything here."

He put a piece of steak in his mouth and made a moaning sound. "Oh man, this is amazing. If I'd known you were eating like this, I would have come to visit sooner." His eyes widened as he remembered the reason he was here. "Ah hell, Sara, I didn't mean – "

"I know you didn't." I smiled despite the ache in my chest. Grief is not a fleeting emotion. This pain would be inside me for a long time, and all I could do was learn to live with it and hope that, someday, I'd be able to breathe again without hurting.

We talked mostly about the people we knew back home for the rest of the meal. After our late lunch, I took them up to my room where we could be alone. Roland and I sat on the bed with pillows piled behind us like we used to do at his house. Peter stretched across the foot of the bed with his head propped up on his hand, looking like he didn't know what to say next.

"Do you want to talk about it?" Roland asked quietly.

"I don't know how." How could I begin to describe how it felt to see Nate standing there as a monster? How it felt when he told me the Master had done this to him because of me?

It took me a while to get the story out. Roland and Peter listened without interrupting while I told them about Nate's phone call a few days ago and how he had arrived last night. Roland's hand covered mine while I relived every horrific detail, and I knew I couldn't get through this without him and Peter.

We spent the afternoon remembering our childhood and sharing memories of Nate. I cried a few times, but I drew strength from their presence and our shared history. Late that afternoon, Tristan came to see me, looking like a man who carried the world on his shoulders. I introduced him to my friends and he graciously welcomed them. He told us he'd given Roland the room across from me and Peter's was down the hall so they would be close to me. Tristan told them they were welcome to stay as long as they wanted. Then he pulled me aside to ask how I was doing.

"I'm okay I guess. How – how is he?"

"He's hungry, but we haven't harmed him. So far he hasn't told us anything helpful."

I tried not to think of Nate somewhere down below, hungry for human blood. "Do you think he will?"

Tristan shook his head wearily. "If we kept him down there long enough, maybe."

"Why would he come here, knowing he would" – I swallowed hard – "knowing he would die?"

"My guess is he was compelled by a mature vampire. New vampires are as susceptible to compulsion as humans."

It was the perfect revenge. Make Nate a vampire and send him here so I would have to kill him or watch him die.

"Sara, he's asking to see you," Tristan said, and his expression told me how he felt about it. "I don't think it's a good idea, but I wanted the decision to be yours."

"Maybe he wants to say good-bye." Even though I knew better, a tiny spark of hope flared.

"He's not Nate anymore, not the Nate you knew." Tristan ran a hand through his hair. "He will only try to hurt you as much as he can before he dies."

I stared at the floor. I ached to see Nate, but I wasn't ready to face the evil thing living in his body. "How long before you . . . ? How long does he have?"

"A day, two at the most. By then we'll know if he is willing to talk. If he was compelled, he may not be able to reveal anything."

Panic gripped me. A day and I would lose him forever? "Couldn't we hold him for a while and see if he talks? Maybe if he gets hungry enough he'll – "

Tristan gripped my shoulders firmly. "Is that what you want, to keep him down in a cell, slowly starving to death? Because that is what will happen, and I can tell you it's not a painless way for a vampire to die."

Tears filled my eyes. "But – "

"I wish more than anything that I could fix this and take your pain away, but keeping the vampire alive will not help you. It will only prolong your grief, and I will not do that." His words were hard, but his eyes were gentle. "The Nate you loved would not want that for you, and he would expect me to do what I can to shield you from that kind of pain."

I pressed my trembling lips together and turned away from him. "Tomorrow. I want to see him tomorrow."

"Are you sure?"

"Yes."

"Okay, I'll arrange it." He laid a hand on my shoulder. "I'm so sorry."

I stared out the window for a long moment after I heard him leave. Why did people always say they were sorry when you lost someone? It wasn't like they were responsible for your pain.

"You all right?" Roland asked.

"No." I was too tired and drained to try to pretend my world wasn't falling apart. I faced him and Peter. "Will you come with me tomorrow to see Nate? I'll understand if you don't want to."

"Of course, we will," he said without hesitation, and Peter nodded.

I went to sit beside him on the bed again. "I'm so glad you guys are here. I don't think I could get through this without you. The people here are nice, but they didn't know Nate."

Roland took my hand in his. "We'll be here as long as you need us . . . and longer if they feed us steak every day."

I let out a shaky laugh. "You and your stomach."

"Speaking of food," Peter cut in. "It must be almost time for dinner."

The last thing I wanted was to be around everyone, but I couldn't expect my friends to go to dinner without me. "Give me a few minutes, and then we'll go down."

I was in the bathroom, splashing water on my face, when I thought I heard a knock on the door. Drying my face, I walked out to find Roland and Peter sitting at the small table with a large covered tray between them.

"A girl named Jordan brought dinner for us," Roland told me. "She said to tell you to let her know if you need anything, but she doesn't walk dogs. You have dogs?"

I shook my head at Jordan's thinly-veiled joke; leave it to her to try to make me laugh. However, I didn't think Roland and Peter would find her werewolf humor funny.

"Just the hellhounds," I said.

Peter made a noise. "I wouldn't exactly call hellhounds dogs. By the way, when do we get to meet them?"

"I'll take you down tomorrow."

"Cool." He lifted the cover off the tray. "Hmm, these look awesome."

Jordan must have known something about werewolf appetites because the tray held five huge double hamburgers with the works and a large basket of fries. Her comments were soon forgotten as the boys dug into the food. I took one burger and nibbled at it, and by the time they had polished off the other burgers, I had barely eaten half of mine. I gave the rest of it to Roland who finished it in no time.

Peter picked up a napkin-wrapped bundle from the tray and looked inside. "A blueberry muffin? Strange thing to bring for dinner."

My heart swelled at Jordan's thoughtfulness. She acted the tough chick all the time, but she was a lot nicer than she let on. I took the muffin from Peter and broke it into three even pieces before I laid them on the floor beside my bed.

"What the – ?" Peter's eyes grew wide when the first little fiend appeared and snatched up his prize before retreating beneath the bed again. "You have imps in a demon hunter home . . . and you're feeding them?"

I watched the second piece of muffin disappear. "They came from home. They stowed away in my stuff."

"And you let them stay in your room?"

"Why not? They practically lived in my room back home."

Peter made a face. "Because they're demons and they would steal the fillings out of your mouth."

"They're pretty quiet and they don't mess with my things. Although, I don't know how it's going to work when Oscar comes to live – " My breath caught. Nate was supposed to bring Oscar when he came for Thanksgiving. Nate, who had been in the middle of his transition when I last spoke to him on the phone, and who had walked around our apartment as a vampire and touched our things, defiling our home. Fresh pain stabbed my chest. A vampire would show no mercy to an animal, especially one I cared about.

"What is it?" Roland asked.

"Oscar and Daisy – he probably killed them," I said in a cracked voice.

"You don't know that. Animals sense evil, so they might have run away when Nate turned."

When Nate turned. I had seen Nate as a vampire with my own eyes, but hearing it from Roland made it all suddenly, agonizingly real. Nate was gone, and my life would never be the same again.

I pushed away from the table and ran to the bathroom where I promptly threw up the little bit of food I'd eaten.

"Sara, you okay?" Roland called through the closed door.

"I just need a minute." I splashed cold water on my face and stared at my pale reflection in the mirror. My lips were almost colorless, and the shadows around my eyes made my face look tired and sickly. But my haggard appearance was nothing compared to the damage inside me. If it wasn't for the constant ache in my chest, I would have believed my heart was broken into pieces.

"I'm really an orphan now," I whispered to the ashen face staring back at me.

I would give anything to bring Nate back. But there was no bad guy to barter with this time, no sacrificing myself to save Nate. The Master had seen to that. He didn't take Nate to replace Eli. He took him to torture me and to show me that no one I loved was safe from him. How many more would he hurt to get to me? Would he go after Roland or Peter next, or maybe the kids at my old school?

I couldn't live with that.

My hands gripped the edge of the sink until they turned white and I shook with helpless rage. *Stop it. That is exactly how he wants you to feel.* I was playing right into his hands, and if I didn't do something about it, he would win. Anguish and fury built in me. I remembered my dad's mutilated body and I imagined what Nate had gone through. Heat spread through me, and I watched my hair lift off my shoulders as tiny blue sparks skimmed across my skin.

Is this why he fears me? I could knock out a baby vampire and my power was getting stronger every day. Someday, I'd be able to take down an older vampire . . . maybe even one as old and strong as a Master. I needed no weapon because my touch was lethal to demons.

I was, in essence, the perfect demon slayer.

And I knew what I had to do.

Chapter 21

I DRIED MY face and opened the door to find Roland hovering outside.

"You look beat, Sara. You should try to get some sleep."

"I am tired," I lied. "I think I'll lie down for a bit. You guys don't have to stay with me, though."

"Pete and I will go across the hall and watch TV for a while. I bet you guys have all the movie channels here. You come over when you finish your nap."

"Okay," I agreed, although sleep was the last thing on my mind.

I waited for several minutes after I heard Roland's door close before I left my room and shut my door quietly behind me. Most people were at dinner so the hallways were almost empty as I made my way down to the lower level that housed the holding cells and interrogation rooms. Down here the walls were made of smooth stone and there were no windows that I could see. I shivered in my sweater, and I didn't know if it was because of the cooler air or what I was about to do.

At the bottom of the stairs a short hallway stretched before me, with a thick metal door at the other end. As I drew close to the door, I could see the intricate runes etched into the metal, preventing anyone but a Mohiri from opening the door, and I could feel the buzz of strong magic running through it when I put my hand over the metal surface. I paused with my hand on the door. When and how had I started to sense magic?

Turning the large iron knob, I pulled the door toward me, revealing a dimly lit room on the other side. What I didn't see until I walked inside was Ben posted to the right of the door. He gave me a stern look when I entered the room.

"You should not be down here."

"I want to see him."

Ben folded his arms across his chest. "I'm sorry, but I can't let you in there without an order from Tristan."

"He's my uncle and I have a right to see him," I argued, wondering how I was going to get past the huge warrior. "Couldn't you make an exception?"

Sympathy flashed in his eyes. "That vampire is not your uncle anymore. I am sorry for your loss, but I cannot allow you to see him unless I receive orders. If you wish, I can contact Tristan and ask him."

My mind worked furiously. Tristan might let me see Nate tonight, but he and Nikolas would insist on accompanying me, and I'd never be able to do what I came to do. I could tell by Ben's determined expression that he was not going to be persuaded to let me in without permission.

I have to get in there.

I was desperate enough to try almost anything to get into those holding cells, so when the idea came to me, I didn't stop to debate whether it was a bad one or not. I moved backward and let my body slump against the wall.

Ben immediately moved toward me. "Are you all right?"

"Just a little dizzy," I said, making my voice sound weak.

He took my arm and guided me to the only bench in the room. "Sit here and I'll call someone to assist you back to your room."

I caught his hand as he reached for his earpiece. "Ben, if this works, I hope you'll forgive me."

"If what – ?" His eyes widened, and I saw shock pass over his face as static crackled over my hand and a small jolt of power shot into him. For a moment, he stood there staring at me, and all I could think was *oh crap!* Then his eyes rolled up in his head and he fell to his knees. He toppled sideways, and I jumped and caught his head before it hit the hard stones. The last thing I wanted was to give him a concussion on top of everything else. I checked his pulse and breathing and smiled grimly. The jolt I gave him was the same kind I'd used on Chris, so I knew Ben wasn't going to be down for long. And he was not going to be happy when he woke up. "Sorry, Ben, but I had to do this," I said softly, pulling off my sweater to pillow his head.

Searching his pockets, I found a set of keys, and as soon as my fingers closed around them, I felt the same magic in them that protected the doors. I stood and adjusted my T-shirt, then opened the door on the other end of the room. It was covered in the same etchings, and it was even heavier than the first door, closing with a solid thump behind me. I found myself in another hallway lined with metal doors. Each door had a small barred window through which I could see an empty windowless cell. Cold hit me in the chest and my heart sped up as I walked past the cells, knowing that one of them held Nate. Fear and anxiety churned my stomach as I tried to mentally prepare for what I was going to face and what I was about to do.

"Come to visit me at last," drawled a cold voice I barely recognized before I reached the last door. I sucked in a sharp breath and stumbled, not as prepared to hear his voice as I thought I was. I took a moment to steel myself then stepped up to the door. The cell was dark, and I flipped a switch beside the door, making light flood the small room and revealing the figure chained by his hands and feet to the back wall. His dark hair was lank, and his face looked paler and thinner than it had yesterday, if that was possible. It was his eyes that shocked me the most. Instead of the familiar bright green, they were dark, almost black, and they stared hungrily at me now, the eyes of a predator.

"How did you know it was me?" I asked, fighting to keep the tremble out of my voice.

"You forget I have a heightened sense of smell now, and you . . . " He lifted his face and sniffed the air. "They were right. You smell delicious."

I shuddered. *Remember, this is not Nate.* "Tristan said you wanted to see me."

Nate chuckled. "I did, but I am surprised he and Nikolas let you come to see me alone. I always knew that warrior had a soft spot for – "

"I didn't come down here to talk about Nikolas," I snapped. I'd come here with a purpose, and I would not let him distract me from it. "Did you have something to say to me?"

He shrugged and his chains clinked. "I have many things to say to you. Where would you like to start?"

"How did this happen to you?"

The question seemed to take him by surprise, and he stared at me for a moment before answering. "I met a beautiful redhead who told me she was going to change my life forever." One corner of his mouth lifted and he leered at me suggestively. "She did not disappoint."

I swallowed dryly. "What was her name?"

"Why? So you can hunt her down like a good little vampire killer?" he scoffed.

"Something like that." *And make her tell me who her Master is before I kill her.*

"Sorry to disappoint you, kid, but I'll take that secret to the grave . . . which should be any day now if your guardians have anything to say about it."

"Why?" I burst out. "Why would you protect someone who sent you here to die?"

He scowled at me. "You would never understand the loyalty and love I have for my maker. She made me strong and gave me back my legs. That was all I ever wanted. I certainly never wanted to be saddled with a sniveling, ungrateful little brat who did nothing but hurt the people who cared about her. Your father died because of you. Even your own mother could not bear to be around you."

"That's not true! My dad and Nate loved me, and I loved them and would have done anything to keep them safe."

"Well, judging by my current accommodations, you aren't doing such a bang-up job."

Tears clouded my vision, and I blinked them away. "I never meant for you . . . for Nate to get hurt. I know you don't care, but I wanted to tell you that."

He let out a humorless laugh. "You're right; I don't care."

"Then I guess we don't have anything else to say to each other." I took a deep tremulous breath and inserted the key into the door lock.

"What are you doing?"

I opened the door and slipped inside, closing it behind me with a loud click that echoed down the empty hallway. Dropping the keys on the floor, I faced the vampire that watched me warily. *Be strong and remember you're doing this for Nate. You owe him this.*

"Like you said, I'm a vampire killer," I said emotionlessly.

"And you are going to kill your own uncle?" He asked with a sneer, but there was less confidence in his voice now.

The rage that had been simmering inside me bubbled to the surface. "You aren't my uncle. You're the demon who stole his body."

"Everything that was your uncle is in me. Do you really want to destroy all that is left of him?"

I clenched my fists and took a step closer. "You might have his memories and his face, but you don't have his soul. There is nothing left of *him* in you." As soon as I said the words, I knew they were true. Even after I'd seen him with fangs bared, even as I stood outside his cell, a tiny part of me believed, or hoped, that Nate was not truly gone forever. Cold acceptance settled over me.

"What are you going to do? Are you really going to put a blade through my heart, your uncle's heart?" he asked, still trying to make me believe he was Nate.

"It's not Nate's heart anymore," I replied flatly walking toward him. "And I don't need a knife."

"What do you mean?"

"You have Nate's memories, so you know what I am. Do you know why demons are so afraid of the Fae?"

Fear crept into his eyes for the first time and his Adam's apple bobbed.

"I'm not just a vampire killer; I'm a one-of-a-kind demon slayer. You took Nate from me, so you have the honor of being my first kill. Well, not my first kill, but the first like this."

His eyes bulged as electricity crackled in the air around me.

"First, I'm going to take care of you. Then, I'm going to leave here and hunt down your maker and your precious Master, and I'm going to kill every blood sucker that gets in my way."

Muffled shouts from the outer room drew my attention from the vampire. It sounded like Ben had awakened and called in reinforcements. If I was going to finish this, I had to do it now.

I turned back to the vampire. "Nate, wherever you are, please forgive me for not keeping you safe." Despite my resolve, tears spilled down my cheeks as I called forth my power.

"Sara, no!" Tristan yelled through the window in the door. "Whatever you're planning to do, you have to stop."

My breath caught but I did not look at him. "I'm going to kill a vampire."

Tristan lowered his voice. "Listen to me, Sara; you don't want to do this. Killing a vampire is one thing, but if you kill Nate, it will haunt you forever."

My hair crackled with static and lifted from my shoulders as the power surrounding me grew. "He's not Nate. He's a monster."

"Yes, he is, but you will see only Nate's face when you remember this. Nate would not want that for you."

"I – "

"Sara, open the door."

I closed my eyes at the sound of Nikolas's deep voice. Something tugged at my chest, and a part of me wanted to run to him, to let him wrap his arms around me and chase away the evil in my life. But a larger part of me knew I would never find my own strength if I hid behind his.

My hands tingled and began to glow from the power coursing through them. I could see the light reflected in the vampire's terrified eyes as he struggled violently in his bonds. Behind me I heard running feet and then the distinct sound of a key being fitted into the lock on the cell door.

The vampire screamed when my hands touched his chest, and he began to writhe convulsively, even though I hadn't yet released the force of my power. Just being touched by Fae magic was unbearable to him. I stared at him for several seconds as I gathered more power and prepared to strike.

The door swung open, and I felt the air shift as someone moved toward me with incredible speed. *No!*

I released my power and felt the vampire jerk as he let out a strangled shriek. The smell of scorched flesh filled my nose, and I heard a thump and a curse somewhere behind me. The vampire hung limply in his chains, but I knew he was still alive because we were connected by the power flowing between us. My mind reeled from the knowledge that I was inside a vampire. I was overcome by the need to see the vamhir demon before I destroyed it, to look upon the thing that had turned a wonderful man into a monster.

Unlike Mori demons that live in the brain, vamhir demons attach themselves to the heart of their victims. My power moved through organs that looked healthy and normal until it found the misshapen lump that barely resembled a human heart. Most of the heart was encased in a thick translucent white membrane that resembled a jellyfish, with tendrils that were fused to the spine and brain stem. I prodded the membrane, and it trembled, making the heart stutter.

This was the powerful vamhir demon? For all a vampire's power and strength, the demon was nothing more than a gelatinous parasite that needed a host to survive. Seeing this one weakened and in its natural form took away the mystery and dissolved some of my fear of vampires. It didn't dampen the pain of losing Nate, but it gave me a deeper understanding of my enemy and showed me the demon's true weakness.

The demon rippled, and I felt the vampire stir. I jabbed at it, and it stilled again. Enough studying it. It was time to end this. I pushed forward until I surrounded the demon without touching it. It quivered as if it knew what I planned to do. My soul wept for the heart that would soon no longer beat, but I felt no empathy or mercy for the creature I was about to destroy.

I love you, Nate, I said silently as my power enveloped the demon.

The demon let out an unearthly scream, twisting and pushing desperately against my hold. I opened myself further and more power poured out of the well deep inside me until it felt like lightning flowed through my veins. In a disconnected part of my mind, I knew I was tapping into a force I had never touched before, and I felt a tiny brush of fear mixed with wild exhilaration. I had never felt so alive or aware of the world around me. I could hear people breathing behind me and a mouse scratching behind the walls. I could feel the living earth beneath the thick stone floor. I smelled the droplets of water in the damp air of the cell and the stench of dead flesh that clung to the vampire. And inside the vampire, I saw life . . . and death.

Alien words filled my head, and I heard a hideous voice that made me want to grab my ears and scream. Something clicked in my mind, like a door opening, and I realized I was hearing the demon's thoughts and memories. . . . *good strong body . . . so thirsty . . . but I don't want to die . . . yes, my maker . . . pain . . . so much pain . . .*

As soon as it had come, the demon's voice faded away and images began to flood my mind so fast they were a blur of color. I reached out and snatched one and stared in confusion at the face of a little girl, no older than two or three. I grabbed another and saw the same little girl, a few years older with chestnut curls and happy green eyes. *It's me,* I thought in wonder, reaching for another image then another.

Me sitting on a chair in a white hospital room, my eyes dark and terrified.

Me curled up in a small bed, clenching a teddy bear.

Me grinning as I cut the cake at my tenth birthday party with Roland and Peter.

Me pulling a gift from beneath the Christmas tree.

Me covered in chocolate batter the first time I tried to make Nate a birthday cake.

Me holding the ragged white cat I rescued when I was fourteen.

Me standing in the doorway, wearing a pale yellow Faerie dress.

They were all Nate's memories of me, of my life with him, and each one of them glowed with a father's love for his child. I'd spent my life missing my dad, and all along Nate had thought of me as a daughter. It filled me with bittersweet joy to realize the depth of his love after he was gone.

More of Nate's memories, dark and terrifying, flooded my mind. I saw an exotic red-haired woman in a revealing black dress. *Ava Bryant,* she said in a sultry voice. The next instant, her face twisted and fangs sprouted from her mouth as she struck. I heard Nate moaning in pain and saying, *I'll never tell you where she is.* The memories became hazy after that, and I knew it was during his transition. The last coherent thought he had before the vamhir demon possessed him completely was how glad he was that I would not be alone.

The images and voices faded away into a gray mist and it was just me and the demon again. The demon looked darker and harder with small cracks forming in its surface, and the heart beat in a weak irregular rhythm. The heart that had once held so much love for me. I would not let it suffer any longer.

It was love, not anger, that filled me as power exploded from me in a white flash so brilliant it blinded me through my closed eyelids. I felt the vampire's death throes, and I knew the instant the demon shattered into nothingness and the heart stopped beating forever. A wail of grief welled up from deep inside me, and I heard a voice from my own memory. *Those who hunt you will ultimately give you the power to become the thing they fear the most.*

*　*　*

Far above me, a pinpoint of light shone like a beacon, and I swam through the murky darkness toward it. My arms and legs were heavy, threatening to drag me back down. It would be so easy to just drift in the warm darkness, but the light called to me. I pushed forward with every ounce of willpower until the light grew brighter and I heard muffled sounds: voices, beeping, music. Wait. Was that . . . Carly Simon?

"It's been two damn days. Why hasn't she woken up?"

"Physically, there is nothing wrong with her," a woman said. "All I can guess is that her mind needs to heal from the trauma she suffered and she will wake when she is ready."

"You guess?"

"Nikolas, calm down. There is nothing to be gained from yelling at the healers. None of us has seen anything like this before."

"Dude, I wouldn't want to wake up either with you shouting like that." Was that Roland?

"I think I just saw her eyes move!"

And Peter?

A hand touched my shoulder. "Sara, it's Roland. Can you hear me?"

I tried to move my hand, but it was made of lead. I wanted to grind my teeth in frustration, but I couldn't do that either.

"There! Her lips moved. See, Pete, I told you the music was a good idea."

I heard people moving around and then warmth encased my hand. "Sara? It's time to wake up, *moy malen'kiy voin.*"

"I'm trying, damn it!" I wanted to say, but no words would come forth.

"Ah, is our beauty still sleeping?" asked a new voice. "Perhaps a kiss from her prince is all she needs."

"This is no time for your humor, Desmund." Nikolas's voice was low and harsh, but his hold on my hand was gentle. Beneath his hard demeanor, I sensed worry and fear. Nikolas, afraid? Impossible.

"On the contrary, laughter is just what she needs. It is far too gloomy in here . . . and what is that awful noise?"

"Hey, she likes this music," Roland retorted defensively.

"If you gentlemen don't keep it down, you are all going to have to leave," the healer interjected with calm authority.

Voices rose in argument, and the room got even noisier. The sounds grated on my ears.

"Stop it," I yelled, but it came out as a hoarse whisper. It was enough to make the room go silent. Forcing my eyes open, I saw an unshaven face and a pair of shadowed gray eyes. "Hi."

Nikolas's hand squeezed mine, and his lips curved into a smile that plucked at an invisible string attached to my heart. "Hi, yourself."

"What's going on? Why is everyone in my room?" I coughed the last word and wondered why my mouth and throat were so parched.

"Here." He placed a hand behind my head to support it and put a glass of water to my lips. I took a long, greedy drink before pushing the glass away.

Someone moved to the other side of the narrow bed, and it took me a second to realize it wasn't my bed at all, but a hospital bed. Why was I in the medical ward? I struggled to remember what could have put me here, but the edges of my mind were shrouded in dense fog.

"Hey, how are you feeling?" Roland asked, his blue eyes cautious. "You scared the crap out of us."

"Roland?" I thought I had been dreaming when I heard his and Peter's voices. "What are you doing here?"

His eyes flicked to Nikolas then back to me. "You don't remember?"

"No, I . . ." Images began to emerge from the shadows: Thanksgiving dinner, a white van, Nate in his wheelchair, Nate standing, Nate chained to a wall . . . I covered my face with my hands as it all came back to me with merciless clarity. "Oh God, I killed Nate." My body shook, and I could not get enough air into my lungs. Nikolas said something, but I all I could hear were the screams of the vamhir demon and the beating of Nate's heart before it went silent. Arms encircled me and I turned toward Nikolas, curling against him as he murmured in my ear. It took several minutes for his repeated words to penetrate the grief choking me. I jerked away and stared at him in confusion.

"What did you say?"

Nikolas wore the trace of a smile. "Nate is alive."

I moved my head slowly from side to side. "That's not possible. I killed him. I felt him die."

"You killed the vampire." Tristan walked over to the bed, wonder shining in his eyes. "We have no idea what you did in that room, but Nate is alive."

"You're not making any sense. How can the vampire be alive if I killed him?"

"Sara, the vampire is not alive. Nate is," Nikolas said slowly. "Nate is human again."

Chapter 22

"WHAT?" I LOOKED from Nikolas to Tristan to Roland, and they all nodded at me in turn. Disbelief flooded me, followed by a spark of hope. "Human? He's human . . . and alive?"

"He smells human to us," Peter said from behind Roland.

I gripped Roland's arm because he was closest. "You've seen him?"

"Ow. Demon strength, remember." He rubbed his arm. "We've seen him a few times. And you should know that he – "

"Where is he? I want to see him." I pushed aside the blanket and sat up. Dizziness assailed me, and I would have toppled out of bed if Nikolas had not been there to catch me.

"Hold on. You're too weak to go anywhere." He held me with gentle firmness. I struggled against him, but it was no use.

"Let me go! I have to see Nate." Twice, I'd thought I lost Nate; first when he'd arrived as a vampire and then when I killed him – or believed I had. And now to find out he was miraculously alive . . . "Let go of me, Nikolas, or I swear I'll never speak to you again." They were harsh words and I didn't mean them, but I was too upset to take them back.

"You never did like to be told what to do."

My head whipped in the direction of the door, but my view was blocked by Tristan. It didn't matter because I'd know that voice anywhere. "Nate?" I said in a small voice.

Tristan moved aside, and I watched breathlessly as Nate approached the bed. He wore a smile that warmed his familiar green eyes, and all traces of malice were gone from his face. Nikolas stepped back to let Nate take his place beside the bed. Nate laid a hand over mine, and I saw tears sparkling in his eyes. "Hey, kiddo."

I reached blindly for him. He wrapped me in strong arms, and we clung to each other like we were each afraid the other would disappear if we let go. "You're really here," I cried into his shirt. "I thought I lost you."

"I thought I lost you, too."

"How is this – ?" The words caught in my throat as I suddenly became aware of what I was seeing. "Nate, you're walking!"

His laugh melted the last of the ice that had filled my chest the moment he'd stood up from his wheelchair. "Tristan says my spine was healed when the vampire demon possessed me. And then you killed the demon."

I fell back against the pillow and rubbed my temple. "I don't understand any of this."

"What do you remember?" Tristan asked.

The healer spoke for the first time since I woke up. "Sara has been unconscious for two days, and this is obviously overtaxing her. Perhaps we should let her rest before – "

"No. I've been asleep long enough." I tried to sit up again, and Roland hit a lever to raise the head of the bed to a sitting position. Once I was comfortable with an extra pillow behind me, I tugged on Nate's hand until he sat beside me. I didn't think I would ever be able to let him out of my sight again.

When I looked away from him, I saw that Tristan, Roland, and Peter had pulled up chairs for themselves and Nikolas stood near the head of the bed. The healer left, and I noticed the lone figure standing quietly by the window.

"Desmund? I thought you hated coming downstairs."

Pushing away from the wall, he sauntered over, one corner of his mouth lifted in a haughty smirk. "Well, they would not accommodate me by moving you upstairs, so I was forced to spend time in this depressing ward." He picked up my hand and put it to his lips. "Welcome back, little one. And if you worry us like that again, I will lock you up myself for the next fifty years."

"Get in line," Nikolas muttered.

Great, all I needed was another male in my life who thought he knew what was best for me. I didn't know whether to scowl at the pair of them or be amazed that they were in agreement on something. Unfortunately, with my penchant for attracting trouble, I'd probably see how serious their threats were sooner rather than later.

Desmund smiled kindly and released my hand. "I will go and let you catch up with your family and friends. Come see me when you are feeling better." I started to say that he didn't have to leave, but he was gone before I could get the words out.

I looked at Nate who was talking quietly to Tristan. *He's really here.* Two days ago, I thought my heart would never be whole again, and yet here it was, bursting with happiness.

"Sara, do you feel up to telling us what happened?" Tristan asked.

"What you did has never been done before, at least it's never been recorded in our history. I don't know where to begin to try to understand it."

"I didn't know I could do that. I knew I could kill demons, but I never dreamed it was possible to make a vampire human again.

I toyed nervously with the edge of the blanket and met Nate's gaze. "I was so upset and angry about what happened to you. I went down there to kill you, not to save you."

He put a hand over mine to stop my fidgeting. "I know," he said without a hint of anger or bitterness. "I remember everything, especially the horrible things I . . . the vampire said to you. I know you did what you had to do."

"What exactly did you do?" Roland prodded.

"Like I said, I planned to kill the vampire. The first time I hit him with my power it was enough to knock him out. While I was connected to him I could see the vamhir demon attached to Nate's heart." I heard Nate inhale sharply, but I couldn't look at him and see the horror on his face. "I was going to hit it again, but then I heard its thoughts. Actually, I think they were its memories."

Tristan put up a hand to interrupt me. "You understood what it was saying?"

"Bits and pieces."

He frowned. "Only our oldest scholars can understand demon tongue, and they spend centuries learning it."

"But we can understand our Mori demons."

"The Mori demon was chosen to create our race because it is compatible with humans. Our demons are born inside us, and we learn to communicate with them as we grow."

I looked from him to Nikolas. "You mean my Mori talks in a whole other language and I didn't even know it?" Nikolas nodded, and I fell silent while I tried to process this new knowledge. There was so much I had to learn about who and what I was.

Peter leaned forward. "What happened after you heard the demon?"

"Then I saw – " I looked at Nate. I needed him to understand why I did what I did. "I saw your memories of me. Then I saw you being changed and the pain you went through. I couldn't let you suffer anymore. I held your heart, and I felt it stop. I thought you died."

"I think I did die, but then I felt something pulling at me. It was so bright and warm that I honestly thought I must be looking at an angel." He wore an expression of someone who has seen something so wondrous they cannot put it into words. "Then heat spread through me and it got so hot I thought I was going to burn from the inside out. The next thing I knew, I woke up on the floor of the cell with Tristan standing over me, looking like he was going to finish the job."

"I almost did," Tristan admitted soberly. "But then I saw his eyes, and I knew something was different, especially after what I'd witnessed."

"What did you see?" I asked him.

"We unlocked the door, but before Nikolas and I could get to you, you sent out enough energy to throw us across the room. You and Nate were inside some kind of energy sphere that glowed so brightly it was impossible to look at directly. We couldn't get within five feet of it without it pushing us back. I've seen many things in my life, but nothing like that."

"You didn't actually see what I did to Nate?"

"No. You were like that for a minute, and then the sphere disappeared and you both fell to the floor. Whatever it was, it melted the irons on Nate's arms and legs without leaving a mark on him."

"A minute?" I leaned back against the pillows, stunned. "It felt like it was a lot longer than that."

"Yes, it did," Nikolas said in a tight voice, and I saw Nate give him an appraising look. Nate and I had so much to talk about, and I could only imagine what he would say when he heard about me and Nikolas. Nate liked Nikolas, but I had a feeling he wasn't going to be too pleased about the whole bond thing.

Roland tugged on my hair playfully. "You learned some new tricks since the last time we saw you."

"This makes what she did to you look like nothing," Peter said with a grin, and Roland nodded vigorously.

"No kidding."

I let out a small laugh, and Roland said, "It's good to hear that again."

"It feels good." How could I not be happy? Nate was back and I was surrounded by people I cared about. The Master knew I was alive, but I was too happy to worry about that now. Nate was safe here, and the Master could not hurt him or use him against me again.

I tugged on Nate's hand. "You're staying here until they get the Master, right?" He had argued so strongly against coming to live here when Nikolas offered it to him back in New Hastings that I was afraid he would refuse now.

He smiled. "I guess I can write as well here as I can anywhere else. Of course, I'll need to get my computer and things from home."

"And don't forget Daisy and – " I broke off when it hit me that I still had no idea if our pets were even alive. "Nate, where are Daisy and Oscar? You didn't . . . ?"

He wore a horrified expression. "No! They ran away as soon as I went home after I was attacked."

"They're fine," Peter said. "Dad and Uncle Brendan went to check out your place and they saw Oscar outside. He wouldn't come near them so Aunt Judith put out some food for him."

"And Mom took Daisy to our place," Roland added.

"Thanks," I told them hoarsely.

Tristan stood. "Why don't we let Sara and Nate have some time alone together? I'm sure they have a lot to talk about."

"Wait. What about Ben? Is he okay?" I asked, remembering the warrior I'd knocked out.

"Ben is fine, although he is a bit put out about being taken down so easily. He understands you were very distraught and not thinking straight." Tristan smiled, but there was disapproval in his words. I had a feeling that once I was better, I was going to get a lecture about using my power on another Mohiri.

I nodded, chastened. "I'll apologize to him as soon as I see him."

"I think Ben would rather you not bring it up again," Nikolas said with a wry smile. "Maybe I should be the one to apologize to him for helping you hone that particular skill in the first place."

Tristan's gaze flicked between me and Nikolas. "Perhaps I should learn exactly what goes on in your training sessions. But right now, Sara needs to rest and talk to Nate. We'll discuss her training in a few days."

"Can I go back to my room? We'd be a lot more comfortable there."

"You should stay here, close to the healers, for a few more hours," Nikolas said before Tristan could respond. I recognized his determined tone, and for once I didn't want to argue with him.

"Okay, but only for a few hours," I conceded. "Then I need to get out of this ward. I've spent way too much time here the last month."

"I've given Nate the apartment next to mine," Tristan told me. "It has two large bedrooms, so you can move in with him if you want to."

While I wanted to be close to Nate, the thought of sharing the same floor with him, Tristan, and Nikolas was too much for me. Under their constant watch, I'd never have any freedom. Besides, I liked having my own space and being near Jordan and the others. And what would I do with the imps if I moved?

I looked at Nate. "If you don't mind, I'd like to stay with the other trainees. We'll see each other all the time anyway."

He nodded and gave me a knowing smile. If anyone knew how much I liked my privacy, it was Nate.

Roland and Peter were reluctant to leave until Nate told them they could have me after dinner. I grumbled that they made me sound like a toy, and they all laughed. The boys left talking about what was on the menu for lunch, and they were stoked when Tristan told them they could request steak if they wanted. Was it really only a few months ago my werewolf friends couldn't imagine associating with the Mohiri? And now they were visiting a Mohiri stronghold and eating meals with them every day.

Nikolas was the last to leave, and I suddenly felt shy being alone in the same room with him and Nate, like bringing home a boy for the first time. Only Nikolas was no boy and I didn't know where to begin to describe our relationship to Nate.

"I'll be close if you need anything." He leaned over me, and my stomach did a little flip. But he only touched his lips to my forehead. "Later, you and I are going to talk about what will happen if you ever pull something like that again." Straightening, he nodded to Nate and left.

Nate raised an eyebrow at me, and I let out a heavy sigh. We had a *lot* to catch up on.

"You might as well sit down. This could take a while."

*   *   *

"So, you only found out a few months ago that your two best friends were werewolves?" Jordan looked at Roland and Peter who were sprawled out on my bed next to me. "And you two had no idea what Sara was?"

I laughed because I knew how odd it must sound to not know your two best friends were werewolves. "Werewolves are very good at hiding their secrets, and even I thought I was human until I met Nikolas."

"Don't they smell like dog or something when they get wet?"

"Jordan," I scolded, and her mouth twitched. The three of them had been making little digs like that at each other all day, and I was getting tired of playing referee.

"And then you found out you are half undine, which is why you can do all the freaky shit you do, and how you were able to make your uncle human again?" I nodded, and she swore. "Half demon, half Fae. That is messed up. No wonder you didn't tell anyone."

"I wanted to tell you. I really did." I found out yesterday that my secret was no longer a secret thanks to my miraculous feat with Nate. People who thought I was a little odd before openly stared at me now, and more than one conversation stopped when I walked into a room. Apparently, Tristan had called everyone together in the dining hall last night to dispel any rumors and given them an abbreviated version of the truth. I was glad I didn't have to hide what I was anymore, but I could do without the instant celebrity status.

Jordan waved a hand. "No, I get it. I'd probably want to keep something like that to myself, too."

"I guess now we know why the vampires want you so bad," Roland said. "If you can make them human again, they must be shaking in their boots."

"No kidding." Peter sat up. "My dad says there is nothing that scares a vampire more than mortality."

Those who hunt you will ultimately give you the power to become the thing they fear the most.

The Hale witch's prediction had not been about my ability to kill vampires, but my ability to make them mortal. But the vampires didn't give me that power; I was born this way. Wasn't I?

I remembered what Aine had said to me the day we met by the lake. *We were unsure of how your body would react to the vampire blood it absorbed.* Aine thought the cold sensation in my chest was a side effect of the vampire blood in my system, but what if that wasn't the only side effect? What if Eli's blood had changed me somehow and made it possible not only for me to understand vamhir demons but to restore a vampire's humanity? But the Master could not possibly have known this would happen to me.

"If the Master ever finds out Nate is human again, he'll know what I can do and he'll go after everyone I care about. I don't want anything to happen to you guys."

Roland plumped up the pillow under his head. "Don't worry about us. Vamps would be nuts to mess with a pack as big as ours."

"How big is your pack?" Jordan asked.

"There are forty-five of us in New Hastings, but we have family spread out across Maine," Peter answered. "About a hundred and ninety of us in all."

"Biggest pack in the US," Roland added proudly.

Jordan leaned her arms on the counter in my kitchenette where she had been raiding my small refrigerator. "So, do you guys have to worry about fleas and ticks?"

"Jordan!"

"What? It's a valid question. They do have fur half the time."

I shook my head at her, and she shrugged. "How often will I get a chance to ask a werewolf questions?"

Roland ignored her question. "We haven't seen much of Nate today. How is he doing with all of this?"

"He seems okay, but I think it's going to take him a while to take it all in." Yesterday, Nate and I had talked for hours. He told me about the female vampire, Ava Bryant, who had approached him, posing as a reporter from New York. It wasn't hard for the beautiful vampire to compel him to go with her. He'd never met her Master, but her love for the other vampire had passed to Nate when she made him. I'd told him over and over how sorry I was for what he went through until he ordered me to stop apologizing. He said it would be different here, but the whole bachelor pad thing wasn't working for him anyway and now he would be near me.

He had been more interested in my life here, more particularly, what was going on between me and Nikolas. Unsurprisingly, he was not happy to learn about the whole bond thing and he said I was way too young to commit to someone. I had to reassure him that I wasn't jumping into anything. I told him Nikolas understood my feelings and we were taking it slow. That seemed to mollify Nate a little, although he did say he and

Nikolas were going to have a man-to-man talk. No amount of pleading on my part would dissuade him.

Nikolas stopped by last night and today to see how I was doing, but for the most part, he was giving me space to be with Nate and my friends. We hadn't been alone together since our moment by the river before Roland and Peter arrived, and I often found myself wondering where he was and what he was doing. When I talked to him today he said he would see me tonight, and I got butterflies whenever I thought about being alone with him again.

"Nate will be fine," Roland assured me. "He can write anywhere, so it's not like he's giving up that."

I brightened. "That's true." I got off the bed and logged into my laptop, hoping to see an email from David. One of the first things I'd done when I got back to my room last night was ask him to find what he could about a female vampire named Ava Bryant. Tristan had his people searching for her, too, and I'd already made him swear to bring her in alive if he found her. I had a very personal score to settle with the vampire who had tried to take Nate from me.

A new mail notification popped up just as someone knocked on the door. I went to answer the door and was surprised when Michael entered my room, wide-eyed and out of breath.

"Sara, I'm glad I found you," he panted, ignoring everyone else. "Sahir sent me to get you."

"Is it Minuet again?"

"No, it's the hellhounds. They got out again and took off into the woods."

"What?" I shoved my feet into a pair of boots. "How the hell did they get out?" I'd taken Roland and Peter to meet them a few hours ago, and I was careful to lock their cage as I always did. And no one besides Sahir and I ever went near them or had keys to their cage.

"I don't know, but they're on the loose," Michael said fearfully. "They wouldn't hurt anyone, would they?"

"No, of course not," I replied sharply as I grabbed my coat. *Would they?* The hellhounds behaved when they were with me, but they weren't exactly house pets.

I hurried to the door and turned to look at the others. "You guys stay here. I'll take care of it and be back as soon as I can."

Roland and Peter were already off the bed. "Screw that," Roland said, pulling on his boots. "You're not going to run around in the woods alone."

Jordan stood and darted out the door. "Where are you going?" I called after her.

"To get my coat."

Michael left the room, and I followed him. "You guys really don't have to come," I told Roland and Peter. "Nothing will hurt me with Hugo and Woolf around."

"Not like we have anything better to do," Peter replied as he entered Roland's room and grabbed their coats.

Jordan came out of her room and shut her door. "Come on, people. Let's go round up Sara's little doggies before they eat someone."

The five of us raced down the stairs, nearly running over two people on the way. Outside, it was a cold, clear night, and the full moon cast a soft bluish glow over the day-old snow on the ground. Our combined breath fogged the air around us as we started across the grounds toward the woods.

I turned to Michael. "Which way did they go?"

He pointed to a spot, and I saw it was the same place we usually entered the woods when I took them for walks. They were most likely following my scent. Still, it was strange they should go that way when my scent was probably a lot stronger between the menagerie and the main building.

I stopped at the edge of the woods and strained to see through the darkness. The thick branches blocked most of the moonlight, and I could barely make out the ghostly gleam of snow on the ground. "Hugo! Woolf!" I called, but there was no answering bark. They could be halfway to the lake by now. I hoped they didn't hurt one of the sentries patrolling the woods.

Groaning, I turned toward the menagerie. "We're going to need a flashlight."

"Here, take mine." Michael pulled a short black flashlight from his pocket and handed it to me. I flicked it on and the powerful beam slid over the ground, cutting through the inky blackness beneath the trees.

"Let's go," I told them. "And don't blame me if you freeze your butts off."

I entered the woods and headed in the direction of the lake with the four of them behind me. Less than fifty yards in, I spotted large footprints in the snow, and I knew they belonged to the hellhounds. The only problem was I couldn't tell if the impressions were fresh or from our walk this afternoon. I looked for my boot prints but couldn't see any. That wasn't surprising because Hugo and Woolf ran around so much they probably obliterated my prints. Stopping, I whistled, and called for them again.

"Damn, it's cold out here," I muttered, blowing on my hands and wishing I'd remembered gloves.

Roland snorted. "Nice of your friend, Sahir, to stay warm and cozy inside while you trek through the woods."

"Sahir wouldn't – " I broke off as it hit me what had been niggling at me since we came outside. I turned to Michael. "Where is Sahir anyway?"

Michael shrugged. "I think he – "

He grunted in pain when I grabbed his arm in a death grip. I gasped and cold air stung my lungs, but that was nothing compared to the lump of ice forming in my chest.

"Vampire!" I spun to the others and cried, "Run!"

"Please, don't leave on our account," said a husky feminine voice as a blond vampire appeared out of nowhere to stand in front of us. "We only just got here."

Her words barely registered before I felt a slight disturbance in the air and four more vampires stepped out from the trees to surround us.

Chapter 23

THIS CAN'T BE real. The perimeters were tightly patrolled day and night. How could vampires get past the armed warriors and get so close to the stronghold?

"Is this her?" the female asked, pointing at me.

"Yes," Michael replied in a small voice.

I sucked in a sharp breath. Behind me, I heard two low growls.

"You rotten little traitorous piece of shit!" Jordan shrieked, leaping at Michael who stumbled backward. One of the vampires moved, and I grabbed Jordan's arm to hold her back.

"I'm sorry," Michael cried to me. "They have Matthew and they'll kill him if I don't help them. He's all I have."

All I could do was stare in horror at the boy waving his arms frantically as he pleaded with me. I had suspected Michael was a bit messed up from losing his family, but in that moment I saw how broken he really was. He was so desperate to believe his brother was alive that he was willing to trust his mortal enemy and sell out his own people for a ghost.

"Touching." The female vampire sneered and motioned to her companions. "Take her and kill the rest."

"You said you wouldn't hurt anyone else!" Michael yelled. "You said you would trade Matthew for her."

The female laughed and her fangs grew. "We don't make deals with the likes of you." She moved in a blur and struck him so hard he flew fifteen feet and hit a tree with a sickening crack. He landed in the snow and lay there unmoving. The vampire turned to me. "Now where – ?"

She gasped and stepped back as loud growls erupted behind me and two massive werewolves appeared where Roland and Peter had stood. I had never seen my friends transform, and it was shocking even for me.

"Werewolves!" the female spat, stunned that she and her companions had not picked up on my friends' scent. She recovered quickly. "Two of you are no match for five of us."

"What the fuck am I, chopped liver?" Jordan's hand moved and the vampire closest to her made a gurgling noise and clutched at a silver knife handle protruding from his chest. The male sank to his knees in the snow and Jordan waved a second knife in front of her. "Now it's four to three."

The female snarled. "Lucky shot, little hunter, but Stephen was a fledgling. You won't take me that easily." She waved the others forward. "What the hell are you waiting for?"

One of the werewolves let out a ferocious growl and jumped over my head to face the dark figures moving in on us. I didn't need to ask to know it was Roland in front of me. Behind me, Peter guarded my back while at my side, Jordan brandished her long knife. I looked down helplessly at my weaponless hands before I realized that a knife in my hand wouldn't help our odds much anyway. The best weapon I had was me.

Roland dove at one of the approaching vampires, and I heard the sound of flesh ripping and felt a spray of hot blood across my cheek. Snarls and shouts filled the woods around me, and it became impossible to make out one flying shape from another.

A cold hand grabbed my wrist and whipped me away from my friends, the sharp claws digging into my skin. I knew immediately this was no baby vampire. Terror gripped me and memories of Eli flooded my mind. *No. Never again.*

Heat roared through me as I opened the barrier holding back my power. Instead of trying to pull away from my attacker, I whirled and placed my free hand on his chest. After my experience with Nate, I knew exactly where the vamhir demon lurked and how to hurt it. Before the vampire knew what was happening, white hot energy burst from my hand and pierced his chest as easily as one of Jordan's blades.

The vampire froze and his hands went slack. I yanked my wrist from his grasp and staggered back a step. It was too dark to see his expression, but I could tell his eyes were still open and staring at me in shock. I had no idea how quickly he'd recover, and I had no weapon to finish him off. I raised both hands to blast him again, and he made a small sound like a smothered scream.

A second later, someone shouldered me aside and a blade sank into the vampire's chest. Jordan pulled her knife free and grabbed my arm. "Come on. We need to get out of here."

I whirled around and realized we were alone except for the dark shapes littering the ground. My stomach dropped. "Where are Roland and Peter?"

"They went after the female." Jordan started pulling me through the trees. "We need to get back and raise the alarm. How the hell did five vampires get past our sentries?"

From deeper in the woods my friends' snarls grew fainter as they pursued the vampire. I dug in my heels. "We can't leave Roland and Peter. And what about Michael?"

Jordan stopped and looked back at me. "Your friends ripped two vampires to shreds; I think they can take care of themselves. And that little traitor can stay – "

I froze, almost doubling over from the cold stabbing me in the chest. "More coming," I croaked.

"Shit! Where?"

I shook my head because my new vampire radar wasn't that specific. The only chance we had was to run and hope it was away from danger. This time, it was me who grabbed Jordan's hand and plunged into the trees. After a dozen or so yards, the cold fist in my chest loosened, which told me we were heading away from the vampires, but still being pursued. That wasn't our only problem. In the dark, everything looked the same and I had no idea where we were going. If we didn't get out of these woods soon, our chances of escape were not good.

I came to a stop and listened to a faint gushing roar off to our right. "The river. Come on." If we were near the river, we couldn't be too far from home, and we only had to follow it downstream to get to safety. Adrenaline rushed through me, and I changed course and headed for the water with Jordan close at my heels.

The cold deepened in my chest again, and I ran with everything in me. My foot snagged on a tree root, I would have gone down if Jordan hadn't caught me. Ignoring the throbbing pain in my ankle, I pushed forward. The roaring grew louder. We were so close.

We burst from the trees and teetered at the top of the steep riverbank for several seconds before we righted ourselves. Gasping for breath, we spun and ran down the narrow path that followed the river. There was barely enough moonlight to see the path, but we couldn't afford to slow down. With every step we took, I sensed the vampires getting closer. They couldn't know where we were or they would have grabbed us already. It was the only thing we had going for us. We'd never be able to outrun them otherwise.

Jordan let out a small scream and stopped abruptly, and I caught myself just in time to keep from plowing into her. I looked past her at the tall shape standing in a patch of moonlight at the bend in the river. My newfound gift told me all I needed to know. Vampire.

I whirled to go back the other way, only to see someone coming up the path toward us. We were trapped. If we ran for the woods, they would catch us for sure. That left only one option.

I grabbed Jordan's arm and, as soon as she turned her head toward me, I yelled, "Jump." She gripped my hand tightly, and we moved as one. My feet left the ground, and there was barely enough time to suck in a deep breath before I hit the river. Freezing water closed over my head. The impact pulled Jordan's hand from mine, and I grabbed for her frantically before my bursting lungs forced me to give up. My head broke the surface, and I sucked in cold air then choked as I swallowed water.

"Jordan!" I sputtered as more water flooded my mouth. The current tugged at my heavy clothes, dragging me back under. I kicked my feet and fought for the surface as the swift river carried me away. A gasp of air then water washed over my head again. Terror filled me and I lost all sense of up and down. My lungs burned and tiny stars exploded before my eyes.

No, not stars. In my panic, I'd summoned the water's magic, and it had answered my call. A cloud of sparkling lights moved rapidly toward me, surrounding me, lifting me. I broke the surface and sucked in a deep breath of cold air that burned my throat.

Gasping, I searched the water for Jordan. A flash of blond in the foaming water ahead of me caught my attention. It disappeared and I thought I'd imagined it. Then I saw it again.

"Jordan!" I pushed forward with renewed strength. A few seconds later my numb fingers snagged the collar of Jordan's jacket, and with a cry, I pulled her to me. Her arm wrapped around my waist and she laid her head on my shoulder as I kept us above water. She was battered and freezing, but alive.

"Hold on to me. I'm going to get us out of this." I took several deep breaths to calm myself and reached out to the magic in the water. I felt it respond almost immediately and watched as millions of golden particles formed a warm glowing shield around us and kept us afloat in the rushing water.

"W-what is that? Is that y-your power?"

"Sort of." Surrounded by the familiar magic, I felt my courage and strength returning. This was my element; there was nothing for me to fear from the water. I was back in control, and the river would take us exactly where I wanted it to.

Minutes later, I saw a glow through the trees ahead. The stronghold. Using my free hand, I directed the water to carry us to the shore below the low bank I often sat on. Our feet touched bottom, and we supported each other as we stumbled across the slippery rocks to collapse on the shore. As soon as we left the water, the cold hit me again and I shivered violently. Rocks dug into my back as I stared up at the clear moonlit sky, but for a full minute I was too exhausted to move.

Stiff from the cold, I got to my feet and pulled Jordan up with me. "We have to get inside and warn everyone." I was still reeling from Michael's betrayal and the fact that so many vampires had gotten past Tristan's security. The stronghold was supposed to be impenetrable, but it looked like no place was safe from the Master.

"Well, hello there," drawled a strange male voice above our heads. I jerked backward and stared in shock at the two vampires standing on the bank. I was so cold I hadn't even sensed them.

"Stay back." I shuffled backward until I felt cold water around my calves. Where the hell was everyone? We had vampires running around the grounds and there wasn't a warrior in sight. My gut told me the situation was a lot worse than I'd thought. There was no way vampires would get this close to me with Nikolas here unless . . . unless something really bad had happened to him. My stomach squeezed painfully.

"Don't come any closer," I yelled at them, my fear for Nikolas overriding my own.

"Or what?" The second vampire let out a laugh as he jumped off the bank and landed a few feet away. "You'll splash us?" Before I could respond, he seized my arm in a steel grip, yanking me against him. Jordan pulled out her knife and waved it at the other vampire who was advancing on her.

"Mmm, you do smell good. I bet you taste amazing." The vampire's nose nuzzled my neck, and I pushed back on the terror threatening to engulf me. He was trying to use my fear against me, to make me so scared I could not fight. A few months ago, he would have succeeded.

I twisted around and put my hands on his chest. I wasn't too scared or cold to notice he had moved faster than a baby vampire but not as fast as a mature vampire. I might not be able to knock him out, but I was prepared to do my damnedest. Keeping my eyes on him, I reached into the water swirling around my knees and sent out a silent, urgent call to the magic that waited to do my bidding. *Come to me. Help me, please,* I cried, terror tinging my inner voice.

Water exploded upward behind me, sending a cold shower down on our heads. The vampire's eyes flew wide and his mouth opened in a silent scream as an ungodly screech rent the air. Before I could turn to see what was behind me, a huge white shape leapt over my head to land on the shore behind the vampire. The snow white kelpie towered above us and shook his magnificent mane before he opened his mouth to emit another earsplitting sound.

"Noooo!" the vampire screamed as Fiannar clamped down on his shoulder and ripped him away from me. The vampire's horrified eyes met mine, and then he was gone. With a flick of his powerful head, Fiannar tossed him out into the river.

"Fiannar," I breathed as the kelpie ran past a stunned Jordan to grab the second vampire who shrieked in terror as he was dragged into the water. The water guardian stopped beside me and gave a slight bow before he disappeared beneath the surface with his struggling captive.

Farther out, the first vampire recovered from his shock and started swimming frantically back to shore. Out of the water rose the black head of Feeorin. The kelpie latched onto the vampire and dragged him screaming underwater.

The whole attack had lasted no more than a minute, and I was left staring at the dark river where the two kelpies had been a moment ago.

"What the *fuck* was that?"

I faced Jordan, who stood with her knife hanging limply from her hand. She sounded like herself for the first time since we'd entered the river.

I started climbing the riverbank. "That was Feeorin and his brother, Fiannar. They're the kelpies who guard the river."

"Oh, is that all?" She tucked her knife away and followed me. "Friends of yours?"

"You could say that."

Almost numb from the cold, we pulled ourselves over the top of the riverbank. We lay there for a minute to catch our breath before we set off running toward the buildings. There could be more vampires lurking around the property, and we had to find help before someone else was attacked. I didn't want to think about Roland and Peter out in the woods dealing with God only knew what. Or Nikolas. Or Nate.

My pace picked up. I had to get to Nate.

Shouts and screams reached us as soon as we left the roaring river behind. Cold blossomed in my chest and I sprinted around the nearest building and came up short at the sight in front of me.

"Oh, God!"

The unimaginable had happened. Westhorne was under attack, and everywhere we looked, warriors battled vampires. The vampires were slow, new, but they made up for that in their numbers. Most warriors fought three or four at one time, their swords glinting in the moonlight as they cut down one vampire after another with deadly precision. The warriors without swords fought with knives or bows. I watched one punch a hole through a vampire's chest with his bare fist. It was a bloodbath.

Movement by a corner of the main building drew my attention. I gasped when I saw Tristan decapitating one vampire only to have two more take its place. Beside him, Celine wielded a sword with deadly accuracy, despite her long red dress. I harbored no love for Celine, but I had to admit the woman could fight and I was glad Tristan had her at his back.

I scanned the grounds for Nikolas, but there was no sign of him or Chris. Knowing them, they were out here somewhere in the middle of all the bloodshed. More than anyone, Nikolas could take care of himself in a fight, but that did not prevent the knot of fear from settling in my stomach. *God, let him be okay.*

Two more warriors joined the fight, and my heart leapt into my throat when I recognized Terrence and Josh. Immediately, the two boys were attacked by three vampires. Terrence swung his sword, and one of the vampires screamed when his arm fell to the ground. Josh leapt to one side, his sword flashing, and one of the vampires staggered back holding his gut. Two of the three vampires howled in pain, but they didn't retreat. Josh moved until he and Terrence were back-to-back, and they waited for the next attack.

"We have to do something," I said. Our friends were fighting for their lives; the people I cared most about in the world were under attack. Nate was inside that building. I just got him back; I could not lose him again.

Jordan opened her mouth to reply when a girl screamed off to our right.

"That's Olivia." She took off in the direction of the scream, away from the main battle. There was nothing to do but follow her. Nate and the others were a big question mark, but Olivia was here and she needed us now.

"Get away from her, you bastard!" Jordan screeched, throwing herself at the vampire latched onto Olivia's throat. The male released Olivia who crumbled to the ground like a rag doll. He swung his arm, and Jordan flew half a dozen feet to land on her back in the snow.

The vampire ignored her and advanced on me. "All this sweet young Mohiri blood . . . delicious," he hissed. He wavered slightly on his feet as if he was drunk and drops of blood – Olivia's blood – dripped from his chin onto the snow. Bile rose in my throat, and my eyes darted to the girl who lay motionless a few feet away. *Please be alive*, I pleaded silently as I backed away from the vampire stalking me hungrily.

My heel struck something, and I flailed as I almost went down. Righting myself, I looked behind me and choked when I saw Mark's sightless eyes and ravaged throat. He and I had not been friends, but something inside me snapped at the sight of his lifeless body. Instead of Mark, I saw my dad lying in the snow covered in his own blood.

White-hot rage exploded in my brain, and my Mori cried out happily as we came together. Its power roared through me, saturating every muscle, every tendon, and bone. I lifted my eyes to the vampire as the world sharpened into brilliant focus around me.

I don't know who was more surprised – the vampire or me – by the fist that slammed into his nose with a satisfying crunch. He howled and put a hand to his bleeding face. A few seconds later, his mouth twisted into a snarl and he came at me again. He was fast, but not fast enough.

The world slowed down around me, and I watched his clawed hand swipe at my face before I tilted to one side to evade it. I kicked out and my booted foot struck him squarely between the legs.

He wheezed and sank to his knees, and I grinned with malicious pleasure to see that Nikolas had been right about the effectiveness of a well-placed kick. Before the vampire could recover, I spun and my other foot connected with his face.

The vampire flailed as he flew backward, right onto the blade in Jordan's hand as she came up behind him. His eyes widened in shock, and he made a choking sound before he fell face first into the snow.

"Liv!" Jordan dropped her knife and ran to Olivia. The rage drained out of me as I went to kneel beside our fallen friend. As soon as I touched Olivia's face I knew her life force was gone. My eyes met Jordan's and I shook my head, unable to speak.

"Can't you help her?" Jordan begged desperately.

"She's gone. I'm sorry."

Jordan's eyes filled with tears for the first time since I'd met her. "You idiot," she whispered hoarsely, brushing Olivia's hair out of her face. "How many times did I tell you to always carry your weapon?" Her breath hitched, and she looked at me. "I always teased her, but she was my friend."

"I know, and she knew it, too." I stood and grabbed Olivia's arms.

"What are you doing?"

"She should be next to Mark." The two of them had finally admitted they were a couple last week, but everyone knew they were crazy about each other long before that. They had died together, and it was only right that they lie beside each other in death.

Jordan got up and took Olivia's legs, and together we carried her over and laid her at Mark's side. I closed his eyes, and Jordan put their hands together. Then she wiped her eyes on her sleeve and cleared her throat. "Come on. We can't stay here."

I cringed at the screams coming from behind us, near the main building. We were out of sight for the moment, but we were stuck between the battle and the woods. An attack could come from either direction, and we were looking a bit worse for wear with only one weapon between us. Using my Mori's strength had left me tired, and our dunk in the river hadn't helped. I wasn't sure either of us would survive another attack.

"Which way should we go?"

Jordan found her knife and wiped it on the snow, leaving bloody streaks behind. "I don't know, but we're sitting ducks out here."

"Lead the way," I said, waving in front of me. Pain shot up my arm, and I grunted loudly.

"Ah shit, did he get you?" Jordan lifted my arm to examine it, and I saw for the first time, the long tears in my coat sleeve. There was blood on my sleeve, but it didn't look too serious. It just hurt like the devil.

"I've had worse than this. Let's go."

"Sara!"

I turned at the sound of my name, and my lips parted in a trembling smile when I saw Chris sprinting toward us from the main building.

"Chris," I yelled hoarsely, running toward him, relieved to see he was okay.

"Behind you!" Jordan shouted, and Chris and I looked at the same time to see two vampires run at him from behind. Neither of them looked older than sixteen, and their slower movements marked them as newly made. Chris brought up his sword and cut them down with little effort. I couldn't help but feel a dull pang of sorrow for the two teenage boys whose life had been cut so short.

Chris waved us toward him. "Let's go. We have to get you two out of here."

Jordan and I were twenty feet from Chris when he suddenly stopped, his body going rigid like he'd been shot. I screamed his name as his face twisted in agony and he sank to his knees. A second later, my eyes were drawn to a slight figure emerging from the woods to our right, walking with purposeful strides toward Chris. It took me another few seconds to recognize the white markings on the person's dark face.

"No!" Power seared my throat and tongue as I sprinted forward and threw my body on top of Chris's to shield him from the Hale witch. My hands found Chris's face, and I opened myself to rip the witch's magic from him before it could burrow inside his mind like a cold maggot. Revulsion filled me when I touched it, but unlike the old magic that had festered inside Desmund, this was new and much weaker. This witch was nowhere near as powerful as the one who had attacked Desmund or the witch who had come after me.

I ignored the cold nausea as I pulled the dark magic into me. It seemed to take on a life of its own, fighting to escape as if it knew its impending fate, but I was a lot stronger than I'd been two months ago when I encountered my first Hale witch. My power incinerated the magic. I heard a scream nearby, but all I cared about was Chris.

"Chris? Chris?" I rolled off him and tapped his cheek a few times before his green eyes opened and he gazed at me in confusion. "Hey. You with me?" I asked him.

He groaned and rubbed his brow. "That is some war cry you have, cousin. What the hell happened? I feel like I have a killer hangover."

"Hale witch." I glanced over at the witch who was lying on his side, facing away from us. "Come on, we have to get up."

"Up?" He blinked in confusion. "Why are you so wet?"

I tugged on his arm. "Long story. Come on. Get up."

"Shit!"

I looked up in time to see Jordan dive away from the attack of a snarling female vampire who had probably been a college freshman a few weeks ago. Jordan rolled in a ball and came to her feet with Chris's sword in her hand.

"This is more like it," she said fiercely as she brandished the weapon with ease. The vampire skidded to a stop and stared at the sword warily. Jordan leapt forward in a burst of speed and sliced off one of the female's arms at the elbow.

"That was for Mark," she shouted over the vampire's screams. "And this is for Olivia!" The sword whistled and the vampire's head separated from its body.

Jordan stood over the corpse, shoulders heaving and silent tears running down her face. Then she spun with the dripping sword in her hand and stalked angrily toward the fallen Hale witch.

"No." I pushed to my feet and caught her arm. She tried to pull out of my grasp, but I held firm. "Trust me; you don't want him in your head. I'll handle this."

The witch had his arms wrapped protectively around his head. I nudged his back with my boot, and he moaned loudly.

"If you can't take it, don't dish it out," I told him pitilessly. "Get up."

He rolled onto his back and uncovered his face. I sucked in a sharp breath when I saw that he was only a boy, maybe sixteen, if that. How young did these guys start in this business?

"Please," he whispered brokenly. "Please finish it. Kill me."

"What?" I took a step back. "I'm not going to kill you. I just wanted to stop you from hurting people. Did you hurt more of my people out in the woods?"

The boy nodded, and I swore furiously at the thought of the warriors lying out in the woods in pain. "You better hope they're alive," I ground out. More screams pierced the air around us. "If we survive this, you are going to show us where they are and then you are going to fix whatever you did to them. You understand me?"

"Please." He sounded more like a young boy than a powerful witch. "They took my mother and my sisters, and they will kill them if I do not do as they ask."

"I'm sorry about your family, but I'll do anything to protect my family, too. You can sacrifice yourself later if you want to, but not until after you help the people you hurt. Now get up."

He stared at me for another minute before he sat up. His strained expression told me that was as far as he could go on his own.

I was loath to touch him, but I could not leave him here and give him the opportunity to escape. Reaching down, I grabbed his hand and pulled him to his feet. He wavered unsteadily and I called Jordan over. "I don't think he has enough juice left in him to try anything, but if he does, you can kick his ass." I gave the boy a hard stare. "You hurt anyone else and you'll deal with me." I had no idea if I could hurt him, but he didn't know that. He nodded submissively.

Jordan gave the boy a warning glare before she took his arm. I hurried back to Chris, relieved to find him sitting up. "Can you walk? We can't stay here."

Shouts reached us before he could answer, and I turned to see Erik and three other members of his team racing toward us. The warriors sped around us and intercepted a group of six vampires advancing on us. My heart thudded when I realized how close we had come to being taken by them. Surrounded by so many vampires, I had a permanent lump of ice in my chest, which rendered my vampire radar useless.

Erik quickly sized up our pathetic group. We had one sword, an injured witch, and our seasoned warrior was down. "Get out of here," he shouted at us. "We've got this."

I glanced around us frantically. In every direction, I could see fighting, hear screams and shouts. Until now, we'd kept away from the main battle, but it looked like it had found us. There was nowhere to run.

"You're going to have to help me up, cousin," Chris said, and I wished I had some of his fortitude. I took his hands and helped him to his feet, putting one of his arms over my shoulders so I could support him. He shook his head to clear it, and despite my fear, I felt the urge to grin at him.

"See, Dimples, I knew I'd end up having to save your ass someday."

He tried to scowl but couldn't quite pull it off. "If I remember correctly, you said it would be from all the women. You didn't say anything about almost getting my brain turned to mush."

"Beggars can't be choosers."

He stumbled, and I shifted to take more of his weight. Damn, Mohiri warriors were not light.

I looked around us. "Where to?" I asked Chris, trying to keep the fear from my voice.

"That way." He pointed to the cluster of low buildings a few hundred yards away on our left that housed the garages. "If we can make it there, we'll be okay."

"If we make it." I took a deep breath to steady me and started in that direction, trying not to stagger under his weight as we moved as fast as we could. I looked straight ahead so I didn't see the battle around us, but there was no way to block out the sounds of fighting and dying. If I survived this, those sounds would haunt me for the rest of my days.

"Sara, we *will* make it." The arm across my shoulders squeezed me. "Nikolas will be so proud of you."

"Have you seen him? Where is he?" I asked anxiously.

"We were coming back from town when someone raised the alarm. We found the main gate open and ten vamps waiting inside. The two of us were holding them off when Desmund showed up to help. Nikolas asked me to come find you."

"You left them there?" My voice rose when I thought of Nikolas and Desmund alone and outnumbered five to one.

"Don't worry about the two of them. Desmund is as good as Nikolas with a sword, and he actually looked like he was enjoying himself. Trust me; he and Nikolas are safer than we are right now."

A menacing growl behind us made the hair on the back of my neck stand on end, and I spun us around, fearing for Jordan who followed us with the witch. My breath hitched at the sight of the black werewolf ripping apart a vampire less than twenty feet from us. Roland made short work of the killing then dropped the body and bounded toward us with Peter close behind him. Both of my friends looked like they'd been through more than one battle tonight. Their fur was wet and dirty and bloody. Peter was limping, and Roland had a nasty cut above one eye that looked like it was already starting to heal.

"Phew, you guys really do smell like wet dog," Jordan declared, stumbling when Peter brushed against her.

Roland came up to me, and I would have hugged him if I wasn't supporting Chris. I put a hand in the rough fur on his back, and he leaned against me.

"I'm so glad to see you guys." I wanted to sob with relief, but now was not the time to break down. My friends were safe and their arrival greatly improved our odds of survival, but we were far from out of danger. We picked up our pace with renewed energy. Roland walked beside me, and Peter took up the rear to protect us from a surprise attack.

"Roland, once we get to the garage, will you go find Nate and keep him safe? Please?" My voice broke on the last word. I hadn't allowed myself to think about Nate, but seeing my friends made me painfully aware that he was the only one whose whereabouts were unknown. I also knew Roland and Peter would not leave me until I was safe, even to help Nate.

Roland growled softly and nodded his large head.

When a high-pitched cackle echoed through the woods a few seconds later, my bladder almost gave away and my heart threatened to break through my ribs. Chris stiffened and tried to stand on his own. Roland's hackles rose as Peter came racing back to us. We all turned to stare at the trees.

"What is that?" Jordan asked.

"You don't want to know," I said through numb lips. "We've got to go – now."

We broke into a run, going as fast as we could with two injured people. I tried not to think about what was out there, but it was impossible to not picture the grinning mouths and the six-inch claws that could rip the roof off a pickup truck.

The sound came again, much closer this time, and I knew we weren't going to reach the buildings in time. Roland and Peter realized it, too, and they moved to take up defensive positions between us and the trees. They had a chance against the creatures, if there weren't too many of them. All I could do was stand there and hold up Chris, who was wheezing from our short run.

Jordan let go of the witch and hefted Chris's sword like it was made for her. She was wet and bloody and tired, yet she stood bravely to face a threat unlike anything she had encountered.

"Jesus!" she hissed when the first massive hyena-like creature stepped from the trees. "What the hell is that?"

No one answered her. We were riveted on two more creatures emerging from the woods, followed by at least ten vampires. Terror slammed into me at the sight of the three massive crocotta.

A large head swung in our direction and spoke in a perfect imitation of Jordan's voice. "Jesus!" it said and giggled.

A second later, roars followed by screams came from the other side of the grounds. What other horrors were the warriors facing? How could we hope to survive this?

God, please help us.

The vampires held back as the crocotta advanced on us. Roland and Peter sprung forward to meet them. One of the crocotta raked its long claws along Peter's flank. Peter howled and clamped down on the crocotta's throat with his own powerful jaws. The two of them went down in a snapping, growling mass of fur, claws, and teeth.

Roland let out a snarl, and he and the second crocotta lunged for each other at the same time. I cried out as the crocotta's mouth latched onto the back of Roland's neck. They hit the ground with a loud thud and rolled over a few times in the snow before Roland was able to shake free of the creature's hold.

I was so fixated on my friends that I forgot about the third crocotta until Jordan screamed my name. She leapt in front of me swinging Chris's sword in a deadly arc. The tip of the sword sliced easily through the shoulder of the creature bearing down on us. The crocotta roared in pain and swiped at her. She dove to the side, but its claws hooked the pocket of her coat and threw her off balance.

Jordan landed hard on her stomach but kept her grip on the sword. In one fluid motion she rolled onto her back and slashed at the crocotta looming over her, cutting a long shallow gash in its chest. Her attack took the crocotta by surprise, but that did not last long. It struck out with a paw and knocked the sword from her hands before it reared up to strike, its mouth opened and drool dribbled between the razor-sharp teeth.

"Jordan!" I screamed. I tried to run to her, but Chris held me back.

A roar split the air, unlike anything I had ever heard. From out of nowhere, a large winged shape dived from the air, dipping so close to our heads that the downdraft from its leathery wings made my hair fly around my face. The crocotta stumbled away from Jordan, and I saw terror in its eyes before it turned to flee. It didn't get far before it was swallowed by flames so hot I felt them from twenty feet away.

"Alex?" I whispered, too awed by his appearance to be terrified he would come after me next.

Engulfed by flames, the crocotta screamed and thrashed violently on the ground. The wyvern circled the dying creature once before taking off toward the vampires that had stopped their advance on us to stare in shock. Flames sprouted from his snout again, and I heard a vampire shriek in agony. The others scattered.

If Alex's appearance shocked me, it was nothing compared to the sight of the golden griffin that dropped from the sky with an enraged squawk and snatched one of the vampires up in her sharp talons. The vampire's screams lasted only seconds before he fell in pieces to the ground. I stared at the gruesome sight and swallowed several times to keep from gagging. If my sweet Minuet could do this, I did not want to imagine what an adult griffin was capable of.

Chris let me go, and I ran to help Jordan to her feet. She retrieved the sword, and the three of us watched the vampires scream and run from the endless attacks from above. The snow-covered ground turned scarlet, and I could not understand why the vampires did not run for their lives, choosing instead to be burned alive or ripped to pieces.

Growling pulled my attention from the vampires to Roland and Peter still locked in deadly battles of their own. Sharp teeth and claws tore at flesh and tried to snap bones. Blood sprayed and hot breath steamed the air. The werewolves and crocotta were evenly matched. We had to do something to help Roland and Peter.

"Jordan, we need to – "

Jordan jumped forward with the sword raised. But not to my friends' defense. I saw the vampire as he swerved around her and came at me. He was not a baby vampire, but he was still young and his sneer was cocky, obviously not seeing either of us as a threat. Jordan staggered slightly as she spun to intercept him, and I knew she was exhausted.

I was running dangerously low on energy, but I stepped away from Chris and summoned what power I could. When the vampire grabbed me, I slammed my hands into his chest and gave him a weak jolt. It wasn't nearly enough power to disable him, but he stopped short and stared at me in surprise.

It was all the opening Jordan needed. Our eyes met briefly, and I stumbled backward as her sword sliced cleanly through his neck. The severed head hit her boot, and she kicked it away before letting out a whoop and shooting me a savage grin.

"You and me are one badass vampire-killing duo."

I tried to smile back as I swayed on my feet, and Chris had to grab me to keep me from falling. "Looks like you'll have to go solo," I panted. I was used up.

Chris yelled Jordan's name, and she spun around as a male and a female vampire weaved their way toward us. Their ability to evade Alex and Minuet and the way they sometimes blurred as they moved told me these were almost mature vampires.

"Give me my sword," Chris commanded, but I knew he was still too weak to fight. Jordan knew it, too, and she shook her head without looking at him. She was going to die defending us.

I heard a whimper to my left and cried out when I saw Peter slumped over one of the crocotta. He was bloody and barely moving. A few feet from them, Roland was locked in a death grip with the second creature. My friends were all going to die before my eyes, and there was nothing I could do to help them.

I felt the air move around me a second before two long furred bodies sailed over my head and hit the ground snarling. Hugo was on the female vampire before she knew what hit her, and with one bite, he tore her head from her shoulders. Woolf went after the male who had already turned tail and run. I watched Hugo give the female's body one last shake before he dropped it and joined Woolf in the pursuit of his prey.

The remaining vampires' courage left them when they saw the two red-eyed hellhounds that had come to join the fight. They turned and fled for the trees with Hugo and Woolf snapping at their heels and Alex and Minuet attacking them from above.

The sound of snapping bones tore my eyes away from the hellhounds, and I spun in time to see the last crocotta sink to the ground. Roland released its broken neck and staggered back from the dead creature.

I fell to my knees beside Peter and ran my hands over his head and sides. My power was so drained I didn't know if I had enough to heal him, but I would give everything in me if I had to.

His large head lifted sluggishly, and his amber eyes met mine before he gave my chin a lick.

"Are you okay?" I asked, and he nodded once. I threw my arms around his thick neck and hugged him tightly. Roland came to sit beside me, and I found myself sandwiched between them and struggling not to fall apart. I'd come so close to losing them again. If Alex, Minuet, and the hellhounds hadn't arrived when they did, we'd all be dead now. I wasn't sure how much more I could take tonight.

"I think it's over," Jordan said in a disbelieving voice.

An eerie silence hung over the grounds. Everywhere I looked, warriors stood with dead vampires at their feet. The quiet was broken only by the distant roars and growls growing fainter by the second.

"Do you think they'll be okay?" I asked no one in particular, staring at the woods.

Chris let out a bark of laughter that was followed by a fit of coughing. When he recovered, he wiped his eyes and smirked at me. "Sara, I'd take you and your pets into battle with me any day."

Jordan harumphed and gave Chris a look of pure chagrin as she stabbed the tip of his sword into the ground so close to his foot, he had to step sideways to avoid losing a toe. "Next time, you can carry your own damn sword, Blondie."

I burst out laughing at the bewildered look on Chris's face, but my laughter faded when a familiar presence brushed across my mind. My heart soared. *He's safe.* I whirled and searched the grounds breathlessly for a glimpse of Nikolas.

He tore around the corner of the main building, carrying a sword in each hand, and wearing a thunderous expression I could see from where we stood twenty yards away. Spotting us, he veered in our direction, and I barely had time to take a breath of air before he was in front of me. He threw down his swords and grabbed my shoulders, ignoring everyone else.

"Are you hurt?" he bit out. His rigid posture and the blazing intensity of his gaze told me he was close to losing it.

"I'm okay, Nikolas; we all are." I laid my hands against his chest and felt his body tremble from the effort to calm down. Rising up on my toes, I whispered in his ear. "Please, don't freak out on me, okay? I don't think I can take it right now."

A sound like a soft growl rumbled deep in his chest, and I took a hasty step back, only to be pulled against him. I started to protest, but my words were smothered and all thought fled when his mouth came down over mine.

Chapter 24

THIS WAS NOTHING like the tender first kiss we had shared. It was hard and urgent, and it sent a shock wave to the center of my being. I gasped and he deepened the kiss, sending heat unfurling in my stomach and melting the bones in my body until my legs couldn't support me anymore. He tightened his hold, and my arms moved of their own volition to wrap around his neck.

As soon as I kissed him back, the tension drained out of him and his mouth became soft and searching. I responded in kind, my heart swelling with love. My body felt like it had been starved for oxygen, and being with him was like taking a deep breath of air. I felt my Mori sigh contentedly and whisper *solmi*, and I trembled when it reached out and embraced Nikolas's Mori for the first time. An answering shiver ran through Nikolas. It was wondrous and frightening to know how deeply connected we were in that moment.

"Damn. Get a room, you two!" Jordan exclaimed, breaking the spell holding us. My whole body grew warm in embarrassment, and I pulled abruptly away from Nikolas. The bewildered look he gave me as he let go told me I wasn't the only one deeply affected by the kiss.

Jordan let out a whistle. "Wow, I think you guys melted the snow."

"Shut up," I muttered, scowling at her. I darted a glance at Roland and Peter, but it was impossible to read their expressions when they were in wolf form. I refused to look at Chris, whom I suspected was enjoying the whole thing despite his weakened condition.

"You missed all the fun," Chris quipped hoarsely to Nikolas. He teetered, and I moved to support him again, but Nikolas nudged me aside and took my place.

Jordan poked me in the side as I walked past her. I stopped, and she leaned in close to my ear. "Two swords. Smoking hot."

Blushing furiously, I went to help the boy witch up from where he had fallen when Jordan let him go to fight the vampires. He was still shaky, and his eyes darted around him in fear.

Nikolas's face hardened when he noticed the Hale witch for the first time. "I can guess what happened," he said harshly.

"No, you can't, my friend. You really can't," Chris wheezed. "Now, can you please get me somewhere I can lie down before I pass out?"

"It looks like you all could use a trip to the healers," Nikolas replied. His eye narrowed when he spotted my torn and bloody sleeve.

"It's just a scratch. I can hardly feel it," I lied. Now that my adrenaline levels were coming down, my arm was starting to hurt like crazy. "We have to go find the people who were out on patrol. They ran into this guy," I pointed to the witch, "and we need to get to them as soon as possible."

"We will find them," said Tristan in a voice I barely recognized. I turned to see him, Celine, and Desmund behind me looking like they were in a lot better shape than me and my friends. Tristan's mouth was a hard line, and I could feel his tightly controlled anger. "I am relieved to see you are all safe. Go to the healers and I'll talk to you when I get back. Maybe we can piece together exactly what happened here tonight."

I chewed my lip, hating what I had to say next. "It was Michael. He helped the vampires."

"Michael?" Tristan could not have looked more shocked, and he wasn't the only one. I understood how they felt. It was hard to imagine the sweet, quiet boy hurting anyone, let alone betraying us to our enemy.

Jordan made a sound of disgust. "Little bastard led us right to them. If he's not dead, I call dibs on finishing the job."

Tristan shook his head in disbelief. "Why would Michael do that?"

"It's not his fault," I said, and everyone stared at me like I had lost my mind. "The vampires got to him somehow and convinced him they had his twin brother, Matthew. They promised to let him go if Michael helped them."

"Still no excuse to betray everyone you know," Jordan replied irately.

"He's messed up, Jordan." I understood her anger. Michael's betrayal cut me deeply as well, but he was obviously delusional and in a lot of pain. The saddest thing was that no one had seen it and helped him before it was too late.

"Where is he now?" Celine asked, and I was surprised she sounded almost civil toward me.

I told them where we had entered the woods and gave them a brief overview of how we had ended up in there. "One of the vampires hit him pretty hard, and I'm not sure if he's alive. We had to leave him."

"We'll find him if he's still out there," Tristan said grimly. "You go to the healers. Nikolas, we could use your help if we have men down out there."

Nikolas nodded, and Jordan took his place supporting Chris. His eyes met mine for a moment, and I knew he was making sure I was okay before he left. It wasn't until I smiled and nodded that he turned away and the four of them headed toward the woods.

Left alone, our group limped toward the main building. We passed dozens of vampire corpses, revealing the sheer size of the force that had attacked us. Most of the vampires had been new, or the outcome would have been a lot different. At least we knew now why so many people had disappeared in the last month. The Master built a disposable army to send against us. What they lacked in speed and strength, he'd hoped they would make up for in numbers and the element of surprise. It had almost worked.

Tears pricked my eyes, and I looked away from the bodies. My life used to be about healing and helping others. Now it was all about killing and destruction. My chest ached and I longed for the days of watching movies at Roland's house and hanging out at the cliffs with Remy. Back then my greatest worry was keeping my secret from Nate and my friends. Now I was afraid of losing one of them.

The main hall was pristine and untouched. Thankfully, none of the vampires had been able to breach the building. Even so, I would not be able to rest until I saw that Nate was okay.

"Sara!" Nate raced down the stairs, and the sight of him safe and unharmed made the last two hours seem like some unreal nightmare. He was shaking when he pulled me into a bone-crushing hug. "I saw you out there with those things, and I thought . . . "

"It'll take more than a few vampires and their pets to take us down," I said with as much lightness as I could muster. He could never know how close he had come to watching us all die. I'd dragged him into this new world, and I had to shelter him from as much of it as I could.

Two younger warriors appeared behind Nate eying the witch. "He stays with me," I told them. They started to protest, but I stood firm. "We need him to help the people he hurt. Don't worry, he won't hurt anyone else." I gave the boy a pointed look. "Will you?"

The witch shook his head and stared at the floor. I'd be afraid to meet the eyes of the people whose home I had attacked, too. He looked so young and vulnerable despite the tattoos, and it pulled at my heart for a few seconds. Then I remembered Olivia and Mark and I hardened again. Sometimes, the lines blurred between good and evil, and this was definitely one of those times. I wanted to hate him for what he'd done, but he was just a boy scared for his own family. I sighed inwardly. It was another reason why I would never be a good warrior.

Roland and Peter disappeared upstairs to change back and dress, and the rest of us went to the medical ward. The healers were busy tending to several injured people when we got there. No one was happy to see the witch, but I assured them he was no longer a threat. We deposited Chris in one of the rooms, and then Jordan and I went to get treated for our own injuries. The boy stayed with me, and he was very subdued, trailing behind me quietly.

A healer gave me some pants and a long-sleeved top to change into, and I went behind a screen to pull off my wet clothes. I longed for a shower, but I settled for warm, dry clothes and washing my face in the sink. I wasn't going anywhere until I knew the fate of the warriors out in the woods.

Nate stayed with me while the healer treated and wrapped my arm and gave me some of the dreaded gunna paste. He and the healer wanted me to rest, but there was no way I could lay still with so many people hurt and missing. I promised to take it easy and went in search of Chris. I found him resting in a bed with his color almost restored. His face lit with a smile when I remarked on how much better he looked.

"Gunna paste never fails."

I made a face at the taste still lingering in my mouth. "We're lucky they have lots of it on hand."

His gaze flicked to the witch, and he grew sober. "You saved my life out there."

"Now we're almost even," I returned lightly. "Besides, what is family for?"

Jordan came in with Roland and Peter, and I could not help but smile when I heard the three of them sharing battle stories like old friends. Maybe they had more in common than just me. The boys told how us they had chased the blond female for a good three miles before they took her down. They came back looking for us and followed our scents to the river.

Jordan and I took up the story and told them about our swim in the river and everything that had happened after. She grew very quiet when I talked about Olivia and Mark. She didn't let her guard down much, but I could tell she was hurting a lot.

It was over an hour later when Nikolas and the others returned carrying Seamus, Niall, and Ben, who were taken to a ward where the healers could tend to them all at once. I grabbed the boy witch by the arm and pushed past everyone crowding outside the door. Desmund stood just inside the doorway and the pain on his face told me how bad it was before I looked at the men. If anyone knew what they were suffering it was him.

I had to hold back a cry when I saw the twins' pale faces and blank staring eyes. Beside them, Ben moaned and pulled at his hair until two healers restrained him. I shoved the boy forward. "Fix them," I ordered in a choked voice.

The healers working on Ben backed up when we approached the bed. Everyone else gave us a wide berth as we stood by the bed and the boy laid a hand on Ben's forehead. The effect was almost immediate. Ben's hands fell to his sides, and in less than thirty seconds, his moaning stopped and color began to return to his face.

The boy lifted his hand from Ben's face. "He will sleep now, and when he wakes he will be well."

I released the breath I was holding, and we moved on to Seamus and Niall where the boy repeated whatever he had done to Ben. Soon all three were sleeping peacefully. After my work to heal Desmund, it was hard to believe how easily the boy reversed the damage he had done.

Two guards stepped forward to take the boy who looked at me fearfully. I gave him a reassuring nod, and he let them lead him away. Tomorrow, I'd talk to Tristan about helping the young witch's family. No matter what he was, he was still just a scared kid and a victim in all of this, too.

After the boy left, a healer told me they'd found Michael. He was suffering from head trauma and internal injuries, but they believed he'd make it. Part of me wondered if it would not be more of a kindness for him to die. He would never be the warrior he dreamed of being; he'd be lucky not to end up in a cell for the rest of his life. He would have to live with the stigma of being a traitor and the knowledge that he had betrayed his people for a brother who had died a long time ago.

Tristan assigned a guard to watch over Michael, even though the healers had heavily sedated him. I watched Tristan look down at the unconscious boy and shake his head sorrowfully. His troubled expression told me he was wondering how they had gone wrong with Michael.

It looked like all the injured had been treated when Terrence and Josh arrived carrying a gravely injured Sahir. I hovered outside the room while the healers went to work on him. Josh told me they had found him in the menagerie and it looked like he had been attacked as he was setting the creatures free. "We found two vamps fried to a crisp beside him. Looks like the wyvern took care of them."

Another agonizing hour passed before the healers announced Sahir was going to make it. I sagged against the wall from relief and exhaustion, and I was still there when Nikolas came looking for me a few minutes later.

"You should be in bed."

"I'm fine," I argued weakly.

"You're practically asleep on your feet," he said firmly. "There is nothing else you can do here tonight. If you don't rest, you'll end up in here yourself."

"Okay," I relented and pushed away from the wall somewhat unsteadily. He moved in to pick me up, and I put up a hand to stop him. "I can walk." I scowled at his dubious expression. "I'm tired, Nikolas, not weak."

He laughed softly. "Sara, no one who knew you would ever accuse you of being weak. Come on, I'll walk you to your room."

It was barely ten o'clock, yet the building was quiet as we made our way to my room. "They're outside, cleaning up," Nikolas explained when I commented on the empty halls. I shuddered at the grisly job the warriors had ahead of them, disposing of all those bodies and collecting our dead. In addition to Olivia and Mark, we had lost three warriors tonight, and their friends were out there right now clearing the battlefield instead of mourning their loss. God, I just wanted this horrible night to be over.

"You're sure you would not feel better staying with Nate tonight?" Nikolas asked as we climbed the stairs to my floor.

I want to stay with you. I wished I could say the words, but I didn't want to sound needy or for him to take it the wrong way. Besides, he was probably going to be busy tonight and he didn't need to be distracted by me.

I shook my head. "I'm sure."

At my door, I turned to face him. I swallowed and raised my eyes to meet his, hoping he wouldn't see how close I was to coming apart.

"You were amazing tonight."

"Really?" I searched his face for some sign he was patronizing me, but I saw only pride.

"The whole time I was out there, all I could think about was getting to you. And then I find you standing in the middle of it all, surrounded by bodies. I heard what you did. Don't ever tell me again that you're not a warrior."

"I did have a lot of help," I said, flushed with pleasure at his praise. It was the first time he had acknowledged my ability to take care of myself, and I was going to remember this moment for a long time. "I was worried about you, too."

His expression was impossible to read and my breath caught when he took a step toward me. He opened his mouth as to say something but changed his mind. Tenderly, he brushed my hair back from my face, his fingers grazing my cheek. "Try to get some sleep."

"I will," I breathed. I entered my room and closed the door behind me, then leaned against it, wondering if he was still out there. After a few minutes, I realized I would have sensed him if he was that close. Shaking my head at my own foolishness, I went to shower off all the battle grime clinging to me.

I was trembling from fatigue when I emerged from the bathroom and fell onto the bed without bothering to turn off the lamp. But though my body was spent, my mind refused to shut down, and it kept replaying every horrific detail of the night when I closed my eyes. After thirty minutes of torture, I grabbed the quilt off the bed and curled up on the couch, flicking through TV channels for anything to distract me. I settled on an English comedy even though I was too tired to try to make out what they were saying.

But even the show's raucous laughter could not keep the dark thoughts away for long, and I found myself thinking about Michael, who had looked so young and innocent in the medical ward. How was it that no one had seen how delusional and desperate he was until it was too late? We had some of the best technology and medicine in the world, yet we had failed to help one troubled boy. In the short time I'd known Michael I had seen how obsessed he was with finding his brother. It was the same obsession I'd seen in myself when I'd searched for my dad's killer. I wished I had said something to Tristan about him. Even though Michael had betrayed me in the worst way, all I wanted to do was cry for the wasted life of the boy I had believed was my friend.

My chest constricted painfully when I let myself think about Olivia and Mark. Olivia had been so animated compared to Mark's quieter personality, but they had been happy together. The two of them were orphans, but unlike me, they had no other family but each other. And now they were gone. They were dead because of me. I should not be here safe with the people I loved while Olivia and Mark lay on cold slabs in the morgue.

I buried my face in the quilt to smother my sobs. I didn't hear the door open or realize I was no longer alone until the couch dipped beside me. I went blindly into Nikolas's arms and pressed my face against his soft sweater.

"I can't do this anymore. I can't bear all these people getting hurt because of me."

"None of this was your fault," he said against my hair. "No one expected the vampires to try something like this. If you have to blame anyone, blame me. I promised you and Nate that you would be safe here."

"I can't blame you." Since the day we met, Nikolas had done everything in his power to protect me. He might choose to ignore the truth, but my conscience would not let me forget so easily. And the truth was this started the night I decided to meet a stranger at the Attic to get answers about my dad. Before that night, Eli and his Master had no idea where or what I really was. Since then, Roland, Peter, and Nate had all been hurt in attempts to get to me. How long would it be before one of them met a worst fate?

"You all could have died tonight," I said, hiccupping loudly. "I couldn't bear it if . . . "

Nikolas wrapped his arms tighter around me. "Nothing will happen to us. Now that we know the lengths this vampire will go to, we will step up security and put every resource we have into finding him. I will never let them take you. That is one promise I will take to my grave."

"Don't say that." I shuddered at the thought of him dying, and the cold realization hit me that he would willingly give up his life to protect me. I would not let him die for me.

The more time that passed, the bolder this Master became. He was never going to stop, and eventually someone I loved would pay the ultimate price. I could not sit back and let that happen. It was time to make some hard decisions and to stop hiding like a frightened rabbit, waiting for the predator to strike.

Nikolas rubbed my back through the quilt. For the first time since I entered the woods with Michael, I felt sheltered and warm. Westhorne was supposed to be my refuge, but tonight had shattered that illusion and opened my eyes to the truth. The only time I felt truly safe was with Nikolas.

He had never wavered or weakened once in the months I'd known him, no matter what danger he faced or how much I'd tried to push him away. When I needed a trainer and a friend he was there. When I thought I'd lost Nate, he was my strength. He sent for Roland and Peter because he knew how much I needed them. He had been patient and put his own feelings aside when I was confused and afraid. He was a warrior in the very best sense of the word.

His hand stilled. "Feel better?" I nodded, and he loosened his embrace.

"Would you . . . stay just a little longer?" I asked when he began to pull away. Tomorrow, I would be strong. Tonight, all I wanted was to feel his arms around me.

"I'll be here as long as you need me." He tugged on the quilt that had fallen off my shoulders, pulling it over both of us. Then he moved us until he reclined against the cushioned armrest with me lying against him. Cocooned in his arms with his heart beating beneath my hand, I felt a sense of wholeness and belonging unlike anything I had ever known. It was incredible and wonderful and a little frightening to care so deeply for another person, especially with a monster out there determined to take everyone I loved from me.

I *love you.* The words hovered on my lips, but something held me back from saying them out loud. I didn't know if it was fear of laying my heart out there or a need to savor these new feelings a little longer before I shared them.

His hand came up to stroke my hair. "Go to sleep, *moy malen'kiy voin.* You've earned it."

"You're always saying stuff in Russian," I murmured. "What did you just say?"

He chuckled. "It means 'my little warrior.'"

"I'm not that little," I retorted then yawned, unable to keep my eyes open. "You're my warrior, too." I felt his arms tighten around me as sleep finally claimed me.

Chapter 25

I STOOD ON the riverbank and stared at the tumbling water without really seeing it. The weak December sun did little to dispel the bite in the air, and I pulled the collar of my warm coat up to cover my ears. It was too cold to be standing outside like this, but I couldn't spend another minute inside with everyone talking about last night. And I couldn't walk around the grounds without seeing the red splotches of snow and other evidence of the battle that took place here.

Was it really less than sixteen hours ago that Jordan and I dragged ourselves from the river at this very spot? I looked down at the sloping bank and saw the gouges in the frozen dirt and the places where our hands had found purchase as we'd pulled our freezing, wet bodies over the top of the bank. Directly below me on the rocky shore was where Feeorin and Fiannar had sprung from the river and saved us from a horrible fate.

In the light of day it was hard to imagine the terrible events of less than a day ago. But I would never forget them. I'd never forget Olivia and Mark and the three warriors who lost their lives here last night. No one was saying it, but everyone knew the attack was an attempt to get to me. No matter what Nikolas had said last night, my conscience felt the weight of those five lost lives.

I hadn't seen Jordan yet today, and she wouldn't answer when I'd knocked at her door. I'd left her alone to grieve for Olivia and Mark, knowing there was nothing I could do to ease her pain. Jordan acted tough all the time, but she had a good heart. She had not only lost two friends, she'd watched one of them die. You'd have to have a heart of stone to not be affected by that.

Movement in the water caught my eye, and I saw Feeorin's head break the surface. The kelpie watched me with his big black eyes, and I smiled wanly at him.

"Thank you," I called to him. A second later, he disappeared from sight.

"Who are you talking to, little one?"

I turned to smile at Desmund as he strode toward me. The warrior's transformation was astounding. I might have helped heal him, but the battle last night had awakened something in him, a fire that had burned low a long time ago. He walked with a strong, confident swagger, and his eyes seemed to be lit from within. If a guy could be breathtaking, Desmund was in that moment.

"Would you believe me if I said I was talking to a kelpie?"

Desmund reached me and smiled down at me. It was funny that I had never realized how tall he was. Or maybe he was just holding himself taller now.

"I would believe anything you say." He took one of my hands and rubbed it between his warmer ones. "Why are you out here alone in the cold?"

I shrugged. "I just needed some fresh air."

"And room to breathe," he added knowingly, and I nodded. "You have many people who care for you, Sara. You cannot fault them for worrying about you after last night."

"I don't. I just can't stop thinking that all of you could have died." I pressed my lips together to contain the emotions simmering just below the surface today.

"I'll have none of that," he declared sternly. Tilting my chin, he forced me to look at him. "It does no good to go back and worry over what did and did not happen. Warriors die. It is a part of life and you cannot save everyone."

I pulled away scowling. "I think I liked you better when you were trying to throw me out of the library."

Two weeks ago, he would have been insulted by that remark. Now he merely chuckled. "You should have thought of that before you fixed me."

"How do you . . . ?"

"I began to improve after I met you. I was too ill at first to make the connection, but when Tristan started to remark upon my improved health I knew it had to be you. He and I talked when you were ill, and he said you had healed me but he didn't know how." His eyes seemed distant for a moment before they focused on me again. "I saw you with that witch last night. He was afraid of you. I have never seen a Hale witch fear anyone."

"He's just a kid and his magic is not very strong, not like the one – "

"The one who attacked me?" he finished for me.

"I was going to say 'the one who attacked *me*,'" I corrected him, and his eyes widened. "I had a run-in with my first Hale witch a few months ago and got a taste of their magic." I described my encounter with the witch, and I saw the pain in his eyes. No one who had not experienced such an attack could ever understand how it felt. That was one thing Desmund and I would share for the rest of our lives.

"I felt the sickness in you, but I didn't know what it was until Tristan told me what had happened to you. That was when I knew I had to try to help you, even if I failed."

"But when and how did you heal me?"

I stamped my feet to warm them. "When I sat beside you at the piano I pulled the magic from you into me. It was pretty nasty stuff. Please, don't ask me to explain how I did it. It took a couple of times to get it all."

He looked away for a long moment, and his eyes were troubled when they met mine again. "I was not very nice to you in the beginning. Why would you put yourself through that for me?"

It stung a little that he questioned my motives, but he had spent a century pushing people away and it would probably take him a little while to get used to relationships again. "Because you're my friend, Desmund."

He pulled me toward him and gave me a tender hug. "You will always have my friendship, little one." Leaning back, he grinned devilishly. "Nikolas will come and toss me in the river if I hold you like this much longer."

"But you're gay. Surely, Nikolas knows nothing is going on between us."

"That does not matter to a bonded male. He will not like to see another male embrace his mate . . . or his mate-to-be. As much as it pains me to say it, he is a good man. I am happy for you."

"Thanks." I blushed and looked away. I hadn't seen Nikolas since I fell asleep in his arms last night. He was gone when I awoke this morning, but sometime during the night he had carried me to my bed. The indentation on the pillow and my dreamless sleep were evidence that he had stayed with me all night.

"Nikolas isn't even here." I glanced around the grounds to be sure, and he was nowhere in sight. I assumed he was working with Tristan to get things in order today.

Desmund laughed like I had made a joke. "You do not see him, but he is watching over you, trust me. After last night, I cannot blame him." He took my arm and began walking us back to the main building. "I need a brandy, and you need a warm fire. What do you say to a game of draughts?"

My head was too full to concentrate on checkers. "Would you play the piano for me instead?"

He gave my arm a little squeeze. "It would be my pleasure."

*   *   *

"Sahir, you're awake." I ran to his hospital bed, and he lifted a hand to take mine. "I was so worried about you when they brought you in here last night." I'd come by to check on him first thing this morning and the healers told me he was still out from the drugs they'd given him. They said the effects should wear off in a few hours.

He let out a small laugh then winced. "Based on how I feel right now, I can only imagine what kind of shape I was in. Last thing I remember is opening the cages and then getting ambushed by a couple of vampires."

"Alex saved your life, did you know that?" His eyes widened, and he shook his head. I told him what Terrence had said about the burnt vampire bodies they'd found next to Sahir. "He and Minuet and the hounds saved us, too. If you hadn't let them out, a lot more of us would be dead." I'd found out that the roars and screams I heard from the other side of the grounds last night were from Alex and the hellhounds mowing down every vampire in their way as they tried to get to me.

"I thought those hounds of yours were going to tear their cage apart. I think they heard the vampires before I did. As soon as I realized we were under attack, I knew they would find you. I don't know what possessed me to release Alex, but I'm glad I did." He smiled weakly. "I told you wyverns love to hunt vampires."

"He looked like he was having fun. Minuet and the hounds came back this morning, but there's been no sign of Alex. I hope he doesn't hurt anyone."

Sahir coughed, and I handed him a glass of water from the table near the bed. After he'd taken a long drink he leaned back with a groan. With the severe injuries he'd sustained, it was going to take him another day to get back on his feet. Still, it was miraculous that he was awake and sitting up already.

"I hear they've already sent a team to find him, and then they are going to send him to Argentina."

I nodded wistfully. "You know, I think I'm actually going to miss him."

"Sara," Tristan called from the doorway, and I turned to look at him. His expression was serious and it spoke of the weight on his shoulders today. I was pretty sure he had slept very little since the attack, and he had no intention of resting until every detail of last night was uncovered. "Michael is awake. I am going to talk to him, but he's asking to see you. You don't have to talk to him if you don't want to."

I thought about the urgent email from David I'd read this morning, the email I'd received last night but not read because Michael had come to get me before I had the chance to open it. *Do not trust this Michael kid. He's been talking to vampires online for at least a month.*

My chest constricted every time I replayed the words in my head. If I'd gotten the email one minute earlier, if Michael had shown up a minute later, we never would have been led into the trap. I would have gone to Tristan and Nikolas and told them about Michael, and the attack might have been averted. Olivia and Mark and the fallen warriors would still be alive.

Misunderstanding my hesitation, Tristan nodded and started to turn away. "No, I want to." I knew Michael's motive for betraying us, but I wanted to hear what he had to say to me. Maybe it could help me understand how I had been so deceived by someone I'd believed was my friend.

I told Sahir I'd see him later. Then I followed Tristan to a room with a guard standing outside. When we stepped inside, I saw Nikolas standing near the door and Celine sitting in a chair not far from him. Nikolas's angry expression made it clear he was not happy about me talking to Michael, but he wasn't going to try to stop me.

"You came?" said a small voice, drawing my attention to the pale blond boy huddled in the hospital bed. Michael had one arm folded over his chest and the other was chained to the bed railing. "I didn't think you would."

"I wasn't sure I would come either." I paused then walked over to stand next to the bed. Up close, he looked even paler than usual, and I could see dark shadows beneath his eyes. "How are you feeling?"

"O-okay." His blue eyes brimmed with tears. "Sara, I-I'm sorry for what I did to you. I know you won't forgive me, but I want you to know that I didn't ever want to hurt you."

"You didn't hurt just me, Michael. Olivia and Mark are dead." The words came out harsher than I'd intended, but the pain of watching Olivia die was still too raw. I didn't know if that was something you ever got over.

Michael's face drained of color, and I realized no one had told him about them. "Oh God," he moaned and tears spilled down his face. "No one was supposed to die. They said if I gave them you, they would give me Matthew."

"And you believed them?" What had he thought the Master planned to do to me once he had me? Or had that not mattered to him?

"I had to." His eyes pleaded with me to understand. "I messed up everything else, and it was my last chance of getting Matthew back."

Tristan stepped forward, looking a lot more composed than I felt. "What do you mean? What did you mess up?"

Michael stared down at the blanket, unable to face Tristan. "I-I was supposed to scare Sara and make her leave. I did things to make her want to go, but she never did."

"What things?" My mind replayed every bad thing that had happened to me in the last month. "Did you have anything to do with us getting attacked in the movie theater?"

He darted a glance at me and looked down again. "I only told them what movie you were going to see. I didn't know they would sic demons on all those people."

I was right. There had been a vampire nearby when we left the movie theater. But what had they thought to gain by sending lamprey demons after us? "What about the vampires at the party we went to? Did you tell them we would be there?"

He shook his head. "I didn't even know you were going to a party. I swear."

"What else did you do?" Tristan asked sternly.

"I gave Sara some drex venom." I gasped loudly, and Michael swung his gaze to me. "It was supposed to make you sad and depressed so you'd want to leave. It's not supposed to make people sick. I didn't know what to do when you got so sick."

"You did that to me?" Drex demons disabled their victims by injecting them with their venom, which was like a powerful psychotropic drug. It should have, at the very most, caused me to have hallucinations. But I had been so sick I could barely move from my bed. I had a suspicion that drex venom and Fae blood did not mix well. No wonder it had taken troll bile to cure me. Trolls are immune to all toxins and poisons.

"Where on earth did you get drex venom?" Celine asked.

"They keep a lot of venoms in the medical ward for making antidotes," Michael said, and I shivered to think of what other poisons he could have used on me. It was a miracle I was still alive.

"What else did you do?"

Michael cowered from the barely contained fury in Nikolas's voice, and it took him several minutes to answer. "I-I let the hellhounds out so they would scare her. I did it when there were lots of warriors around to keep her from getting hurt."

"How did you do that without anyone seeing you?" Tristan asked calmly, shooting Nikolas a look that said "let me handle this."

"They let me hang out in the control room sometimes, and I saw Ben entering in his security code when he was on duty. After that, it was easy to log on from my laptop."

While everyone digested how easily a fifteen-year-old computer nerd had broken into their top-notch security system, I thought of something else. "You set the karks on me, didn't you?"

"I sprayed some scarab demon pheromone on you. I used just a drop to get them worked up. I had no idea they'd go nuts like that."

I threw up my hands. "I don't get it. The vampires wanted me dead and you had so many chances to finish me off. Why didn't you just kill me and be done with it?"

He recoiled as if I'd slapped him. "I couldn't do that. I never wanted to hurt you at all. I just wanted you to leave so they would see I did what they asked me and let Matthew go. And they said they wanted you alive."

"So after all that, they suddenly decided to come here to get me themselves. Why?"

He looked away again, and his chest rose as he took a deep breath.

"They asked about your uncle . . . and I told them he was human again. They wanted to know how, but I didn't know how it happened. That's when they told me I had to bring you to them or Matthew would die."

They know what I can do. A fist-sized lump of ice formed in my stomach. It was no wonder they were desperate enough to attack a Mohiri stronghold.

Tristan walked over to stand beside me. "How did you make contact with them in the first place?"

Michael swallowed hard. "I was on a forum where you look for missing people. I posted about Matthew a bunch of times, and a month ago, someone contacted me. They said if I helped them, they would tell me where to find Matthew."

"Oh, Michael." I knew the kind of message board he was talking about. It wasn't a normal missing persons website. The people on there were looking for family and friends who they believed were taken by aliens or something supernatural. I'd used them myself when I was looking for a sign of Madeline's whereabouts.

He shook his head fervently. "You don't understand. They sent me pictures of him. He's alive."

The denial in his eyes tore at my heart. "If you posted an old picture of Matthew, it would be easy for them to find someone who looks like he would today."

"You're wrong! You think I don't know my own twin?" He twisted his fingers in the blanket. "I failed him."

I glanced helplessly at Tristan. "Michael, you see now that the vampires were using you, right? They never had Matthew."

"You're wrong!" he yelled, getting agitated. "I saw him. I talked to him."

"They tricked you."

"No!" Michael's eyes blazed and for the first time, I saw the madness in them. "He's alive and now he's going to die because I couldn't give them you." His screams grew louder, and he began to thrash wildly in his restraints. His sweet face suddenly twisted into one I didn't recognize. "This is all your fault. Why couldn't you just leave? *You* killed him, Sara! You killed my brother."

I put my hands over my mouth and backed away from the bed as two healers ran into the room. One held Michael down while the other injected him with a sedative. The powerful drug kicked in quickly and soon the only sound in the room was my ragged breathing. Nikolas made a move toward me, but I shook my head.

"What will you do with him now?" I asked Tristan.

Tristan looked at me with eyes full of sorrow. "We have a facility in Mumbai where they've had some success rehabilitating some of the older orphans we've found. I'll contact Janek and have him take Michael there."

He ran a hand through his hair. "Sara, what he said . . . "

"He's delusional, I know." Michael's outburst had hurt, but not because I believed him when he said it was my fault. It hurt me to see how much pain he was in.

Celine stood and waved a hand at the unconscious boy. "Please tell me it's not that easy to get to our children and turn them against us."

Her insensitivity rubbed against my already frayed nerves. "He's sick and they used that against him. How about a little compassion?"

"You expect me to show compassion to the person who betrayed us?"

Tristan stepped in before I could reply. "The welfare of the boy was our responsibility, Celine, and we failed him. I don't believe our young people are at risk. This was a special case." He tilted his head toward the door. "And I think we should continue this conversation elsewhere."

"I'm done here," Celine said angrily and swept out of the room.

I walked out behind her and waited for Tristan and Nikolas. They walked out, deep in conversation, and I was about to excuse myself, but I stopped when I heard what they were saying.

"If they know what Sara did to Nate, they will stop at nothing to get to her," Nikolas said in a low voice.

Tristan nodded. "I've already spoken to the rest of the Council. We are doubling our force here and bringing in five special teams to hunt this vampire."

Nikolas's brows drew together. "It's not enough. You saw the small army he was able to assemble and send against us. One child Hale witch brought down half our sentries without blinking. I'm shocked it hasn't been tried before. You can be sure they will try to use them again now that they know how effective they are. And the only person who can go up against a Hale witch is the one we are trying to keep safe."

"What do you propose?"

Nikolas's eyes met mine, and the hard set of his jaw told me he was going to say something he knew I would not like. "We need to move her to a new location, somewhere known only to a handful of us. Overseas would be best."

"Hold on." I stepped up to them. "I'm not moving again, especially not to some strange place where I'll be on lockdown twenty-four seven."

"Nikolas makes a good point, Sara," Tristan said like he was actually considering it. "It would not be permanent, just until we deal with this Master."

"That could take years. I am not going to spend the rest of my life running and hiding while you two hunt this vampire. Forget it."

Nikolas shook his head. "Actually, I will be coming with you."

It should have made me ecstatic that we would be together, but all I saw was a future where I was a virtual prisoner. "So, I'll be back to having a bodyguard again," I said bitterly. "Why don't we invite Chris along, too, and it'll be just like old times?"

"We can bring Chris if you'd like," Nikolas replied, deliberately ignoring my angry sarcasm. "He likes to travel abroad."

"What if I *don't* like to travel abroad?"

"You can hardly say that when you've never left US soil," Nikolas pointed out with infuriating certainty. "I'm sure we can find plenty of places you will enjoy. We can even bring your two beasts if you want."

"This would be the best way to keep you safe," Tristan added, and I felt my freedom slipping away. "I promise we will do whatever we can to end this and bring you home soon."

"But what about Nate? I just got him back. I can't leave him like this, especially if he'll be in danger here."

Tristan gave me a reassuring smile. "I've already told Nate he has a home with us as long as he wants to stay. But if he wants to go with you, he has that option."

"How can you expect me to run away like a coward and leave everyone else here to face this?" I cried desperately. "Please don't ask me to do that."

Tristan shook his head. "No one here would ever call you cowardly, Sara, especially after what you did last night. But being a warrior means you must also know when to retreat. This is one of those times."

My throat constricted painfully, and I could only nod mutely. I did not trust myself not to cry if I spoke. Neither of them said it, but the message was clear; it didn't matter how well I'd fought. I still wasn't good enough in their eyes. They weren't planning to send the other trainees away, even after Olivia and Mark had died. *Because they think I am the only one too weak to protect myself.*

I turned toward the door. "Sara, please understand," Tristan called after me, but I refused to stay there another second.

"I'll talk to her. She'll come around," Nikolas said in a lowered voice.

I turned back and glared at Nikolas through angry tears. "I will never be okay with this or having no control over my own life. If you don't know that, then you don't know me at all."

*   *   *

I chewed my bottom lip thoughtfully as I surveyed the bounty spread out on my desk: seven hundred dollars in cash, fourteen large diamonds, and a tiny vial of troll bile. The cash wouldn't get me far, even if I stretched it, but I'd already been in touch with one of my old contacts about the diamonds and he said he could get me a hefty price, after they were authenticated of course. The only problem was it would take a few days to set it up and I wasn't sure how much time I had.

The troll bile would fetch enough money to allow me to disappear for a long time if I wanted to. But it would also draw way too much attention. I decided to hang onto it and use it only in an absolute emergency.

My eyes went to the email from David two hours ago that was still open on my monitor.

We found her. I'm running some checks now to verify the information, but so far it looks solid. She's in Albuquerque, but I'm not sure how long she will stay there. Are you sure you want to do this?

He'd done it. He'd actually found Madeline. Now, it was my turn. I was going to track her down and make her do something good for once in her life. The way I saw it, she owed me. My mother was the only one who supposedly knew the identity of the Master. She was going to tell me who he was and then I would tell Tristan, who would take care of the rest. It didn't matter that neither of them knew of my plan yet. In fact, that was exactly how I wanted it.

I scooped up the glittering diamonds and dropped them into a small pouch, which I stuffed in a pocket of my old backpack along with the money and the troll bile. I scanned the room as I thought about what I needed to bring with me. I needed to travel light and fast, so a few changes of clothes and some toiletries were all I could manage.

I looked longingly at my laptop and sighed. It was thin and light and it would fit in my backpack, but I could not risk the possibility of Tristan's security guys tracking it somehow. David was setting me up with a clean laptop and some burner phones, and letting me know where to pick them up. I had to have a way to communicate with him and know what was going on out there. It helped to have a friend with his talents, especially on this mission. Of course, I needed to get out of here first, and that was going to be tricky. I still hadn't worked that part out yet.

A knock at the door pulled me from my musing, and I rushed to throw the backpack in the closet. "Come in," I called after I picked up a book and lay down on the bed.

Roland poked his head in before stepping into the room. "We're leaving tomorrow and you're hiding in your room?"

I laid the book on my chest. "Sorry, I didn't mean to ignore you. It's just been a rough few days and I wanted to veg for a while."

He cocked an eyebrow. "You mean you wanted some time alone to plan your little getaway."

"What?" I swallowed nervously. "What are you talking about?"

"Nikolas told me he's taking you away. He said you were upset."

"So?" I avoided his gaze so he couldn't see the hurt in mine. I hadn't seen Nikolas since I'd left him that morning. A few hours ago, he'd knocked at my door, but I didn't answer. He'd known I was here the same way I knew it was him on the other side of the door, but he left after a few minutes. I hated putting distance between us, and I felt his absence like a gaping hole in my chest. But he knew me too well and I'd never be able to hide my intentions from him. If he got wind of what I was planning, he'd have me on a plane for parts unknown tonight. I couldn't let that happen.

Roland snorted loudly. "I know you too well to expect you to go meekly along with that. Fess up. What's the plan?"

I struggled to keep an innocent expression. "There is no plan, Roland. I'm just reading. See?" I held up the book for emphasis.

"You know, I'd find that story a whole lot more believable if that book wasn't upside-down."

I glanced at the jumbled text in front of me and flushed.

"Busted." He sat on the foot of my bed and fixed me with a serious look. "You can't really be thinking of running off on your own after what just happened?"

Abandoning all pretenses, I tossed the book aside and sat up. "It's because of what happened that I have to go. We have to stop this Master before more people get hurt. I'm going to find Madeline and make her give up his identity."

"What makes you think you can find her when the rest of the Mohiri can't?"

"Madeline is smart, and she's watching for the Mohiri and the Master. One sign of them and she is in the wind again." I smiled self-confidently. "She won't be looking for me."

"Yeah, but first you have to find her, and she's managed to stay out of sight for ten years."

"No one stays out of sight unless they are living totally off the grid, and I know for a fact that my dear mother has not been living in a cave. My friend, David, has been tracking her for a month, and it didn't take him long to pick up her trail."

Roland frowned. "David, the hacker guy? If he knows where she is, tell Tristan and let him deal with it."

"No." I got off the bed and began pacing the room. I wasn't going to sit back anymore and do nothing. I couldn't. Besides, Madeline was too smart for that and she'd see her father coming from a mile off. "Like I said, she'll be watching for him. And I'll be damned if I let them ship me off to God-knows-where while everyone else puts themselves in danger. You know me, Roland. I can't live like that."

"But you can leave Nikolas? I saw the way you looked at him last night. You love him, don't you?"

I stopped pacing and swallowed past the lump in my throat. "Yes. But it's not enough." The idea of leaving Nikolas was tearing me up inside. I loved him more than I'd thought it was possible to love someone. But if I stayed and let him protect me the way he wanted to, I'd soon feel smothered and I'd eventually start to resent him. For this thing between us to work, we had to see each other as equals. That would never happen if we did things his way.

Roland pointed to one of the pictures above my desk. "What about Nate? You're going to leave him, too?"

I sank down in my desk chair and put my head in my hands. "It's not like I want to leave him, Roland. I almost lost him, and it kills me to hurt him like this. But I'm doing this for him, too. He's a prisoner here as long as the Master is out there. After last night, I don't think he's safe anywhere."

"You're set on this, aren't you?"

"Yes." Once I set my mind on a course, there was no changing it, and he knew it. The last thing I wanted was to leave Nikolas and Nate, or Tristan or Jordan or Desmund. But this wasn't about what I wanted. I knew with every fiber of my being that I *had* to do this.

"Fine. Then I'm going with you."

Hope flared in my chest, and I jerked my head up to stare at him. But just as quickly as the hope had ignited, I stamped it out. As much as I didn't want to do this alone, I could not drag him into it. "No, I can't let you do that."

He crossed his arms and his mouth formed a stubborn line. "If *I* don't go, *you* don't go."

"But what about your mom and school? You can't miss your senior year."

"Mom will understand . . . eventually. And school sucks without you."

I chewed my nail anxiously. I was more than a little nervous about what I planned to do, and it would be a lot less scary with Roland by my side. There was no one I'd trust more with my life than my best friend. Well, almost no one. I forced myself not to think about Nikolas.

"Okay."

It was Roland's turn to get up and pace. "Sara, are you sure you want to do this?"

I set my shoulders and met his blue eyes filled with worry. "This vampire killed my dad *and* tried to take Nate from me. He's tried more than once to kill me. He declared war on my family, and I am not going to sit around and wait to see what horrible thing he does next. This time, I'm taking the fight to him."

"That's what I'm afraid of," he muttered. "So let me see if I have this right. We're going to hunt down your mother *and* a vampire Master while half the blood suckers in the country are looking for you? Not to mention the Mohiri?"

The last four months, I had been hunted and terrorized and I had witnessed more brutality and death than anyone should see in a lifetime. I was tired of being afraid, tired of feeling weak, tired of crying. Roland was right; we were going to be constantly looking over our shoulders. I'd just have to make sure to stay a few steps ahead of them all. And the last thing the Master would expect is for me to leave the stronghold and go out on my own. If we were lucky, we could find Madeline and be back here before he even knew I was gone.

"That's the plan."

Roland groaned. "You forget one very important thing," he said dejectedly. "That vampire is not all you have to worry about. Nikolas is going to come after you, and he's going to be royally pissed. There's gonna be hell to pay if either of them gets their hands on you?"

"Have a little faith, Roland." I lifted my chin and smiled at him. "They're going to have to catch me first."

~ The End ~

ABOUT THE AUTHOR

When she is not at her job as a computer programmer, Karen Lynch can be found writing, reading and baking. A native of Newfoundland, Canada, she currently lives in Charlotte, North Carolina with her cats and two crazy loveable German Shepherds: Rudy and Sophie.

YA LYNC
Lynch, Karen,
Refuge /

SEP 1 7 2018

CPSIA information can be obtained
at www.ICGtesting.com
Printed in the USA
LVHW02s1546120818
586746LV00010B/569/P